The Space Between

Jenn Crowell

Carnelian Press
FOREST GROVE, OREGON

For Mike

used to huddle in—across the back of her IKEA couch. And after that?

She'll write a few faculty evaluations, no doubt. Pour a single glass of red wine, rather than the four-plus she'd downed at Bill's posthumous retrospective, where Jascha had needed to steady her back to the car. Clasp her hands behind her head to free her dark hair from its elegant bun. Light a candle on the pale laminate coffee table. Allow herself the mannered release of a brief cry: five minutes, no more.

These days, every letter Gloria sends, every phone call she makes to him, exudes a cheerful air of pluckish resolve. When she came back to London last month for the Christmas holidays after a mere season spent away, she looked like a phoenix arisen: slender instead of gaunt, chatty rather than confessional. Ticking the transformations off on her fingers. "No more chain-smoking, no more sobbing in public, no more bathrobe as permanent catatonic attire."

"Also," Curran, the eight-year-old, broke in, "she makes proper dinner again. And Scotch eggs at breakfast."

Clearly repatriation suited her. Sure, there was the occasional skirmish with her mum ("Love her to pieces, but we work better at pond's length"), and that terrifying moment on the Beltway when she'd momentarily blanked on American road rules ("I never drove much as a teenager—too busy in the backseat with some mohawked fuckwit"), but overall her reports from the field waxed philosophical and proud.

Tired tired tired, but rocking this single parenthood gig. Still ache for him so hard it hurts, but no longer plagued by that desperate, needy urge to … you know. (A coy reference to the sloppy, impulsive kiss she'd given him after those four glasses of wine.)

As Bill's former colleague, Jascha should have patted her soothingly on the shoulder and stepped away to hail her a cab home.

But what he did was kiss her back—not an indulgent peck, but one so gasping and urgent and deep that, when they pulled apart, strands of her hair were still in his mouth.

"Our fifteen minutes of fame," he and Gloria now jokingly call it, placing their misguided dalliance in an East End car park squarely in mutual grief territory. That electric frisson of empathy—*yes, I know, I know. I know*? Better channeled into solid war-veteran camaraderie than tossed to the winds of flighty flirtation.

At least, this is what he tells himself.

But as the clock creeps toward time-zone magic hour, Jascha can't help wondering what it would be like to kiss her without tasting tears and bad merlot, to feel her hands slide over him in languid delight rather than frantic clutch. A fantasy not only blasphemous, given today's date, but also laughably unrealistic, given how quickly and fully they've switched roles: from widower font of wisdom to wounded albatross, from quavery-lipped waif to bereavement rockstar.

Hell, when his own terrible anniversary came around this past August, Gloria had been the one to console *him*, sitting atop her pile of unpacked moving boxes with the phone tucked under her chin for two hours, holding space as he brokenly rambled. "Almost half a decade, and you'd think I'd ... Jesus, this is pathetic, innit? I shouldn't keep you. I'm sorry."

Her voice like burnout velvet: soothing and centered, but raspy-ragged too. "Don't be."

I should phone her, Jascha thinks now. She may not need me, but the least I can do is return the favor.

Five past one here, which is five past eight there. Jascha nudges the speed-dial shyly with his thumb.

Ring-ring-ring, on the cusp of voicemail. Click-shuffle. "H-hello?"

"Hey, Glor. You holding up all right?"

"Lost my edges. I can't find my edges."

Shit. Maybe she's drunk after all. "How much did you have?"

"Just one glass, but I'm serious. My edges, Jascha, they're gone."
Gloria pushes out her words with such huffed precision there's no
doubt now that she's sober.

"Tell me what you mean," Jascha says, sitting up.

"I tried to feel them, but I couldn't. I looked in the mirror, and I
wasn't there."

High, then? "Thought you were punk growing up, not a raver."
He chuckles, partially to test her, and partially to quell his own
growing alarm.

"Please. You have to believe me." Her voice ascends into a wail.

"I believe you," Jascha says softly. "Just need you to back up a
little, so I can understand what—"

"I dropped off Curran. I came home. I ate my Thai takeout and
read a little, and then I went into the bathroom to brush my teeth
and get ready for bed and have my ritual cry, and when I looked up
from the sink there was—" Gulpy swallow of a gasp. "There's a
stranger in the mirror. She looks like me, and she moves when I
move, but she's not me."

He thinks of pulpy psychological suspense novels, women-in-
jeopardy films. Were Gloria herself at the moment, she'd snicker at
this, put on the throaty announcer voice, mime the cover model's
terror-stricken face. But, clearly, on some level—Jascha has to
concede—she isn't herself, and so he has to press on.

"Where are you now?" he asks. "Still in the bathroom?"

"Yeah. On the floor. Can't look. Scares me too much." Her
inhales are pained, her exhales quavery.

"Okay. You don't have to look."

"I tried," Gloria says. "I traced her. I slammed the glass."

Dear God. "How hard?"

"Not very. I'm telling you, Jasch, my edges, they're missing." Her words catch in a whimper. "I'm staring at the tiles on the wall and they don't look real, and I don't feel real. What's happening to me?"

No way he can sidestep. No way around admitting. "I ... I don't know."

Brittle moan. "Oh, my God."

"Sweetheart," he says quickly, the word stripped bare of anything but soothing. "Just—"

"What?" Challenging tinge. Jascha pictures squared shoulders, a haughty face, a wry scowl—anything except the reality of Gloria huddled, knees drawn up, beneath the sink.

"Close your eyes. Breathe."

Halting shudder. "Where am I?" The question like a child's riddle, only crucial, only deep-dark.

"Washington, D.C. On your bathroom floor."

"Tell me my name."

"You've forgotten it?"

"No. Just want to hear. Maybe if I hear it, from someone else, I'll ..."

"Your name," he says softly, "is Gloria ..." He stops. "Wait. I don't know your middle—"

"Jacqueline. After du Pre."

"The cellist?"

"Yeah."

"Hell of a legacy, that."

"Right?" She almost laughs, reassuring him, but then there comes another terrified suck-in of breath. "Shit. What if I *am* like her, and it's some terrible neurological disorder that's going to kill me slowly after a long—"

"Gloria Jacqueline Burgess," he says, "you are not dying."

"Better not be. Too much goddamn dying going on."

Finally, an answer Jascha can give with certainty. "I know."

"I know you know."

"Feel any different?"

He swears he can hear the flicker of her eyes reopening.

"I'm still not here. Air and air and air. That's all there is. No boundary between." Panicked word-rush. "*Fuck.* Maybe if I did something, opened myself up, I could—"

"No." Jascha's voice is an immediate shout. "No."

"I have to," Gloria whispers. "I don't care if it hurts, I don't care if there's blood."

"Well, I do."

"You wouldn't if you were like … like this." The phone clatters.

"Don't hang up. Don't you dare."

Soft scuffle. "Not hanging up. Just crawling over."

"To what?"

"The tub ledge."

"For what? A razor?"

Stubborn silence.

"Put it back. Right now."

"I have to," Gloria whispers again. "I need to."

"What you need," Jascha says, "is to go to hospital."

"No. Had enough of them with Bill."

"Don't be an idiot."

"You said I'm not dying."

"Yeah, but you're not exactly well at the moment, either."

"I can't go. I *can't.*"

"Why not?"

"They'll lock me up. I'll lose Curran. I'll lose my job. I'll be—"

"Safe."

"No."

"Curran needs you to be safe."

Long, fraught pause.

Please, Jascha thinks. I'll stop kissing you in my head. I'll cheer you on for your own first date, I'll be the best man at your wedding. I'll make you an ice sculpture for your fiftieth anniversary party, just please don't.

Delicate porcelain clink. "I ... I set it down."

His breath unfolds in a sigh. "Good girl."

"Jascha, I'm so scared."

"Shh. Just stand up. I'll talk you through it."

Jascha coaxes her back into her shoes, back into her coat. Reminds her to take her wallet with her. Nudges her gently to lock the front door.

During the hunt for her keys, Gloria dawdles on the threshold. "Are you *sure* I should do this?"

"Yes. But don't drive. Take a cab, or—"

"Hospital's only a few blocks away. I'll walk."

"Okay. Would your mum come down from Baltimore and meet you there? If you rang her?"

"I—I can't."

"Why? Is she gone for the weekend?"

"No. Just too hard."

"Then I'll do it. Give me her number." Jascha turns over his grant application. Takes down the digits Gloria reads off from her address book.

"Here goes nothing," she whispers as she heads out the door.

"I'm sure your Elgar concerto will be just stunning, Ms. du Pre."

"Thanks." *A lot, asshole,* he waits for her to add, proving she's back to her old self, but no luck. "I'm so sorry, Jascha."

"Don't be."

"What do I tell them?"

"Just tell them how it feels."

"It feels like I'm broken."

"You aren't broken," he says. "You're brave as fuck."

In response, a series of jarring beeps, signaling the near-demise of her cordless battery.

"My phone's about to die."

Hurried swallow. Huge leap.

"I love you," Jascha whispers.

Click.

Brilliant move there, wanker, he chastises himself as he dials Gloria's mum. She's probably rolling her eyes and thinking, *Way to make it all about you in my time of need, Jasch.*

Of course, she may not have even heard him. Or just took his amorous confession for business as usual, like the casual *x*'s and *o*'s they often use to sign their letters to each other.

Not that it matters right now. What matters is that she has someone with her.

"Hello?" Gloria's mother answers the phone with her usual breathy mellifluence.

Jascha pauses, unsure whether to greet her as Caroline or Mrs. Merchant. He's only met her once, when he came by to pick up Gloria the night of Bill's retrospective. She'd ushered him into the kitchen, chatty and exuberant to the point of overcompensation, babbling on about how she'd smartened Gloria up for the show. "You should see her! I talked her out of her usual boring black, and into hitting Harvey Nic's for a—"

Makeover? He couldn't believe it when Gloria shyly entered the room, looking gorgeous in a fitted-but-classic dress the color of a pomegranate, her dark hair upswept.

"Mrs. Merchant?" he says now, playing it safe. "I don't know if you remember me, but my name's Jascha Kremsky."

"Oh, of course I remember!" she says brightly. "Gloria never stops talking about you. Said she was so relieved that you were going to call her tonight to check in."

Jascha swallows. "Umm, about that. I did just speak to her, and ..."

He chokes out the story of what happened, fully expecting Caroline to gasp in shock. But instead there's a long pause on the other end of the line, so long Jascha wonders if their international connection has broken up.

Finally Caroline lets out a grave sigh. "She's been through so much already, my girl. I just can't ..."

Her voice cracks. "Can't thank you enough, Jascha. I'll drive down there straightaway."

◦◦◦

No sooner has Jascha hung up and fallen asleep, the old nightmare rises up from the murk, running the same relentless reel of mental celluloid:

Sluice-slick motorway.

Rain-spattered windscreen.

Frantic turn of the steering wheel.

Metal's crunch slam shatter.

Jascha's eyes fly open. He half-gasps, half-growls, arms slashing through space only to land on the mattress in defeated splay, his heart stubbornly thrumming in his achy chest.

As his pulse calms, as his fingers ease out of fists, he pictures Gloria, woozily curled on a hospital bed, coming down from a similar terror. His still-wild eyes mentally trace her, their gaze softening, luxuriating in every detail: pale face, black hair thicket, serious but sensual mouth, still able to (he hopes; he prays) summon a dry wit. Fragile but fierce, even in this odd delirium.

Alive. Alive. Alive.

CHAPTER THREE

Holy shit. He told me he loved me.

I mean, he's said it before. Same way I have to him, with a quick "Got to run, love ya" to conclude a non-crisis phone call.

But not like this. Unless I'm imagining? Which is totally possible, given the shape my brain is in.

Damn it. Of all the times for my phone's battery to croak.

I want to know exactly how he meant it. I want him to continue talking me through this. I want to tell him I love him, too.

But I can't. Every street corner, every crosswalk, I have to navigate alone.

When I finally enter the emergency department, I'm tempted to turn around and bail through the automatic doors.

Then, in the waiting room, I spy a blond-haired little boy begging his mother for a snack from the vending machine. ("We've been here forever! Can't I just have one bag of Cheetos? *Pleeease?*")

Put an English accent on him and swap the Cheetos for a Cadbury Flake chocolate bar, and that'd be my son, right down to his towhead.

My son. Who needs me to be safe.

But I can't face the reception desk just yet. I pace back and forth in front of the wall rack full of old magazines, as if each step taken will shore up my courage. But all it does is wind up my sense of agitation.

Back and forth, back and forth. My eyes dart. My fists jam themselves into my coat pockets. I'd shudder with gratitude at having returned to my body, if it weren't for the fact that said body is abuzz with cagey fear.

"Mom," I hear the boy whisper. "What's wrong with that lady?"

His puzzled question—coupled with his mother's mortified look of *Don't be rude! She can't help it if she's batty!*—is all the push I need.

I yank my hands free from my pockets, fold my arms across my chest as if bracing for a terrible impact, and make my way over to the reception desk.

In line ahead of me, a man with a bandaged wrist is trying the patience of the nurse behind the glass. "But they *told* me I wouldn't have a copay!"

"Sir," she says with a sigh that stops just short of gritted teeth, "that's between you and your insurance company."

Oh, yeah. Those guys. I'm still not used to having to deal with them, after so many years spent in England with free healthcare.

"So you're gonna what, expect me to cough up the money and wait to get reimbursed later?"

As his voice rises, my eyes well. I wrap my arms tighter around myself. Pinch the skin above my elbow, testing for an edge.

Nothing.

And I'm up.

"Can I help you, ma'am?"

I dig my fingernails in harder. Still nothing.

"Ma'am?"

"I ... I ..."

Where did my words go? I'm not used to language being a struggle. I did my university thesis on James Joyce. I explored so many things, so effortlessly, inside my own mind, before it became this jagged splinter of a—

"I'm sick," I finally choke out.

Idiot. Of course you are, or else you wouldn't be in an emergency room. Pull it together. She needs details.

My mouth twists. My lips quake.

"I think I'm … having … some kind of … breakdown." All I can manage is a whisper.

"Okay." She's stunningly calm. "Just step over here."

She guides me to a triage cubicle, where a burly, affable-faced man sits sandwiched between a computer and one of those everything-but-the-kitchen-sink wheeled medical carts they use to assess vital signs.

"Hey," he says, looking up. "Have a seat, and we'll getcha checked in."

I lower myself down into a chair with a precarious wobble. My gaze doesn't know where to flicker—too many public health posters about hand-washing and worker's compensation rights; too many wall tiles that could morph into terrifying dislocated blobs again—so I fix it on my lap.

But not before I catch the nurse mouth two words to him: *Psych consult.*

Never in my life have I been so ashamed.

To his credit, the guy runs down his bureaucratic checklist with the same matter-of-factness as if I'd come in with a physical injury. "First things first. What's your name?"

I imagine Jascha saying it.

"Gloria ... Jacqueline ... Burgess."

"And your date of birth?"

Numbers jumble in my head.

"I'm thirty-one. My birthday's in ... July." Come on, come on.

"I'm sorry. I can't—"

"That's okay."

No, it isn't.

He tries a different tack. "Do you know the year?"

I haltingly force out four correct digits.

"And how about the president?"

"John Major."

Soon as I say it, I realize I've just made myself look like even more of a raving lunatic.

"Sorry," I mutter. "I lived in England for a long time."

He's totally unfazed. "When'd you move back?"

"Last ... summer." My mouth and brain fumble for the timeline. "Five ... months ago."

"Wow. That must have been quite the transition."

I give a vague nod. Stare across the top of his head at a poster on the opposite wall that reads *RATE YOUR PAIN*.

Below it, a continuum of ten faces line up as helpful examples. Mr. One looks like a rich geriatric playboy who just had a marathon debauchery session with his gold-digging young wife and might be suffering just the slightest bit of oh-so-worth it Viagra overkill; Mr. Ten looks like he's about to rip someone else's head off just before his own explodes in agony.

When my husband was dying, he got so sick of Rate Your Pain that when it was actually manageable he'd give the nurses cheeky answers. My favorite was the time he recited pi to the eighth decimal.

I couldn't do that now if you paid me.

"Okie-doke." The printer on the desk spits out a laminated paper bracelet, which the intake guy attaches to my wrist.

Gulp. No turning back.

⟨∼

Once my insurance card's been photocopied, they escort me to a mental health observation room, which is basically a glass-walled fishbowl with a stripped-down bed and excruciatingly bright recessed lighting.

A nurse draws the blinds closed (from the outside, so I can't reach them) and hands me a gown. "I'll need you to take off everything except your underwear."

At least she doesn't watch. I fumble to unbutton my crisp cotton blouse. Unhook my bra. Unzip my wool gabardine skirt. Struggle to roll down my stockings. Step, more precarious wobble, out of my heels.

I haven't worn one of these diamond-print sacks since I was in the hospital giving birth to Curran. The back's woefully skimpy, and my fingers can only master the most inelegant of loose knots, but at least it's not a straitjacket.

The nurse pops back in. Notices my headmistress bun. "Oh. Sorry. And your hair pins, too." As if in consolation, she hands me a pair of socks.

"How long until I can see a doctor?" I whisper.

"Hard to say. Friday nights are always busy."

When she leaves, the heavy door thunk-clicks behind her.

Shit. Is it locked?

From outside, the blinds open, exposing me again.

No. I've made a horrible mistake. I need to go home. I want to be curled up with a book and another glass of wine, cozy in my own bed, not this one that has straps hanging off its mattress like canvas spider legs.

I should be scared of that, but the thought of being tied down almost sounds soothing. A sensation of tautness, affirming my edges. Like being held.

Mom would hold me.

I wrap my arms around myself. Wander back and forth in front of the window, my turns rounded and gentle, aiming for a lulling rhythm.

Doesn't help. Where is she?

The meander's now a pace. Sharp corners.

In my mind, I'm a six-year-old lost at a carnival, tearfully bleating, *I want my mommy.*

Stop it. You're a grown woman. Someone's mother.

Curran needs you to be safe.

But this feels so vulnerable.

I bow my head. Raise my hands to my face. Dig my fingernails into my scalp. Lean against the fishbowl window.

For a split second, I contemplate banging my skull against its glass.

But instead I march over to the door and smack the red call button with my palm like I'm ringing the buzzer on a game show.

Nurse is on it. "What can I do for you?"

My hands rise to my hair again. My eyes squinch shut.

"It hurts," I half-whimper, half-wail.

"Stay right where you are." Her voice is simultaneously calm and forceful. "I'll get you some medication."

Thunk-click.

I keep my eyes closed. I don't move. Feels like hours.

"Here."

My eyes fly open. I take the pair of paper cups she offers.

One shake onto my tongue. One watery swallow.

"I brought you a blanket, too."

Ooh, it's warm. Delicious. I drape it around my shoulders. Huddle inside it while I pace.

Eventually, the whip-turns slow to a stagger. My chin nods. I feel wrapped in a thick, foggy membrane.

Whoa. My balance starts to buckle. Better lie down.

I slump-roll onto the hard mattress. Burrow into the pillow's crackly case. Yank the blanket over myself.

Mmph. Sleepytime.

⁓

I wake to the sound of my mother giving the ER staff hell, her voice equal parts tender and fierce in its urgency. "Why do you have my daughter in that glassed-in room, like some zoo animal?"

"It's standard protocol for psychiatric patients, ma'am."

There's a sharp, almost elegant intake of breath, during which I can picture her straightening her posture, squaring her shoulders, rallying herself for what lies ahead. "All right. May I go in?"

The locked door clicks open. Perfectly coiffed even at this late hour, Mom rushes to the bed.

"Gloria. Sweetheart." Everyone's calling me sweetheart tonight.

My hand fumbles needily for hers. My fraught voice slurs. "I'm … so … sorry."

"Hush." She caresses my cheek. "There's nothing to apologize for. You just relax."

Easier said than done, I think, but then my sedative proves me wrong by working its magic yet again.

⁓

Floaty oblivion. I could get used to this.

Inside my fog, I hear a vague *thunk-clink,* followed by the somber murmur of Mom giving the doctor my quickie biography.

17

"She's had an extraordinarily difficult year. Her husband died of leukemia, she moved back here after living in England for over a decade, and now she's a single mother with a very demanding job."

"Any history of mental illness in the family?"

Way to cut to the chase.

"Her …" I can almost hear Mom swallow. "Her father committed suicide when Gloria was twenty-one."

God damn it. I struggle to prop up on one elbow and make myself heard.

"I don't want to kill myself. I just want whatever this is to stop."

"And it will, honey." Mom shoots a look at the doctor that says, *You'd better have a plan.*

I rub a hand over my bleary eyes. "Let's just go home."

"Actually," the doctor says, "I think you need to be admitted to our behavioral health unit."

Now there's a euphemism.

"The psych ward, you mean?" Mom's not playing around.

He nods.

"For how long?"

"That depends. If Gloria signs in as a voluntary patient, she can leave as soon as she and the staff mutually decide she's ready."

Stop talking about me like I'm not here. "And if I don't?"

"Then we're looking at a minimum seventy-two hour hold."

Hell with that.

I sit up slowly, blanket clutched around myself. "Okay."

"So you want to—"

Preserve what's left of my dignity? "Yes."

He hands me his clipboard. Taps the signature line at the bottom of the page with his pen. "Right there'll do it."

My hands shake so badly I can barely scrawl my name. The letters jagged and ugly, with no hint of my usual precise penmanship.

Frowning, I pause. Take a deep breath, and pass the clipboard back to him.

"Trust me," he says. "You'll be glad you did this."

"Can you guarantee that in writing? On my chart or something?"

He chuckles. "I know it's scary, checking yourself in, but most people find a brief stay to be a huge help."

And the ones who don't? The ones like my dad, who never get better?

"I hope so," I whisper.

If he heard me, he doesn't acknowledge. Just thrusts out his hand to shake mine.

"Well, good luck to you."

Thunk-click.

❧

After he's gone, I lean against my mother and sob.

"Oh, hey, now." She rocks me back and forth, rubbing my back. "Shh."

"My life is over."

"No, it's not. I promise you it isn't."

I think of the answering machine message she left for me while I was at work, so I could come home to it tonight. *Gloria, I know this is the day of emotional reckoning, and I know you've got zero tolerance for inspirational pep talks, but I just have to say how proud of you I am. You may feel like you barely survived the past year, but you're thriving, and Curran's thriving, and I just couldn't be more ... Oh, hell, this thing's beeping at me. Don't drink too much wine, all right? I love you.*

"Mom," I whisper now, "are you still proud of me?"

She bites her lip. Tucks a strand of hair behind my ear.

"More than ever, darling girl," she whispers back. "More than ever."

My nurse guesstimates that a room on the unit will be available in about an hour. While we wait, Mom and I hash out the logistical details.

She'll take my keys and sleep at my apartment. Bring me some clothes in the morning on the way to fetch Curran from his friend Quinn's house in Rockville. Drive up to Baltimore to pack her own overnight bag, then come back down to stay. "As long as you need me."

"What about your classes?" Mom teaches cello at the Peabody Conservatory during the week.

"I'll cancel them."

God, I'm such a burden.

"Jascha loves me," I mumble.

"Of course he does, sweetheart." She strokes my hair. "We all do."

"Even like this?"

"Even like this."

An orderly comes in pushing a wheelchair. "Your bed's ready upstairs."

No. It's too soon. Let me stay here a little longer, huddled in my rabbit warren of waffle-weave cotton.

Once I'm in the wheelchair, I can see a security guard waiting outside the fishbowl. Mom and I glance at each other.

"Is that really necessary?" she asks the orderly. "I mean, look at the poor girl. She couldn't make a run for it if she wanted."

"Sorry," the orderly says. "Hospital policy."

There's that phrase, trotted out again. Eroding my liberty, in the name of better safe than sorry.

Am I really doing the right thing?

Yes, Jascha's voice says in my head.

"May I at least go upstairs with Gloria?" my mother asks.

"Sorry," the orderly says again.

I'm almost relieved. This is far too embarrassing already.

The orderly steps behind the wheelchair. "Ready?" he asks me.

No, but I nod anyway.

"You'll be fine, darling," my mother says, her face wan, her voice suddenly thin and uncertain.

She reaches out a hand to give me a restrained cheek-pat, but I grab it and clutch her manicured fingers so tightly I feel her wince.

"You *will*," she repeats, her eyes welling up as she reluctantly slips free from my grasp.

Guard at my side, I'm rolled through back hallways and staff-only entrances, into a service elevator (what, are they ashamed of us?), and up to a set of locked double doors.

The orderly swipes his electronic keycard. Nudges the wheelchair into an anteroom full of lockers, and then through another secured entryway.

Inside the actual ward, it's all middle-of-the-night hush, the only light a faint glow from the nurse's station. I was expecting a snake pit, but the place looks no different from the oncology floor I more or less lived on when my husband was dying. Even the common area with its round tables and plastic chairs and stacks of magazines could double for a regular cafeteria or waiting area. In a sense, this is disconcerting, but in another it's comforting. I'm just in for brain chemo—with a private room, no less.

The sedation is still potent enough that I basically ooze from the wheelchair onto my new bed.

"Easy there," the night nurse says. "I know you're doped, so I'll try to make this quick, okay?"

She checks my blood pressure. Asks if I have any allergies. The usual medical rundown, and then—

"Any self-harm urges?"

"At … all? Ever?" My words are a thick-mouthed mumble.

"Right now."

"Oh. No."

"And this is all you came in with?" She gestures toward the paper bag the orderly hands her.

"That's it, yeah."

I watch as she removes each item and takes inventory of my lingerie and heels and work clothes.

Less than eight hours ago, I chaired a faculty meeting and ran to catch the Metro just in time. I moved through the world with a proud confidence that rounded off the hard edges of this day's commemorated mourning. Those heels clacked. That winter coat swished.

And now look at me, bare-thighed in a skimpy gown, my feet clad in gray ER-issue socks with the gripper bottoms like the kind my son used to wear as a toddler, my only adornment an admission bracelet and my wedding ring.

My *wedding* ring. Will I have to take it off?

I gaze down at the modest glint of the tiny diamond. Bill was a twenty-three-year-old fresh out of art school when we got married. Had to scrape to buy it, because his father wasn't keen on the art degree or me. I was a surly punk then, it's true, the chip on my shoulder more like a boulder, my jewelry preferences running more toward nostril safety pins than feminine sparkles, but I'd shrieked with pure girlish delight when I opened that velvety box.

As if reading my thoughts, the nurse's eyes drift to my left hand. "You might want to keep your valuables in the hospital safe," she suggests. "Things have a habit of going missing around here."

I picture the ring ripped off my finger by a fellow patient in a rage. I picture it twirling down the shower drain with a clink, lost in a moment overtaken by lost edges. And then I think of the three hundred and sixty-six days that I have now lived without him, and of Jascha's final words to me before my phone battery choked, and I say a silent prayer of remembrance and slowly work the band down my knuckles till it slips free.

⁓

Once in bed, I drift off within minutes, into a fog heavy as a London cliché. Next thing I know there's a knock at the door.

"Whaa?" I groan, one hand flailing off the edge of the mattress, as I open my eyes to sunlight.

Middle-aged guy in a white coat (yes, really) pokes his head around the door. "Good morning. I'm Dr. Marshall. Mind if I come in for a chat?"

I slide further under the covers, squinting at him. "Umm ..."

"I'm an early bird, I know. I'm sorry."

"No, it's not that. I just ..." Haven't chatted with a man in my nightgown in what feels like centuries? Don't exactly care to do so with one who's getting paid to figure out what's wrong with my psyche?

"I can come back in an hour or so if you'd rather."

"Please. That'd be great."

I sit up slowly and swing my legs over the side of the bed. Scuff one toe across the vinyl floor.

I can feel it. Kind of.

A second knock at the door.

"Hey there." It's the night nurse. "I'm just about to go off shift, but I wanted to make sure you got these goodies your mom dropped off."

She hands me my Whole Foods grocery bag from last night, in

which three days' worth of oversized pullovers and soft sweatpants and pajamas are immaculately folded, along with a little zippered makeup case full of travel-size shampoos and soaps from Lush.

"We had to confiscate the stuff that had laces and ties," the nurse says. "She went all out."

A lump rises in my throat. "That's my mom."

"You doing all right with your safety, hon?" There's a hint of Baltimore in the nurse's pronunciation on the last word.

"Yeah. Yeah, I think so."

"Good deal. Why don't you wash up and grab some breakfast?"

The shower in my attached bathroom has water pressure no better than a trickle. I was hoping for a hard sting, a constant patter of droplets that would shock me back into myself, but no luck.

At least it's warm. The gels and potions my mother sent me slide over my hair and spill across my shoulders, dripping their way down my knees, soaking me with a protective, rose-scented sheen.

I rub myself dry with a scanty hospital towel, grateful for its invigorating coarseness. By the time I'm dressed in my classy sweatshirt-and-workout-pants combo, my body has begun to wake up, just a little.

I drag a comb along the strands of my wet, tangly hair. Gather up my toothbrush and baking soda paste.

And then it dawns on me: in order to scrub the vile, scummy taste of sleep and tranquilizer chalk from my mouth, I'm going to have to face the mirror.

As I approach it, I keep my head down. Focus on the simple, mindless mechanics: flick of the wrist to turn on the faucet, uncap, squeeze.

By reflex, I glance up.

The woman reflected has dark circles under her eyes and an exhausted, vaguely feral gaze. There's a smudge of toothpaste grazing her upper lip. She looks haunted.

I feel haunted.

My free hand grips the edge of the sink. *Is* it my hand? It's attached to my wrist, but it looks foreign.

Please, God. Not again.

I press my palm into the porcelain. My knuckles cramp. There. Okay.

One last spit. I wipe my mouth with the towel. Impulsively reach up to touch the mirror with my fingers. Safety glass, I'm sure.

How's your safety, hon?

Shaky.

I step away from the sink, backing up until I reach the bed. I lower myself onto it slowly. Rustle-rummage in the paper bag until I hit chenille.

My British-heating-or-lack-thereof-is-a-bitch socks. Ahh. So much better than the grippies.

I hear the thrum of meal carts rumbling past the nurse's station. My stomach rumbles back. I pull the fuzzy pale-blue fabric up past my ankles and head for the door.

⌒〜

The mental health tech who hands me my tray looks like she's barely out of her teens. "It'll all be random for today," she says, "but you can fill out a menu for tomorrow."

Chaos, followed by certainty. I like the sound of that.

I take a seat at an empty table furthest away from any of the other patients. I've come at the tail end of breakfast, so there are only a few of them quietly chatting.

I open my plate's domed lid to find one tough sausage link and a piece of soggy toast, accompanied by a container of chemical-laden fat-free yogurt and a cup of coffee that looks like sludge. Wouldn't touch it back on the other side of the keycard door, but right now I'm so hungry the platter and its plastic silverware look like a high-end brunch.

As I scarf it all down with grotesque abandon, I listen to snatches of the other table's conversation.

"Last time I was in, they had me on some shit that made me gain twenty pounds in a month."

"Which doc did you have?"

"McCann."

"Ugh. She's the worst. I'm lucky I got Marshall."

"*I'm* lucky I didn't get diabetes."

"Ain't that the truth."

I'm relieved to hear a vote of confidence for my assigned doctor, but I'm shocked and saddened to hear the rest of it. Cycling in and out of here? Risking lifelong illnesses to rid yourself of your torment?

That won't be me. That can't be.

Thankfully they move on to a more benign topic of conversation: how much it sucks to have to stop smoking while in the hospital. "Nicotine patch? Ha, yeah, good luck. Barely takes the edge off."

Now *that* I can relate to. I smoked like a fiend after Bill died. Only thing that helped me kick it was the fear of Curran getting sick from second-hand exposure. That, and Jascha cheering me on.

I wish I could call him. Just to check in. Just to hear his voice. But there's no phone in my room (safety risk, I guess?) and my spare international calling card's in my wallet, locked deep in the bowels of the hospital safe.

Mom would gladly bring me another one. But she'd have Curran with her, and the "Rules and Regulations for Unit Four West" poster taped up at the nurse's station clearly states, *No visitors under age 16 allowed.*

I could ask them to make an exception. But I'd just cry. And Curran would get scared. And that'd be so horrible it wouldn't be worth it.

No. I have to get my act together. Focus. But how?

Ah-ha. My dietary dance card, blank and ready for filling-in.

Hamburgers, chicken fingers, vanilla pudding. The stuff of primary school cafeterias everywhere. I tick the box for orange herbal tea, figuring it's better than the coffee.

"Community meeting's about to start," the tech, whose nametag reads *KELSEY*, chirps.

I take that as my cue to get up and slide my tray back into the cart and head for my room. I hate to come off like an antisocial snot, but I can't handle the idea of sitting in a circle and sharing my goals for the day, which are basically just: *Find out what the hell is wrong, so they can fix it and I can go home to my kid.*

❧

I'm halfway down the hall when Dr. Marshall catches me. "Is this a better time to talk?"

Might as well get the diagnostic party started. "Sure."

Back in my room, he takes the chair by the desk. I've never seen a hospital room with a desk in it before; maybe we're supposed to study?

I'm tempted to ask him, but he beats me to the questions. "So, you had a pretty rough night last night, huh?"

Nah, I just signed myself onto a psych ward for fun.

"Yeah." I stare down at my lap. "Yeah, I did."

"What would you say was the worst part? The tipping point that made you decide to go to the ER?"

I don't want to think about it. I can't even put words to it for a minute.

"I felt ... so unreal," I say slowly, "that I wanted to open myself up with a razor to … see where my boundaries were."

Spoken aloud, it sounds completely and utterly insane.

"Was it a sense of being detached, as though you were looking at yourself as a disembodied—"

"Yes." My voice rises with excitement at being understood. "That's—that's a *thing*?"

He nods. "It's a symptom, though not a common one."

Oh, God. So I *do* have some rare disease.

"Twelve hours ago I was fine," I say. "I'm not kidding you."

Dr. Marshall chews his lip pensively. "And in your everyday life, do you tend to mentally zone out? Feel physically distant?"

"No. No." I shake my head vigorously. "If anything I'm the opposite. Very 'on.'"

Bloody hell, I can still hear Bill laughing, as I rolled over on top of him under the duvet on our French Riviera honeymoon, breathless. *You don't do anything halfway, do you, love?*

Nope.

"And your tox screen in the ER came back negative."

"Right." I'm not sure what was more sadly hilarious: attempting to pee in a cup while edge-less as part of the admission process, or the fact that they were ruling out the possibility of my being pregnant on my one-year anniversary of widowhood-induced celibacy.

"So no drug use?"

I shake my head again.

"Alcohol?"

Stupid yuppie biodynamic hooch. Is that why I'm screwed? "Just a glass of wine earlier that evening."

Dr. Marshall mulls this over. "Well," he says, "given the sudden onset, I'd like to perform some tests to rule out physical causes. If that's all right with you?"

"Yes. Please. Let's get to the bottom of this."

CHAPTER FOUR

Noon here, which is seven in the morning there.

Jascha rolls over in bed. Fumbles hungrily for his phone as it rings. Maybe it's Caroline. Maybe it's Gloria herself. Maybe—

"Jaschechka, where are you? Is bingo hall day. You promised."

Ahh, hell.

"Sorry, Mama. I … I overslept."

"Well, hurry. First round starts in an hour."

He'd hoped his mother's favorite game would take his fretful mind off Gloria, but all it does is remind him of the time she came with them and mortified Vera by stamping *F U* on her bingo card when some serious geriatric players tsked at her for laughing too loudly during a number announcement.

"Sixty-nine."

No comment, he hears Gloria snicker in his head.

"Twelve."

His mother gives her correctly numbered square a vigorous daub. "Jascha, what on earth is wrong?"

"Work's ridiculous right now. New exhibition coming up."

She shakes her head. "Terrible liar, you are."

"Seventeen."

"I'm not lying."

"Not telling truth, either."

"Okay, fine." He leans across the table to whisper so the elderly bingo patrol won't give him a telling-off. "It's Gloria."

Vera sighs. "What's she gone and done now?"

"Eighty-eight."

"Fallen ill."

"Not surprised. Too skinny, that girl. And too many cigarettes, just like your father."

"She quit them."

"Seventy."

"So did he, but he still got emphysema."

"It's not emphysema," Jascha says peevishly. "She's having some kind of—"

"Forty."

"Breakdown. Neurological problem. I dunno."

"Twenty."

"But at least she's getting help."

"What sort of help?" Vera's eyes narrow. "They're not sending her to *psikhushka*, are they? Please say *nyet*."

Jascha gives his mother's arm a soothing pat. "Stalin's dead, remember? Psych wards aren't punishments anymore."

"But you're worried."

"Of course I'm worried. She could have had a stroke, or a seizure, or a—"

"Nine."

"*Boshe moi*," his mother says. My God. "Have you spoken to her recently?"

Jascha shakes his head. "No word from her mum. And I don't know if she has access to a phone where she is."

"Why not ring hospital front desk? Have them transfer you?"

"They'd do that?"

"Oh, sure. When Maeve Kilburn from bridge club had hip replacement, I phoned to see how she was doing, and they sent me over to her room number straightaway."

"I'm guessing Maeve Kilburn wasn't on a locked ward, though."

Vera sighs. "Is worth a shot at least, *da*?"

"Yeah. You mind if I step out and—"

"No, no. Just bring me some crisps and Tizer from the snack bar while you're up, *pazhalsta*."

☙

Once outside, Jascha steps into the nearest phone box. Swipes his card and rings the directory enquiry service. "I'd like a foreign number, please. For a hospital in Washington, D.C."

"Which one, sir?"

"Umm ... I'm not sure."

The woman on the other end patiently runs down a list. "Sibley Memorial? Georgetown? Washington Medical Center?"

"Let's try the last one."

Please, please, please.

"Yes, there's a patient here with that name," the hospital switchboard operator informs him. "Hold on. I'll transfer you."

Beep, beep, ring.

"Four West." The woman who answers this time sounds as haggard as Jascha feels.

"May I speak with Gloria Burgess?"

"Last name Sturgess, you said?"

"No. Burgess."

"Could you speak up, sir? I can barely hear you."

Damn international reception. "Gloria Burgess," he shouts over the line's crackle.

"Sorry. She's not available right now."

Not available, meaning what?

He pictures her sullen and shut-down, refusing to answer anyone's calls, not even her mother's.

Or worse: curled up in a fetal position, all babble and sob and shiver.

"Would you like to leave a message?"

"Yes. Please. Tell her Jascha Kremsky phoned."

"No luck," Jascha says, sighing, as he returns to their bingo table with his mother's snack-stand order.

"Speak for yourself." Vera holds up her blacked-out card, victorious. "I just won full house round."

CHAPTER FIVE

During the forty-five minutes I am required to remain completely still in the claustrophobic MRI chamber, I close my eyes and imagine my dead husband is here in this black liminal space with me.

A year ago, I would have daydreamed about crawling into his lap, all sobs and fervent kisses, but what I pretend now is that we're cozied up with non-sludgy coffees, knees touching, fingers brushing, as we chat.

You've got circles under your eyes. The first thing Bill says. The last thing he ever said to me.

I was doing so well, I tell him. You should have seen it, honey. I ran a school. Curran and I had a blast sightseeing at the Smithsonian. Mom and I reconnected!

You're joking.

Nope. You'd have been so proud of me.

Still am.

Shut up. You're just saying that.

I'm not. Why would I lie?

Because you're the dearest man in the world and I've got my head in a fucking magnet doughnut. Where's the pride in that?

You're taking care of yourself.

Yeah, by checking myself into a—

Hush. That's strength.

Now you sound like Jascha.

I can't thank him enough.

Did you put him up to this? Pull him aside in the studio and ask him to look after me once you were gone?

No. But I'm glad he is.

You heard what he told me, right? I mean, I doubt he meant it *that* way, but ...

Would it make you happy if he did?

Umm ...

Honest answer, now.

Shit, this is embarrassing.

I'll take that as a yes.

Sorry.

Don't be.

They made me take my ring off, too.

It's all right, love.

Really?

Really. Hand me that permission form, Headmistress. I'll write you one.

No. Just hold me.

God, your hair feels brilliant.

Mom raided Lush.

Has she got Curran?

Yeah. I'm so scared for him. For me.

Don't be, I wait for Bill to say, but the only sound I hear is a loud whirr, followed by the clicking on of a microphone, and the radiologist's voice. "All done."

Next up: the EEG, otherwise known as reclining in a quasi-dentist's chair while a lab technician turns my hair into alien tentacles, slathering my skull with goo.

I try to pretend I'm at the Aveda salon on Wisconsin Avenue. Just getting my complimentary scalp massage. Twenty electrodes for fashion accessories, no extra charge.

Now that I'm wired up, I am supposed to "just relax." She'll tell me when to look at the flashy lights. Fireworks, like the ones at Jascha's mother's New Year's Eve party last week.

I can't believe I was just there. Normal. On a North London balcony, fussing at Curran to be careful with the sparklers. Hugging Jascha at midnight. Wishing I could kiss him instead.

"You're doing a great job," the tech says.

I'm a good girl. Even if the sign at the entrance of my ward says *BEHAVIORAL HEALTH UNIT.* Behavioral! Like we're naughty children.

Here come the lights. *Be careful, baby.* Writing his name in the sky. In case his dad could see it.

"Feel anything different?"

"No," I say. "Am I supposed to?"

"The flashes can occasionally trigger seizure activity. So please let me know if you experience any unusual sensations."

Wait, what? Am I going to lose my edges again?

I grip the arms of the chair. Curl my toes. Clench my teeth. Everything I can do to feel resistance, to sense boundary.

The fireworks flicker, then extinguish. Whew.

"Okay. Now I'd like you to breathe deeply for a while."

I inhale. Push out. A steady, comforting rhythm, like in labor.

"Even more deeply. We need you to hyperventilate."

Huh? Weird. "Why, if you don't mind my asking?"

"That's another potential trigger."

I picture a bullet leaving a gun. Grip everything again.

My chest tightens. My breath whistles, all strangled gasp, as the corners of my vision blacken.

What's happening? Where are my hands? Where's the mirror? I need to see.

It's all right, love. Really.

No, it's not.

"Hey, whoa. I've got all the data I need. You can stop now."

No, I can't.

My eyes screw shut. My lips whisper things I can't even parse out. My hands dig into the chair arms, fingernails scratching at the vinyl.

"Open your eyes for me, Gloria. Can you open them?"

Yes.

"Now slow your breathing down."

My breath is not behaving. It is an incorrigible girl, gasping like she's coming, gasping like she's leaving.

"Am I dying?" I manage to heave.

"You're having a panic attack."

The blackness recedes enough that I can see her turn nimbly toward the nearby counter, and then swiftly back to me.

"Here." A chalky tablet. My tongue soaks it in.

I'm not in an Aveda salon. I'm in hell.

Back in my room, I lie there for what feels like forever, my hair matted and slimy on the pillow, my throat and chest still full of wince and throb.

I'm about to force myself into another shower when Dr. Marshall's face appears at the door. "Got a sec to discuss your test results?"

Ack, that was fast. Bad omen?

I sit up slowly. "Go ahead."

"It's good news. No tumors, no epilepsy, no MS."

Part of me is elated. Another remains unrelieved. If there's no physical cause, that means—

"I'm just crazy?"

"More like in crisis." He takes a seat at the desk again.

"I don't understand," I say, voice quaking. "I get grief. I've been there. But *this*? Losing touch with reality, with my body, with myself? No frame of reference. At all."

"That's because what you experienced," he says, "is a disorder called depersonalization and derealization."

My first thought is: Whoa, there's a mouthful.

My second is: Curran.

"Please tell me it's not genetic."

"It isn't."

Whew. "But is it permanent?"

"My sense," Dr. Marshall says, "is that this was an isolated episode brought on by stress."

"I was doing *so* well," I protest.

He leans forward. "It takes a tremendous amount of energy trying to prove yourself, doesn't it?"

His query feels like a stab. *Now* I'm in my body, fighting the urge to scream and shake and whimper, every nerve pressed down, rubbed raw, abraded by brutal touch.

"Look," I say. "I lost not only my husband to leukemia, but my father to suicide. I don't bust my ass for some widowhood gold star; I do it so my son never has to experience that pain."

"At a great cost to your own well-being."

"I'm not the one who matters."

"Not the only one, no. But ..." Dr. Marshall leans back in his chair, hand to his temple in *Thinker* pose, no doubt contemplating the question of *How on earth do I get this exasperatingly stubborn woman to admit her grand plan backfired?*

"Okay," he says finally, with a little rise of inspiration in his voice. "You fly a lot, right? Back and forth to England?"

I nod.

"So I'm guessing you've sat through the big long safety spiel during takeoff enough times that it's just background noise at this point."

"Are you kidding? I'm usually too busy nagging my son to turn off his stash of 'portable electronic devices'"—here I crook my fingers into flight attendant air-quotes—"to even hear it."

Dr. Marshall chuckles. "Well, that's not the only request they make of parents, right? There's also the reminder about oxygen masks, and how we're supposed to secure our own before we attend to our children's."

"Yeah, in a plane crash."

"You don't think the metaphor holds true for obstacles in everyday life?"

My shoulders slump.

"I think," I say slowly, "that I'm too exhausted to think in metaphors right now."

He gives me a soft smile. "You don't have to prove anything here. Rest, take advantage of the groups."

"For how long?"

"I'd recommend you give this place a shot until at least Monday."

❧

Two more days. Cut off from everyone I love.

I'd cry, but I'm too numb for tears. Instead I stand in the shower until it runs cold, my Medusa tresses sopping.

And then I go out to the nurse's station and ask to use the desk phone. "It's a local call. I won't be long."

When I dial my own number, Curran's the one who answers.

"Mum! You're not dead! When Gran said 'Sit down I have something to tell you'"—he rushes the words together—"I thought for sure you were."

If my heart's going to break, at least I'm in a hospital.

"Nope," I say, forcing brightness. "Not even a little bit."

"But you're sick."

"Yes."

"What kind of sick? I asked Gran but she just kinda went err, umm."

Err, umm is right. I stand in silence, a torrent of words swirling through my head until the best ones emerge like a miracle.

"Well," I say slowly, "my brain has been playing some pretty weird tricks on me."

"Is it cancer?"

Our go-to fear.

"No, baby. It's not cancer."

"Promise?"

"Promise. They took a picture of my brain to make sure."

"Wicked! Did it hurt? How did they do it? Put a spy camera in there? Is it still turned on?"

Oh, eight-year-old boys. "They did a special X-ray, honey. Nothing that exciting."

"Aww. But you're coming home soon, right?"

What's soon in a child's mind? Three days could feel like an eternity, but in comparison to the two-week hospital stays his father logged, they're an eye-blink.

"Monday, the doctor says."

"So you'll be well enough to take me to Quinn's birthday party next weekend?"

Priorities, priorities. "Absolutely."

"Brilliant. Yay. Hold on, Gran wants to talk to you."

No. Stay with me. "Bye, lovey. Be good."

"Gloria." Over to Mom. "How are you, sweetheart?"

My faux brightness collapses. Now the tears come.

The nurse at the desk looks up. Hands me a tissue with impressive nonchalance.

Equally impressive is my mother's lack of crooned platitudes, her abundance of quiet, space-holding calm.

It's not until after my gaspy hiccups subside that she finally speaks again.

"What can I do to help?" she asks, her voice urgent but gentle. "What would make this easier for you?"

I dab my eyes. Blow my nose. Choke out one potent word.

"Jascha."

"Okay." Mom doesn't skip a beat. "I'll call him. See if he can fly over."

CHAPTER SIX

Of course Jascha can. Of course he will.

The only last-minute flights the airlines have on offer all cost a thousand-plus pounds. Onto his credit card the cheapest booking goes. One-way only. No idea how long she'll need or want him to stay.

He jots down his departure time. Makes a list of surprises to bring in his suitcase: Cadbury Flake bars for Curran, who constantly pines for British chocolate; a copy of the latest Booker Prize winner for Gloria, who could no doubt use some engrossing reading to alleviate the hours of hospital boredom.

On his way home from picking up the presents that evening, he drops by his mother's again.

She opens the door in her dressing gown and slippers. "Jascha, is half-past eight! Am almost ready for bed. What are you doing here?"

"I have to go to Gloria, Mamochka. She needs me there."

"And you want to be there."

"Sure, but that's not—"

"No lies, now. I can see it in your face."

His cheeks go hot as he looks away. "You probably think this whole thing is ridiculous."

"Well," Vera says, sighing a little, "she would not be first choice of girl to start over with, if I was one picking. But she has good heart underneath that rude mouth, *da*?"

"She really does."

"And that little boy. So precious. Yes, you should go to them."

"Promise me you'll take care of yourself while I'm there," Jascha says. "Watch your blood sugars. Keep all your GP appointments."

"Yes, yes. And most important, get beauty sleep." She pretends to wave him off, then pulls him into a fierce hug. "Don't stay away *too* long. You don't want to get in trouble with work."

Work. Christ. That's right.

Soon as he gets home, Jascha dials his assistant and terrible matchmaker, Tim.

"Hey, Jasch. How'd it go with Perky Baps?"

"Last thing on my mind at the moment."

"Don't tell me you lost your nerve. That was *not* an easy gig to arrange."

"Listen," Jascha says. "I'm not ringing to give you a recap. I'm ringing because I have to hand the South London Subversives exhibition off to you."

"What? Why?"

"Family emergency."

"Your mum go into diabetic shock again?"

"No. It's Gloria."

"Ahh, hell. Not that bird." Tim's never been a fan, nor has Perky Baps been the first attempt he's made at getting Jascha's mind off her.

"She's in hospital," Jascha says now.

"So you're going to dash across the Atlantic and leave me on my own a week before opening night?"

"I'm sorry."

"Really? That's all you can say?"

"It'll be a good opportunity for you."

"Don't try to spin this. You're not giving me a leg up; you're being an impulsive idiot."

"She's got an eight-year-old son, Tim," Jascha reminds him.

"Shit."

"Yeah."

"Okay. I'll spot you. But I won't make excuses."

"I'm not asking you to."

"If the board gets wind of this, you might well get sacked. You willing to take that risk?"

"Wouldn't have phoned if I weren't."

"Jesus." He whistles under his breath. "Fingers crossed for you both, mate."

❧

One p.m. in London, eight a.m. in Washington.

Jascha's trapped on a plane next to a plump, chatty woman who won't shut up about how much she loathes flying. "But at least air travel's safer than driving. Or so I'm told."

Yes. He has statistical proof, in the form of two matching headstones.

Once his seatmate has stopped nattering and gotten settled perusing her *Hello!* magazine, Jascha punches his cabin-issue travel pillow into shape against the pulled-down window shade next to him. It's been a long, brutal weekend, and he wants to greet Gloria refreshed and attentive, not sleep-deprived and haggard.

The nightmare, of course, has different ideas.

Firm, gloved hands pinning him down on a gurney.

My wife. My daughter. Where are they?

His neck cranes, stubborn even as the shock hits.

Where. Are. They?

Lie still, sir.

"Sir?"

Jascha jerks awake at the sound of a flight attendant's voice.

"I'm sorry to startle you, sir. Would you care for a beverage?"

Absolutely. A stiff one.

CHAPTER SEVEN

On Sunday morning, Kelsey the teenage tech encourages me to attend community meeting after breakfast, but I skip out so I can call Mom.

"He's on his way," she reassures me. "Gets into Dulles around dinnertime."

Now I'm pinching the inside of my elbow in giddy disbelief instead of dislocation.

"You look a million times better than you did yesterday," the nurse at the desk says to me after I hang up.

"Why? Because my hair's not in tentacles?"

"No. Because you're smiling."

~

My spirits have buoyed enough that I even decide to give morning groups a shot.

First up is art therapy, The woman who leads the workshop is a quirkily vacuous creature equal parts grunge and princess: olive-colored babydoll dress, faux-vintage choker, black lace tights, matching Converse sneakers.

"Today we're going to make a gratefulness tree." She gestures toward the back of the conference room door, on which is tacked a long, narrow sheet of paper with the trunk and branches of a tree sketched in brown marker.

I want to snicker, but then I think: *Dear God, I am so grateful I could fill the whole damn thing.*

Grunge Princess passes out a stack of autumn leaves and some Sharpies.

I grab one of each and immediately write, in my returned-to-normal script, *Curran*. And then: *Jascha*. And then, after a wry headshake: *Mom*.

"Your handwriting is beautiful," Grunge Princess coos.

I blush. "I used to be an English teacher, before I became a school principal."

One who's due back at work Monday. Tomorrow.

Crap. What will I—can I—tell them?

❧

As I dial my assistant headmistress's home number at the nurse's station half an hour later, my hands shake and my mouth goes dry.

"Please tell me this isn't about that boy in Year One with special snowflake food allergies," Julia says in her crisp British accent when she answers.

Before today, I would have eye-rolled along with her, but I now feel chastened by my current medical status.

"He's not a special snowflake," I say. "Peanut allergies are serious business."

"Right. Of course. Sorry." Julia's words are a staccato *Don't get me fired, please don't get me fired* scramble. "Is he okay? Are *you* okay?"

"He's fine," I say, "but I've been better, Jules."

"Oh?"

"Yeah. I had to go to A and E Friday night, and they decided to keep me through the weekend on a ..." Think fast. Watch it. "Keep me under observation."

"Goodness. Whatever for?"

"A, umm, neurological issue."

Coward, I scold myself.

"But you're all right now?"

Ah, the perennial stoic assumption. Of course you're all right, no matter what happened, because you've made your lip stiff as crinoline.

"Oh, sure," I say. "Just needed a bit of ..."

Now *I'm* scrambling, this time for sufficient medicalese. "A bit of cognitive rest."

Well-played, Gloria Jacqueline du Pre.

"Mmm. And you'll be back soon?"

"Discharged on Monday." It's a hedgy answer, but I have every intention of being at work Tuesday morning.

Next up: *Psychoeducation*, as per the whiteboard in the group meeting room.

"*Psycho* education?" a rough-hewn man asks in bewilderment as we take our places around the conference table. "You really think we need lessons in bein' crazy, when we're sittin' in this place?"

Our straight-talking leader, a woman with bleached blond hair and a Long Island accent, shakes her head. "Education on understanding your illness, bud, not tips on how to make it worse."

She turns to a bespectacled, solemn-faced man in his mid-fifties who reminds me of my dad. Not in a bad way, just an eerie one.

"Peter, you shared with me a really great insight when we talked at lunch. You feel comfortable offering it to the rest of the group?"

He stares down at his folder of patient handouts. His thin mouth twists, pensive.

"All right," he says tentatively, glancing back up.

"Good for you. Takes a lotta courage. Doesn't it, guys?"

A tableful of nods. I nod with them, because she's right.

"So, I ..." He looks down again. "I spent a long time—years, we're talking—acting like there were only two ways things could be: totally fine or a complete mess. And I just cycled through life"—here he makes a precise circular motion with his hand—"believing those were the only two choices. I was on top of it all, or I was ruined."

"What made you wake up from that illusion, you think?"

"Being ... being here. Being humbled by this illness."

I wonder about my father, about the different path his own life could have taken, if he'd had this space to confess in, rather than simply the inept and inappropriate sounding board of his young daughter.

"Anybody else relate to that?" the leader asks.

Slowly, I raise my hand.

CHAPTER EIGHT

The passport control queue is moving at a snail's pace. Jascha checks his watch every few minutes, praying he'll get to the hospital in time before visiting hours end.

"Jascha!" Caroline waves a cashmere-clad arm at him at the baggage claim.

He staggers dazedly over, dragging his suitcase by its cheap cord.

"Welcome to America." She plants a kiss on his cheek. "Or as Gloria calls it, the land of the free and fucked-up."

Classic. "Thanks. Where's Curran?"

"Fetching the luggage cart."

Sure enough, here the boy comes, steering like he's driving a race car.

"Watch out," Caroline tsks as he parks it. "You'll run somebody over."

Soon as she says it, she claps a mortified hand over her mouth. "God. I'm so sorry. I didn't mean to—"

"Don't worry about it," Jascha says.

He's barely gotten the words out before Curran slams into him with the fiercest of hugs, flinging his arms around Jascha's waist.

"You came," he whispers.

Jascha rifles Curran's hair. "Not only that, but I brought presents."

Once he and Curran have squished into the backseat of Caroline's car, Jascha opens his messenger bag and produces a Cadbury Flake bar with a flourish. "Ta-da."

"Yes!" Curran yells triumphantly. "May I have it now, Gran?"

Caroline gives him an indulgent smile from the driver's seat. "Just this once."

He munches in contentment next to Jascha in the January dark as Caroline deftly merges lanes on the motorway.

It's been years since Jascha navigated driving with such matter-of-fact assuredness, and he's simultaneously soothed and envious.

"Are we all going in to see Mum?" Curran asks, voice hopeful, once he's finished off his chocolate.

"Curran," Caroline says crisply. "You know you're not allowed, sweetheart."

"Why not? I got to visit Dad."

"Right," Jascha says, "but that was a different situation."

"Because he was dying, you mean."

"Well, that, and ..." Jascha trails off, not sure how much to divulge in Gloria's absence.

"What? They let my friend Quinn visit his mum when she had a baby this autumn, and that's the opposite of dying. So why can't I go?"

Caroline sighs. "Every hospital has different rules."

"But I think it was the *same* hospital."

"Okay, look, mate," Jascha says. "I know you think the rule is rubbish, but—"

"Do *you* think it's rubbish?"

To bar an eight-year-old from visiting an adult psychiatric unit? No, but he can't say that.

"I think," Jascha says slowly, "that you need to hold on and be patient a little longer."

"Jascha's right. Mummy'll be home soon enough." Caroline pulls up to the curb of the hospital entrance.

"Do *you* want to visit for a bit?" Jascha asks her. "I could wait with Curran in the lobby, while you—"

"No," Caroline whispers. "Just go to her."

CHAPTER NINE

By six-thirty, an hour after Jascha was due to land, I've started to worry. Traffic's always bad in D.C., but it's a Sunday, not the workweek.

Maybe immigration was a bitch.

Maybe his luggage disappeared.

Maybe he …

My thoughts loop as I pace in the hallway that runs past the nurse's station.

After a few rounds of back-and-forth, Peter, the solemn middle-aged guy who looks like my dad, comes out of one of the group rooms and falls into step with me.

"It's flower arranging tonight," he says dryly.

"Be still my heart. How could you turn down *that* therapeutic opportunity?"

He chuckles. "Quite easily. Mind if I join you on your evening constitutional?"

"Not at all."

We pass the nurse's station, where a particularly bitchy tech glances up from the computer. "Why aren't you two in group?" Her voice midway between strong suggestion and interrogation.

"I'm waiting for my visitor," I say.

"I'm pacing in solidarity," Peter adds.

She shakes her head. "All right. Just don't forget meds at eight."

Ahh, meds. One of the few time markers available to us, aside from meals.

"You take any?" Peter asks, as we head back down the hall.

"Only when I freak out."

"They've had me on every antidepressant in the Merck Manual. This last one seems to be taking the edge off, finally."

"How long have you been here?"

"Almost a month. I'm the elder statesman of Four West."

A month? I can't even imagine.

"Wow. Does your family visit, at least?"

He shakes his head. "My daughter's off at college. And my wife ... she's ... well, we're separated. Until I get this under control."

"No pressure there, huh?"

"Actually, it's good. In a way. Forced me to face all this."

I'm filled with a mixture of empathy for and envy of Peter and his daughter, who still have the potential for a relationship, no matter how rocky. "My visitor would say you're brave as fuck."

"Would he, now? He sounds like quite a catch."

I'm about to respond with hearty agreement, but then—

"Wait? How did you guess?"

Peter shrugs. "Fatherly intuition? It doesn't take a Merck Manual to diagnose the look of anticipation on your youthful face."

I grin. "Please. I've got about ten years on your daughter."

"Compared to me, that's still young, dear."

"Yeah, but I got started early on everything. I feel old."

I don't realize just how much so until I say it. At thirty-one, I've raised a child on two continents and midwifed a spouse through a terminal illness—and that's not even counting all the years I spent as precocious caretaker to my father in his darkest moments. No wonder I'm crashing out and craving rest.

Seven o'clock now. Other patients are spilling out into the hallway from group, some ambling, some slumped.

"I might go to the next session," Peter says. "Will you be all right pacing solo?"

I'm not sure, but I nod anyway.

He squeezes my shoulder. "Enjoy your visit."

Am I even having a visit? My maybe-thoughts race again as I make a slow final turn, telling myself that if Jascha's not here by the time I get to the nurse's station, I'll go to group with Peter.

When I reach the end of the hallway, I see that Grunge Princess has hung up our paper tree, right next to a plaque bragging about the unit's positive outcomes.

I slide my hand over Mom's leaf, all prickly gratitude. I stroke Curran's name, silently whispering *One more day, hang in there, baby.* And then, dreamy as a schoolgirl, I let a long caress linger over Jascha's.

He's coming, I tell myself for the millionth time, as I turn around and head slowly, dejectedly toward the nurse's station. It seems beyond silly to keep issuing these internal reminders, but I desperately need them, because for the last forty-eight hours, none of my perceptions have been trustworthy.

Which is why, when I approach the front desk and glimpse Jascha standing there, I take a step back, barely believing.

His eyes have circles dark as his hair. He's wearing his *Exoticize This: Experimental Multi(cultural) Arts Fest 1994* T-shirt and leather jacket. And his arms are subtly but unmistakably outstretched.

I want to dash into them, but instead I shuffle forward, bewildered, until I'm close enough to lean into the hug he offers.

At first he holds me lightly, as if he's afraid I might shatter, but then I wrap my arms around his waist beneath his coat, resting my cheek on his shoulder, and then he clasps me hard and I squeeze back and the world recedes into blackness again, this time soft and welcoming as his palm cradling the back of my head.

CHAPTER TEN

Jascha could hold her forever, were it not for the fact that a burly bloke is trying to edge past them and head for the medication window. "Step aside, lovebirds. I gotta get my drugs."

Gloria pulls away so they can back up to let the guy through.

"Come on," she says hoarsely. "We can talk in my room."

The unadorned walls are painted the color of blue hour, soothing but deep. Other than that, it's all blond laminate shelving and a sink and mirror. Shades of Scandinavian prison.

"You can sit down." Gloria gestures toward the chair by her desk.

Jascha's grateful for the directive; it dampens down his urge to sit next to her on the bed.

She perches on the edge of the mattress, legs crossed. Beneath the hems of her long black yoga trousers, a pair of fuzzy socks peek out.

Head lowered, Gloria picks at a lint-ball on one heel.

"So, umm, listen," she says. "What you told me the other night, right before my phone croaked. I know you probably just said it to say it, to keep me from—"

"No." He scrapes his chair closer. "I mean, yes, I did want to keep you from ... from ..."

His words dissolve. He slides his hands underneath the baggy sleeves of her pullover to slip them up, revealing the miracle of her bare, unscathed forearms.

Gloria bites her lip. Blinks.

Jascha ducks his head. Presses his mouth to the pale vein at her wrist. Looks up again.

"My edges," she says. "I can feel them."

 ❧

It's quite possibly the most oddly erotic thing anyone has ever said to him. So intense Jascha has to push his chair back.

Gloria gets up and walks over to him shyly. His knees widen of their own accord so she can nestle between them.

She rests one palm against his cheek. Brushes his hair back from his temple with the other.

"Sweetheart," she murmurs, like he did to her two nights ago. "You look so tired."

"I tried to sleep on the plane, but—"

"Never works," Gloria says. "Except the time Mom paid for me to fly business class."

His stomach growls.

"Let me guess. Dinner in coach was inedible?"

Jascha nods.

"Well, we can fix that."

 ❧

As they walk down the corridor toward the common area, Jascha reaches for Gloria's hand. She gives it a tight squeeze, then lets their linked fingers swing languidly between them. A small, mundane affection he'd once taken completely for granted, strolling along the seaside with Marianne.

The plastic bowl of snacks set out on a table by the telly contains nothing but lukewarm string cheese and spotty bananas.

"What a load of crap," Gloria mutters.

"*She's* got ice cream," Jascha says, pointing to a girl who's watching a celebrity newsmagazine show while eating spoonfuls of vanilla out of a paper cup with what looks like a miniature wooden tongue depressor.

"Where'd you get *that*?" Gloria breathes.

"Nurse's station," the girl says, mouth full. "They're feeling generous tonight."

Gloria grabs Jascha's hand again and marches toward the front desk.

"Any chance we could snag some dessert from the freezer?" she asks sweetly.

The nurse on duty looks up at Jascha. "I can't hand out food to visitors."

"Seriously? He just—"

"It's fine," Jascha says.

"No," Gloria says, her voice rising. "This man"—she points to Jascha—"flew three thousand miles on less than twenty-four hours' notice to hang out with me on a locked unit. If that's not worthy of a rule-bending ice cream, I don't know what is."

Jascha isn't sure whether to groan or grin.

"Vanilla, or strawberry sorbet?" The nurse fights to hide her own smile.

"Don't get the sorbet," the girl bellows from the commons. "It tastes like chemtrails."

Jascha and Gloria glance at each other quizzically, then turn back to the nurse.

"Vanilla," they both say at the same time.

◦∿

"Next up: rehab reports and fabulous fashion!" the television host intones, as Jascha and Gloria cozy up together on a couch in the commons.

"Is this the weirdest date you've ever been on?" Gloria asks, scraping the last melty bits from the bottom of her ice cream cup.

"By far."

"Same here. *Too* weird?"

"Not a bit."

◦∿

When it's time to go, Jascha lingers at the front desk, reluctant. "What time are they setting you free tomorrow?"

"Dunno." Gloria shrugs. "Dr. Marshall's a morning person, so that should work in my favor."

"Well, ring home soon as you know."

"Kiss for luck?" Her voice is equal parts slyness and shyness.

Jascha reaches up to brush a lock of hair from her forehead. Presses his lips chastely against her temple, ever mindful of the nurse keeping watch. "Will that do?"

"For now," Gloria whispers, hugging him goodbye so tightly the metal clasp on her hospital bracelet rasps against the back of his neck.

◦∿

By the time he walks back to Gloria's flat, Curran's already in bed and Caroline is busy tucking sheets onto the couch.

"For me," she says to Jascha. "You can take her room."

"Are you sure?" Jascha asks.

"Of course I'm sure. Your back's got to be in agony after that long flight."

She leads him down the hall, past the *TOP SECRET! KEEP OUT!* sign affixed on Curran's door.

"I planned to tidy up in here before you came," Caroline says, stepping into the master suite, "but I couldn't bring myself to. It just seemed … wrong, somehow, to disturb Gloria's things."

She's two blocks away, not dead, Jascha wants to retort, but he has to admit there's a comfort in the chaos, even if it does mean he'll have to clear a mountain of books and papers from Gloria's bed in order to sleep in it.

He and Caroline work in silence, stacking novels and biographies on her nightstand, sorting her work folders into piles.

"That damn job," Caroline says softly. "If I'd known what it would do to her, I never would have sent her the listing."

And he never would have loaded up the car that night for an August weekend at the seaside.

"God." Caroline tosses a final folder atop Gloria's dresser. "I feel so guilty."

"Me, too," Jascha says.

She glances over at him. "What do *you* have to feel guilty about?"

More than you could possibly know.

"She may have heard about the job from you," he says, "but I'm the one who convinced her to take it."

"You did? I'd have thought for sure that you'd be begging her not to go."

"I won't lie," Jascha says. "I didn't want her to leave. But I wasn't about to let her to waste a brilliant opportunity."

Caroline's face softens. "Did she want to move here? Or was she just humoring me?"

"She really did."

"Now *you're* humoring me."

"No." Jascha lowers himself onto the bed. "I stood with her in the embassy queue to renew her American passport. I drove her to the airport. She was so nervous she dropped her tickets and birth certificate on the floor every five seconds, but they were excited nerves."

"Then why did you have to convince her?"

"She was scared. Had a lot of doubts. Would Curran hate it here, would her colleagues think she was incompetent, could she really jump from being an English teacher to running a school.

"But she was elated, too. Said it felt amazing to be more than the widow of the gone-too-soon artist bloke, or Curran's mum, or the odd-one-out American teacher. To be someone's dream candidate." He can't help blushing. "I mean, she was mine, too, but …"

Caroline leans down. Takes his face in her hands.

"Listen," she says. "I won't lie, either. I had my doubts about you in the beginning. But you've dispelled every one of them."

She kisses him on same temple he kissed Gloria on earlier. "Thank you," she says. "For helping her come back to me. For coming over to support her. You're a gem, Jascha. An absolute gem."

After Caroline heads for the couch, Jascha pulls back Gloria's teal abstract-swirl-printed duvet and edges gently, gingerly between its matching sheets. He half-expects the pillowcase to smell of nicotine, but then remembers, with more than a hint of pride, how he'd convinced her to give up cigarettes this past autumn.

Argh! her withdrawal-jittery letters read. *I'm jumping out of my skin! I don't know what to do with my hands!*

I'll give you something to do with them, he'd almost written back.

Now that he's finally in her bed, all he wants is pure, unadulterated sleep. But the only thing he can do is set the alarm on his watch for the morning, and pray for brevity and mercy as his senses slip under.

CHAPTER ELEVEN

After Jascha leaves, I head down to Peter's room and knock on his door.

He answers it with one hand over his temples, his face pained.

"Hey," I say. "You up for a loop before bed? Might help you shake that—"

"Not a headache," Peter mumbles. "Hard night."

"Oh, man. I'm sorry."

A wan smile. "Not your fault."

"Wanna talk about it? There's still some ice cream up at the nurse's station."

"Dear," he says quietly. "Please. There's no need to waste your last few hours of insurance-funded rest playing surrogate therapist."

And with that, his door closes again.

The rest of my loop is a slow, pensive one. On the last turn, our group leader with the Long Island accent stops me. "You look mighty downcast for someone who's a short day from freedom, missy."

Yeah, so? my inner sixteen-year-old scowls. I'm about to let her out to play, all crossed arms and cocked head, but my outer thirty-year-old beats her to the punch with a rational, reasonable, unexpected request.

"Do you think we could maybe ... umm ... talk for a minute?"

"You bet." I love the matter-of-factness in her voice, blessedly free of any *Finally, you've come around and opened up!* fawning.

We snag a window seat at the far end of the corridor near the pay phone.

"So what's up?"

"I think Peter's mad at me."

Long Island raises one heavily plucked eyebrow. "That's a pretty big assumption. Care to fill me in?"

While I tell her the story of what happened, she pulls one leg across the other and leans back against the wall.

"Okay, so listen," she says when I've finished. "You gotta practice some healthy detachment here, girlfriend."

"Huh? Detachment's why I'm in this place."

"Right, but this isn't about you. Peter's pissed at his depression, not his walking buddy. And he was probably trying to protect you from that anger."

My chest floods with longing: for my father to have been so self-aware, for him to have even *wanted* to protect me, much less taken steps to do it.

"He's a really good guy," I whisper, swallowing down the lump in my throat.

"Sure he is. But you're not here to be his confidante. You're here to get your bearings, so you can go back out into the world and do more of that hard but important work I keep harping on."

Christ. "Let me guess. Therapy."

"What's with the eye-roll, Miss Thang?"

"I'm a single mom. And a school principal. I don't have time for—"

"You can't get a babysitter an hour a week? It's an investment in your well-being."

"More like a luxury."

"Would you say that to a diabetic who needed insulin? A cancer patient who needed chemo?"

Ouch. She's got me there. "No."

"Well, then, don't say it about mental health."

Long Island pushes herself up from the window seat, employee lanyard swinging. "I'll bet you a vanilla ice cream from the nurses' station freezer that you'll find therapy useful."

I make a face. "Those things are vile."

"Thai takeout?"

"Okay, now we're talking."

At breakfast the next morning, Peter arrives late, looking sheepish and groggy, and deposits a cafeteria milk carton on my tray.

"Peace offering," he says quietly. "I'm lactose-intolerant, but they gave it to me by accident. Figured you'd like it in your tea, having lived in England and all."

"Thanks," I say, equally quietly, as I pour the watery skim into my cup.

"Do you mind if I sit with you?"

I shake my head.

Peter scrapes a chair free from the table and lowers himself into it.

"My daughter was supposed to call last night," he says. "Never did."

"I'm sorry." I can't bring myself to tell him that I don't blame her. I'd have been tempted to do the same at that age.

"She's probably busy with her January term. Mini-mester, they call it. Personally I think it's an excuse to get back to the dorms and party."

"Sounds about right." I slide my untouched breakfast to the side and turn to the rest of the group. "Anyone see Dr. Marshall?"

"I heard the charge nurse say he wouldn't be in until ten," Kelsey says from her post by the food cart.

"What?" I huff. "Any other day he'd be waking me at the ass-crack of dawn to discuss my 'situational stressors.'"

"They live to torture us here," the girl who had the ice cream last night says. "I swear they're part of the Illuminati."

"The what?" I ask.

"A cabal of evil imperialist reptiles-in-disguise who secretly rule the planet," Peter says. "She gave us the whole list of offenders during the group you missed yesterday: Queen Elizabeth, George Bush ..."

"Don't forget Hillary Clinton."

"Oh, my God," I mutter, taking a sip of my Brit tea for fortification.

"Sure you don't want to stick around a little longer, Gloria?" Kelsey asks.

"Not if you paid me."

⁊

I do, however, decide to attend community meeting in honor of my last day.

We all take a seat in the semicircle Kelsey has drawn around a whiteboard.

"Quick reminder of how this works for the new folks," she chirps. "Tell us your name, your goal for the day, and your mood on a scale of one to ten."

Ah, so it's Rate Your Pain for psych patients. Awesome.

Peter is a three; Ice Cream Girl is a fifteen.

I am a cautiously optimistic seven.

Next up: goals.

The responses are quiet, halting, poignant.

"To ask the doc about switching to a med that won't make my hands shake so much."

"To stay out of bed." (Peter.)

"To hit the AA meeting."

"Gloria," Kelsey says softly. "Your turn."

The words tumble from me, all warm maternal rush. "I'm counting the minutes till I can see my son again."

"And jump your hot boyfriend," Ice Cream Girl snickers.

"Tamara!" Kelsey scolds her.

My face flushes. "Umm, isn't it time for art therapy?"

"Any requests for background music while we do free drawing?" Grunge Princess asks us a few minutes later.

"Country Q106!" Tamara's favorite radio station.

"How about classical?" Peter suggests.

Much better. I'm about to reach for a sheet of paper when Kelsey pokes her head in.

"Gloria? They're working on your discharge."

"Sounds like a personal problem," Tamara mutters.

Well-played, my sister in smart-assery.

Kelsey motions for me to come with her. I'd expected to feel elated when this moment arrived, but what I actually feel is a twinge of fear at being sent back out into the world, along with a sudden burst of tenderness toward my fellow Four West comrades: Tamara, cracking a stick of gum while working intently on a poster for mind control awareness; Peter, patting me on the arm with a soulful good-luck smile.

Hell, I'm even feeling it for Grunge Princess, but all I can give is a quick wave before I'm off.

"I'm guessing your boyfriend's picking you up?" Kelsey asks once we're back in my room.

"I mean, you *do* have a boyfriend, right?" she adds shyly. "Tamara wasn't just being Tamara when she—"

"Oh, no. I mean, yeah, he's definitely ..." My voice trails off as my mouth breaks into a grin.

She grins back, waggling the top of her uncapped pen at me. "Look at *you*, all glowy."

We work down the inventory list on her clipboard, checking off each piece of my admission-night clothing as she pulls it from a big plastic tub like the kind you'd store off-season sweaters or Christmas ornaments in, then stuffs it into a trash bag.

"Let's see, we've got a coat—you'll want that, it's chilly out. And a pair of pantyhose. And ooh, these are nice heels. Where'd you find them? Ann Taylor?"

"Marks and Spencer."

"That the new place over at Tyson's Corner?"

"It's a British store. Solid. Nothing glamorous."

I say this like a Fashion Week reviewer, but the mere prospect of wearing shoes feels glamorous right now, after three days spent scuffing around in socks.

Knock, knock.

It's Dr. Marshall, bearing a sheaf of paperwork.

"Ready for your pink slip?" he asks.

"Yes. Please. Fire me already."

"Okay. First up." He hands me a square sheet with his signature attached. "I wrote you a short-term script for anxiety meds."

"Do I have to take them?"

"Only if you feel the need. We just want to make sure you're covered in the first week or two home."

Next he passes over a sheet of official letterhead. "Documentation of your condition for your employer. In case you plan to take time off."

"I don't," I say. "But thanks. For everything."

Dr. Marshall smiles. "You're welcome. Oh, and before I forget." One last square of paper. "A therapist referral."

I will myself not to crumple it and shoot a basket into the trash.

⟡

Jascha arrives just as Kelsey's snipping off my patient wristband with a pair of scissors.

"You're good to go," she announces. "Take care of yourself out there, okay?"

Jascha hoists the garbage bag full of my clothes over his shoulder like Santa Claus. I put on the pair of flats he brought me so I wouldn't have to wobble home in my Marks and Sparks heels.

And then I step over the *Patients, Do Not Cross* white line taped a few feet away from the unit entrance, and let the security guard swipe us out through the first set of double doors, and then the second, ushering me back to autonomy and freedom.

⟡

The lights in the elevator are excruciatingly bright. We squash in next to an elderly woman with a walker and a new dad carrying an *It's A Girl!* balloon.

Next to me, Jascha bows his head at the sight of the pink Mylar.

I know that hurts, I want to say to him. *Love, I'm sorry.*

But then the metal doors slide open, like on the Tube, and we're pushed out into a lobby full of other broken people, and my breath catches as I think: Holy shit, this is happening so fast.

At the financial services desk, I give my name and wait for a tired-looking middle-aged woman to retrieve everything deemed too dear to stay in my possession while I was upstairs.

"Just these two items."

My wallet. Along with a small plastic bag, in which gold and white glints.

My wedding ring. I take it from her slowly, my thumb brushing the tiny circlet. "Thanks."

And then I tuck it lovingly into my purse, and look over at Jascha, and say, "Let's get the hell out of here."

Cars and faces and honking horns and construction jackhammers. Sound rattling my bones, sight rushing at me.

I sway in the crosswalk. Squint to dial back the onslaught.

"Lean into me," Jascha says, draping an arm around my shoulder. "I've got you."

I don't want to lean. I don't want to *have* to lean. But I do it anyway, and find that he's right, that—for now, at least—his sheltering embrace can keep me from falling into the overwhelming sea of bodies and stoplights.

My lobby. My elevator. Whew. It's coming back to me.

And there it is, my door. Same one I stumbled out of three nights ago, terrified yet sleepwalky.

I open it to find my living room-dining room-kitchen combo transformed, so blandly immaculate it might as well be the leasing office's model: books stacked precisely on the coffee table, rendered mere ornamentation; the stove's electric coils shiny as my wedding ring.

"Jesus," I mutter. "It's like I don't even live here."

"Your mum insisted on one final hoovering." Jascha gestures toward the precise-as-plaid vacuum marks on the carpet.

"Is she still here?"

Before Jascha can reply, Mom answers the question for me by rushing in from the hall, overnight bag on her shoulder.

"There's my girl." She drops the duffel to the floor and draws me into a hug.

I rest my cheek against her shoulder. Hold on tight as she strokes the back of my head.

"You're going home?" I whisper.

"Mmm-hmm. Figured you and Jascha might like some time together before Curran gets out of school."

I lift my chin. "How did you—"

"Guess?" My mother gives me a droll smile. "Please. You two were a matter of when, not if."

After she leaves, Jascha and I stand in the middle of the room, staring at each other.

He clears his throat. Shifts the garbage bag of my clothes to his other shoulder. "I'll, umm, get these into the wash. Why don't you go relax?"

"I forget how."

"Hot bath?"

Oh, my God. A hot bath. My hair's practically curling at the ends in anticipation. "Genius. I'm on it."

"Wait," Jascha calls after me as I head down the hall.

I turn to see him holding out a hefty novel I've been dying to read for weeks.

"Ooh, the new Booker Prize winner!"

"Forgot to give it to you while you were in hospital. Better late than never, innit?"

I kiss him lightly on the mouth in thanks. "Damn straight."

⟨~

Before I can luxuriate, though, I have to face the mirror again. The one whose glass can't keep me safe.

I flip on the bathroom light. Step toward the shimmery rectangle with trepidation. Reach up to touch my reflection, fingers trailing down my own cheek soothingly, as if to say: *It's all right, beautiful. We're together. We're here.*

I'm together. I'm here.

On the sink, right by the toothbrush holder, my mother has placed a small etched-glass jar of Lush bath bombs. As if she knew this would be the first thing I'd want to do.

I run the water hot as it will go. Pluck a random globe from the colorful collection and drop it into the tub.

Oh, that bomb's delectable, all milky, honey-scented slosh. I flex my toes against the faucet. Sink down just enough for the water to lap over my breasts.

"Not drowning yourself in there, are you?" Jascha calls from the laundry closet.

"Very funny, asshole," I call back.

"Ahh, the endearing words I've been waiting days for you to utter again."

God, I love him.

After I read for a bit, my tired gaze meanders up the wall to the top shelf of the shower caddy, on which sits a dark green bar of soap that's got to be Jascha's.

I can't help smiling. It's been so long since these tiny reminders have brought me anything but the gut-punch of sorrow. Too damn long.

I lean an arm out to set the book on the tile floor, and sit up slowly.

The grin on my face evaporates as soon as I spy my razor, still on the edge of the tub.

My stomach drops. I duck my head.

Beneath the water, my pale calves are studded with three days' worth of dark stubble.

I glance up at the razor again.

Come on. Just get it over with. You don't want to gross him out when he finally sees you naked, do you?

I pull the plug on the drain, dry myself off with a towel that, while a thin cheapie by normal standards, feels so obscenely plush in psych-ward comparison that my skin positively tingles, and tie my robe loosely around myself.

Ligature clearance! Yeah! Worthy of an imaginary fist-pump.

I balance on the edge of the tub. Smear my legs with gel. Pinch the razor's lavender-colored handle gingerly between my fingers. Let the blade hover above my shin.

It's a stupid bonus sample from a Walgreens value pack, not a weapon. Breathe.

I let out my breath.

Careful. Steady.

I glide the razor up the front of my calf, then down the back.

So far, so good. The blade quickly clogs. Eww.

I rinse it under the tap. Move on to the other leg.

Now I'm humming. Glide, rinse, glide. Not quite so careful, not quite so steady this round. My hand swoops down to catch the stubborn bits behind my ankle. *Gotcha!*

And then the pain of the nick hits, and I glimpse a modest-wedding-diamond-sized droplet of my own burgundy blood glistening on my Achilles tendon.

"Ouch," I whisper, both mesmerized and terrified.

It takes a minute for my motherly wound-tending instincts to kick in, but when they do I'm an efficient force of nature. Dab, dab, dab with a torn-off piece of toilet paper. Open the sink cabinet and then the first aid kit. Pluck a Star Wars Band-Aid from the box, rip its seal, slap it on.

Done. Victory. Whew.

I stealth across the hall to my bedroom, careful not to let Jascha see me. My own shyness comes as a surprise—after all we've been through in the past few days, after all those months of built-up and played-down longing, what need do I have to mince around prudishly?

It's just awkward. I mean, the poor dude's first time in my knickers consists of him tossing my dirty ones into the washer. Ick.

What to wear, what to wear? I open and close dresser drawers, amazed at all my choices. I've never been a fashionista, but this is like a shopping spree. Real blouses with buttons! Belts! Scarves! The non-nuthouse options are endless.

I haven't felt this playful in … well, forever. My shyness dissipating, I open the door to the closet and survey its contents in lip-chewing debate. Should I go formal headmistress, or coy cardigan, or faint echo of my punk teen years? What are you aiming for here, Gloria Jacqueline not-du Pre?

I want to feel alive in my own skin again. I want to make Jascha hard.

CHAPTER TWELVE

When he's finished with the laundry, Jascha knocks on Gloria's closed bedroom door.

"Mind if I use your phone to ring Tim? I'll pay you back." He knows from their late-night chats just how ridiculous international charges can be.

"Of course," she calls back. "Don't sweat it."

Tim answers on the first ring. "How's your girl doing?"

Wow. He actually asked. "Brilliantly. Just got out this morning."

"I'm guessing you'll want to stay on a few more days?" Surprisingly, Tim says this with nary a trace of a disapproving sneer. "Help her settle in?"

"Yeah. Exactly." Jascha swallows. "If that's all right with the powers that be."

"I talked to the board. They're cool, as long as you get your arse back here by opening night to wrangle the press."

Oh, thank God. "Owe you big-time, mate."

❧

"What's the word on work?"

From his seat at the dining room table, Jascha looks up to see Gloria enter the kitchen in knee-length boots and a tastefully clingy dress.

Pick your jaw up off the floor, wanker. "You were … umm … asking me something?"

Her pale face flushes a little. "For an update. On whether you still have a job."

"I do. As long as I'm back by Saturday."

"Awesome."

Gloria sidles over to the table. Slides onto Jascha's lap facing him, straddling his hips with a grin.

"Three whole days together." She drapes her arms around his neck. Kisses her way along his jaw in between words. "Whatever … shall … we … do?"

Her skirt rides up against the waistband of Jascha's jeans as she presses into him.

"Jesus, Glor," he half-moans, half-mutters.

She slides one hand down to his hard-on. "Mmm, now there's an edge."

Jascha runs his palms along the insides of her thighs. "You have no idea how long I've wanted this."

"Oh, yes, I do." Her teeth playfully graze his ear.

Who knew it would be this easy? No more mournfulness. No more hesitation.

He pushes himself up from the table and carries Gloria down the hall, her legs wrapped round his waist, his palms cupping the delicious curve of her arse.

And now he stands at the foot of her bed. What next?

If she were Marianne, he'd lay her down gently, all croons and caresses, but Gloria strikes him as the type for whom that move would produce nothing but an eye-roll.

Jascha takes a deep breath. Drops her roughly onto the mattress.

For one blissful second, Gloria's eyes flicker closed and her lips curve into a muted yet intense smile of anticipation as he dives down atop her.

But then Jascha bumps her shoulder with his own, hard, and she whacks her head on the wall above her pillow, and they both start helplessly laughing.

"Goddamn edges." Gloria rubs her temple.

"Shit. Are you okay?"

"I'll live."

Jascha flops onto his side next to her. "Sorry. I was just trying to cure you."

"By what? Giving me a concussion?"

"Note to self: Traumatic brain injuries make for terrible foreplay."

She turns her cheek to meet his gaze. Clasps his free hand. Gives it a little shake. "Hey, so. Serious subject before we go for take two."

He props up on one elbow. "Yeah?"

"We're gonna have to make a drugstore run if we want to do anything more than foreplay."

Jascha's brows furrow. "Wha—"

"Condoms."

Oh. Right. Four years of celibacy preceeded by six of marriage have kept those off his radar. "You're not on the pill or anything?"

She snorts. "Why would I be?"

"I dunno. Migraines? Screwy periods?" Jascha pauses. "Or, umm, maybe …"

"I slept with someone other than myself and didn't tell you?" Gloria laughs. "I would have told you, believe me."

His face flushes. "It's not like I've been suspicious. I just didn't want to assume you hadn't, you know? I mean, here you were, doing brilliantly back in the homeland, all confident and gorgeous …"

Gloria rolls over to face him.

"I've cried every night since I moved here, Jasch. Every fucking night. And not just till the kitchen timer went off after five minutes, either."

"Because you missed Bill?"

"Yeah. Always. That goes without saying. But also—"

"You missed London? Your old job?"

"No, dumbass." Her voice chokes up. "I missed *you*."

"Oh, love." Jascha gathers her into his arms.

"There *was* one time when I was ..." Gloria buries her face in his shoulder. "Tempted. At a stupid networking party. All these British expats, crammed onto the rooftop of the organizer's condo in Adams Morgan."

"Where?"

"Trendy neighborhood not far from here. Islington-ish, only a tad grittier."

He strokes her back. "Like Shoreditch?"

"Yeah, kinda. Anyway. There was this guy. Young. Really young. Twenty-three, tops. I felt like such a cradle-robber."

"What?" Jascha can't help laughing. He's seen Gloria's passport; she's only thirty-one.

"I know it sounds stupid, but listen. He had that youthful sense of invincibility going on. Not cocky, just clueless. Never been hurt yet. Sitting on the railing with his shirt sleeves rolled up. Going on about his budding journalism career. You know what he said to me, as a pickup line?"

"I shudder to think. Tell me."

Gloria leans back so Jascha can see her imitation of the bloke. "He looks at me and goes"—she puts on a perfect Oxbridge-schooled accent—"'Well, if *I* ruled the Guardian masthead, you'd have a permanent column.'"

"Shut up."

"Yes. And I've had one glass of Tanqueray—*one*, I swear—so I play along and ask, 'In which department?'"

"Uh-oh."

"And bless his heart, he tilts his head and squints in the sun and says, 'Literary style.'"

"Mmm, well-played."

"Right? Under all that bravado, there was a sweetness. Reminded me of Bill. Made me wanna grab his hand and make a break for the stairwell and have at it like I was his age again."

"But you didn't."

"Nope."

"Because you wanted to stay—"

"Faithful? Oh, it would have been an homage to my boy, at that point. I could almost hear him in my head, saying 'Go on, love, you've been patient enough.'"

"So if you didn't feel guilty, then what stopped you?"

"I knew it'd be pointless. A stupid nostalgia fuck. A—"

"Pitiful attempt to reclaim your old life that would just make you feel even more like shit?"

"Exactly." Gloria fiddles with a button on his shirt.

Jascha grabs her hand to stop her. Kisses her knuckles in the hopes that she'll interpret his defensive reflex as ardor.

"I felt that with Perky Baps, too," he says. "Tim kept telling me, 'You need to relax, mate. Take yourself back to when it was effortless.'"

And ditch that godawful American single mum who's too much trouble, he'd also told Jascha, but Jascha figures it's best not to include that quote.

"Did you boff her?" Gloria asks.

"What?" He laughs. "No."

"Did you want to?"

"For about five seconds. Then I realized I'd just be thinking of you the entire time."

"Oh, stop." Gloria ducks her face into the pillow, bashful.

Jascha nudges her foot with his. "Hey. We've an hour or so left before it's time to fetch Curran. Shall we go out for lunch?"

She lifts her head. "Out, as in on a date? Like the ones normal people have, that aren't in psych wards or parking garages?"

"Just like."

They walk in the opposite direction of the hospital, clasping each other's hands in the January chill. Glancing over at each other every few seconds, as if to ask: *Are you sure? Is this real?*

The cafe she's chosen is dimly lit but high-ceilinged and full of echoes. Traditional white-collar workday fare: five hundred ways to customize your panini, five hundred add-ins for a healthy smoothie.

"Real silverware again," Gloria sighs as they take their seats at a booth. "Finally."

"You know," Jascha says, "if you took the rest of the week off, we could do this every afternoon."

"God, I wish." She blots her mouth with her napkin. "But I can't."

"Why not?"

Gloria plucks a menu card off the table and holds it up, pointing to the dollar sign on an entrée's price. "We're in the land of the free and fucked-up, darlin'."

"I thought you worked for a British company?"

"Oh, I do. Until cost-cutting measures come into play, and then they're proud to be in A-mur-ica."

"Lovely."

"Yeah. Care to take a stab at how much time off I get per calendar year?"

Umm ...

"Go on, guess."

"A month?"

"Haha, I wish."

"Three weeks?"

"Two. And that has to cover everything. Not just vacation, but routine doctor's appointments, and car oil changes, and meeting with the accountant, and the times when Curran's home sick and my mom can't drive down from Baltimore to watch him, and—"

"How'd you manage to come visit at Christmas, then?"

"Went into work coughing like Typhoid Mary through all of December to save up enough time."

"Jesus. So much for the dream job."

"Eh, I knew that going in." She grimaces. "Plus, fool that I am, I figured that after Bill died the universe would cut me a break and spare us any more crises. How's that for wishful thinking?"

"You weren't a fool, Glor. And there's no point in beating yourself up after the fact."

"Yeah, you're right." Gloria takes a long, contemplative sip of her coffee. "What really scares me is the prospect of how much my little spa weekend just cost."

Shit. The States' lack of national health service has been off his radar longer than condoms. "You've private insurance, yeah?"

She nods. "Didn't take any chances there. Got the Diamond Preferred All Access Backstage Pass policy. Which will cover maybe the price of that ice cream we shared if I'm lucky, but—"

"One step at a time. You just got released, what, three hours ago?"

"I know. I just can't stop worrying." Gloria ducks her chin in shy admission. "It's kinda making me want a cigarette."

Jascha pushes his plate of horseradish roast beef on sourdough aside and reaches over to silence her fingers' restless drumming on the table.

His thumb brushes her knuckles. He lets it play against the bare spot once covered by her wedding ring.

"Don't even think it," he says. "There are far, far better things to do with that lovely mouth of yours."

Gloria slides her hand out of his, reluctantly but firmly. "Not right now, though. We need to pick up Curran."

❧

On the walk over, she's chatty with anticipation at the thought of seeing her son—"Poor kid, I'm gonna embarrass the hell out of him with reunion kisses"—but as soon as they near her school's block, she freezes on the pavement at the corner.

"What's wrong?" Jascha asks.

Gloria stays silent, her gaze focused on the empty playground across the street where a group of well-heeled parents and foreign nannies have congregated to wait for students at the end of the day.

"You'll be fine."

"No," she whispers. "It'll be too awkward."

"With Curran?"

She shakes her head. "My staff. Julia. Everyone asking questions. Wanting to know how I am."

Jascha squeezes her hand. "You can do it."

"No." She pulls away from him. "I'm not ready, Jascha. Tomorrow I will be. But not now."

"Curran's been counting the minutes till he sees you. Why make him wait any longer than he has to?"

Gloria's face crumples. "Please. Please. just walk him home for me, so I can take a little time to—"

"All right. But do something for me?"

"Anything."

"Ring that therapist the hospital recommended."

She sighs. "Okay."

"Promise, now. You won't dismiss it as some daft American thing?"

"I make no guarantees about that. But yeah, I'll call."

"Good." Jascha kisses her lightly on the mouth. "See you in a bit."

CHAPTER THIRTEEN

Well, that made me feel like Mom of the Year. Guess I do need some therapy.

One, two, three rings, and then the woman's answering machine kicks in. What a relief.

"Hello, you've reached the office of Laurie Breggin, LCSW. I am currently taking new patients …"

Damn. I was hoping she'd be booked up and I'd get a free pass.

"I look forward to speaking with you soon. Have a wonderful day."

At least she doesn't sound like she's twelve. There's some soothing gravitas in her voice's timbre. Like one of those relaxation audiotapes they played for us in the hospital that almost put me to sleep.

Can I snooze on Laurie Breggin's couch and call it therapy? Will the Diamond Preferred All Access Backstage Pass pay for that?

You need to take this seriously, I tell myself. If not for your own well-being, then at least for Curran's.

❧

A few minutes later, I'm sitting cross-legged on the couch, reading the novel Jascha gave me, when I hear the front door open.

"Hey, Glor," Jascha calls. "I brought you another present."

The novel falls to the floor as I rocket up, holding out my arms to Curran.

He rushes into them. I hug him so hard I lift him off the ground. Bury my face in his hair.

Oh, my God. He's here. I'm here. We're here together.

Curran's arms cling round my neck. My cheek nuzzles the top of his head. My hand strokes his back as he hiccups through tears.

"It's okay, baby," I whisper, setting him down again. "Take a breath. I'm not going anywhere."

❧

Once he calms down, we all settle in for a game of Monopoly—the U.K. version, of course.

I've just scored Park Lane—boom!—when Jascha pushes back his chair.

"Conceding defeat?" I ask.

"Just realized I should ring my mum before she goes to bed. If that's okay."

"Absolutely."

He gets up and heads for the kitchen to stretch his legs while he talks. "*Ochen harosho*, Mama. She got out today. Doing great. ... What?" His mouth softens into a smile. "Yeah. Yeah, we are."

❧

Come dinnertime, we order in pizza and put on a movie.

"Mum, do I have to do my maths homework tonight?" Curran asks from where he lies sprawled on the floor in front of the television.

"Nah. I think we can let Monopoly count just this once." I reach for the blanket my mother left folded on the couch, and drape it over myself. "Tomorrow, though, it's back to the grind for both of us."

"Jascha, too?"

"I'm staying till Friday," Jascha says.

"Brilliant!" Curran grins. "Let's watch another film after this."

"It's almost time for bed," I remind him.

"Aww, but—"

"Actually," Jascha says, "I should go pick up your mum's medicine from the chemist's."

He leans over the arm of the couch to peer at the rough map I sketch him. "Walgreens, okay. Do I need to show them an insurance card or something?"

"Nah. I'm on file."

He leans down to kiss me goodbye, but then glances at Curran and quickly pulls away. "Back in a bit."

"Don't forget the, umm …"

"What?" As it dawns on him, Jascha gives the slyest of smiles and a nod of anticipation. "Oh. Right."

CHAPTER FOURTEEN

While he waits for Gloria's prescription to be filled, Jascha wanders the drugstore aisles, amazed by their random American excess. Microwave popcorn! Beach towels! Eyeliner!

And condoms. Bloody expensive condoms, in a dizzying array of flavors and styles. Jesus. When did blokes become connoisseurs? Back in his uni days, you bought whatever the vending machine in the bar's toilets dispensed, prayed you could stay sober enough to remember to put it on, and that was that.

Jascha grabs a box of the most bog standard he can find. Middle-of-the-road, neither the black lambskin Pleasure Tip XL ones that cost as much as a bottle of wine, nor the "barely a step up from your proctologist's rubber glove" house brand.

Next up to be tossed into his basket: a bottle of mouthwash. That takeaway pizza was delicious, but heavy on the garlic.

He pays for both items at the self-serve check stand. Scans the mouthwash first as a test.

Beep. No robotic announcement of each item and its price, thank God. Last thing Jascha needs is for the entire store to reverberate with "Haven't Been Laid in Years Super 10-Pack."

He carries his plastic bag to the pharmacy counter, where the young female cashier looks up and bellows, "Pharmacy consult, Tanisha!"

A willowy African-American woman in a lab coat comes over, pill bottle in hand. "Okay. So this is Valium. You can use it every four to six hours for panic attacks."

Let's hope Gloria won't need it that often.

⌒

Jascha returns to the flat to find her in Curran's room, sat down on the end of his bed reading to him.

"Hold my place, sweetie." Gloria hands the book to Curran. "I'll be right back."

She steps into the hall, motioning Jascha to the side so they'll be out of Curran's earshot.

"We should tell him," she says quietly.

"Before the morning, when it'll get awkward."

"Right."

"How do you want to—"

"Let's just be matter-of-fact."

Jascha nods. Takes a deep breath.

They walk back into Curran's room together, close but not cloying so.

Gloria sits on the bed again. Jascha stands next to her.

"So, listen, kiddo," she says. "Jascha and I have something we'd like to talk to you about."

"You mean that you're together?"

Whoa. Jascha knew Curran was a perceptive child, but damn.

"Umm … right," Gloria says, flustered. "I realize it's kind of sudden, especially with everything else going on right now."

Curran grins. "I was hoping."

"You were?" Jascha's voice rises in flattered amazement.

"Yep."

Jascha swallows. "Well, thanks, mate. I never want you to feel like—"

"It's cool." He nudges his mother's arm. "Can we get back to our reading, Mum?"

⌒

"Well, that was easy," Gloria says, as she and Jascha head for the living room.

"Thank God. I was having kittens."

"He adores you. Always has. When he gets homesick, you're on the top of his list of things he misses."

"Above Cadbury Flake bars?"

"Okay, maybe a tie with those." She flops down on the couch. Pats the free cushion, beckoning to Jascha.

When he hesitates, Gloria raises an eyebrow. "C'mon. I don't bite." Sly smile. "Unless that's your deal."

What *is* his deal? It's been so long he can't remember.

Jascha sits down next to her. Draws her still-stocking-clad feet into his lap. Walks his fingers flirtatiously along her ankle, tracing the delicate bones in a slow circle.

Gloria's shoulders shiver a little. She tips her head back against the couch arm, her smile soft now, her hair falling rakishly over one eye.

"I'm so nervous," she says.

"Me, too."

"And so rusty."

Jascha chuckles. "You're only a year out of practice. How rusty do you think *I* am, after almost five?"

"Oh, I dunno. You were definitely rocking it this afternoon before you accidentally slammed my head into a wall."

"Thanks. That's comforting."

Gloria sits up, encircling her drawn knees with her arms. "How much are you willing to bet that Bill and Marianne are looking down at us and laughing?"

"Or rolling their eyes and sighing, 'Just get on with getting it on already.'"

"It's so weird. I've wanted this forever, but now I'm all …"

Jascha looks down. "Yeah."

"You want a glass of wine?"

"Sure."

Gloria hops up. Heads for the refrigerator. "Should I take my wonder drug too, ya think?"

"I wouldn't. Unless you really need it."

"Nah. I don't want to get all sloppy."

She grabs a pair of goblets from the cupboard. Fills them from a bottle of red. Holds it up to read the label.

"Biodynamic, sulfite-free, organic merlot. Warning: May induce depersonalization and derealization on shitty anniversaries. You still game?"

"Absolutely. Bring it here."

Gloria comes back over. Sits down and hands him a glass. "To us?"

"To us."

Clink. "Cheers."

"*Nasdarovye.*" Jascha takes a sip. "Whoa."

"Way better than that cheap plonk we served at Bill's retrospective, innit?"

"Indeed." He sets his glass on the coffee table. "You know what this feels like?"

"Hmm?"

"An open marriage."

Gloria sputters with laughter on a sip of her wine.

"It sounds daft, I know."

"No, no." She places her glass next to his. "I get it. They're still here, in a way. Sweetly permissive, but lingering."

JENN CROWELL

"Like voyeurs? Shadows?"

"Echoes. Of grace notes."

"Yeah."

"Would it be massively inappropriate to ask what she was ... like?"

Jascha raises an eyebrow. "In bed, you mean?"

"Sorry. I'm just curious whether ..." Gloria blushes. "Whether I've got a legacy to uphold."

Poor thing. She's just as insecure as he is.

"All our memories are legacies at this point, Glor."

"Funny how our brains do that, huh?" She reaches for her wine glass again. "Edit all the awkwardness out. Soft-focus Vaseline-lens perfection. Never mind the times one of you farted in the middle of a hot and heavy moment, or begged off with a headache, or cried because you'd just had a baby and felt saggy and leaky, or—"

"Don't forget clumsy make-up sex." Like the last time he and Marianne made love, the night before the accident.

"Nope. Can't say I've had the pleasure of that experience."

"Come on. Don't tell me you and Bill never fought."

"Not really." Gloria shrugs. "We were content, and content to be boring."

"So no 'Yes, Headmistress, may I please have another?'"

She snickers. "Hardly. The only time that got even remotely kinky was when ..."

Gloria looks down into her drink.

"When he was in the hospital," she whispers. "For the last time. Dying. He was in so much pain, toward the end. Being in his body was nothing but agony. Not just the kind morphine can take away, either."

Yes. Jascha knows that opiate-hazy torment.

"One night I just slid under the blankets. Had to crouch carefully

90

so as not to hurt him more. You get bone pain at that point, right, so if I leaned on him the wrong way, any way …"

Gloria's eyes well up. Her voice quavers with elegiac tremor.

"He was worried," she says. "Everything worried him in his fever. And I said 'Shh, love, just let me,' and ducked my head down, because how could I not, how could I deprive him of one last tiny little shard"—she pinches a minuscule amount between her thumb and forefinger—"of pleasure?"

On the last two words, her tone shifts upward, brightening into tenderness and wonder.

Warmed by wine, drowsy from the time difference (nine o'clock here, which is two in the morning in London), Jascha feels a surge of desire strong as a pulse. Not a cheap hard-on brought on by Gloria's bald, transgressive tale of giving her husband head while risking a nurse or oncologist walking in, but an appreciation so deep it goes beyond erotic.

"Look at me," she says, with a self-deprecating headshake. "Babbling morbidly at you, when I'm sure you'd rather I—"

"What? Hide it all and just play into my headmistress fantasy?"

Jascha slides closer to her. Plucks her drink from her hand and sets it back on the table.

"Honey," he says, taking her face in his hands, "I want you dirty-mouthed and erudite and mournful and everything in between. You don't have to hide any of it."

Gloria lets out a tiny whimper deep in her throat. Breaks into a soft smile. "Thank you."

❧

One last fortifying sip of wine, and then they amble down the hall, fingers laced.

Their shyness kicks back in as soon as they're standing in Gloria's bedroom, the brand-new box of condoms deposited ceremoniously on the nightstand.

"Can you give me a sec?" Jascha asks, gesturing toward the bathroom door.

"Sure."

Drain the lizard? Check. Swish of mouthwash? Check? Pep talk in the mirror?

Oh, for fuck's sake. Just go out there and ravish the woman like you're in a Mills and Boon novel.

Without cracking her head open, of course.

Jascha reenters her room to find it lit by a single candle on the dresser. Gloria sits on her knees on the bed, wearing a short, lace-trimmed black silk slip.

"Hope this isn't too cheesy," she says.

"No. Umm. Wow. Not even a little bit."

When Jascha comes over to stand in front of her, Gloria reaches up to run her palms across his chest.

Shit. The scars. Can she feel them?

Don't freak out. Now's not the time.

Jascha gathers her hands in his. Brings them to his mouth, nuzzling her knuckles.

"Mmm." Gloria lets out a pleased little sigh. Straightens up tall enough to slip free and drape her arms around his neck.

They kiss so slowly and deliberately it almost hurts. Her shoulders yielding back onto the mattress at his touch—careful, careful—as her spine elongates down with a dancer's grace.

All that dark hair, fanning out onto the teal duvet. *Boshe moi.* It's like a flipping dream.

Jascha leans over her, propped on his elbows. Strokes a stray lock from her forehead.

Gloria reaches a hand down to work his belt buckle open.

"Christ," she mutters as she fumbles. "I forgot how hard these are to undo from this angle."

"Here. Let me." Jascha stands up. Takes off his belt. Flings it on the duvet.

Gloria's gaze flickers toward the coiled heap of black leather. "Sure you don't want to live dangerously by boring-people standards and put that to good use?"

A delicious thought. Followed by a pathetic one: If her wrists are tied, she can't reach under my shirt.

"Not yet," he says. "I just want to feel you."

"Well, the sentiment's mutual," Gloria murmurs, stretching out with with a suggestive hip-arch that almost kills him, "so take your damn pants off already."

"Yes, Headmistress." Jascha scrambles out of his jeans. Kicks off his socks. Sprawls on his side next to her. "Now where were we?"

Jascha encircles Gloria's head with one arm. Skims the other down the slickly sensuous fabric of her camisole, fingers trailing from the notch of her collarbone, along the hollow between her breasts, across the taut-yet-soft flesh of her belly, and under the slip's bottom hem. Drags his nails up the inside of her thigh.

Gloria closes her eyes. Lets out a breath so deep he can see her chest rise and fall.

Jascha strokes a nervous, tilted hand between her legs. Startles to find that she's not wearing knickers.

"Holy hell," he sighs out, as his eager fingers marvel at her wetness.

She opens her eyes again.

"All right, yeah?" Warm, seeking slide. "Not too much?"

She shakes her head. "Not ..." Tiny smile as her words echo his from earlier. "Not even a little bit."

Jascha would have pegged Gloria as, if not a screamer, then at least on the vocal side, but she's remarkably quiet as his fingers play. Downright solemn, even.

After a few fumbling minutes, the lines in her forehead and between her eyes furrow and deepen. Her throat works. The muscles in her thighs clench.

"That's it," Jascha murmurs, kissing her temple. "Let those edges go."

Gloria chokes down a gasp. "Not until you're inside."

But I'm already in—

Oh. *Oh.*

"Okay." Jascha's voice and hands shake with excitement. "Hold that brilliant thought."

He practically trips over himself stepping out of his briefs. Tears open the box of condoms and shakes one into his palm.

Watch it. Easy, wanker. You don't want to—

Too late. The metallic wrapper rips. "Son of a *bitch*."

Gloria laughs. "You want some help?"

"Just keep looking delectable. I'll get it sorted."

Take two. Unroll. Roll. Adjust. Whew.

When he dives, her eyes widen. "Oh, my God." Her voice stunned at first, then elated. "Oh, my *God.*"

"I know," Jascha whispers. "I know."

Slammed hips. Teeth sunk into the vulnerable curve where shoulder meets neck. Kissing to avoid crying out. Crying out anyway.

And then, huddling together in the shiver-shudder afterwards. Stroking each other's faces. Bodies striped dusky by the candle's thrown shadow.

"How did we ever take this for granted?" Gloria whispers. "Before?"

"I don't know, but I'm never taking it for granted again."

"Me, either."

Even the mundane post-coital routine—sink wash-up, step aside so she can have a pee—feels refreshing to return to.

"Take your shirt off and stay a while." Gloria gives Jascha's sleeve a playful tug.

He swats her equally playfully on the bare arse. Heads back into the bedroom. Turns down the duvet's top edge like a hotel housekeeper.

"Your bed, madam," he says as Gloria walks in, sweeping his arm in presentation flourish.

"Well, aren't you chivalrous." She kisses Jascha lightly, her mouth tasting of toothpaste, then crawls beneath the covers and settles in with a long stretch. "Oh, my God." She moans out the words as if she's just had another orgasm.

"What?" Jascha says.

"This mattress. It doesn't suck. I mean, it does, because I bought it from IKEA in that sad discount corner right before you get to the checkout. But compared to the nasty vinyl psych ward ones ... holy shit."

Gloria plumps her pillow into just the right shape. Curls up on her side. "Only thing that would make this better is you." She pats the other pillow.

Jascha sits down on the bed next to her.

"I should warn you," he says. "I'm a really rough sleeper."

Understatement of the century, but not a lie.

"Don't sweat it. I sleep like the dead."

Aghast at her own choice of words, Gloria backtracks. "Christ. You know what I mean."

Jascha chuckles. "I'm going to set my alarm for five. So I can be up and ready to coax you out of bed by six."

"Yeah, good luck with that."

Still in his shirt, Jascha slips into bed next to her. Wraps his arm around her waist.

Gloria nestles her cheek against his chest. "Mmm. I've missed this."

Her fingers toy with his shirt buttons. "Why so shy, darlin'?"

"I'm not."

Jascha wills himself to relax as she opens each one, working downward from his collar. When she reaches the scars at his sternum, he waits for a drawn breath of shock, but Gloria simply brushes a gentle palm across the scalpel lines.

"What happened here?" she whispers.

"They, umm ..."

Lie still, sir.

"They had to crack my ribs. To save me."

Gloria watches him with exquisite tenderness. "You're a fucking miracle."

And then, as if to prove it, she dips her head down and presses her mouth to the marred flesh.

Jascha almost cries out again, but instead he gasps, "Gloriochka."

She looks up, puzzled. "What'd you just call me?"

"An impromptu Russified nickname." He blushes. "Daft, I know."

She smiles. "Say it again?"

"Gloriochka."

"Again?" Her smile deepens. "Please. I love it."

Gloriochka, he whispers, against her ear, along the nape of her neck, *Gloriochka*, over and over, until both of them sink into satiated, entwined slumber.

Five a.m. The alarm on his watch blares.

"Mmph." Jascha slams his hand down on the nightstand to silence it.

Gloria wasn't kidding about sleeping like the dead. She barely even twitches.

He swings his legs over onto the floor. Rubs his hands over his face. Blinks to clear the blur.

And then it occurs to him: He just slept for six solid, dreamless hours.

Jascha pushes his hair back from his forehead. Allows himself the indulgence of a small, amazed half-smile, half-exhaled breath.

And then he hefts himself up and gets to work.

$\backsim$

Wine glasses and pizza plates into the dishwasher. Coffeemaker started. Quick scrub-down in the shower, then a shave.

Jascha swills his way through some dark roast while on the phone with British Airways, booking his Friday flight back to London. Alas.

Six a.m. Down the hall, Gloria's alarm buzzes. Switches off. Buzzes again.

Jascha pours a fresh mug and carries it into the bedroom. Lowers himself onto the mattress, careful not to spill.

He rubs Gloria's back with his free hand. "Wakey, wakey."

"Urgh." Gloria rolls over. Buries her face in the pillow.

"None of that, now." Jascha jostles her harder.

She swats at him. "Go away."

"I have caffeine." He brings the coffee in close enough for her to smell its aroma.

That does the trick. Squinting, Gloria sits up, the duvet sliding to her waist, the spaghetti strap of her camisole falling off one shoulder.

After a few sips, her voice softens. "Thanks, love. This is delicious."

"Still not too late to take a sick day." Jascha reaches over to adjust the rogue strap.

Gloria sighs. "I've gotta go in. No way around it."

He shakes her knee. "Well, then you'd better get moving."

CHAPTER FIFTEEN

The beautiful thing about a hot shower is that you can sob in it and pretend your tears are simple rivulets of water, nothing more.

I feel stupid crying. But all of Jascha's little sweetnesses remind me of Bill. Remind me that the universe is an unrepentant asshole who can just take it all away on a whim.

Two minutes, and I'm done. Before it's even time to rinse out my conditioner. Atta girl.

"Any requests for breakfast?" Jascha calls from the kitchen.

I pull the shower curtain open. Step onto the bathmat, and reach for a piece of toilet paper with which to blow my nose. "More sleep?"

My brain's like booze-flavored cotton candy. Come on, Gloriochka. (Could that nickname be any more adorable?) Think. What's your headmistress prep routine?

Ooh, I can blow-dry my hair now that I'm not in a nuthouse! We'll start with that.

"Mum?" Hesitant knock at the bedroom door.

I scramble to throw on my robe and stow the box of condoms in the top drawer of my nightstand. "Yes?"

Curran pokes his head in. "Do we have PE this afternoon?"

Hell if I know, kid. "What day is it again?"

"Tuesday."

Tuesday, Tuesday. I attempt to visualize the whiteboard full of class schedules that hangs on my office wall. Year Four, PE … "Yep. You do. Be sure to pack your uniform."

Whew. Maternal failure averted.

Is mascara pushing it? I don't want to stab myself in the bleary eye.

I do need some lipstick, though. Won't help to return to my post all pale and haunted.

There we go. Much better.

In the kitchen, I find Curran now munching on cereal and toast, and Jascha setting me out a second cup of coffee.

"Damn," I say. "I could get used to this whole having a househusband thing."

"Husband?" Curran's spoon drops into his milk. "Wait, are you and Jascha married now?"

"No," I say, laughing. "It's just an expression."

Jascha rubs my shoulders from behind. "When's your lunch break today, Gloriochka?"

"What lunch break? I've got a backlog a mile long."

"You should take one. I'll come get you. Noon-ish?"

Oh, twist my arm.

~

The minute I enter the school lobby, I'm swarmed by students.

"Miss, is it true you got abducted by aliens?" one little boy asks.

Wait, huh? "What on earth gave you that idea, Jamie?"

"Quinn said Curran said something about a spy camera in your brain."

Oh, for the love of God. "Sorry to disappoint you, but I was just out sick for the day."

My office looks just as I left it: endless stacks of file folders, sticky notes all over the edges of my computer monitor, framed photo of Curran on my desk.

I drop my bag on the floor next to my chair and check my voicemail.

Twelve of them. Daunting, but doable. Just prioritize.

I'm about to write out an index card of my top tasks for the morning when Julia enters, bearing a scone on a paper plate.

"Oh, bless your heart," I say, standing up again.

I expect her to simply hand it over and launch into her list of nascent emergencies that must be staved off, but instead she envelops me in a hug. Whoa.

"It's so good to have you back," she sighs.

"It's good to be back, Jules. Whatcha got for me?"

"Phone interview for the *Post*'s school choices guide at eleven-thirty."

Ouch. No pressure there.

"And Peanut Allergy Mum's still on the warpath."

No doubt because you dismissed her son's condition as a fussy annoyance. "I'll handle it."

"Brilliant. Thank you."

Julia dashes off to wrangle her own to-do list, and I head back to hacking through the voicemail jungle.

Table booked for this spring's education expo? Done.

Revision of the school prospectus? On it.

Proposed extracurricular clubs approved? Bam.

Now I remember why I took this job despite its shitty hours and lack of vacation time: the undeniable thrill of competent leadership.

By nine a.m., I've found my groove as a multitasking fiend, absorbed in typing and note-taking and phone-answering.

Brring! "British Academy of Washington."

"Ms. Burgess." Crisp female voice tinged with default exasperation.

"This is Marjorie Kent. Mother of Jonathan Kent."

Jonathan, with the peanut allergy. I lean back in my chair, settling in for what I sense will be a long conversation.

"Yes. Hi. Glad to finally get a chance to—"

"I tried all day yesterday to reach you. And every time I speak to your assistant, she waves me off."

"I'm so sorry. I've been on ..." Careful, Gloria Jacqueline du Pre. "Medical leave."

Marjorie's tone softens, just a touch. "Then surely you can understand how critical it is for my son's school environment, the place he spends more time in than his own home, to not threaten his physical safety."

"Absolutely. I do."

"You're committed?"

"One hundred percent. I've got an article on the dangers of anaphylaxis right here on my desk, photocopied and ready to go to every faculty member, and I'm revising our lunch policy as we speak."

"Thank God. Jon's last school acted like I was asking them to provide full tuition and renovate the entire campus." She lets out a small, bitter laugh.

"I've got your back, Mrs. Kent. Trust me."

After she thanks me about fifteen times, I hang up and do a victory office-chair swivel. Crisis dodged. You're on fire, Gloriochka.

By eleven a.m., though, it's all gone to hell. I catch the daughter of one of our major donors smoking in the girls' bathroom. My computer crashes just as I'm about to save the "No Peanuts, Please!" cafeteria memorandum.

And then Melinda Lewisham, Curran's math teacher, comes into my office on her break to discuss yesterday's incomplete homework.

"He told me you said he could skip it. Really took me aback. I'd expect that sort of made-up excuse from some of the other boys, but not Curran."

"He wasn't making it up," I say slowly.

"What? Surely you're joking."

I shake my head.

"Well, this puts us in an awkward position, doesn't it?"

Yeah. One I've got to get out of.

If I wanted, I could be a royal bitch and pull the *I'm-your-superior* card, but no way would I be able to live with myself. I'm already walking a fine line having Curran enrolled at my school, period.

Alternatively, I could remind Melinda I was out sick. But that in itself is a pitiful explanation. It's January, for Christ's sake. Epicenter of flu season. If every kid got a free pass because his parents came down with something, she'd have a class full of high achievers turned slackers.

Nope. I'm going to have to spill my guts.

"Listen, Mel," I say, "I don't condone what I let him get away with. And I won't let him do it again. But I wasn't just out with a cold. I was in the hospital."

"What?" Melinda's voice rises in shock. "Oh, my God, Gloria. What happened? Are you okay?"

Kinda.

"Yeah. Yeah, I'm fine now. Got out yesterday."

"No wonder Curran seemed so distracted! Poor thing. I won't mark him down for an incomplete."

"Thanks. Appreciate it. And like I said, won't happen again."

Assuming this never happens to me again.

◦〜

Eleven-twenty. Almost time for my interview with the *Post*. I hunch over my desk, rubbing my hands over the bridge of my nose.

Maybe I should take my anxiety medication. Did I pack the bottle in my bag? Please say yes.

When I reach into its front pouch, my hand lands on a folded scrap of paper. I pull it out and unfold it to find a card festooned with primary-hued marker spirals and exclamation points.

Best! Mum! Ever!

Oh, my heart.

Eleven twenty-five. I get up and close the door to my office.

My chest has started to tighten. At least I'm still in my body, right? Every edge constricted and taut.

You can do this. And afterwards, you'll get to have lunch with Jascha.

The thought of that reward—the invigorating chill of a walk, his hand in mine—settles me a little. I sit back down. Caress a heart Curran drew on his card.

Brring. Brring.

Hurry and answer.

Brring. I pick up the phone.

And then completely blank on the name of the school I run.

Quick. Think of the city. "Wash ..."

Wait. Wrong order.

"British School of Washington."

Academy, stupid. Academy.

"May I speak with Gloria Burgess, please?"

"That's, umm ..." My tongue feels like mush. "Speaking."

"This is Brian Jones from the *Post* education section."

"Oh. Right. Hi."

"Is now still a good time to talk?"

Not really, but let's get it over with. "Sure."

"Well, what we'd like for our school choice pull-out section are profiles of what makes each school unique. Anyone can research achievement test scores, but we want to give parents a true sense of why they should pony up for private tuition that costs an arm and a leg. No offense."

"None taken." Our substantial employee discount is the only reason Curran's able to attend my school.

"So why don't you give me a quick rundown of what makes the British Academy special?"

Time for my speech. The one I can normally do in my sleep, without so much as a glance at our marketing flyer.

But my mind won't summon the outline, and my mouth can't summon the words.

"Hello? Ms. Burgess?"

More like Ms. du Pre.

Pull your shit together. Now.

"Sorry," I say. "Our phone lines have been a bit finicky lately."

Not a lie—I've got a work order in to the telecom company—but I'm sure as hell using it as an excuse.

"Okay, so." I take a breath. "We're unusual in that we offer a U.S.-based education completely aligned with all curricular standards in the …"

In the what? I've got brain freeze so bad you'd think I'd just taken a bite of Häagen-Dazs straight from the container.

"In the U.K."

"And the benefits of that alignment are?"

Too many to list. Hit the bullet points.

Cradling Curran's drawing, my hand uncontrollably shakes.

Think. What is it you wanted for him? Want for him?

"Rigor. Coupled with … flexibility." Good save. "A young person who graduates from our school at eighteen leaves having completed the equivalent of … of …"

Come on, come on.

"Of the first two years at an American college."

"Wow. That's impressive."

You like that, you should see our headmistress's ability to flounder. "Yeah. During what would normally be their junior and senior years of high school, our kids study something called ..."

Breathe. What are they called? You know this.

O-levels? Jesus. No, idiot. They phased those out in England ages ago.

"A-levels." Whew.

"Is it similar to an International Baccalaureate program?"

Bless you, Brian Jones. "Yes, as a matter of fact. Only with a wider range of course options. A-level study gives bright and self-motivated students an opportunity to ..."

I gag down a hard swallow. Almost done. "To specialize."

Only thing I'm specializing in right now is fumbling babble. "Any other questions?"

"None that I can think of at the moment. Those are some great features to highlight."

Thanks, Brian. "Did you get the sample info pack I sent you?"

Click, click, click of computer keys in the background. "You know, I don't think I ... Nope. Never got it."

"Huh. I could have sworn I ..." Mailed it out in between brain scans and glueing gratitude leaves? "Sorry. I'll put one in the mail today. Full color glossy. Lots of great photos for you to use."

"Perfect."

After we hang up, I bow my head and lean my face into my hands.

What the hell is wrong with me? A week ago, I would have breezed through that interview, but now I'm a wreck.

Over a five-minute chat. With a reporter whose beat is the exact topic I normally happily geek out over.

I rest my head on my arms. Breathe in, breathe out.

Fifteen more minutes, and Jascha will be here, and you'll get a break. So sit up and stop wallowing and redo the peanut policy.

Oh, God. If we prohibit nuts at school, that means I'll have to go, too.

You aren't crazy. It was a mere one-off. Stress. Remember?

I reach back into my bag. Dig around for the medication bottle. Nowhere. Shit.

The phone on my desk rings again.

"British Academy of Washington." There ya go. Not a single beat skipped.

"Ms. Burgess." A male voice, pissed-off-ness disguised as crispness. Classic Brit. "This is Harrison Bingham. Madeline Bingham's father."

Madeline, who an hour ago sat atop the bathroom radiator in a haze of smoke, one lace-stockinged leg crossed archly over the other, her honeyed voice dripping entitlement. "It's just a fag, Miss, not a line of coke. Daddy lets me have them all the time."

And now Daddy's livid that I dared send his precious little girl packing for a day of in-school suspension. "But she's a model student!"

"Academically, yes, she's one of our stars. But substance abuse on campus isn't exactly model behavior."

"Substance abuse?" he scoffs. "We're talking about a single cigarette. Don't tell me you never smoked any at school growing up."

He's got me there. I had way more than one as a teenager. And I feel like a hypocrite coming down on Madeline when I craved another just yesterday. But still.

"My personal adolescent history is beside the point. It's my job to keep the Academy a safe and healthy environment." Thank you, Marjorie Kent, for your vicarious jolt of righteous indignation. "And that means holding students responsible for their unsafe behaviors."

"By expelling them from class?"

"Suspending. Temporarily." For one freaking day.

"Well." Mr. Bingham's breath is a huff. "If that's how you insist on handling such a minor infraction, I've no choice but to reevaluate my contribution level for the coming year."

Asshole. He didn't.

"That's certainly your prerogative, sir. But my decision still stands. Madeline can return to regular classes tomorrow."

And you can't buy good sense. Jesus. This part of my job I didn't miss while I was in the bin.

Where are my fucking pills?

I turn my bag upside down and dump its contents on my desk. Wallet, lipstick, novel Jascha bought me, random file folder, cough drop, keys.

But no pill bottle.

My chest is closing up.

The walls look weird.

Please, not again.

What time is it? Where's Jascha?

Relax. He said noon-ish.

But I need him now.

Heels clacking in the hallway. Laughter.

You have to pull it together.

How?

Breathe.

I'm scared. Even though I know it's stupid, I'm so scared.

Of what?

Walls. Voices. Moving. The sight of my own shaky hands.

Get up. Open your door. Fake it till you make it. Or at least till Jascha gets here.

Instead, I crawl under my desk.

CHAPTER SIXTEEN

First thing Jascha does after Gloria and Curran leave for school is tidy the kitchen. The second is go back to bed.

Her bed. With the faint scent of her hair—rosemary-mint shampoo mixed with arousal-induced sweat—on the pillowcase.

So good. He drifts straightaway. Floats in blessed black nothingness, allowed respite yet again.

Until the alarm on his watch buzzes.

12:15. Shit. Gloria's probably wondering where he is.

Jascha sprints the five blocks to her school. Takes the front steps of the main building two at a time.

Forget checking in at the secretary's office; he dashes right for Gloria's own closed office door.

He gives a firm knock. "Gloriochka?"

No answer.

Students are pouring down the hall now, bound for the lunchroom, all exuberant chatter.

"Did you hear about Madeline? In-school suspension. For one stupid fag!"

"*Nooo.* Her dad's gonna be right vexed."

After they all turn the corner, Jascha knocks again, louder this time. "It's me. Jasch."

Oh, hell. Just go in.

He jiggles the thankfully unlocked doorknob. Steps inside, closes it quickly behind him, and rushes toward her desk.

But Gloria's not at it.

Maybe's she's in the toilets? Or a meeting?

From the direction of her empty office chair comes the soft but unmistakable sound of a shuddery hiccup.

Jascha walks slowly closer, close enough to glimpse the dumped-out contents of her bag strewn atop the desk.

"Gloria?" Holding his breath, he comes around the side of the desk, almost kicking a wastebasket. "Honey?"

Jascha's breath unfolds when he sees Gloria crouched in the space between the desk and the pushed-out chair. Knees to her chest, arms round her knees. Hair obscuring her face.

"Hey." Jascha grips the seat of the chair to brace himself, and lowers down next to Gloria. "What's wrong?"

She doesn't move. Doesn't speak.

Jascha strokes her hair. "Hard first day back?"

Nothing.

"Talk to me, Gloriochka." He tilts her chin up to face him. "Please."

Gloria's gaze is stark and unblinking. Her lips tremble.

"Losing my words," she chokes out. "Can't do this."

"Do what? Work?"

A staccato little nod. "Not ... yet."

"Okay." He kisses her on the forehead. "It's okay. I'll take you home."

"Have to tell ... Julia." Her lashes blink hard now.

"We'll do that. Here." Jascha scoots back and stands, offering Gloria a hand up from the floor. "Careful." She almost bumps her skull on the desk's keyboard tray. "Duck. There you go."

Once they're both upright, he gathers her into his arms.

"Too soon," Gloria sighs ruefully against his shoulder. "I should have …"

"Shh. Let's just get out of here."

CHAPTER SEVENTEEN

I should be worried about discretion as I shuffle down the hall holding Jascha's hand, but I'm honestly so numb and needy I don't care. Not even when two of my students whisper behind us on their way to art class.

"Look, Miss has a boyfriend!"

"I thought she was married. You think she's cheating?"

"Dunno, but he's cute."

That last comment makes me smile just enough to rally myself as I reach Julia's office.

"There you are." She looks up from her computer. "I was about to come find you and ask how the *Post* phone interview went."

"F-fine."

"Then why do you look gutted?"

I swallow. My free hand flails. "I, umm ..."

No crying, now.

"I think I came back too ... I think I need to take ..."

"Another day off?"

I nod.

"Then by all means take one, dear."

"You'll be—you're sure?" Look at me, stammering and asking my subordinate for permission. "I mean, you'll be okay?"

A small smile. "Well, I'd much rather have you at the helm, but I'll certainly manage. Peanut Allergy Mum's been placated, I assume?"

"Yep."

"And Madeline's still on suspension until tomorrow?"

"Uh-huh."

"Then I think we're sorted. Unless there's anything else you want me to take care of?"

There is, but I'm having trouble remembering what.

An errand? Yeah. But to which place?

Office supply store? No, I sent our secretary last week.

Post office? Yes. Pickup or drop-off? Wait, it's coming to me ...

"The mark—marketing package," I say. "For Brian Jones."

Julia scribbles a quick note. "Got it." Then she turns to Jascha. "Take good care of our Gloria, all right?"

⁊

There's one more to-do scratched off the list, at least: unveiling my mystery man and sudden lack of wedding ring.

I want to joke about it to Jascha, but my sense of humor has evaporated along with my ability to articulate. All the things that make me me, torn asunder.

By the time we get back to my apartment, I feel ready to fall over. Wrung-out as the washcloth I once sponged along Bill's feverish face in the middle of the night, praying for the red number-line on the thermometer to drop.

He got to one hundred point six before he died. Once you're there, it's not even fever anymore, but something else. Fury made molten. My palms stung with heat when they rested on the insides of his gaunt thighs, that last time I took him in my mouth.

I need my brain to stop.

"Here." Jascha walks me into the kitchen, pours me a glass of water, and reaches for the bottle of pills on the counter.

There those little fuckers are. I greedily swallow the one he hands over.

Then I go into the bedroom and kick off my flats and roll down my stockings and unzip my skirt and sit on the bed, slumped in nothing but my blouse and underwear.

Jascha comes in and sits next to me. Rubs my back gently, then says, "I think you need to take off the rest of this week."

I shoot him a skeptical look. "You're just campaigning for extra time with me."

He sighs. "The only thing I'm campaigning for is you getting better. *Really* getting better, not just throwing yourself back into work as if none of this ever happened."

"I told you," I snap. "I can't afford to—"

"You can't afford *not* to."

"But—"

"Think about it. What's going to threaten your job more: asking for extra time to regroup, or another repeat of today?"

Damn it. Jascha's got me there.

I stare down into my lap. "Okay, but what do I tell Julia? And the HR department? And Yvonne?" My supervisor in England.

"The truth."

"How?"

"Just show them the letter your doctor wrote."

"You make it sound so easy," I mutter.

"There's no shame in this, Gloriochka."

"Bullshit." I draw away from his touch.

"No, really. If you had been my employer, or Bill's, back when—"

"You guys were freelance artists. You didn't have anyone to answer to."

113

Another sigh, this one more exasperated. "But let's say we did. Would you have looked at that sheet of paper stating he was battling leukemia, or I had just spent six months in rehab relearning how to walk after an accident, and said, 'Sorry, how awful, my sympathies, but you're too much of a liability now, so allow me to show you the door?'"

"No. Of course not."

"Well, then, what makes you think that will happen to you?"

"Don't be naive," I bristle. "We're not talking about cancer or physical injuries. We're talking about a psychiatric breakdown."

"A temporary one."

"Yeah, but it could still scare them off."

"You don't know that."

"I work with children, Jascha."

"And you've done it for ten years without a problem."

I blow out my breath. "Okay. Okay."

He pats my knee. "Tell you what. I'll grab us some takeaway while you rest for a bit, and then we'll go back to your office so you can talk to Julia before we pick up Curran. Sound good?"

"Yeah. Except for the whole talking to Julia part."

"You'll feel better once you get it over with." Jascha kisses me on the forehead before heading out.

Two hours later, I'm well-rested and well-fed, but still nervous as hell when I enter Julia's office.

"Gloria." She looks up. "I thought you were planning to take the afternoon off."

"I am." I swallow. "I still am. I just wanted to …"

Julia gestures toward the chair across from her. "Why don't you sit down?"

Don't talk to me like I'm a child, I want to snap, but I sit anyway.

"You need to know," I blurt out. "I need to tell you."

"Tell me what, love?"

"Why I need more time off."

Her brows furrow. "More than just a day, you mean?"

I nod. Pull Dr. Marshall's letter from my work bag.

"Here. Read this. It'll explain." Because I can't.

Julia puts on her glasses. Reviews the statement with sharp-eyed precision. No perfunctory skim for her.

Once she's finished, she lets out a deep, inscrutable sigh. Sets the page on her desk blotter. Leans forward on her elbows.

"I'm so sorry," I whisper.

"Whatever for?" she asks gently.

"Falling apart today. Dancing around why I was in the hospital."

"I wondered," Julia says. "When you came back to work so soon, looking physically fine. But I didn't want to meddle."

"It's kind of a relief," I murmur. "Not having to pretend anymore."

"You don't ever have to pretend around me, Gloria." She reaches over to rest a hand on my arm. "My older brother back home has paranoid schizophrenia. He's been in and out of mental health facilities since his early twenties."

"I won't be like that," I say desperately. "It's just a—"

"I know." She puts up a palm. "I know. I'm just saying, I understand. And I'll vouch for you with HR and Yvonne if they give you grief."

"Seriously?"

"Of course."

"Thank you," I sigh. "It'll only be till Monday."

❦

My relief's short-lived, though, because now I have to explain to Curran why I'm taking the week off.

"What the hell do I say?" I whisper to Jascha as we make our way outside to the pickup area. "It's not like I can just pass *him* the medical letter."

"How much does he know already?"

"Just that my brain was being a jerk and all my tests came back negative." I glance over at him. "Let me guess. You think I should go for broke."

"In an age-appropriate way."

"But—"

"Curran's s a bright kid. He'll know if you're bullshitting him."

Yeah. I'm just gonna have to suck it up.

I reach for Jascha's hand. "Will you help me?"

He gives my hand a reassuring squeeze back. "Of course."

❧

We find Curran huddled under an awning next to Melinda Lewisham, who's got her arm draped soothingly around him.

"He's been a bit rattled ever since he found out you left early," she says to me.

"You told him?"

"I—I went to your office to say hi at recess." Curran's lower lip trembles. "And you weren't there."

Jesus, Mel. You could have said I was in a meeting.

"Come on, lovey." I stroke the top of his head. "Let's go home and have a chat."

❧

I sit Curran down on his bed, Jascha beside me.

"Okay." I take a deep breath. "I need ... I need to be honest with you about something."

"What is it?" Curran whispers.

I bite my lip. "You remember how I said my brain was playing weird tricks on me, right?"

He nods.

"Well, the kind of tricks it was playing made me need to stay on a special unit in the hospital. One for … for …"

I give Jascha a *Help me out here* look.

"People who are mentally unwell," he says.

Curran's eyes widen. "Like that lady we always see in the Metro station who keeps going on about how the CIA's out to get her?"

Yes. No. Umm …

"Well, that's one way people can act when they're ill." Jascha saves me yet again. "But your mum—"

"Wasn't like that," I say. "At all."

"Then how *were* you?"

Contemplating a razor. Staring in horror at my foreign face, my suddenly unfamiliar hands. Gasping in terror as if I were dying.

Hell, just the memory of those moments is still terrifying now. I can't even speak.

Jascha rubs my shoulder. "Have you ever had a really bad nightmare?" he asks Curran. "One where everything seemed creepy and confusing and all you wanted was to wake up, but you couldn't?"

Slowly, Curran nods again.

"That's what it felt like for your mum."

"Okay," Curran says, "but I still don't get why you went into hospital."

"Because …" I swallow.

"When you're scared and freaked out," Jascha says, "you don't always think clearly, mate. Your mind can tell you some real rubbish. To the point that you might not be safe on your own."

"Did they lock you up?" Curran asks.

Way to cut to the chase, buddy.

"I chose to go," I say, "but yeah. There were locks on the doors. And lots of rules."

"Like me not being able to visit."

"Right."

"Were they—were they mean to you? Was it scary there?"

I shake my head. "Just different. And hard, because I had to be away from you guys. But I needed to be there, same as your dad needed to be in the hospital for his chemo."

"Will you have to go back like he did?"

"Nope. My doctor thinks it was just a one-time thing."

"Then how come you left school early today?"

All my potential answers are self-flagellating, so I let Jascha take this one.

"Your mum got a bit overwhelmed," he says. "From coming back to work too soon."

"Like when you tried to do PE right after getting over the flu last year," I remind Curran.

"That was the worst." He turns to Jascha to clarify. "I spewed sick all over my brand-new trainers."

"Which is what my brain pretty much did this morning," I say.

Curran giggles. "Brain barf."

I should have known better than to run with such a disgusting metaphor. "So, yeah. I'm going to take the rest of this week off. But I don't want you to worry, okay? Jascha will be here, and—"

"Can I take the week off, too?"

"He looks terribly worried, Gloriochka," Jascha says dryly.

Relieved, I pull Curran toward me. Kiss the top of his head. "Nice try, kiddo," I half-whisper, half-laugh. "Nice try."

I'm just about to order more takeout for dinner when the phone rings. 301 area code, so local, but no one I recognize.

Please don't be Harrison Bingham phoning to berate me some more. Please.

"Hello." Soothing-but-grounded female voice. "This is Laurie Breggin at Healing Roots Counseling, returning a call from Gloria Burgess."

Healing Roots? You've got to be kidding me. Sounds like a New Age bookstore or a mountain retreat center that holds drum circles.

Don't laugh. She might be decent. At the very least give her credit for not phrasing her greeting as a question in perky, quasi-validating uptalk. I had an Australian professor in college who did that. Drove me up the freaking wall. *I think you should structure your thesis statement differently? So that it reflects a wider range of critical approaches?* Jesus, stop asking permission to express an opinion and just tell me why my essay's weak.

"Hello?"

I startle. "Hi. Yes. This is Gloria."

"Did I catch you at a bad time?"

"Not at all. I mean, things haven't been …" I swallow. "Haven't been the greatest lately, otherwise I wouldn't have called, but …"

Quit while you're ahead, Gloria Jacqueline du Pre.

"I understand. And I've got an appointment available tomorrow at nine if you'd like it."

Wow. That's quick. From the way everyone on Four West talked, waiting less than a month for a slot in a shrink's diary to open up was the equivalent of discovering a unicorn crapping gold-encrusted crack on the upper Metro platform at L'Enfant Plaza.

Better run with this good fortune. "I would."

⟨⟩

Jascha comes with me the next morning, for moral support. It's elbow to elbow on the Metro in rush hour, with the usual mix of characters: the earnest-to-the-point-of creepy guy handing out religious pamphlets, the woman with airbrushed fingernails longer than my hair who's got her headphones cranked up so loud we can all hear her commute jam, the Hill interns with their ties and wedge heels and rapidly wearying young faces.

My favorite train operator is on the Orange line today, rasping out over the loudspeaker at 8:20. "Ten minutes, friends. You still have time to get a cup of coffee."

Once we're on the Red line, approaching Silver Spring and therapyland, the crowd opens up a little. Jascha snags a seat and pulls me down into his lap.

"Come here, you." He wraps his arms around my waist, gathering me close.

An older lady shoots us a look as if to say, *Knock it off. You're not teenagers.*

But I feel like one. Careless and giddy, for the first time in I don't know how long.

⁓

My giddiness dissipates, though, soon as I'm sitting in the waiting room of Healing Roots *(don't laugh, don't laugh)* Counseling.

"This is the dumbest thing ever," I say to Jascha. "We should skive off."

"No." Jascha pats my hand. "It'll be good for you."

Psychiatric Brussels sprouts. Yum.

The walls are painted soothing pink. Self-help paperbacks with names like *Freedom From Codependency* and *The Gift of Inner Wisdom* sit tucked in a bookcase.

"Let's go sightseeing," I say. "C'mon."

Jascha looks me up and down. "I'm perfectly content with the sight I'm seeing at the moment."

"National Gallery of Art," I say, refusing to be buttered up. "All classics, no bullshit. Picasso. Dalí. Special history of sculpture exhibit, closing tomorrow."

"Wait, what?" Jascha's eyes widen like Curran's at the sight of a Cadbury Flake bar.

"Gloria?"

At the sound of my name, I look up to see a woman in her late forties come toward me.

Definite urban hippie vibe. Long silvery hair, spiral pendant, leggings paired with metallic paisley clogs. Fifty bucks says she's got a Zen sand tray and a dreamcatcher in her office.

Is this the part where I run? There's no *Patients, Do Not Cross* line like in the hospital, so I should be safe.

"Laurie Breggin." She offers me a surprisingly strong handshake.

"Hi." I'm suddenly withdrawn. Not like my surly adolescent self, but my deeply introverted childhood one.

"Why don't you come on back?" Laurie beckons like she's about to seat me at a restaurant or give me a haircut or perform any number of other mundane matter-of-fact.

Jascha points to his chair, as if to say *I'll be stationed right here.* Mouths *Good luck.*

Thanks, love. I think I'll need it.

❧

"So. Why don't you tell me a little bit about what brought you here today."

Oh, God. Do I have to give the biographical sketch again? Run down the timelines and lists of symptoms and personal history and blah fucking blah fucking blah?

At least she gets bonus points for no dreamcatcher. Let's go in with an open mind here, Gloriochka.

"I, umm …" My gaze flickers away from Laurie, toward the window that looks out on University Avenue and the late-to-work bustling crowd. "I spent last weekend at Washington Medical Center, on the …"

Psych unit. Just spit it out. It's shop talk to her.

But I can't.

"On Four West," she says gently.

Thanks, Laurie. "Right."

"Was that your first admission?"

Still looking away, I nod. "They recommended I see you."

"Well, I'm glad you came."

That makes one of us.

"Did they send you my chart, by chance?" Maybe she can read the Cliff's Notes. Speed this up.

Laurie shakes her head. "I can't access your medical information unless you sign a release."

"I'll sign it. Do you have a form or something I can fill out? Boxes to tick?"

"I do have a new client intake sheet, yes, but I'd much rather focus on your emotional experience of what just—"

"Look." I turn back to her. "I'm sorry, but this is really weird for me, okay? And exhausting. I got asked question after question while I was inpatient, often multiple times by multiple people, and I'd really rather—"

"Write down the key information for me and get that part over with?"

Whoa. She's good.

"Yes." I smile in spite of myself. "Thank you."

"Of course." Laurie hands me a clipboard with a sheet of paper and a pen. "Feel free."

In my best script, I write:

I'm thirty-one. I'm widowed (thanks, leukemia) and have an eight-year-old son who means more to me than anything in the world. I lived in England for ten years, until last summer when I came back here.

As I write, my cursive grows longer and loopier.

You guys like family-of-origin stuff, right? Well, here ya go: My mom's exasperating but painfully well-intentioned. My dad's dead. Suicide. Don't worry, I don't feel like following in his footsteps. I just ... lost myself for a bit. "Depersonalization and derealization disorder." Triple D.

Now I'm printing, fast and loose.

I'm a workaholic, but I'm working on it. No big "treatment goals." Just need to regroup. My boyfriend's flying back to London tomorrow and it's going be hard. Is this good enough? My hand hurts.

I hand the clipboard over to Laurie. She takes her time reading, her expression one of engagement and curiosity.

When she's finished, she looks up and says, "Yes. More than good enough. You've delineated your situation beautifully." Hint of a smile. "And I can tell your sense of humor is a real strength."

I look down into my lap. "I don't feel particularly strong lately."

"Ah, but feeling fragile doesn't mean you're fundamentally weak."

Wait, what? I raise my head slowly, taking in her words. "Wow. Could you ... run that by me again, please?"

"Sure." Laurie repeats the words, each one clear and deliberate. "You may feel fragile given all you've been through, but that feeling isn't a fact."

When I open my mouth to protest, she puts up a hand. "Hang on, bear with me. I'm not saying the feeling isn't valid or doesn't exist. I'm saying its content isn't a literal commentary on you as a person."

O … kay. "I think you just broke my brain." Not that it takes much these days.

"Let's look at it another way. Human beings have a natural craving for order and coherent narrative, right?"

"Of course. Since antiquity." Be still my English major heart. Now I'm with her.

"I take it that's a better metaphor for you?"

"Oh, yeah. Analyzing narrative's what I used to guide my students through all the time when I taught."

"Great. We'll run with that." Laurie looks relieved. "I'm guessing you focused on the aesthetic properties of narrative, yes? Whether it 'worked' as a plot, whether it compelled the reader, whether it reflected a theme?"

"Exactly." Ooh, this is like a graduate seminar. Totally worth the copay.

"Well, when we look at narratives from a psychodynamic perspective instead of a literary one, we examine for themes, too, but with a different aim."

"Let me guess," I say slowly. "You want to pinpoint the stories I'm telling about myself."

"Bingo."

Yay, I won. Can we stop so I can take my man to see Picasso now, please?

"I love that you said stories, plural," Laurie says. "Because we tell more than one at a time, and they intersect and diverge at various points."

"Like a Venn diagram?"

"Sort of. Only messier."

Now I'm twitchy again. Messy (outside of lax housekeeping, of which I'm horribly guilty) scares me.

"More like a frayed braid," Laurie clarifies. "You look nervous. Are we going too fast?"

I glance away. "I dunno."

"How you are you feeling in your body right now?"

My fingers fold over themselves. I dig my nails into my palms. Ouch. Still here.

"It's good. I mean, it's okay." Liar.

"So if I asked you to give me a summary of the dominant story, the one you're connecting with most at the moment ..." Christ, her voice is so gentle. "Could you tell me one? What would it say, about you as the protagonist?"

Blink blink blink. Hey, now, no tears. Just look at University Avenue. All those other fools muddling through the world with their briefcases and paper coffee cups and suddenly delicious-looking cigarettes.

My head jerks back to face Laurie. "She worked her ass off, but failed anyway."

"So the major theme's failure. And shame?"

I nod.

"About checking into Four West?"

I nod again.

"Because needing to be there says something about you, too."

"Yeah."

"What?"

"That I'm like my dad. A toxic waste of space."

"Whoa." Laurie raises an eyebrow. "That's a huge logical jump if ever I've seen one."

My shoulders tighten. No, really, can we stop now?

And yet: I want to push through it.

"I worked really hard." How many times can I say it, pleading, praying that that knowledge, that defense, will shore me up? "To keep from being him. But I still ..."

"Recognized you needed help and asked for it?" Laurie shifts in her chair, getting more comfortable. "What you did this past weekend wasn't proof of failure, but a sign of success."

Oh, come on.

"And yes, I get that it doesn't feel like one. There's no buzz of achievement or accomplishment like when the boss hands you a promotion. Nobody says, 'Yay, go me, I signed myself into a place with locked doors and shitty food and draconian rules that make me feel like a condescended-to child!'"

Aww, hell. I really am starting to like her.

"Do they?"

I manage a tiny smile. "No."

"And yet, I'm talking to you in person instead of reading your obituary and thinking, 'Wow, what a loss. Such a vibrant young woman. If only she'd come forward and let someone know she was—'"

"I *told* you." The words come out way more pissy than I intend. "I've never been suicidal."

"Maybe not, but Washington Med doesn't hospitalize people for mild depression or transient Triple D. Great term, by the way. Mind if I borrow it?"

"Go ahead." I want to cross my arms and glare, but alas, I already respect Laurie too much to turn sulky teen on her.

"Believe me, I've worked that ER. With the number of psych crises that come in every day, and the constant shortage of beds, they triage hardcore. No admissions without a documented danger to self or others."

I picture the razor. Give a reflexive shudder.

"I ... I did have thoughts of hurting myself," I say. "Which is different from suicidal ideation."

Vigorous nod. "Yeah. I get that. But even without intent, you still could have done some real damage."

Jesus. I don't even want to imagine.

"Look," Laurie says, "I'm not telling you this to be morbid or scare you. I'm telling you as part of an alternate story: one in which you aren't a waste of space, in which staying alive—staying able to bring the gifts you have to offer the world—is a triumph."

Goddamn it. Now I'm tearing up for real.

"And I'm pretty sure your exasperating mom and your dear little boy who serves as a touchstone and that sweet-looking guy out in the waiting room would agree."

"Yeah. I guess so." I swipe at my watery eye with my thumb. "Could I possibly get a tissue?"

"Of course." Laurie plucks an entire box off her desk and leans over to hand it to me. "Just in case you need more."

"Thanks." I blow my nose. "Sorry."

"No need to apologize."

"I'm just sick of crying. Done so much of it in the last year."

"So your husband died recently?"

Sniffling, I nod. "Last January."

"Ah. Anniversaries are always tricky."

You're telling me.

"And your current relationship is relatively new?"

"Yes and no." I give her a brief recap: the fifteen minutes of fame, our New Year's Eve balcony cowardice, his words just before my phone shut off, our reunion at the Four West nurse's station.

"Wow. Now there's a story. I can see why you'd be anxious at the thought of him leaving tomorrow."

"Yeah," I say with a sigh. "I mean, on the one hand, I'm not losing him permanently to leukemia, just temporarily to the Atlantic Ocean."

"And on the other?"

"I've just barely *gotten* him, you know? And it's so wonderful."

Every last trace of sullen teenager melts from my voice. "All those things I missed. Lunch dates and inside jokes and playing board games with my son and mind-blowing sex and ..." My face goes hot. "Sorry. Was that last bit TMI?"

Laurie chuckles. "There's no such thing as TMI in therapy."

Whew. "I'm tempted to ask him to stay longer."

"What's making you reluctant?"

"He'll lose his job if he's not back by Saturday."

"Wow, yeah, that'd make me reluctant, too. But if his job security wasn't an issue? How would you feel then?"

"Oh, man. I don't know." I sigh again. "I want him here, obviously. And it's a huge help to have him here. But I don't want to be too"—I make a face—"clingy."

"Okay." Laurie's all excited, like I just said the secret prize-winning word of the day and confetti and dollar bills are about to descend from the ceiling. "Let's unpack that statement, those semantics, for a minute. 'Clingy' means what to you?"

Dad pushing my University of London acceptance letter to the side of his desk. *You're sure, love? It's much harder academically across the pond.*

I've got a 4.0 here, Dad. I think I'll manage.

His eyes locked on me, despondent. *I wish I could say the same.*

"Holding someone back," I say. "Out of your own selfishness. Your own fear."

"Of not being able to cope without them?"

I nod.

"Is it true?"

"That I'm afraid?"

"That you won't be able to cope without your boyfriend here."

"Sometimes I feel like I won't."

"But feelings aren't facts, remember?"

Argh. "Okay," I say. "If—I mean, when—he leaves tomorrow, I'm not going to fall apart. It'll just be incredibly painful."

"And you've weathered that sort of pain before. After your husband died."

"Yeah, I was doing a pretty good job of it up until about a week ago."

"Perfect. Keep the focus on your own long-term competence. Big picture, not just the last few days."

"That's really hard when …" I trail off.

"I know. But be gentle with yourself. You're more than just the sum of what's happened to you."

Oh, God. "I'm gonna cry again. Shit."

"It's okay."

No, it isn't.

I reach for another tissue. "I wasn't expecting this to be so … to stir up so much—"

"We'll go slowly. There's no need to condense it all into one session."

"How—how long do we have left?"

"Today?" Laurie checks her watch. "About thirty seconds."

Good. I let out a shaky breath.

"Thanks," I whisper. "For not pouncing on the stuff about my dad."

"Of course. You didn't look anywhere near ready to go there. And I won't push you."

"Thanks," I whisper again.

"Well, let's book another appointment, at least." She reaches for her calendar. "I've got a one o'clock a week from next Tuesday. How's that?"

Umm …

"Or I have Thursday at eleven? Friday at ten?"

"No evenings or weekends?"

Laurie shakes her head. "Sorry."

Crap. Are we in or are we in, Gloriochka?

"Okay," I say, sighing. "Tuesday at one it is."

When I return to the waiting room, Jascha peers at me with furrowy concern. "Have you been crying?"

"Eh." I shrug. "Cathartic tears. It's all good."

"She wasn't too hippie-dippy, then?"

"Nah. I like her." I grab his hand and tug him toward the door. "C'mon, darlin'. Your art awaits."

CHAPTER EIGHTEEN

A day so luminous Jascha can't believe it's happening:

Viewing Salvador Dalí canvases in the flesh.

Wandering the outdoor sculpture garden, arm in arm with Gloria.

People-watching on the Metro, bags of takeaway in their laps. ("Watch out, Gloom and Doom Prophet's working the aisles again.")

Fucking with her balanced on the edge of the bathroom sink. Her hair in his fist. His mouth to her ear. "Office door's closed, Headmistress. No one will hear you."

And then: that glorious moment when, given permission, somehow released, she tips her head back against the infamous mirror and finally lets out a ragged scream.

Afterwards, they flop on their stomachs, exhausted, on Gloria's bed. Cheek pressed against the duvet, she watches Jascha with a tiny, blissed-out smile.

"You're having a melancholy Russian moment, aren't you?" she asks.

"That obvious?"

"Mmm."

"I just can't stop thinking about how I have to get on a plane in twenty-four hours."

"Don't remind me." She sighs. "I'm trying not to think about it, either. To just relish the time we've got. But—"

"I can't leave you," Jascha blurts out. "Not now."

Holy hell. Where'd *that* come from?

"Jasch. Honey." Gloria bites her lip. "Don't worry. I'll manage."

"I'm not worried about you. I mean, I *am*. More like concerned, maybe? Hard not to be, after what happened. But that isn't …"

Christ. Spit it out, man.

Jascha rolls over onto his side. Props up on one elbow.

"Okay," he says. "This is going to sound horribly sentimental, and I know you're going to roll your eyes and laugh."

"I won't. Promise." Gloria turns over to face him, posed with rapt attention.

He swallows. How to explain? It's all so bound up with the accident, tangled as his totaled Audi's gnarled metal.

"When Marianne and Elizabeth died," Jascha says slowly, "I was furious. At an arsehole God who'd left me completely bereft. At my mum who kept yammering on about how I'd find a reason to live if I just held on long enough. All that forcible-bootstrapping-disguised-as-inspirational-pep-talk crap."

"But you hung on."

"Mainly because I couldn't stand the thought of leaving Vera to grow old alone."

"Hey, whatever keeps you going."

"Yeah. It gave me a sense of purpose, but only for a little while. I mean, I love my mum dearly, but taking her to bingo and doctor's appointments wasn't my Reason with a capital R, you know?"

Gloria nods.

"So then I thought, okay, maybe art's my purpose. Total cliché, right, channeling your pain, but I reckoned it was worth a shot. Even if all I wound up creating was—"

"Pretentious wankery?"

Jascha snorts. "Jesus, Gloriochka, tell me how you really feel about my life's work."

"Sorry."

"No. No. It's okay. Guilty as charged. And again, I enjoyed my work at first. Threw myself into it. Even slept at the studio some nights."

Tossing and turning on a pulled-out futon. The nightmare taunting: *Anywhere you try to hide, I can find. No matter how clever the refuge. No matter how sacred the space.*

"I was kidding myself," Jascha says. "Chasing some daft arrogant notion of becoming the next YBA"—Young British Artist, epitome of hyped trend-setting—"when honestly I was lonely as fuck."

Now it's dawning on Gloria where he's going. He can see it in the way her face shifts into softness, the way she props up on her elbow to mirror his own position, the way her shoulders bunch up in anticipation of what he's about to confess.

"Took me four long, excruciating years," he says. "But now I know. My reason ... It's you and Curran."

Gloria's brows furrow. She presses a hand to her heart. "Oh, Jasch."

"You can laugh," Jascha says. "I know it's treacly as all hell."

"No." Her smile deepens. Her voice goes breathy with wonder. "No. It's ..."

Gloria runs a hand over her eyes. "Wow. I can't ... I just ..." She trails off, shaking her head a little.

And then she leans over and grabs his face in her hands and draws him in for a hard, urgent kiss, then pulls back and whispers, "Cancel your ticket. Call Tim. Let's make this happen."

Jascha's breath catches. His pulse hammers.

"Seriously?" he chokes out.

"Seriously."

Boshe moi. Suddenly all the logistical issues he'd conveniently ignored in his fervor start rearing their pesky heads. "My passport stamp says I'm only authorized to stay for six months. Is that enough time to find a job?"

"Honey, D.C.'s crawling with arts admin positions. Funding agencies, the National Archives ... They'll eat you up." Wicked grin. "But not as much as I will."

She makes it sound so simple. So easy.

"I need to think on this, Gloriochka," he says.

Gloria frowns. "Excuse me? You're the one who just said you can't—"

"I know, I know." Jascha's almost sorry he mentioned it now. "I was caught up, okay?"

"So you didn't ... didn't mean it." Her voice trembles.

Jesus. What a mess he's made.

Jascha takes her face in his hands. "Love, I *want* to stay. Please don't doubt me on that front. I just ..."

"What?"

"This is a huge leap. Way bigger than my flying over on short notice."

Gloria jerks away. "You think I don't realize that?"

"Please," Jascha says. "Give me some time. A few more Russian moments of contemplation."

She chews her lip in what looks like her own bout of pensiveness, but Jascha can feel the scowl of petulance brewing beneath it.

"There's heaps at stake here," he adds. "It's only fair."

A soft, resigned sigh. Gloria flops onto her back.

"Yeah," she concedes. "I guess it is."

For the rest of that night, the temptation and trepidation gnaw at Jascha in equal measure. As he roughhouses with Curran, as he makes love to Gloria again, his id insistently wheedles: *This could be yours, all the time. Come on. You know you want nothing more.*

But then, while he watches her sleep, the what-ifs creep in. What if he doesn't find a job? What if it's too soon? What if it all blows up in their faces?

Gloria rolls over against him. Flings her arm across his chest.

She's so unlike anyone he's ever met. Mouthy as hell, all unbridled ardor. Heart stitched permanently on her sleeve. It's refreshing yet terrifying.

Just because she's up for this, Jascha reminds himself, doesn't mean you have to be.

So much to fear. So much to let go of: his career, his flat, his comfortable if introverted life in London.

Not to mention his elderly mum. Christ.

And yet: so much to gain.

Jascha remembers himself ten years ago, a skittish, fumbling new husband and father. Holding back. Keeping his affection in reserve, until it was too late.

Compared to that fatal blunder, the potential mistake in front of him pales to the point of near-invisibility, eclipsed by the riotous color-whirl of the beauty that could be.

Gloria's eyelids flutter. Her cheek nudges itself into the hollow of his neck.

"Yes," he says aloud.

"Huh?" She tips her head back, groggy but curious.

"Yes," he says again, louder this time.

JENN CROWELL

Gloria blinks. Gives him a drowsy smile. "Yes to what?"

Jascha tucks her head back against his shoulder. "To here. To us."

⟋⟍

The announcement's got to be made to Curran, but Jascha can't help worrying what his response will be. Staying a little longer's one thing—he doesn't doubt Curran will welcome that—but Mum's new boyfriend moving in is another entirely.

"He thinks of you as a father figure already," Gloria says, linking her arm soothingly through Jascha's as they cross the road. "It's not like you're some guy I picked up at a bar two days ago. You've been part of his life for a year."

Good point, but still. The boy's been through so much turmoil. What if …

Stop it. Just stop.

"Mum!" The minute Curran spies Gloria, he rushes toward her with a gleeful yelp. "You came!"

"Of course I did." She gathers him into a cozy hug.

Jascha steps back to give them space as Curran's teacher (Mrs. Lewis? Lewisham? Yes, that's it) comes over to say hello.

"This young man"—she gestures toward Curran—"did an outstanding job on his multi-digit subtraction homework." Gloria made damn sure he finished it last night.

"Jascha helped me," Curran says. "Loads."

"Don't sell yourself short, mate." Jascha drapes an arm around him. "You did all the hard work."

With a wave goodbye to Mrs. Lewisham, the three of them trudge toward home in the cold, Curran in the middle.

Another experience Jascha will never again take for granted: two tall shadows and one small one nestled together, reflected on the sunny pavement.

136

Let's hope their news won't blow it all.

"Anyone else up for a hot chocolate?" Gloria asks. "I'm freezing."

"Yes, please!" Curran chirps.

There we go. Genius idea. Combine it with something light and fun.

After ordering, they all squish around a tiny table—so tiny their knees touch—at the coffee shop in the lobby of Gloria's building.

"You should have worn gloves, Mum," Curran tsks at her. "Like you're always after me to."

"Do as I say, not as I do, right?" Gloria winces as she rubs her bare knuckles, their pale skin purpled by chill.

"Here. Let me." Jascha blows on her hands softly, then gathers them in his.

"Oh, that's better," she sighs. "Thanks, love."

Jascha expects Curran to look irritated at their public display of affection, but instead he simply sips away at his cocoa, content.

"How's that shot of Nutella in there?" Jascha asks. He'd convinced Curran to try it.

"Sooo good." He kicks his backpack to the side to make a bit more foot room. "Can we do this again after school tomorrow? Before your plane leaves?"

Jascha and Gloria glance at each other.

"Sure," Jascha says. "But my plane's not leaving."

"Did your flight get cancelled? That happened to Quinn's family once. They were going to Florida, Disney World and all that, for their Christmas holiday. Oh, his mum was so vexed. She never uses f-bombs. Unlike Mum, who says it—"

"All the time, yeah, I know," Gloria says dryly.

"But Mrs. Matthews, she marched right up to the ticket counter and said 'Are you bloody joking? I paid an extra tariff for priority seating and everything, and now you f…'" He blushes. "Can *I* say it, Mum?"

She pats his arm. "We get the picture, sweetie. Let Jascha explain, okay?"

"My flight didn't get cancelled," Jascha says, chuckling. "I cancelled it myself."

"So you can stay longer?" Curran's eyes light up.

Jascha nods.

"How long? Till Quinn's birthday party on Sunday? It's gonna be brilliant. With bounce houses!"

Oh, this child.

"I'll definitely still be here for the party," Jascha says. "In fact, I'll be here until July."

"With us? Like, in our flat?"

Jascha nods. "And maybe longer. Depending on whether I can get a job."

"He will," Gloria says.

"And then he'll be here for good?"

"That's the plan," Jascha says, ready to follow up with caveats about how he realizes this is a huge change and Curran might feel like he's going to replace his father and Jascha totally understands if he's ambivalent or even angry.

But before Jascha can so much as say "Listen, I," the boy jumps up from the table, dumping his hot chocolate everywhere, and dashes over to hug Jascha hard around the neck.

"I'm so glad," Curran whispers.

"Me too, mate." Jascha pats him on the back.

Curran casts a nervous glance at the mess. "Sorry about the table, Mummy."

"It's okay." Gloria beams at the two of them. "I'll go grab some napkins."

Jascha watches as she heads toward the cluster of condiments and straws by the till. She thinks he's not looking, Jascha knows, which is why, when he looks, he can see her surreptitious grab of an extra napkin with which to blot the (grateful, he also knows) dampness from her eyes.

⁐

Barely any time to bask in that moment, though, because when Jascha gets back to her (their?) flat he has to make a series of phone calls: not just the one to the airline canceling his flight home, but also several to London to break the news.

"Oh, Jaschechka," his mother sighs. "Following heart is not same thing as being bossed about by it."

"Come on," Jascha says. "You were the one who convinced me to fly out here."

"For a little while. Not this crazy 'six months, maybe longer' business."

"I'll make sure you're taken care of, Mama. Hire you some help."

"With what money?"

"I can get a job."

"In another country? Just like that?"

"You and Papa did."

"As dishwasher at a pub. As cleaning lady in hotel. You deserve better."

"And I'll find it. Gloria's well-connected to the expat community here."

"What about her little boy? How does he feel about all this?"

"Over the moon."

At that, Vera's voice warms. "Maybe you three come back instead? To London?"

"Or you could move here."

His mother laughs. "Very funny. Am quite done with new citizenships, thank you."

"Well, we have options. I'm not deserting you."

"Never said you were. Am just thinking of what might go wrong."
Classic Russian.

"Mamochka, please. For once, finally, things are going right."

"And you're happy."

"More than I've ever been. Since ... you know."

"Well, then," Vera says. "Is settled. Am still worried, but you have my blessing."

Whew. Next up: Tim.

"You're fucking kidding me. Please say you are."

"Not even a little."

"Jesus. I could understand if she was still horribly sick. I'd even argue for you taking longer leave. But chucking it all? No way, man."

"I'm not chucking it all. I'm gaining it."

"Yeah, keep telling yourself that. And talk to me in six months when you're still unemployed and you have to fly home and rebuild all the bridges you burned."

"I'll find work," Jascha says for what feels like the millionth time today.

"Will you? They're spoilt for choice in Washington, same as here. You really think a museum will pick a random foreign bloke they'll have to arrange a visa for over a Yank who's ready to start tomorrow?"

"Won't know unless I try."

"I wouldn't. You're up-and-coming here. Remember Veronica, that *Observer* journalist?"

"The one you made out with at the Christmas networking party," Jascha says, sighing.

"Wish I'd done more than that. She was totty as hell."

"I'm not racking up a massive bill on Gloria's phone just to hear your exploits. What's totty Veronica got to do with me?"

"She rang earlier today. Says you're tapped for the shortlist of YBAs in their 'Creatives to Watch in 1996' piece coming out next month."

"Whatever."

"*Whatever?* That's a game-changer, man. I'd give my right ball to be on that list."

"Go ahead, then. I'm done chasing accolades. I just want to be with—"

"She's nothing but a liability, Jascha. First a single mum, and now mental. I mean, sure, I'm guessing she's brilliant at putting that dirty mouth to use in bed, but—"

"Fuck you." Jascha slams the phone down.

"Please tell me you didn't say that to Vera," Gloria says, coming into the kitchen.

"God, no. Started out tetchy, but she came around."

Gloria sighs. "Guess I should suck it up and tell my mom, too."

CHAPTER NINETEEN

Why am I so nervous? I'm a grown damn adult. I've got every right to make this sort of choice about my life.

But how do I tell her?

"Oh! Sweetheart." Mom's voice rises in surprise and delight at my calling her of my own volition. "Having an easier time of it today?"

"Yeah. Much better. In fact, I was wondering if you might be up for lunch tomorrow."

"Of course I am. But wouldn't you rather spend time with Jascha before he flies out in the evening?"

"Actually ..." I take a deep breath. "It's a non-issue. Jascha's not leaving tomorrow."

"What? I thought he had to be back in London Saturday. For his art show."

"He did. But—"

"They gave him extra time off? Oh, how kind."

"No. No." Gulp. "He quit."

"Why on earth would he do a thing like that?"

"He decided to move in with me."

"*He* decided. On his own. With no regard for—"

"No. I mean, *we* decided. Together."

"And this is ... permanent?"

"Once he gets a new job, yeah, it will be."

"But there's no guarantee he'll find one."

"There's no guarantee with anything, Mom. And to me this risk is absolutely worth it."

"What about Curran? What about Jascha's mother back in England? He can't just leave her behind."

"Curran's thrilled, and Vera gave us her blessing." Suddenly timid, I pause. "Like I hope you will."

"I wish I could, but …" Mom's voice puckers with distaste. "It's so soon. So fast. And this could be a real burden on your financial situation."

"Oh, for Christ's sake. Jascha's sitting next to me perusing the want ads as we speak. And it's not like him living here adds any extra burden to my budget. I mean, he's got the tall, broad-shouldered, hunky Slavic thing going on in spades"—at this, I hear Jascha snicker from behind his newspaper—"but the man doesn't eat *that* much."

Success. Mom laughs. "Fine. You've got me. Not saying I'm not still concerned, of course, or that I think it's a wise idea, but—"

"Duly noted. There's no need to worry, Mom."

That hurdle crossed, I spend the rest of the evening in thrall to tiny domestic delights.

I make us all dinner (just spaghetti and frozen breadsticks, but hey). I fold a load of laundry, sneaking one of Jascha's T-shirts into my own pajama drawer. I quiz Curran on his spelling words, then get my ass handed to me in a game of Scrabble (by a man whose first language isn't even English, no less).

Jascha takes pity on me and does the dishes while I bribe Curran into the tub with an extra chapter of bedtime read-aloud if he washes fast enough. From behind the bathroom door, I can hear him bellowing Oasis over the sound of the running water.

I sneak up behind Jascha at the sink and kiss the back of his neck. He shivers so hard he almost drops a plate.

"*Boshe moi*," he whispers. "I still can't believe …"

"Me, either." I rest my palms on his shoulders. Give them a giddy squeeze.

Curran's exuberant voice ramps up to a near-bellow as he reaches the chorus of "Wonderwall."

"You'd better be soaping up in there, Liam Gallagher!" I yell.

"Already finished," Curran calls back. "But I can't find any clean towels."

Oops. Guess I missed that load.

"I'll get him one," Jascha says.

A minute later, I hear Curran giggling as Jascha tells him the story of how Vera misheard and thought the name of the song was actually "Wonderbra."

My boys, I think, shaking my head as I take Jascha's place at the sink to scrub out a stockpot. My ridiculous, lovely boys.

On Sunday, the day of Curran's friend Quinn's birthday party, I ask my mom to drive us all. Embarrassing as that request is to make, I don't feel ready to navigate the Beltway yet.

"So is this Rockville place the one from the REM song?" Jascha asks as we cross into Montgomery County.

"It is indeed."

Of course we then have to sing the chorus as if we're Curran performing in the bathtub.

"You two," Mom says, shaking her head.

She turns down a weather report on the radio—"Snow's predicted in the metro region later this evening …"—so she can find a parking spot in the Matthews' crowded cul-de-sac.

"Not a single space," Mom sighs. "Must be quite the event."

Uh-oh. My stomach churns at the thought of running into the entire Year Four class and their parents.

"There's a spot, Gran."

Curran dashes out of the car, dragging Jascha with him. "C'mon! C'mon!"

Mom turns to me. "Pick you up at three, right?"

Feeling like a teenager getting driven to the mall, I nod. "Thanks, Mom."

❦

I hurry to catch up with Jascha so I can introduce him properly when Quinn's mother, Fiona, answers the door.

"Welcome to the madhouse," she greets us in her dry English accent. "Feeling better, Gloria?"

Now that I've been released from another madhouse, sure. "Getting there."

Curran's beside himself with excitement. "Have the bounce houses gone up yet, Mrs. Matthews?"

"They have, pet. Just nip round the side gate."

As Curran scampers off, Jascha glances at me.

"Oh. Sorry, Fee. This is my partner, Jascha."

To her credit, Fiona doesn't raise an eyebrow. "Lovely to meet you." She rubs her hands briskly over her arms. "Let's get in from this Arctic chill, shall we?"

❦

She leads us down their sprawling colonial's long center hallway toward the kitchen, where her American husband Jason is busy setting out a platter of fruit arranged in smiley-face patterns and

145

cupcakes festooned with gummy-worm light-sabers.

"Are we the only parents here?" I ask.

Fiona nods. "I invited the rest to stay, but they all wanted to make supermarket runs for milk and loo paper before the blizzard hits."

"It's not going to be a blizzard," Jason says, chuckling, as he pulls a stack of juice boxes from the fridge.

"I'll get those." Fiona nudges him aside. "Go supervise the sprogs."

She's barely arranged drinks on the kitchen's center island when the doorbell rings. "That'd be the takeaway pizza. I'll be right back."

"You should talk to Jason," I say to Jascha after the couple has reported to their respective duty stations.

Jascha shuffles from side to side, clearly uncomfortable with the whole forced-dude-socialization idea.

"He owns a staffing agency."

Jascha frowns. "You mean, like crappy temp jobs?"

"No. Permanent. High-end."

"*Oh.*" His face perks up a little as he heads for the backyard.

Fiona returns carrying a stack of cardboard boxes. "Let's just hope they don't wake the baby trooping back in for their pepperoni. Could you grab that fine china for me, Glor?"

"Sure." I set out the Star Wars-themed paper plates.

"Thanks. You want a mimosa or something?"

"I'd love one."

"Okay. Hang on." She opens the sliding glass door and calls to the kids. "Pizza time, you lot!"

We're almost trampled by the stampede.

"Ooh, light-saber cupcakes!"

"Don't shove, boys." Jason's directing traffic. "Quinn, let your little brother in there."

Fiona hands me a champagne flute. "Quick. Let's escape to the lounge while we can."

⟋⟋

At first it feels a little weird, sipping alcohol in the middle of the day with someone who's the mother of both my son's best friend and one of my students. But, suburban excess aside, I genuinely like Fiona.

"I don't mean to be nosy," she says, taking a sip of her non-boozy mimosa version, "but what on earth was the business with the spy camera Quinn and Curran kept going on about?"

"Oh. That." I fake a casual, unconcerned laugh. "Just got a scan to rule out a few things. Which I thankfully don't have."

"Smart of you to get checked, though. My sister was in denial about her MS symptoms for ages, and now she's—"

"Mummy!" Fiona's three-year-old, Bertie, comes stomping into the room, his chubby cheeks tear-stained. "Quinn not letting me do bounce house!"

Fiona strokes his hair. "That's because it's for bigger kids, love."

"But I'm big!"

"Toddler logic." She sighs. "Let me get him settled in the playroom. I'll be right back."

After she leaves, I stare down into my drink. Debate whether I should tell her the full truth.

Maybe she'll be understanding, since, like Julia, she's got a sibling with a chronic illness.

But what if she isn't? What if she stops trusting me to hold sleepovers and park dates with Quinn? Or whispers to other parents at the school about how "unstable" I am?

God. What to do?

From the kitchen, I hear Jason and Jascha networking. "Send me a resume. Here, I'll give you my card."

"Thanks. Really appreciate it."

No. I can't wreck this.

Upstairs, the baby lets out a thin wail.

"Christ." Fiona rushes toward the stairs, dabbing a Star Wars napkin at her damp blouse to stem the tide of leaky milk. "Be there fast as I can, kitten!"

I tip my head back against the couch cushion. Close my eyes. Listen to Fiona coo at her daughter. "All right, poppet. There we are, Tessie-bean."

At the sound of approaching footsteps, I startle to find Jascha before me, hand extended to pull me up.

"Come check out the funfair," he says. "You have to see it to believe it."

He wasn't kidding. The backyard's been transformed into a full-on carnival, with little booths set up for party games, and a popcorn machine, and even—

Bumper cars? Holy shit.

Kidlet shrieks fill the bracingly cold air. Through the mesh window of an inflatable castle, I can see Curran alternating between tumbles and leaps.

"Rental company thought we were insane doing this in January," Jason says as he hands out fake paper tickets. "But better to set it all up on solid ground now than deal with soggy slush later."

Curran's head emerges from the front curtain of the bounce house. "Jascha!" he breathlessly squeals when he sees us, almost forgetting to put his shoes back on in his rush over to where we stand. "Let's do the bumper cars together!"

CHAPTER TWENTY

Sure, Jascha wants to say. I'd love to, he wants to answer.

But he can't answer. Can't say it.

And even worse: Can't do it.

"Sorry, mate." A rueful headshake's all he manages. "Not this time."

Not ever. At least that's what it feels like.

"Why not?" God, that puzzled, pouty face. Breaking him.

Jascha swallows. "I just …"

"Please." Curran grabs Jascha's arm. Shakes his sleeve. "Please, Jascha."

"Don't bug him, honey." Gloria pats Curran's shoulder in gentle admonishment.

Poor kid. He didn't ask for this.

"I wish I could," Jascha says. "Really, I do. But—"

"You get sick on them?"

"Umm … not exactly." How can he explain?

"Then why can't you?"

"I *said* don't bug him." Gloria's tone ratchets up to a snap. "If he doesn't want to, he doesn't want to, okay?"

Curran crosses his arms. His lower lip trembles as he glowers. "*Dad* would have."

And with that gauntlet thrown down, he slinks off dejectedly toward the games booth.

⁓

Jascha and Gloria turn toward each other at the same time. He can't see his own expression, but he guesses it's remarkably close to her wide-eyed, downturned-lipped one of *Oh, shit.*

She blows out a slow sigh. "Guess it was only a matter of time, huh?"

Jascha's face burns. "I'll go find him and tell him I'll do it."

"Oh, no, you won't." Gloria grabs his arm. "You looked like you were about to faint just watching those things crash into each other."

Christ. Really? What a pitiful sod he is.

"I'm sorry, Gloriochka," he whispers.

"For what? Not wanting to relive the worst moment of your life?" She gives Jascha's arm a soothing squeeze. "I wouldn't either."

"Yeah, but—"

"He's just being a brat. I'll go tell him to knock it off."

"No," Jascha says. "I should talk to him. He needs to know why, or else he'll just keep taking it personally."

Gloria nods. "Good call."

Now it's Jascha's turn for a deep blown-out breath. "Wish me luck."

⁓

Jascha finds Curran at the front of the queue for the darts challenge.

"Why so sad, buddy?" Jason asks as he hands Curran his first round.

Curran says nothing. Draws his arm back and slams a bull's-eye onto the board.

"Nice," Jascha says. "Imagining my face, were you?"

The boy fights not to smile. "A little."

"Come on. Let's go talk." Jascha motions for him to step aside so Quinn can take a turn.

"I don't want to miss the cake," Curran protests.

"We won't miss the cake. I promise."

❧

They find a quiet spot inside in the empty formal living room. Jascha sinks into an overstuffed chair and pats the ottoman next to him, beckoning Curran to sit down.

He does so gingerly, perched on the edge as if poised to make a quick getaway—not just for cake, but also for an end to the conversation.

"Sorry, Jascha." Curran's voice is rote.

"No need for that," Jascha says. "I don't blame you for being frustrated. But I do want you to understand."

Curran stares down at the Oriental rug. Traces its pattern with the toe of his shoe. "Understand what?"

"Why I couldn't go on the ride."

Curran looks up again, his curiosity piqued. "Yeah. How come? If you wanted to, and they don't make you ill, then—"

"I'm too afraid," Jascha blurts out.

Curran's brows furrow. "But you're a grownup. You don't act afraid of anything."

Act, being the key word.

"And what's so scary about them? Quinn's brother Bertie's only three, and he's not frightened one bit."

"Well," Jascha says, sighing a little, "I doubt Bertie's been through what I have."

He leans forward. Rests his arms on his knees, lacing his fingers together to stop his hands' nervous shake.

151

"Your mum's told you about my other family, right?" Jascha asks Curran. "From before we all met?"

Curran nods. "I asked her how you guys got to be such good friends. And she said it was because you had a wife and little girl who died, so you both knew what the other was going through."

"Right. But did she tell you how they—"

His question is interrupted by the fussing of a baby in the hallway. Jascha looks over to see Quinn's mum walking back and forth as she pats the back of a pink-wrapped bundle.

Dear God. That's hardly helping.

"No," Curran says. "How did they?"

"In ..." Jascha stares down at his laced hands. "In a car accident. Where I was driving."

"Oh, man." Curran breathes out the words. "I'd be scared to get in *any* car after that."

"I was, for a while."

"But you drive now. Back in England, anyway. And you're cool with it."

As long as it's not raining. "Sure. That's a lot different than getting slammed by bumper cars, though."

"Can't you just remind yourself it's a only ride?" The boy's question comes across as honest curiosity, not a dismissive scoff.

"I'd like to," Jascha says slowly. "I just don't think I'm quite there yet."

Four, almost five, fucking years. You'd think he would be.

In the hallway, the baby's finally quieted.

From the kitchen, Quinn's dad shouts out, "Who's ready for cake?"

Curran gives Jascha a querying look, as if to ask, *Class dismissed?*

"Go for it," Jascha says.

When Curran jumps up, Jascha expects him to dash off. Instead, he leans over and gives Jascha a hug so tight his ribs twinge.

"Bouncy castle afterwards?" Jascha whispers in his ear. "You and me?"

He can feel Curran's grin against his shoulder. "Deal."

⟨∼

After Curran leaves, Jascha sits there for a while, listening from afar to the off-key bellowed rendition of "Happy Birthday," which for some inscrutable reason the children end with "Cha-cha-cha!"

She'd have been ten this year. Double digits. *Happy birthday, dear Elizabeth ...*

Fiona pokes her head in. "Would you mind holding Tess for a moment? She's just fallen asleep on my shoulder and I desperately need to use the toilet."

"Umm ... sure."

When Fiona passes the baby over, Jascha's hit with waves of nostalgia so strong he's afraid he might drop her.

"Look at you. You're a natural."

He sinks back into the chair and props his feet up on the ottoman. Cradles the baby's downy head against his chest.

She lets out a tiny sigh. *Boshe moi.* This is hard.

Thankfully Gloria comes in and sits on the chair's wide arm next to him.

"Fiona'll be back in a few," she says. "She's on camera duty for present-opening."

Jascha nods. "I don't know how long I can ..."

Gloria glances at the baby, then back up at him. "Want me to take her?"

No. Yes. "Please."

She kisses the top of Jascha's head, then reaches over so he can carefully transfer the baby into her arms. "Reminders all over the place today, huh?"

Try every day.

The baby—what's her name? Tess?—starts to stir, whimpering a bit. Gloria does the gentle, side-to-side bounce Jascha remembers well from when he walked the floor with a colicky Elizabeth.

"There we go," she croons, stroking Tess's fuzzy hair till she settles back down. "That's it, sweet girl."

This is killing him. *Stop,* Jascha wants to say. *Take her upstairs. Outside. Anywhere away from here. From me.*

And yet he can't help but imagine: Gloria, doing this out on their flat's balcony in spring. Holding not a party guest's infant daughter, but their own.

"Ever think of having another?" Jascha asks. Trying to keep the query casual.

Gloria bites her lip, obviously flustered. "Umm ..." Her face flushes. "Do we really need to have this conversation? Here, right now?"

Jesus. Him and his big blurting mouth. "No."

CHAPTER TWENTY-ONE

This baby's positively yummy, but I have to hand her back to Fiona before I tear up from guilt.

Tonight. I'll talk to him. It'll hurt, but I have to be honest.

I'm halfway down the hall when Tess wakes up. Fretful as I feel, rubbing her bow-shaped mouth against my sweater in increasingly frantic search for milky fulfillment.

"I got nothing, darlin'," I whisper. "Sorry."

Inconsolable now, she sucks at her tiny fingers with desperate smacks as I carry her into the family room.

"Oh, kitten," Fiona coos, holding out her arms for Tess. "Ready to belly up to the milk bar again?"

She waits until all the kids have dashed back outside for one last round of bounce-crash-win before the carnival leaves town.

"Thank God. Now I can get my baps out without flashing a roomful of boys." Fiona struggles with the snaps on her bra. Leans back onto a pillow. Exhales deeply as her milk lets down. "Ahh, there we go. I was so full they started getting all porn star-y."

I chuckle. "Want another faux-mosa?"

"Please. Sparkling water and orange juice are in the fridge."

As I mix her drink, I can't help remembering how Bill lavished me with attention in those early days postpartum. *Can I fetch you a pillow, love? Glass of water?* Bringing me little plates of cheese and baguette when I was stuck on the couch nursing for hours.

I've no doubt Jascha would do the same. Hell, he'd probably feed the baguette to me.

Stop it. Don't go there.

Fiona sighs as I hand her the glass flute. "Ta. You're an angel."

She looks heavy-lidded and content, almost stoned, all that oxytocin rush flooding her. "So tell me about Jascha."

Wow, you *are* nosy, Fee. Normally I'd be happy to wax poetic about him, but right now I don't know what to say.

"He's a … a friend from London."

"But he's not English."

Of course she'd zero in on his hint of an accent. I'd explain that he moved to the U.K. when he was younger than Curran, but I know in Fiona's mind that won't count. "Russian."

"Mmm. That's romantic."

I give her a wan smile. "Yeah. I guess."

"Honeymoon phase starting to wear off, is it?"

Now I give her an ashamed nod. "Never really left it with my late husband."

Why am I telling her all this? She's not my therapist.

"Well," Fiona says dryly, "you were a one-in-a-million couple, then."

Yes. We were.

Come on. Think of something else to think about. To talk about.

I glance over at the pile of opened presents left abandoned on the carpet. "Looks like the Target toy aisle exploded."

"Doesn't it? All those bloody Pogs. Nothing but decorated cardboard circles. I said to Jason, 'Why are we even paying for this crap?' If I were crafty I could make the stupid things myself."

"Emphasis on *if.*"

"Exactly." She fumbles to re-snap her bra now that Tess has

finished nursing. "Mind holding the little piglet for a sec whilst I get myself sorted?"

Before I can answer, Fiona hefts the baby over to me.

Christ, her soft cheek smells so good nestled against my neck. I bury my face in her hair. Pat her back gently.

Bad move. With a hiccupy heave, Tess spews chunky spit-up all over my shoulder.

"Crikey. Should have warned you. She's a reflux volcano." Fiona pulls her shirt down and looks around frantically for a burp cloth. "Ah, hell. Not even a Star Wars napkin in sight. I'm sorry, Glor."

"Don't worry about it." Hurray for reality checks.

After I've dabbed my sweater with a kitchen towel and Fiona's insisted on blotting the spot with a stain stick, I stand by the sliding glass door and survey the funfair spectacle.

Inside the bounce house, I can see both Curran and Jascha, jumping and laughing and slamming into each other.

Aww. At least they're back to their usual mutual adoration after their earlier emotional scuffle.

The doorbell rings. "I'll bet that's Asher's mum. He's got karate at three." Fiona heads off to answer, Tess draped over her shoulder.

An unmistakable voice floats back to me. "Sorry to interrupt the festivities. I know I'm a smidge early. Are Curran and Gloria ready?"

I open the sliding door. "Five-minute warning!" I yell to Curran. "Gran's here!"

"Look at you, all posh with a chauffeur," Fiona says when I meet Mom in the foyer.

"I'm more than happy to do it. Gloria's just not quite comfortable driving yet after—"

I shoot Mom a *Shut the hell up, don't you dare mention it* look.

"All those years in England," I say to Fiona. "There's a reason I live right by a Metro station."

"Well, don't be a stranger. We'd love to see you again."

"Next time," I say, "I'll take sleepover duty with the boys."

"You sure? It's no trouble to host them here."

"I owe you one, Fee. Seriously."

Fiona gives me a quick, awkward hug goodbye, best as she can with the baby. "So glad you're on the mend. I'll give Curran his party favor bag and send him out." Soft smile. "Along with your big kid."

⁓

"You smell of vomit," my mother says as we walk to the car. "Did Curran get sick in the bouncy castle?"

I shake my head. "Fiona's baby puked on me."

Watching Mom unlock the driver's side door, I'm seized with maternal longing. For her.

"Mom," I say softly. "Can I have a hug?"

She almost drops her keys in surprise. "Of course you can."

The embrace she draws me into is firm, not fawning. Nary a hair-stroke or cheek-pat, just a tight, grounding hold.

"What's wrong, honey?" Mom asks after we pull back.

My mouth works hard to articulate, with no luck.

"Come on. Let's go talk in the car."

⁓

We've got only a few minutes at best before Curran and Jascha burst in and destroy our sanctuary, so I babble it all out fast: bumper cars and *My dad would have!* and *What's this business about the spy camera?* and Tess's delicious infant scent and *Ever think about having another?* and the stony awkwardness that then immediately descended.

To her credit, my mother doesn't make sympathetic clucking noises or murmur banal endearments or give hollow reassurances that everything will be fine.

She simply rubs her hands over her face, and lets out a deep breath, and says, "Gloria, Gloria, Gloria. I don't envy you all this tricky relational navigating you've got heaped on your plate. But I do have a few thoughts."

"Tell me," I say.

"You actually want to hear my opinion?"

"Yes. Immortalize this date on the calendar."

Mom grins. "Okay, one: It's probably good Curran got that rage out of the way. Two: Fiona seems like a charming woman, but if she's going to hold a brief lapse in mental health against you, she's not the sort of person you really want to be friends with or whose child you want Curran palling around with, yes?"

"Umm … yeah. Pretty much."

"And three." She stops for a second, watching the front door to the house open, and Curran and Jascha step outside.

As they wave goodbye to Fiona, Mom turns to me and puts her hand on my arm and says with breathless urgency, "You don't owe him, Gloria. If you truly want to have another baby, I will welcome a new grandchild with absolute delight and support you every step of the way. But if you flat-out don't want to, or are even just uncertain, I need you to remember this: It is not your job to heal his past. Do you understand?"

They're coming down the walk toward us now.

My mother's sharp eyes lock on mine. "Do you *understand* me?"

"Mum, Mum!" I hear Curran squeal, as he holds up his bag of party favors. "We got Pogs!"

Slowly, I nod.

CHAPTER TWENTY-TWO

"You go on ahead," Jascha says to Gloria and Curran, once they're back in their building's lobby. "I want to stop at the coffee shop and grab a Sunday paper."

"Okay," Gloria says with a shrug, walking off with her hands stuffed in her pockets.

Christ, she looks almost eager to ditch him.

Can't say he blames her. Best give her a little space.

Jascha lingers at the newsagent's for a bit, reading inane tabloid headlines before buying a copy of the *Post*.

In the lift, hefty stack of job adverts tucked under his arm, Jascha can't help picturing Gloria holding the baby. And then: her aggravated sigh.

Serves you right, after your umpteenth impulsive move. You've been a couple for what, a week?

Bill wouldn't have done that! Jascha imagines Gloria saying, in mirror image of Curran's earlier taunt.

The lift dings, signaling his floor.

Steady on, man. Let's just wait and see how it goes.

❧

He opens the door to the sound of Curran campaigning for hot cocoa. "It's the perfect thing for when it's about to snow!"

"Not when you've already had a massive sugar binge, it isn't," Gloria says. "Get started on your homework."

Jascha sets the newspaper on the kitchen counter next to her. "Can we talk?" he whispers. "While he's working on it?"

"About what?" Her tone is merely curious.

"Our ... the ... from earlier."

"*Oh.*" She pushes her hair back from her face. "Of course. Yeah."

They head back to the bedroom, where Gloria sits cross-legged on the unmade duvet, hugging a pillow. Jascha joins her, keeping more distance than usual.

"I'm sorry," he says. "I shouldn't have sprung that on you. I was just caught up in ... with the baby ... after Curran's—"

"I know. And it's a fair question." She looks away. "Just one you're not going to like the answer to."

"What do you mean?"

"I can't do it, Jascha."

"Don't sell yourself short," Jascha says. "You're a fantastic mum, and you won't be unwell forever."

"It's not that."

Gloria shifts back to face him. "I've known this about myself for a long time."

"Known what?"

"That I'm only up for one."

Jascha swallows. "You're sure."

She nods. "Believe me, I agonized over it. Worrying if I was making a mistake denying Curran a sibling. Looking at my old college roommates who nailed that statistical average of 2.5 kids like clockwork, and telling myself: 'See, they're fulfilled even though they're frazzled.' But I had to be honest with myself, you know? I wasn't them and I wasn't ever going to be."

Her eyes well up. Her lip trembles.

"I'm sorry, Jascha."

Gloria bows her head. Clutches the pillow more tightly.

"I mean, I know that's what you want," she whispers. "Another girl."

Jascha slides closer to her. "I've already got the girl I want."

"Don't." Now Gloria's crying in earnest. "Please don't bullshit me."

"I'm not. I swear to you." He takes her face in his hands. Tilts it up so he can kiss her forehead, and then her tear-stained cheeks. "Look, if you were to change your mind, I'd chuck that box of condoms in the bin and say let's go for it. But the last thing I want is for you to go along *with* it, just for my sake."

She sniffles. "Good. Because I couldn't live with myself if I did."

"I know." Jascha strokes her hair. "Shh. It's okay."

"Really?"

"Really."

"So Curran and I ..." Gloria swallows. "We're enough."

Oh, honey. *Honey.* "More than."

She leans into his arms. Sobs harder for a moment, then goes limp, finally calm.

"I was so worried," Gloria says hoarsely. "I thought for sure you were gonna bail."

"Never."

"So you don't think any less of me?"

"Absolutely not. If anything, I think more."

Gloria lifts her head with a look of puzzlement. "Why?" she asks, breathy with disbelief.

"Because it's bloody brave to admit what you just did."

She gives him a sly smile. "Brave as fuck?"

Knock, knock. "Yeees?" Gloria calls.

Curran pokes his head in. "I need help with my maths problems, Jascha."

"I'm on it, mate."

"Why's Mum crying?"

Gloria wipes one damp eye. "Happy tears, baby."

For the rest of the night, they settle back into their cozy routine. Well, routine save for the snow, which is coming down like mad.

Curran busies himself keeping watch on the balcony. "Mum's gotta cancel school now," he calls to Jascha. "Who's she on the phone with? Miss Julia?"

"Nope," Jascha calls back from where he stands in the kitchen making pancakes (breakfast for dinner having been everyone's vote). "Gran."

Gloria's been talking with Caroline for a while, holed up in the bedroom. Odd. Normally her mother's chattiness drives her round the bend.

"Aren't you guys cold?" Ah, here she is, scuffing back in in her slippers and yoga trousers and a fresh shirt that doesn't smell of baby puke. "It's freezing in here."

"Shut the door, Curran," Jascha yells.

Slam. He comes inside and sidles up to the kitchen counter. "You know what would be delicious with pancakes?"

"Finished homework," Gloria says.

"He still has his spelling to do." Jascha reaches for a spatula.

"But that snow's reaaally piling up on the roads. I'll bet—"

"Sit your ass down, mister." She gestures toward a chair.

"Ouch," Jascha says. "No mercy from the headmistress."

Gloria sneaks up behind him and wraps her arms around his waist. "In your dreams, maybe."

You don't want to know about my dreams, sweetheart.

He's about to deposit the last pancake onto a stacked plate when the phone rings again.

"That's probably Julia," Gloria says. "Wanting to know when we should call it."

"Now," Curran suggests cheerfully. "Now would be brilliant."

"Less talking, more spelling." She picks up the phone. "Hello?"

Jascha watches as her mouth twists into a perplexing half-smile, half-scowl. "Tim. Umm. Hi."

What the hell? Why's *he* phoning?

"I've been better, quite honestly," Gloria says into the receiver. "What? No, I can't guarantee he won't tell you to eff off this time."

"But here you go. And thanks for asking." She hands the phone to Jascha, who takes it into the hallway.

"You'd best have a good reason, man. How'd you get this number, anyway?"

Tim chuckles. "From you."

"From *me*?"

"Yeah. In case I needed to confer with you about the exhibition. Back when we were—"

Still amiable colleagues, maybe even friends? "Make it fast, arsehole."

"Jesus. Calm down. I just rang to apologize."

Is this a joke?

"I was totally out of line. I mean, the girl's still not my cup of tea, but she hardly deserved me talking crap about her in her darkest hour."

"No," Jascha says crisply, "she didn't."

"Would it help if I wrote you a reference? For your job applications?"

"Yeah," Jascha says slowly. "Yeah, I think it could."

"Then consider it done. You might have dodgy taste in women, but you're a dead good manager and artist, Jascha. Everyone was gutted to hear you'd gone. Asking about you left and right at the exhibition last night."

Not that that matters now, really, but Jascha can't help but feel touched. To say nothing of excited that it might all be coming together, between Jason's hiring agency and Tim's offer to vouch for him. "Thanks."

❦

"Aww," Gloria says when Jascha returns to the dining table with the good news. "I knew there was a decent human being somewhere in there under that misogynist snark."

Jascha's barely sampled a bite of his own cooking when the phone rings a third time. He pushes his chair back.

"I'll get it, love," Gloria says. "Stay here and eat."

She picks up the phone. "Hey, Jules. Whatcha think about this white stuff falling from the sky?"

"Please, please, please," Curran whispers.

"Ten *inches?*" Gloria shrieks. "You've got to be kidding."

That's what she said, Jascha almost smirks, but refrains.

"Good God. We'll be lucky to open at all this week." She nods. "Yeah, go ahead and call the radio and TV stations."

Jascha leans across the table and gives Curran a high-five. "Monopoly marathon, here we come."

CHAPTER TWENTY-THREE

While Jascha gets Curran settled in bed—no easy task, since it's now no longer a school night—I go soak in the tub with my Booker Prize winner for a bit.

Closed door. Slosh and silence. It feels good, surprisingly good, to have some alone time.

I return to our room wrapped in only a towel. Jascha lies on the bed, watching me with an approving smile.

When I sit down on the edge of the mattress, he reaches up to caress my bare shoulder blade. Lets his fingers trail down my back, toying with the point where the towel's fabric tucks in on itself.

I bow my head. Let out a small sigh.

Jascha sits up. Rests his palms on my shoulders and kisses the side of my neck.

"Jasch." I duck out of his reach. "I'm not up for anything tonight."

"No?" He draws his hand away, sounding less disappointed than surprised. Understandable, given that this is the first time in a week I've not been.

I bite my lip. "Sorry."

"Not because of what we talked about earlier, is it?"

"Nah. Just need to pace myself a little." I give him a wan but hopefully reassuring smile as I crawl into bed.

Two a.m. I'm up for the third time to pee, worse than when I was pregnant. Too much quasi-honeymoon debauchery. I really will have to pace myself.

(Fiona: "Honeymoon phase starting to wear off, is it?")

No. Shut up. We're fine.

(Mom, on the phone tonight, when I told her how the one-kid-only conversation went: "Good girl. I'm impressed. With you both.")

See? We're *fine*.

I've just finished washing my hands when, from the bedroom, comes the most horrible sound I've ever heard.

Barely human. Animalistic with terror. Part groan, part cry, part growl.

Jascha?

I hurry to turn off the faucet. Keep the light on in the bathroom so I can see what's going on.

When I run back to the bed, I find him thrashing on the mattress, hard as Bill did when his fever spiked and he had a grand mal seizure.

Shit. Is Jascha having one now?

No. His eyes are closed. His back's not arched.

But his arms bat and flail against an invisible assailant. His head whips back and forth.

I lower myself gingerly down next to him. Rest my palm atop his scarred chest.

I feel helpless as I did watching Bill seize.

"Jasch?" I whisper. "Honey?"

No response. He's lost, somewhere else.

"Jascha," I say, louder now.

Did he hear me this time? Maybe. His frantic headshake's finally tapered off to a slow stutter of the chin.

"Please," he gasps, eyes still shut tight. "Please. I need to see them."

Oh, God. It's a nightmare about the accident.

What do I do? How can I bring him out of it?

I lean over. Pull the cord to turn on the bedside lamp.

Jascha's eyes fly open. He clutches my hand.

"Marianne," he whispers. "My angel."

Literally. Does he realize that, in his stupor?

I don't think so. He's staring up at me with the most poignant, tender look of relief and adoration that it hurts to hold his gaze.

"No," I whisper gently.

Jascha smiles. "Not a scratch on you."

That's because I'm not her! I suddenly want to scream.

Keep your cool. He can't help it. Just ...

"Tell me what month it is."

Jascha rubs shaky fingers over his forehead. "August," he mumbles. "We're headed to the seaside."

"No," I snap. "It's January. There's five inches of snow on the ground."

"Don't be vexed, Mare." His eyes flicker closed again.

"Look at me." I give his shoulder a hard shake. "Fucking *look* at me, Jascha."

It's the f-bomb that jerks him back. Jascha shivers. Blinks. Opens his eyes.

"Gloriochka," he rasps. Not just my name, but its intimate diminutive.

"That's right." I give his hand an encouraging squeeze.

"Gloriochka," he repeats, as if desperate to ground himself in the present.

"Yeah, darlin'. I'm here." I duck under the duvet and crawl on top of him, straddling his hips. Guide his palm to the hollow between my breasts, where my frantic heart pounds. "Feel that? Feel me?"

Jascha nods.

"Good." I lie down all the way atop him. Stroke his sweaty hair back from his forehead. "Just try to relax, okay?"

Jascha dutifully forces out a deep breath, but beneath me his shoulders remain clenched. "Feels like I'm still … back there."

My poor boy. What can I do? I have to do *something*. To soothe his fear. To assuage my own helplessness.

But what?

As he chokes out another pained quaver, I can feel him inadvertently harden with adrenaline along the inside of my thigh.

I lean my mouth against Jascha's ear. Pray what I'm about to suggest won't sound too bizarre.

"Would it help," I whisper, "if we made love?"

A strangled nod. I lift up a little.

Careful, Gloria. Just do what you did for Bill, that final time. Last thing you need is—

No. What if that's not enough? Look at him. How ravaged he is.

I look at him. And then reach down, and guide him inside me in an act of impulsive grace, spurning the box of condoms in the nightstand drawer so that he can slip unencumbered into welcoming warmth.

Jascha's barely aware, too busy moving in halting yet frantic thrust.

"Easy, easy," I murmur. "Let me."

I sit up and lean over him, letting my hair spill around him the way he adores.

Sure enough, a delighted moan escapes Jascha's throat. He finally calms, little by little, as my hips glide over his, rocking this horrible sorrow to sleep.

"There you go," I croon, as if he's Fiona's fretful baby. "There's my love."

When his body stiffens and tremors again, it's such a sweet relief it almost rivals the moment I slid under the blanket in Bill's hospital room.

I collapse onto my elbows atop Jascha, cheek slumped against his, luxuriating not only in my own pleasure—the undeniable thrill of fucking unadulterated, all heat and gush—but also in the knowledge that I've coaxed him back into himself.

As I move to get up, Jascha clutches my hand. "Don't go. Please."

"I'm just gonna turn off the bathroom light. I'll be right back."

After I flip the switch, I stand in the dark for a few seconds, dazed and sticky-thighed, letting out several shaky breaths.

So much anguish. So much need.

He's not your suicidal dad. He's your lover. Your struggling partner. Go back out there.

I go back out. Slip under the duvet, into Jascha's waiting arms.

"Thank you," he whispers against my hair.

⟡

Come morning, I'm the first one up for a change, followed by Curran.

"Jascha's still asleep?" he asks, trudging into the kitchen with a yawn.

"Yeah. He had a ..." I pause, not sure how to explain, or even if I should. "He got to bed late."

"Oh." Totally nonplussed. "Can you make me Scotch eggs?"

"I can indeed." I lean down to kiss the top of his head. "And I'll even throw in a hot chocolate. No extra charge."

After breakfast, we take our mugs to the couch and cozy up for a game I often let my students play back when I taught English. Exquisite Corpse, it was called. A tad too morbid for me now, all things considered, so now Curran and I just refer to it as Story Dominoes.

He writes the first line on a sheet of paper. Hands it to me.

There once was a boy who …

Drove his mother completely batty but was too adorable for her to ever be mad at him, I add.

"Hey!" Curran giggles.

His mum was a very funny and smart lady who swore rather a lot, he writes.

"This is supposed to be fiction," I remind him, then write: *Especially when she burnt the Scotch eggs.*

Within a few more lines, we've descended into sci-fi pastiche madness in which aliens arrive on the planet in search of scorched British breakfast followed by world domination (*And then the boy's mother put down her saucepan and looked out the window and was so shocked to see the spaceship that she couldn't even say "What the fuck?"*).

"This is really nice, Mum," Curran sighs once we've exhausted our ridiculous plot options.

"What is, baby? The story?"

He gestures toward the mugs of cocoa, the paper in my lap, the two of us. *"This.* Don't you think?"

"Yeah," I say softly, nodding. "I do."

So much so that I'm almost disappointed when I hear the shower running down the hall.

No, I want to tell Jascha. Sleep longer. Give me a chance to just putter around alone with my kiddo, away from your brooding intensity.

The urge makes me feel like a jerk. Hell, that intensity was part of what drew me *to* Jascha. And it's not like he can help reacting the way he did yesterday, to the bumper cars or the baby or the nightmare.

Whoa. When you add them all up, it feels like a monolith of not mourning, so much, as … what? Post-traumatic stress?

The shower turns off with a screech.

"Let's do another one, Mum," Curran nudges me as he flips to a fresh sheet of paper.

"Hold that thought, honey." I reluctantly push myself up from the couch. "I need to go talk to Jascha for a minute."

❧

I enter the bedroom to find Jascha sitting on the mattress, barefoot in jeans, towel round his neck, his bare shoulders slumped.

"Hey," I say softly.

His gaze flits up. "Hey."

I sit down next to him. Fight the urge to pat his knee or stroke his shoulder.

The silence is excruciating.

"Well," Jascha says, finally blowing out a sigh as he swings his head up all the way. "Guess now you know just how rough of a sleeper I am."

I swallow. "How often does it happen?"

Jascha shrugs. "Comes and goes."

"Is that your stoic downplaying answer, or an honest one?"

He laughs under his breath. "Jesus, Gloria."

"No, really. What are we talking here? Every few months?"

"It …" He stares down at his hands, which now dangle between his knees. "I had nightmares constantly right after the accident. The nurses would have to, umm, sedate me."

Jascha's fingers snarl at each other now, twisting and anxious.

"After a while they tapered off to only a few times a month." *Only?*

"What triggers them?" I ask. "Stuff that reminds you of what happened?"

"Yeah. But they stopped once you came home from hospital."

"For a week."

"Last night was just a one-off."

"How do you know?" I whisper. "How do I know you won't wind up like that every time we take Curran to a birthday party?"

"Not every birthday party's going to be an over-the-top funfair."

"What if it is? You can't hide out from every single thing that triggers a memory, Jasch."

He scowls. "I don't."

"Then why did you pass me Fiona's baby? Why did you pass on doing bumper cars with Curran?"

"It was too much, all right?" Jascha's voice shakes. "Sometimes it's just too much. Can't you respect that?"

"I respect *why*. But I'm not going to just sit here and say, 'Oh, sure, honey, go ahead and keep constricting your life out of irrational fear, no problem.' You need to get help, Jascha."

"How? I don't even know what *would* help."

"We'll figure out what will."

"I don't want to be a burden," Jascha whispers.

"You're not. Trust me. My dad languishing for twenty years with zero self-insight and no treatment options around for miles was a burden, okay, not—"

"But this is the land of the free and fucked-up. You said it yourself: no national health care, barely any days off. When I get a job, will it even pay for my treatment?"

"Stop it." I put my hands on his shoulders. "Just stop, okay? You're making excuses, same as I did when I was afraid to go to the ER or take time off work, and I'm gonna call you on it just like you did for me."

Jascha looks away sheepishly. I turn his chin back to face my gaze.

"I love you, you stubborn, stoic pain in the ass. And I can't stand to see you like this."

"It's not that bad," he says quietly.

"You're only saying that because you're so used it. But I'm not. And last night, watching you thrashing around, screaming for them ..."

My throat catches. "It was terrifying, Jascha. It was really fucking hard."

Jascha blinks. "I'm—"

I put up a hand to silence him. "Please don't say you're sorry. It's not like you could control it."

"I know," he says. "But I *am* sorry. I'll make some calls. I'll take care of this, Gloriochka. Promise."

CHAPTER TWENTY-FOUR

Jascha sits hunched over the kitchen table all afternoon, pen in hand, alternating between circling job adverts in the newspaper and underlining doctors' offices in the phone book.

Every so often, Curran shuffles over and sets a Monopoly figurine in front of him with a none-too-subtle plink.

"Sorry, mate," Jascha says. "I'm in research mode."

Curran sighs. "So much for the game marathon."

Gloria does the ritual read-aloud that evening, so that Jascha can continue his job-and-shrink search. He's so engrossed in jotting down names and numbers that he doesn't realize she's reentered the room until she slips up behind his chair and drapes her arms around his neck.

"Off to bed?" Jascha murmurs, flipping to the next page in the phone directory.

"Yeah. Come with." She hugs Jascha's shoulders.

"Thought you needed to pace yourself."

"I do. I just want you next to me, is all."

Hard to argue with that. Except …

"You're not worried?" he asks.

Gloria's brow furrows. "Why would I be worried?"

"About a …" Jascha looks away. "A repeat of last night."

Gloria pushes aside the phone directory. Perches on the edge of the table in front of him.

"Look," she says. "I know I came down pretty hard on you earlier. But please don't ever think I'm not willing to be here for you."

Jascha strokes her hand. "I never thought that, Gloriochka. Even when you were giving me hell."

"Good. Because I'm here for the long haul. And yeah, I'd be worried if you weren't up for doing *this*." Gloria gestures toward his list of doctors' offices. "But you are."

Jascha sighs. "It's humbling as fuck."

"I know, honey. Believe me, I know." She slides off the table. Gives his arm a rallying shake. "That phone book'll still be here in the morning. Let's get some rest."

And rest Jascha does. Not a single frame of frantic celluloid. Not a second of terror. Just gentle morning sunlight waking him to the sight of his girl curled next to him.

His girl, to whom he swore he'd get help, no matter how tempted he felt to shrug the whole thing off.

Jascha gets up. Makes a pot of coffee. Rings all twenty clinics on his list.

Not once does he reach an actual human being; they must still be holed up at home, thanks to what Gloria and her colleague Julia have dubbed Snowpocalypse.

Still, he's done it. Proved himself via the ritual exercise. Taken this first step.

The rest of the day is full of lighthearted ease: more Monopoly and Scrabble rounds, more hot cocoa. Jascha takes a cabin fever-stricken Curran out into their floor's long main hallway for some mock sword-fighting, complete with *Ching! Sching!* sound effects.

"Now, now, boys, do I need to send you to the office?" The door opens to reveal Gloria standing there in mock admonishment.

"But, Headmistress." Jascha puts on an angelic grin. "Fencing counts as PE in the revised British National Curriculum, remember?"

"Oh, I'll revise your curriculum, all right." She waves them inside with an affectionate headshake. "Who wants more pancakes for dinner?"

And then, at two a.m.:

Blue ambulance light. Gloved medic hands.

Lie still, sir.

Jascha's shoulders struggle. His words half-spit, half-growl.

Where. Are. They?

Being taken care of. Like we need to take care of you.

Screw that.

"Jascha?"

How do they know his name?

Brighter light. Harsher glare.

His pupils are dilated.

Firm hand on his chest.

We may need to restrain him.

"Let me up! Let me up, goddamn it!"

His neck tightens. His fist clenches. Slams forward in a punch.

And then draws back, as Jascha falls back, his eyes flying open to witness an even more nightmarish sight.

Gloria, huddled on her knees next to him, shuddering with shock, a hand pressed to her bloodied lip.

CHAPTER TWENTY-FIVE

I tried to stop him, but he moved too fast. I tried to stop him, but there was no him to stop. Just a runaway train, a charging bull.

My tongue tastes like metal. Did he …?

No. He couldn't have.

"Gloriochka?" Jascha's voice is hoarse, stuporous.

I pull my hand slowly away from my mouth. Look down to find my fingertips covered in blood.

Oh. My. God.

Jascha's eyes widen. He pushes himself groggily up into a sitting position. "What—what … happened?"

"You busted my fucking lip open." My voice rises in shaky disbelief and more than a touch of fury.

Before he can respond, I run to the bathroom. Back to the damn mirror.

Just like before, I'm too scared to look. I spit into the sink instead, little dribbles of pinkish foam.

Warm washcloth. It stings but also comforts. Dab, dab, dab.

I finally lower the wet cotton and make a good hard appraisal.

The wound's ugly, yeah, but I know from raising a boy that gashes often look worse than they are. No damage to my teeth. That's good.

I feel numb, almost clinical.

But then I think of Jascha tracing my lips with his fingers, running his tongue along their tender insides, and my heart swells and breaks.

Dab. Wince. Dab.

Footsteps scuff closer.

"Gloria?" Jascha whispers. No intimate nickname now.

"Yeah," I say hoarsely.

"How bad is it? Do you need to go to A and E?"

"It's not that bad." Physically, at least.

When I turn around, he's right in front of me, poised to stroke my cheek or caress my hair or make any number of other soft, conciliatory gestures, but I want none of it.

I put up a palm. "Don't touch me."

Without so much as another glance at Jascha, I walk out of the bedroom, along the hall, and into the kitchen, where I fashion a makeshift cold pack with paper towel-wrapped ice cubes.

Ow. Bracing. Ow.

My eyes well up. I shuffle into the living room and lower myself onto the couch. Wrap a throw blanket around myself and burrow into the cushions as I watch Jascha come down the hall.

"Can we talk? I mean, will it hurt too much?" His voice trembles. "I won't touch you. I promise."

Last thing I want to do is have a conversation about this at the moment, when my thoughts are a blur from pain, but we really should. "O-okay."

Jascha flicks on a lamp. Sits gingerly on the edge of the furthest couch cushion from me, his head in his hands.

"I'm so sorry," he whispers. "I can't even begin to tell you how much."

I nod.

"I didn't mean to hurt you. Hell, I didn't even realize it *was* you.

In the dream, there's medics, trying to hold me down, and I just—I struggle."

I nod again. Jascha looks up at me.

"Whatever it takes to keep you safe, I'll do it," he says. "I'll sleep on the couch. I'll ring twenty more clinics."

All I can do is just keep nodding.

"Your ice is about to melt. Hang on."

He gets up and returns with a fresh cold compress. Deposits it on the coffee table, refraining from touching me, true to his word.

So honest. So earnest. So good.

"Hold me," I whisper. "Please."

Jascha swallows. "You're … sure?"

No mere nod this time. "Yes."

He lowers himself back down onto the couch. Slides closer. I slide closer still. He drapes a cautious arm around me.

More. Need more. I lean into him, seeking. He scoops me into his lap. Draws my cheek against his shoulder, pressing the ice gently to my mouth's insistent throb.

When I shiver, Jascha wraps his arms around me even tighter. Kisses the top of my head. "Any better?"

Better enough. For now.

He carries me into the bedroom. Tucks me in with one final compress-dab and hair-stroke. "Do you want one of your pills?"

"Probably should."

Jascha returns with a cup of water. Holds my head up and guides a straw toward the non-injured side of my mouth.

Still I wince and splutter. The devastated look on his face hurts worse than the actual ache.

"I love you, Gloriochka," he says quietly.

I love you, too, I want to reply, but I collapse into the shelter of sleep before my bruised lips can form the words.

In the morning, I wake and wonder: Was *I* the one who had the nightmare?

Then I roll over, and grit my teeth as my still-tender face brushes the pillow, and remember: It was a nightmare, yes, but also terribly real.

My hand skims the empty side of the mattress. Where Jascha should be. I'm used to this *he's-not-here* longing, but never have I felt it for this reason.

I'm sorry. I didn't mean to hurt you. I'll do whatever it takes to keep you safe.

I believed him last night, and I believe him now. He's not a domestic abuser spouting *Baby, it'll never happen again* lines while bringing me roses.

And yet there's still danger. Because, no matter how repugnant the idea might be to him when he's wide awake, all bets are off when he's asleep. I'm not just unsafe then; I'm a nonentity. Just a warm blur of a body who stands in for whomever his dreams demand: Marianne, the medics.

Jesus. How are we going to get through this?

First things first. I have to cover up my bruises so Curran won't see.

This is where I could really use Mom's help, but she'd probably be aghast and order me to break things off with Jascha immediately.

Flying solo, I smear on enough foundation and lipstick to pass for a televangelist's wife.

Yeah. Like that won't look suspicious.

If school were in session, I could say I have an important meeting and need to be in uber-headmistress mode, but school's not yet reopened.

Guess I'll just go out and face the awkward music.

"There she is," Jascha says softly when I enter the kitchen.

Curran glances up from the Monopoly board. "What happened, Mum? You look like you got in a fight."

Well. So much for that.

"I, umm …"

Should I lie? I don't want to scare him. And it's being taken care of. We're working this out.

Right? Right.

"I tripped," I say. "On the bathroom floor, in the dark."

"Oops." He takes this in stride. I'm not the most graceful of creatures even when my brain's behaving itself. I've been known to knock entire stockpots of stew off the top of the stove, and there's a scar on the underside of my chin from where, as a teenager, I fell flat on my face on our icy front walk when I came home drunk from a party.

"Does it hurt?" Curran asks.

"A little."

I hear Jascha suck in his breath. He watches me with a stricken, sorrowful look.

"Anybody want a hot cocoa?" I ask, far too brightly.

By lunchtime, we're all cranky and snappish at each other.

"Mum, I'm borrred!"

"Then read a book."

"We could always sword-fight in the hallway again." Jascha suggests.

"Knock yourselves out," I say. "I'm going down to the lobby."

"What for?" Curran asks.

"A goddamn break, that's what."

～

Amazingly, the newsstand's open. I contemplate buying a paper or even a trashy magazine, but instead I find myself depositing a pack of cigarettes on the counter.

"Thought you quit," the cashier says.

"I did."

I take my guilty pleasure—which feels more like self-medicating than indulging, honestly—and head outside. Coatless.

Sharp air feels good, though. And they've deiced the pavement, so I should be able to stay vertical.

I reach into my pocket for the pack. Realize: Shit! No lighter anymore.

I go back in and buy one. Vice indulgence, take two.

Oh, Christ, that's good. A delicate affair, keeping the ciggie away from the bad side of my mouth, but still.

What settles over me isn't quite calm, so much as solidification. Steadiness. I can handle this. I can bear this.

One more for good measure, and then I head back upstairs to my loves.

～

"I'm really sorry, guys," I tell them soon as I step inside. I'd lean down to kiss the tops of their heads, but I don't want them to smell the smoke on me.

"It's okay," Jascha murmurs. "We've all been cooped up in here way too long."

"I kicked Jascha's butt in Monopoly, though," Curran says cheerfully.

"Oh, but just wait till we play Scrabble. You fancy a round, Gloriochka?"

"Yeah. Of course. Just hang on a sec."

I take a detour into the bathroom. Pop two aspirin in the hopes that it'll at least put a small dent in my lip's perpetual ache. Gingerly swish with mouthwash to cover my nicotine tracks.

This is horrible.

⟡

Once in the game, the first word I spell is *miasma*.

"Are you sure that's real?" Curran asks. "I mean, I know you're like a human dictionary, Mum, but ..."

"Yes," Jascha says. "It's a word."

Noun, meaning an oppressive or unpleasant atmosphere.

We eye each other across the table. Jascha reaches for a tile, and builds off the *L* in Curran's "lie" to fashion "love."

I will not cry. I will not cry.

⟡

"You were smoking downstairs, weren't you?" Jascha asks me, once we're finished with the game and Curran's off in his room building Star Wars Legos.

I shrug. "Only had two."

He frowns. "Gloria ..."

"What?" I let out a brittle laugh. "Relapse is part of recovery. They told us that in the hospital."

"Throw out the rest. Please."

"You're really gonna give me shit about this after what happened last night? Seriously?" I pull the pack from my back jeans pocket. Slap it onto the table. "Here, Mr. Virtuous. Happy now?"

Before he can answer, I get up and storm down the hall and

sequester myself in the bedroom. Curl up on top of the duvet with my hands braced in my hair. Angry tears spill down my cheeks, trickling over my overdone lipstick to saltily pool in the jagged corner of my lip.

I expect Jascha to come knock on the door, but instead I hear him in the kitchen, making more calls.

"Hello, yes, my name is Jascha Kremsky, and I'm phoning to find out whether you're currently accepting new patients."

I close my eyes.

"You're not? Ah, okay. Might there be a colleague you could recommend who is?"

He's trying so hard.

"Excellent. Thank you. I'll get in touch with her."

And then, a few minutes later: "I actually don't have insurance at the moment, so … Are there discounts, or concessions, or … anything?" A small sigh. "No. All right. Well, thank you for your time."

Now there's the knock at the door.

I push myself up into a sitting position. "I'm done being a bitch. You can come in."

Jascha sits beside me, taking in the sight of my eyes swollen as my lip.

"I'm coming up empty," he says softly. "Every last one of them has a waiting list, or only takes people with health coverage, or charges an ungodly rate for private pay, or …"

Jascha looks away. "I'm not making excuses. I swear. That's what they're telling me."

"I know," I whisper. "I heard you on the phone. Don't sweat it, okay? We've got credit cards."

"I don't want to go bankrupt, Gloria."

"I don't either," I say. "But I'd rather be financially broke than have this break us."

He nods. Reaches up to brush his fingers gently along the curve of my jaw and up over my chin, carefully palpating, gauging, the damage he's inadvertently done.

It's agony, but I don't pull back. My eyes stay locked on his.

Down the hall, the phone rings. I hear the scamper of youthful sock feet, followed by Curran's yell. "Jascha! Call for you!"

CHAPTER TWENTY-SIX

Finally a good lead. Nice-sounding bloke who's willing to work sliding-scale, with an appointment available two weeks from today.

That's longer than Jascha would like to wait, but beggars can't be choosers.

"Found one," he sighs to Gloria after he sets down the phone.

"Found one what?" Curran asks, from where he sits on the living room floor flipping through video cases to pick the evening's movie.

"A therapist," Jascha says. Why dodge?

Curran's brows wrinkle. "Is that like a doctor?"

"Not ... exactly." Jascha comes and sits down next to him. "I mean, they *are* professionals whose job it is to help patients get better, only they help with ..."

He looks over at Gloria for backup.

"Emotions," she says quietly. "That are causing problems in people's lives."

"So a feelings doctor."

"Right," Jascha says, nodding vigorously.

"Did you see any of those when you were in hospital, Mum?"

"Yeah," Gloria says. "I did. And I think it would be really good for Jascha to talk to one."

"About the accident," Curran says. "The being afraid of stuff."

Damn, this kid is sharp.

"Yes," Jascha says. "I want to get past that, as fast as I can."

"Good, because I want you to, too." Curran reaches for another stack of videos. "You think they'll put a spy camera in your brain?"

Jascha laughs. "If they do, I'll leave it turned on, just for you."

⟨∿

Gloria's mouth hurts too much to do read-aloud duty that night, so Jascha draws her a hot bath with one of those scented fizzy-bomb things and takes over getting Curran to bed. Brings Gloria a glass of wine when he's finished.

"Well, well," she murmurs, taking a faux-regal sip as the foamy bubbles lap around her neck. "This is all very posh."

"When you're done," Jascha says softly, "we should ice your lip again."

Definitely not posh, that. More like heartrending. The tiny whimper Gloria can't conceal when he presses the cold cubes to her bruised lip damn near crushes him.

"I need to shave my legs, too," she huffs out, once the skin-shock's subsided. "Was so out of it this morning, I forgot."

Jascha does it for her, each calf draped in turn across a towel in his lap. Careful, so careful, not to slip or nick.

"Fringe benefit of having a sculptor for a boyfriend," Gloria murmurs, tipping her head back against the tile wall. "You're better at this than I am."

At least he's gotten something right. Jascha gives her soapy foot a gentle squeeze, then pulls the plug on the drain.

⟨∿

While she dries off, Jascha lights the candle that sits atop her dresser. Turns the duvet down neatly.

Gloria enters wearing her robe and an apprehensive look.

"I'm not trying to set the stage for anything," Jascha says quickly. "Just thought you might like."

"I—I do." She flicks her still-damp hair from her shoulders. "It's ... it's lovely."

Gloria sits on the end of the bed, hands laced primly on her knees.

"I'm going to miss you tonight," she says.

Jascha stares down at the carpet. "So will I."

"How long until your appointment with that guy you found?"

"Two weeks."

She sighs. Leans forward to rest her cheek gingerly against his waist. "God, this sucks."

"I know." He strokes her hair. "I know."

"Can you at least stay with me till I fall asleep?"

Now it's Jascha's turn to sigh. "I would, but I don't want to risk—"

"Falling asleep too, and potentially ..."

"Yeah."

Gloria pulls back. "Okay." She gives a resigned nod. "Okay."

Jascha kisses her on the forehead. "I'll bring you coffee in the morning. How's that?"

Her voice is tiny. "Sure."

CHAPTER TWENTY-SEVEN

True to his word, he's sitting on the edge of my bed with a mug when I wake.

"Did you have another one?" I rasp out.

Jascha frowns. "Good morning to you, too. Is our every conversation going to revolve around this now?"

How can it not?

I rub a hand over my eyes with a scowl. "I was just wondering."

He sighs. "Yeah. Yeah, I did."

"I'm sorry, love." I reach up to caress his face with my free hand.

Jascha grabs it. Kisses my palm. "Don't be. You're safe. That's the most important thing."

He's right, of course, but what a price to pay for that guarantee.

Come on, I scold myself in the shower. It's not like you've lost Jascha completely, like you did with Bill. You're together. Sharing a life. So what if he has to sleep on the couch for a while?

Maybe it's just this hothouse atmosphere, I think, as I make myself up like the Whore of Babylon to cover my bruises. Being stuck in an apartment without a natural rhythm to the day would be enough to make anyone rethink their relationship. (Thanks a lot, Snowpocalypse.)

Things will get better. We'll settle in. Learn to navigate all these choppy waters we didn't realize we were sailing off into when we giddily pushed away from shore. It's been what, barely two weeks since we became an official, non-fifteen-minutes-of-fame couple? Not even.

Equilibrium takes time. At least, that's what our fearless Long Island-accented group leader said in the hospital. Had it been Grunge Princess spouting aphorisms, I'd have written them off, but Long Island looked like she'd been around the block.

You've got this, Gloriochka. Just keep your cool and some perspective.

⌒

Ten a.m. Curran looks up from his video game. "Ooh! Go check the mail, Mum!"

Yes, this is how desperate for amusement my household has become on our fourth day of weather-induced confinement.

Taking the elevator downstairs is the new equivalent of hitching up the ol' pioneer wagon and riding into town. I force myself to power-walk past the newsstand and its tempting Marlboro Lights, and head for the rows of mailboxes.

Inside mine I find a solitary envelope.

Please be junk. Please be junk.

Nope. The return address bears the logo of Washington Medical Center.

Please be a *THIS IS NOT A BILL* statement. Please be …

Nope again. There's a tear-off payment coupon affixed to the top of the price breakdown.

And the "Payment Amount Due" box shows a number equal to one month of my salary.

My stomach drops. My hand flies to my mouth.

Don't panic. Maybe it's a clerical error. Maybe they just forgot to deduct the amount my Diamond Preferred All Access Backstage Pass policy already paid.

I skim the lengthy list of services rendered. ER triage. Fifty-minute "initial patient intake session" with Dr. Marshall. The MRI. The EEG. Every tablet in a paper cup they handed me.

Followed by a series of insurance credits.

The math adds up. One month's worth is what I owe.

Shit. I knew this was coming, but I didn't realize it'd be this bad. Or expect Jascha to be living with me, needing his own series of fifty-minute sessions for God knows how long.

Don't bring him into this. He never asked to be traumatized. And you promised him the cost of getting help wouldn't be an issue.

Except now it is.

I tuck the offending envelope under my arm and head for the newsstand, where I buy a coffee and take a seat in the back corner, far away from the table where we sat when Jascha announced to Curran he was moving here.

God, we were so elated. So hopeful. So naive.

I unfold the hospital bill and lay it out next to my to-go cup. Rest my head in my hands.

What the hell am I going to do?

Let's think this through. Logically.

Can I pay the balance due? Yeah, but it'll drain most of my savings.

What if something else comes up after that? What if Jascha needs sessions with the therapist once a week, or twice a week, or even in one of those Monday through Friday, nine-to-five intensive programs I overheard nurses on my unit discussing with patients as options?

I could sell my car. But I frequently have to drive way the hell out into the suburbs, far fringes of Northern Virginia, for educational choice expos and faculty recruitment fairs.

I could pull Curran out of school, put him in the neighborhood elementary. But the poor kid's been put through so many changes already, and I really want him to have the continuity of a British education in case we ever decide to return to the U.K.

God, I feel like such a privileged snot, no different from Quinn's family with their ostentatious birthday carnival. Do we have it on the actual date in January, or wait for perfect spring break weather? Shall we get the deluxe bouncy castle, or the bog standard one?

At least Fiona and Jason both have jobs. And permanent residency here. And while their marriage probably isn't perfect, what with the stress of three kids, I'm guessing they can sleep in the same bedroom without fear of accidentally attacking each other in said sleep.

Christ. I should have just screwed that Oxbridge boy-toy I met on the Adams Morgan rooftop. Or resigned myself to a life of stable widowhood abstinence. What was I thinking, asking Jascha to fly over here, and then encouraging his wish to stay?

You were thinking you loved him.

Kinda hard not to. The man's equal parts snarky and romantic, gets along splendidly with my son, and takes both my psych ward admission and dead husband in stride. I mean, hell, if that's not the dictionary definition of a keeper, I don't know what is.

And yet. And yet and yet and yet.

I take a strong sip of my coffee. Think of Peter, elder statesman of Four West, and his wife, who separated so he could get his illness under control. Who said it was actually good for him, in a way.

Tough love. Or, reframed: love tough enough to brave, to find clarity in, distance.

❧

"That was quite the mail pilgrimage," Jascha says when I reenter the apartment.

"Yeah. Had to fortify myself with more coffee."

"Why? What'd you get?"

"Health insurance statement."

"Uh-oh. How bad?"

I fling the envelope onto the counter. "You don't wanna know. Where's Curran?"

"In his room, Lego-ing. Why?"

"We need to talk."

Jascha's brow furrows. "You and I do?"

I swallow hard. Nod.

❧

We close the door to the bedroom. Sit next to each other on the edge of the mattress, bodies angled so we can catch and hold each other's gazes.

I put a hand on Jascha's arm. Swallow hard again.

"You're scaring me here, Gloriochka," he says.

I give a hoarse, nervous laugh. "Trust me, you're not the only one who's scared."

"About what? The medical bill?"

"Everything."

Jascha reaches up to touch my cheek. "Please don't be."

Again: How can I not?

"I ... I'm in over my head," I say. "*We* are."

At that last point, he looks skeptical. "It's been a tumultuous few weeks, sure. But we're handling it."

"Really? You think so?"

Jascha nods. "I take it you don't."

"I think you should go back to London," I blurt out.

So much for the gentle lead-ins, the delicate warm-up.

Jascha rears back, shaking his head a little. "What?" Disbelieving laugh. "Come on, honey. I know things are rough right now, but you can't possibly be serious."

"Yes," I say softly. "I am."

He drops his face into his palms. His shoulders slump.

Shit. Oh, sweetheart. Look at you, all that armor chinking.

I slide closer. Draw Jascha's bent head against my chest. Hug his shoulders. Kiss the back of his neck.

"Just until this gets sorted out," I whisper.

"It's got nothing to do with the money, does it?" His words are fraught gasps.

"Yes and no."

Jascha looks up, his face puzzled.

"I'm not gonna lie," I say. "You getting treatment for free in England would be a load off my mind and my bank account, but that's not … not the only reason."

Jascha blinks. "What—"

My words tumble out in a pent-up rush. "I can't live with you while this is going on. I can't kiss you goodnight and watch you head down the hall to the couch every night. I just can't."

"So you'd rather—rather have me across an ocean."

Slowly, I nod.

Jascha rests his face against my chest again. Begins to quietly sob.

"I'm sorry." Now I'm crying too. "I'm so fucking sorry."

I lean down to bury my damp face in the top of Jascha's head, but he sits up to stop me.

"What if I just moved out for a bit?" he asks desperately. "Got my own flat."

"No one'll rent to you until you have a steady income."

"I can stay in a hotel till I find work."

"You'll burn through your credit card in a week."

"Jesus, Gloria." He stands up and starts to pace. "You told me to rip up my ticket. You told me to go ahead and quit my job. You told me not to worry about—"

"I know what I told you," I snap. "And I meant it."

"But now you're backtracking because shit just got real."

"That's not fair, Jascha."

"No? I was terrified and overwhelmed, too, going to visit you when you were a virtual prisoner on that locked ward, but I still showed up."

"Yeah, well, you didn't get beaten up."

Now it's sinking in. Jascha rubs a hand over his damp face.

"Okay," he says softly. "Okay."

Then he comes over, rests his palms on my shoulders, and kisses me so gently on the bruised side of my mouth that I almost cry out from the tenderness. Both kinds.

While Jascha calls airlines about ticket prices, I check on Curran in his room.

"Look at you." I put on a too-broad smile. "That Millennium Falcon's really coming along."

He doesn't return the grin. "I heard you and Jascha fighting."

"Yeah. I'm sorry about that."

Curran frowns. "You and Dad never fought."

I let out a sigh. "We led pretty uncomplicated lives, your dad and I. Before he got sick, at least."

He sets his Lego work-in-progress on the nightstand. "Everything's okay, though, right? I mean, you and Jascha made up."

"Mmm-hmm."

Curran flops onto his back on the bed. "Good."

Well, sort of.

Jascha pokes his head in the door. "Got one for 3:45 tomorrow afternoon."

I nod. No use in prolonging the agony, we decided.

"One what?" Curran asks, sitting up again.

Jascha and I glance at each other. We'd planned on breaking the news at bedtime, but I guess we might as well get it over with now.

I pat the duvet. Jascha comes and sits between me and Curran.

"Listen, mate," he says. "I've got to go back to London for a while."

"But I thought you were—"

"I know." Jascha puts a hand up. "I know."

"Is that what you and Mum were having a row about?"

"We ... it ..." My voice chokes. "There's been a lot of really difficult stuff to deal with lately, kiddo, and we're both under a lot of stress."

Curran's eyes widen. "You're not breaking up, are you?"

"No, no, no." Jascha clutches my hand, seeking confirmation. I squeeze it back, hard.

"Then you should stay."

"Honey," I whisper. "It's complicated." In ways I can't explain without needlessly scaring you.

"I want to stay." Jascha's voice shakes worse than mine. "But it's best—it'll *be* best—if I get the help I need from a feelings doctor back in England."

"Because it's expensive, and you haven't a job yet."

We'll run with that. "Right."

Curran chews his lip. "Will you be back for my birthday?"

"I'll try my absolute hardest."

I'm wrapping up another paper towel full of ice cubes to put on my lip when I glance at the microwave clock. *3:45.*

Twenty-four hours from now, he'll be on that plane.

No. Don't treat this like mourning. Jascha's not dying. You're not losing him for good. Besides, you're the one who asked him to leave, remember?

All too well, but I still can't help it.

The final dinner, the final Scrabble game, the final bedtime read-aloud. He does so many chapters, with over-the-top funny voices and monster growls, that I can hear his voice going hoarse from the living room, where I sit drinking a glass of wine, because what the hell else are you going to do the night before you say goodbye to your lover for God knows how long?

Put your kitchen timer on for five minutes and sniffle silently into your hands till it dings, that's what.

Curran, as they finish up: "I wish you didn't have to go, Jascha. Mum's crap at video games, and I'll miss you."

I set the timer for five more.

Once Curran falls asleep, we make love so slowly, so gently, it hurts worse than when Jascha unknowingly threw that punch. Our reverent, needy bodies fumbling, savoring.

Afterwards we huddle against each other, his palms in the small of my back, my leg wrapped round his waist. He murmurs to me in Russian, hushed, fraught words I don't literally understand but can intuit from their timbre.

"Stay," I choke out. "With me. For tonight."

Jascha's face crumples as if I'm the one who just clocked him.

"I can't," he says hoarsely. "You know I can't, Gloriochka."

And then he kisses me one last time and crawls out from under the duvet.

CHAPTER TWENTY-EIGHT

The roads are such a mess from Snowpocalypse's thaw that, on the way to Dulles, Jascha grips the passenger-side door handle with one hand while crossing himself with the other.

"I know Vera drags you to Mass every so often," Gloria says, chuckling, "but I didn't realize you were *that* religious."

"Maybe we should have taken the Metro," he says. "Are you sure you feel up for this?"

"I'm fine. We'll be fine." Gloria reaches across the gearshift to pat his knee.

He sucks in his breath. Doesn't let it out until she puts her palm back on the steering wheel.

Intellectually, Jascha knows she's right. For all her skittishness about driving again last week, Gloria's remarkably confident now, even in the ice and slush. Is it because she's keen to send him off?

No. Don't think like that. Just be glad she's recovered so quickly.

Curran pokes him from behind. "Promise you'll write to me."

"Of course."

"And send more Cadbury Flake bars?"

"Not *too* many," Gloria says. "Right, Jasch?"

"Yeah. I'll ration them out so your … dentist doesn't get too … vexed." His words are punctuated by shaky gulps every time they travel through an icy intersection or over a sludgy puddle.

Gloria glances at him. "You okay?"

Fucking fantastic.

"Please be careful," he whispers.

"I know how to drive, honey."

"Not saying you don't. It just looks—"

"Jesus!" She honks the horn as a BMW cuts in front of them.

Jascha's stomach lurches. He buries his face in the crook of his propped elbow, bracing himself against the frosty window as his lips mouth silent, sputtery prayers.

Nausea washes over him. His palms prickle.

Meanwhile, Gloria nonchalantly chastises the driver in front of her. "Yeah, I see your diplomatic license plate, Mr. Overcompensation. Slow your ass down."

Another backseat poke from Curran. "Earth to Jascha."

And then: "Is he gonna be carsick, Mummy? He doesn't look well. At all."

Blackness. Another swerve. The car stops.

"Jasch." Firm shake of his free arm.

Jascha opens his eyes. Blinks. Finds the car parked outside a petrol station convenience store.

"I'm sorry, Gloriochka," he says.

She looks relieved. *At least he called me by the right name this time,* Jascha imagines her thinking.

Christ. What a wretched thing to find relief in.

He unbuckles his seatbelt. Slumps forward. Rests his head on his arms on the dashboard.

"You deserve better than this," he rasps. "Than me."

Gloria leans over and embraces him, resting her face against the back of his neck.

"Shut up," she says. "I love you."

"Me, too." Curran.

Jascha rubs a sweaty palm roughly over his eyes. "Have you got any of those anxiety tablets handy?"

"Yeah, in my purse. Want one?"

"Please."

Gloria sends Curran into the shop with a five dollar bill and strict orders to buy a bottle of water, and a bottle of water only ("No candy bars and no beer, got it?").

"Hey, now. I wouldn't turn down a beer." Jascha's tight chest twinges with every word.

"It's American, remember? Complete crap."

"Not everything American is," he says, looking over at Gloria with a soft smile.

She blushes. "Hopeless romantic, even in your darkest hour."

Curran returns as promised with the bottle of water. Opens it for Jascha, trying his hardest not to spill.

Gloria hands Jascha one of the tablets. "Don't be surprised if this makes you fall out into the plane aisle from over-sedation."

His flight's a cheap red-eye. Sounds like a plan.

❧

A plan which, once sitting in the airport lounge, Jascha wants nothing more than to jettison. Every departure called on the tannoy brings him a step closer to his own; every squeal of the microphone makes him hope for an announced delay.

Curran sits on one side of him, leaning in to demonstrate his strategic thumb prowess on his Game Boy, which he'd thoughtfully loaned Jascha for the rest of the drive ("Maybe it'll distract you, give you something to look at instead of the road.").

Meanwhile, Gloria sits on Jascha's other side, pensive-faced and twitchy, twisting her hands in her lap. When she gets up to go to the loo, she returns a few minutes later with reddened eyes and the slightest hint of a sniffle.

"Had to go snort a few lines," she says by way of wry explanation as she sits back down.

Jascha shakes his head. Hands Curran the last of his wallet's spare quarters and tells him to go select whatever he fancies from the vending machine. "Spend them up, mate. They're no good where I'm headed."

He expects Gloria to protest, but she says nothing.

After Curran dashes across the hall, Jascha laces his fingers through hers. Brings them up to his mouth and kisses her knuckles.

Gloria bows her head. Lets out a tiny half-gulp, half-whimper.

The tannoy announces a flight to Milan.

"How's your lip doing?" Of all the poignant, potent, meaningful things he could possibly say right now, that's what tumbles out.

She shrugs. "Better than my heart, at least."

Jascha squeezes her hand. "I'll ring you every night."

"Seriously?" Gloria laughs a little.

"What? You don't want me to?"

"Of course I want you to. But you can't possibly be up till one a.m. every night and still get to work in the morning on—"

She stops. "Oh. Umm. Right. Nonissue." The fretful lines in her forehead deepen. "Shit. I've ruined everything for you, haven't I?"

"Hush. You've done no such thing."

"Ta-da." Curran comes up and dumps an assortment of crisps and candy in Jascha's lap. "For you. Since the food on planes is such rubbish."

"Aww, bless." Jascha pockets the stash in his messenger bag.

The tannoy calls a flight to Paris. He wants to make an off-kilter *Casablanca* joke *(We'll always have the Four West psych ward?)*, but there's a catch in his throat.

Gloria leans her head against his shoulder. Lets out a deep sigh.

Jascha drapes an arm around her. "I bet Tim'll help me find something. And I've loads of contacts from grad school."

Is the pep talk for her, or for him?

◦~

The tannoy calls Tokyo, then Frankfurt, then finally, London.

Jascha wants to dawdle, draw it out till final boarding call, scramble to snatch one last moment. But what's the point in wearying everyone? They've already sat here for an hour, holding hands, making small talk, playing Game Boy, blinking ferociously.

And now it's time to stand.

Soon as he's on his feet, Curran wraps his arms around Jascha's waist. "Don't go. Please. I'll save up my allowance so you can pay for the feelings doctor."

Jascha pats the boy's head. Fights to choke down the lump in his throat.

"That's right generous of you, mate, but I've got to go back." He tilts Curran's chin to face him. "Just for a little while, all right?"

Curran gives a resigned nod.

"You'll keep at those maths, and keep your mum out of trouble?"

Another nod, this one accompanied by a small smile.

"Good man."

Jascha turns to Gloria. Clasps both her hands.

"Give my love to Vera," she says.

"I will."

"And tell Tim he'd better continue his upward trend of being less of a jerk."

"I will."

Their shoulders drop. Their grips on each other tighten. They look at each other as if to say, *What the hell are we doing, saying goodbye like the taciturn Brits we'll never be?*

And then she barrels into his arms, and he kisses her on the mouth, and she grabs the back of his shirt in her fists, and he strokes her hair over and over and over until the tannoy squawks out, "Second boarding call for London."

They pull apart.

"Go easy on the coke-snorting," Jascha murmurs.

"I'll try. Call me when you land?"

"It'll be middle of the night your time."

"I don't care."

One last kiss, this time on Gloria's forehead. One last embrace, the three of them squashed together.

My family. My reason.

It's all he can do walking down the Jetway to not look back.

⟳

Jascha arrives exhausted at his flat early Saturday morning to find a *FOR LET* sign in the window.

Shit. He'll have to talk to the property management company. Tell them to take it off the market now that he's back.

Not right now, though. Now he needs to ring Gloria.

Eight a.m. here, which is three a.m. there. Jascha winces, both at the time difference itself and the fact that it separates them once again.

Maybe you should wait till a more reasonable hour.

No. She told me to phone. Told me she didn't care how late.

He undresses, crawls into bed, and dials Gloria's number.

Two rings, then three. Then voicemail.

"Hey, sweetheart, I made it back. Your wonder drug only knocked me out for five minutes, but I dreamt of you, so it was five minutes of bliss." Jascha yawns. "Okay. Need proper sleep now. I miss—"

Her answering machine beeps at him to hurry the hell up.

"Miss you both already."

❧

He's just drifted off when he hears footsteps in the kitchen. Jascha rockets up, clutching the duvet around himself as he debates whether to grab the nightstand lamp as a self-defense weapon.

"All new appliances were installed two years ago, along with this lovely tile backsplash and laminate flooring."

Jesus. It's the letting agent, showing interested renters around.

Jascha scrambles to pull on jeans and a T-shirt. Pads barefoot and scruffy-haired into the kitchen.

"Excuse me," he says, "but have you got an appointment?"

The agent, a woman with heavily penciled eyebrows and a Burberry scarf, takes a step back. "I was told the current occupant had moved abroad and there were no entry restrictions."

Right. Of course she was.

Jascha rubs a hand over his face. "Well, the umm, the situation's … changed."

She sets her business card on the counter. "Then you'd best be in touch with the office. They've got showings scheduled all this coming week."

❧

After a hasty apology to the poor couple who'd come to view his flat, Jascha jumps in the shower, dresses, and heads down to the property management office.

"Sir, you gave notice a week ago," another Burberry bird sighs from behind her desk.

"I know I did. But there's been unexpected … Plans have …" He swallows. "Please. I've been a solid tenant for almost five years."

"And you've resumed employment in the U.K.?"

Shit. "Not yet."

"Then I'm sorry. We've a stack of qualified applicants this high"—she places a palm several inches above the top of her desk—"seeking a Chelsea flat of yours' size and price point."

Before Jascha can protest again, she shuts her folder primly. "Good luck to you."

☙

Jascha spends the rest of the afternoon slamming the few things he'd planned to keep into boxes and cursing under his breath.

Around dinnertime, he phones Tim. Leaves a message. *Hey, I'm in town. Ring me soon as you get this.*

Tim returns his call half an hour later. "Back to pack up your stuff? I've someone interested in your car if it's still up for sale."

"Yeah. It is. But not for the reason you might think."

"Wait, what?" A brief pause, during which the reality must be sinking in. "You're back for good?"

"More or less."

"Christ, she's really playing you, isn't she?"

"No. It's complicated."

Tim snickers. "Of course it is."

"Please, save the 'I told you so' glee and just tell me: Do I stand a snowball's chance in hell of getting rehired, or not?"

Another pause, this one longer.

"Wish I could say yes, mate, but I honestly don't know. I mean, if it were up to me, you'd be back on Monday, but ..." He sighs. "Look, we both know what the only sensible thing to do is."

"No, I don't. I've jet lag from hell. Enlighten me."

"Hash it out this evening over a pint."

CHAPTER TWENTY-NINE

I wake up Saturday morning with swollen eyes and Curran's elbow in my ribs. Only way he'd sleep last night is if I stayed with him.

What had begun as petulant sighs at read-aloud time—*Aww, man, I wish Jascha were here to do it*—turned into an uncharacteristic full-on meltdown, with thrown pillows and accusatory wails. *You sent him away, didn't you, Mum? You're mental! I hate you! I want Jascha!*

And then, collapsing into my arms: *I want Dad. I miss London. I love you, Mummy. I'm really, really sorry.*

Me, too, baby, I whispered. *Me, too.*

Curran rolls over now with a small half-moan, half grumble, his eyelids flickering.

"Hey, sweetpea." I stroke his hair. "How'd you sleep?"

"Okay, I guess." He almost elbows me again as he yawns, then snuggles closer.

"Any requests for breakfast? I think we've still got enough eggs for—"

"I didn't mean it when I called you mental last night, Mum," he whispers. "I really didn't."

"Shh. I know."

"Everything was just making me so mad."

"You've been incredibly brave these past few weeks, kiddo. Put up with a lot. And I don't hold it against you one bit for needing to blow off some steam."

I prop up on one elbow. Give Curran's arm a nudge. "Whatcha wanna to do now that Snowpocalypse is over? Whole weekend's wide open."

He shrugs. "Dunno."

"Well, let's think. There's that movie you've been wanting to see."

Curran buries his face in the pillow. "I don't wanna see it without Jascha."

"Okay, now, listen." I nudge him till he reluctantly opens his eyes. "I want Jascha here just as much as you do, but we're not going to sit around with our lives on hold till he comes back. Do you understand me?"

Curran nods.

"Good. And you'd better weigh in with an idea quick, because otherwise I'm dragging you to see *Sense and Sensibility*."

He looks horrified. "You mean that boring-looking film with the rich English ladies in fancy dresses?"

"Yep. That's the one." I sit up as if raring to go.

"Okay, okay. We'll see mine."

❦

It's not until we're almost out the door that it dawns on me: I haven't heard from Jascha.

When I check my voicemail, I find an adorably rambling, drowsy message from him with a timestamp of three a.m. my time. Something about how dreaming of me was bliss?

"Mum, we're gonna miss the previews if we don't hurry up!"

"We won't miss them. Just give me a sec."

So much for following my own edict about not scheduling our lives around Jascha's absence. I dial the international calling code.

Voicemail on his end, too. Hmm. It's six in the evening there. Maybe he turned in early from jet lag? Or—

Beep.

"Hey, darlin', it's me," I murmur. "Sorry I didn't answer when you called before. We had ..."

I pause, mindful of Curran next to me. "A tough time last night. Headed to go watch stuff blow up on a giant cinema screen now, but—"

"I promise not to tell you the plot in case you wanna see it!" Curran yells in the direction of the receiver.

"Yeah, we'll see how that goes." I tuck the phone under my shoulder so I can pull on my coat and check my watch.

Movie starts in ten minutes. Shit. "Gotta go. Love you. Talk soon, okay?"

CHAPTER THIRTY

A new message comes in just after Jascha hangs up with Tim. It's Gloria, sounding harried and awkward in her attempt to impersonate their former breezy goodbyes to each other.

Love you. Talk soon, okay? What the hell.

Come on. She's gutted as you are. You know that. She just doesn't have the luxury of indulging her sorrow, not with an eight-year-old boy tugging at her sleeve.

An eight-year-old boy, who's both a son to him and an ocean away.

Jascha sets the phone back in its cradle. Pushes his hair back hard with his hands, and returns to taping shut boxes until it's time to head down to his local for that hashing-out pint.

His resolve to pace himself dissolves halfway through the first pitcher. Now he knows how Gloria felt, plowing through all that crap wine at Bill's retrospective.

"Complicated, huh?" Tim says, plunking his glass down. "How much so are we talking?"

Umm …

"She kicked you out. That much I can guess."

Jascha takes a deep sip. "Thought we were analyzing my job prospects, not dissecting my love life."

"Debrief first, strategy later. Why'd she do it? Still mercurial from her illness?"

"Thanks for not calling it a crackup," Jascha says dryly.

"I'm trying here, man."

Yeah, he actually is, Jascha has to admit.

"Thanks. And all her little door-slamming fits aside, she wasn't being mercurial this time, believe me."

Tim raises an eyebrow. "Oh? What'd you do to her, Jasch?"

His question's a chiding chuckle, but Jascha can't dodge with an equally blasé answer. He should, if he wants Tim to still go to bat for him, but the pint's two-thirds gone now and he's gripped by a strange, sudden urge to confess.

"I ..."

He rubs his hands over his face. "This is gonna sound horrid if I don't back up a little—I mean, it probably will even if I do, but ..."

Tim flags the barman for a second round.

"You can't possibly be a bigger arsehole than me," he says. "Out with it."

Jascha slams back another glass.

"Okay," he says. "I'm not just some poor sod who lost his wife and kid in a motorway smash-up. I was the one driving, and I almost died too, and I have nightmares that won't leave me the fuck alone."

"Jesus," Tim whispers. "I'm so sor—"

"No." Jascha puts a hand up. "Save the sympathetic noises. I appreciate them, all right, but let me finish."

Tim nods.

"Your beloved Perky Baps would have run screaming from all that baggage, but a certain mercurial American single mum whom you're so fond of talking shit about didn't. I've got surgical scars all over my chest"—he gestures toward his ribs—"from where they had to crack me open. Ugly as sin. First time she sees them, what does Gloria do? Kisses them without batting an eyelash."

"I *knew* she was kinky," Tim mutters.

"Okay, but see, that's the beautiful thing. She wasn't fetishizing it. She just saw what was there, and treated it with the perfect balance of ..." Don't you dare tear up. "I dunno? Nonchalance and reverence, I guess."

Tim nods slowly. "Yeah. That's brilliant. Bet it felt like a relief."

"Not just relief." Jascha's starting to slur a bit. "Absolution."

"Oh, now we're in dangerous territory, my friend."

"I'm not saying it was easy, all right? I woke up from my nightmares calling her my late wife's name."

"*That's* what made her send you packing?" Tim shakes his head. "Some muse she is. I mean, every bloke's done the awkward ex name slip-up at some point."

"No. I mean I was so disoriented I literally thought Gloria was my late wife. She'd have to talk me down till I was back in the right country—hell, the right year."

"Whoa." Tim rears back. "That's like war veteran syndrome, mate."

"Yeah, well, it gets worse."

Tim leans forward again. Tops up Jascha's beer, as if he senses he needs fortification to continue.

Which of course he does. Swig. Gulp.

"One night," Jascha says softly, "I dreamt about the medics holding me down so they could work on me at the accident site."

"You have memories of that?" Tim asks, equally softly.

"Little bit. I was going into shock when they found me. No idea what had happened. Completely flipped out. Throwing punches at anyone who came near me."

He swallows. Stares down. Draws a damp ring on the tabletop.

"Which," he whispers, "is no real threat when you're that critically ill. But when you're back to full strength …"

"Oh, shit," Tim says. "You didn't."

Jascha nods. "I was thrashing about in my sleep. She was trying to calm me, but I thought she was one of them. Clocked her straight in the face."

He rests his head on the table for a moment to regain what's left of his composure. Lifts it again to haltingly continue.

"I—I wake up, and here Gloria is, kneeling next to me, with a hand over her mouth. And then she pulls it away, and I see …" Jascha swallows. "See the blood."

"Fuck. How badly did you hurt her?"

"Not very, thank God. Missed her teeth. Superficial. But it looked horrible."

"And the damage had been done, so to speak."

Jascha nods. "I started sleeping on the couch to protect her. She started smoking again from the stress. We had to make up a bullshit story to her kid about why she had bruises. Meanwhile, her medical bills are pouring in, and I'm trying to find a job, and the snowfall of the century's slamming Washington, so we're all three stuck in her flat for a week."

"Crikey Moses. Perfect storm, innit? Pun not intended."

"Yeah, but I'm telling you, even with all that, they feel like my family."

Tim slides the pitcher out of Jascha's grasp. "So you wanna go back. That's the goal."

"Absolutely."

"Does *she* want you to come back?"

"Yeah. Eventually. After we've had some space and I've gotten some help."

He glances warily over at Tim. "I'm a fucking monster, aren't I?"

Tim shakes his head. "A monster wouldn't be this torn up about it, Jasch."

"Yeah, but still. I'm—"

"Afraid you'll fail the got-myself-sorted test and she'll say no?" Tim sighs. "That's the wrong tree to bark up, man."

Jascha's head feels fuzzy and witless. "Whaddya mean?"

"Sorting yourself out for her. *Just* for her."

"I'm not."

"Bullshit. You put up with this nightmare business for how many years?"

"Four. Almost five."

"And I bet you'd have kept doing had it not been for Miss Mercurial's ultimatum."

Jascha shrugs. "Better late than never, yeah?"

"Fair enough. I'd just hate to see you caught up in pleading your case like some desperate solicitor, biting your nails waiting for her verdict on whether you've exorcised your demons."

"Please," Jascha says. "The only nail-biting I'll be doing is over whether I'll get my bloody job back."

He pauses. "I mean, you *do* think I'll get it back, right?"

Tim takes a long sip of his drink. "Like I said, if it were up to me ..."

"But it's not."

"Nope."

"And if you had to guess?"

"Honestly?" Tim sighs. "You're an odds-beating kinda bloke, but I'd say the odds aren't good."

At least he didn't say *I told you so.* Jascha reaches for the pitcher again.

"Whoa, easy there," Tim says. "You've already had—"

"I'm Russian, remember? This stuff's like water in my blood."

"Yeah, well," Tim says, "I don't want it sneaking up on you and making you drunk-dial her later."

⁓

After Tim drives him home, Jascha lies in the middle of the living room's laminate floor ("Recently installed!" he can hear the letting agent chirp) and, feeling not drunk so much as woozily chagrined, half-slurs, half-belts along with "Don't Go Back to Rockville" on the stereo.

Not the cheerfully plaintive chorus he and Gloria sang in her car last weekend, but one of the muttered, mordant verses about bleeding a lost lover dry.

Is that what he did to her? Not just literally, in a moment of unknowing delirium, but metaphorically, in deliberate desperation? Pushing her to the edge of her precious edges. His phoenix-muse, his saving grace.

Christ. What an idiot he's been.

On the coffee table, his phone rings.

Jascha rolls over. Reaches a hand up for it.

In the CD player now, Michael Stipe wails apologies on "So Central Rain."

Could always pick up and just let that speak for him. Like a teenager with a bespoke playlist: handwritten titles, earnest liner notes.

Or he could beg and plead until his words dissolve into laughably overwrought sensual rhapsodies: *the scent of the taste of the feel of your* …

Or he could roll over onto his back again and rub a hand over his eyes and listen to the pounding piano-and-drums crescendo, feeling like a coward as he lets the phone ring and ring and ring.

CHAPTER THIRTY-ONE

Midnight here, which is five a.m. there.

I'm huddled in a heap on the couch, watching *Saturday Night Live* and draining the last dregs from my bottle of anniversary wine, Triple D risk be damned.

Hell, a little depersonalization and derealization sounds good right about now. Just not the disorder part. Got that in spades in my life already, thank you very much.

Have I made a complete shambles of it all? Please tell me I haven't.

On the screen, a red-haired chanteuse looks like she's fucking a piano bench. What the?

And now she's singing, all breathy poignance, about how no one's picking up the phone and she's feeling all the things that she never thought that she could feel.

Nope, nope, nope. I've no idea of what you speak, my histrionic, flame-tressed friend. Nothing to see here, move along.

I switch her off with the remote. Carry the wine bottle to the trash, let it fall with a gravitas-laden thud. Feign knocking my palms together in careless brush-off: Whew, there's that, done.

Blustery Sunday. I keep busy: walks in the park with Curran, reviews of mid-year faculty evaluations, folding laundry. A quiet, cozy rhythm, just like what we had before.

Was it really so bad, that life? Was it so truly bereft and sorrow-tinged that returning to it should feel like a horrible backslide?

No, and no.

But then Curran melts down again while doing his math homework. "I need Jascha! He's the only one that can help me!"

I'm about to snap at him that he'll just have to deal when the phone rings.

"Gloriochka." Jascha's voice is soft.

"Hey," I say. "Can you talk our kid down from long division for a minute?"

"Umm … sure."

I pass the phone over. Watch Curran catch his breath and quiet as Jascha's guidance sinks in.

"Okay. … Oh, okay, that makes sense." Enthusiastic grin, coupled with a grateful nod. "Yeah, I get it now."

And then, a shy pause. "I miss you."

Guilt gut-punches me. I turn my back. Bow my head.

"Mum?" Curran calls out. "D'you wanna talk to him?"

D'you even need to ask? I reach for the phone and head down the hallway with it tucked between my chin and shoulder.

"Hey," I say again, the crappiest nonchalance impersonator ever. "Thanks for that."

"Of course."

I sit cross-legged on my bed, curled in on myself. "How's the jet lag?"

"Eh, not horrible, but I don't think I did my reacclimation any favors."

"Lemme guess. Tim took you out on a try-to-forget-the-girl bender."

When Jascha answers, his voice sounds nervous, cornered. "Yeah."

"Is that why you didn't pick up last night?" My words come out brittle and shrewish.

"Jesus, Gloria. It's not like I was out on the prowl for a do-over with Perky Baps."

"Pun not intended."

He chuckles ruefully under his breath. "No arguing with you, is there?"

"I don't want to argue. I just ..."

The chuckle turns to a sigh. "I know."

And then: a long silence. I wish I could be transparent as Curran—*I miss you!*—but that feels far too vulnerable, too heart-on-sleeve.

"Still there?" Jascha whispers.

"Uh-huh," I whisper back.

"If it hurts too much to talk, I can ..." He stops. Qualifies. "Because of your lip."

"My lip's okay." Hitting the yellowy, old-bruise stage. Pun not intended.

"And Curran?"

"He's dealing."

I can hear Jascha swallow. "Dunno if you realize this, but you ..." His voice lifts in skeptical-but-amazed wonder. "You called him 'our' kid."

"Yeah," I say quietly. "Because he is."

"Mum!" A bellow from the kitchen. "Can you please proofread my essay?"

"Speaking of," I say. "Hang on."

I cover the receiver with one hand. Bellow back. "I'll be right there!"

"Listen," Jascha says, when I return to him. "I don't want us to be stuck in some weird orbit, obsessing over phone tag."

"No. I don't either."

"I mean, I'd talk to you every free second if I could—"

"When you're sober."

Another rueful laugh. "Right."

"Same here. On both counts."

"Wait, you got drunk, too?"

"Nah, just finished off the last of that evil Triple D wine. A judicious, mom-on-duty bender, if you will."

"Wish I could have been there to help you with that."

I remember our mouths liquidy from luxurious sips, his tongue slowly licking a spill from my bare collarbone. "So, umm ... you were saying something about ... phone tag?"

"Yeah. Yeah." He startles out of what I know is his own heated reverie. "I'm just thinking, you'll be so busy with work and Curran, and I honestly won't be able to afford ..."

Jascha stops. "Sorry. That probably sounded like a dig, huh?"

"A little. Maybe?"

"Fuck. Okay. Let me start over." Jascha blows out a breath. "I'd hate for us to hang on to some rigid idea that if we don't talk every single day we're disappearing from each other's lives and it's all been blown to hell."

Adventures in object permanence. "I agree. Totally. Maybe we should make a schedule or something?"

"Like you ring me at the weekend, and I ring you mid-week?"

"Yeah. A standing date." I blush a little. "Well, not a date. Last thing I need is Curran walking in on me giving you transatlantic phone."

"Hey, if it's after he's in bed ..."

"He goes to bed at two a.m. your time."

"For that, my dirty-minded darling, I would set an alarm."

God, it feels good to let go the solemnness for a minute, to relish some devilish levity. "Switch the schedule around, then? I call you on Wednesday soon as I get home from work, and you call me on Saturday when a late night's no problem?"

"Sounds brilliant."

"And you'll keep me posted on the getting help situation?"

"Mum!" Curran calls. "Are you done yet?"

"Just a second!" I call back.

"Absolutely," Jascha says. "You'll be the first to know when I find something." He clears his throat. "I mean, assuming I *do* find—"

"You will. No default East European pessimism, you hear me?"

He puts on an air of schoolboy petulance, all rote agreement. "*Yes, Headmistress.*"

"Good."

"It's been more than one second, Mum!"

"Christ. I gotta go proofread." In my haste, I almost cut things short with another breezy goodbye, but then I stop myself. "Jasch?"

"Yeah?"

"I love you so goddamn much."

I return to work on Monday wearing extra layers of foundation, a scarf, and a pair of intricate earrings, all in the hopes that they'll draw the attention away from my faded, but still definitely there, bruises.

"You're looking lovely this morning," Charlotte, the school secretary, remarks.

"Thanks," I mumble, headed straight for the hideout of my office.

Julia's not far behind. She edges in with a *British reticence be damned, we need to talk* look on her face.

"What the bloody hell happened to you?" she asks, the minute I close the door.

Bloody hell, that's what.

"I ... I fell," I say quickly. "On the pavement outside my building, before they deiced it from Snowpocalypse."

"No offense, dearie, but a fall's not what this looks like."

"No offense, Julia, but you need to back off."

Her face blanches. "I—I wasn't ... I didn't mean to imply ... I'm just, well, concerned, you know, that other faculty and staff might get the wrong idea and—"

"Talk?" I give her a hard stare. "They've been talking about me for the last few weeks already, I'm sure." My stare goes harder. "Haven't they?"

Julia's mouth twists. "Erm, well, a bit. But I put a stop to that straightaway."

"Then you can put a stop to any rumors if they come up again." I grab her arm, more desperately than I intend. "Please, Jules. I'm up to my eyeballs in medical bills. I can't lose my job."

Julia swallows. "All right," she says slowly. "I'll vouch for you again, but I have to know the truth."

Scared as I am, I have to admit that's only fair.

I back up against my desk. Can't hide behind it and my seniority, but at least I can park my ass on the edge to steady myself.

"My boyfriend," I whisper. "But he didn't mean to."

When Julia opens her mouth to chastise me about being in denial, I put a hand up to stop her. "Yes, I know that sounds like a horrible case of classic Stockholm syndrome, okay? Just listen."

Suddenly, eerily calm, I explain it all to her: Jascha's accident, his constant nightmares, the accidentally thrown punch.

"He's back in England now," I add. "Getting himself sorted."

"Well, good."

I gesture toward my lip. "Is it horribly obvious?"

Julia pats me on the shoulder. "Only to your trusty detail-oriented assistant."

222

❧

And to my mother.

I don't think much of it when she calls mid-morning with a cheerful offer to drive down and take me to lunch, but the minute she sits across from me in the cafe, her eyes widen.

"Oh, Gloria." Amused-yet-worried sigh. "Don't tell me you face-planted on the ice again."

Yep, never gets old, I want to casually respond, but I know that if I do it'll be a face-plant into brush-off failure.

I shake my head.

"Well, then, what on earth happened?"

I duck my chin. Pretend to memorize the outline of my paper napkin, then start shredding it.

"Answer me." *Young lady,* I imagine her tsking, as if I'm sixteen and coming home late again.

My eyes well up. "Jascha."

"Oh, that smarmy bastard," Mom sneers. "Acting like a font of boundless sensitivity, fooling us both. Say the word, and I'll fly across the Atlantic and …"

She pauses. "You *did* send him back to England, right?"

I nod.

"Good girl." Mom reaches for my hand across the table. Gives it an approving squeeze. "*Good* girl."

I feel like a dog being plied with treats for pissing on the newspaper instead of the couch.

"But, umm …" I look down again. "We didn't split up."

Mom jerks her hand back. "What?"

"It wasn't his fault. Not really."

"Stop it." She scowls. "You're deluding yourself."

"No, Mom. I'm serious."

My plea makes her soften a little. She leans forward.

"Tell me what happened," she says.

I run through it all like I did for Julia. When I finish, I expect more self-righteous sneers from Mom. *I told you not to try and heal his past!*

Instead she reaches over a second time and takes my hand again.

"I completely fucked up, didn't I?" I say.

Mom shakes her head. "I'd hardly call finding a middle ground between showing no mercy and drowning in empathy a fuck-up, darling. Especially given the household you grew up in."

She's got a point.

"Now, rest assured, however," she continues, "that if he pulls any crap dodging his own responsibility, I will make good on my promise to cross the Atlantic and give him a piece of my mind."

Mom takes a breath and a sip of her water. "You're still going to therapy, right? Please tell me you are."

"Yes," I sigh. "Got an appointment tomorrow."

In my fifty minutes with Laurie, when I tell the story of what happened between me and Jascha for the third time, my recap is numb, almost rote. No intense protests, no quavers.

I'm not deliberately trying to mislead her or downplay; I just need to detach.

Which, damn her, she won't let me do. Every sentence I finish, she follows with, "And how did that make you feel?"

Gutted. Afraid. Uncertain. Inept.

I shrug. Talk a good game full of buzzwords about exercising boundaries and taking initiative. "I mean, really, if I did the right thing, if I'm handling it well, the feelings don't really matter, do they?"

"Oh, I'd be inclined to disagree." Laurie's voice is so coyly demure I want to smack her.

"Can we just agree to disagree, then?"

Laurie reaches for her calendar. "Let's schedule another session."

⟜

And then, when I step into the elevator afterwards, I run into Peter from Four West.

I do a double-take. "You're … out."

He nods. "Got released just before the snow hit."

"That's awesome." Bruised lip be damned, I can't help smiling. "You going to therapy in this building?"

Another nod. "Three times a week."

The elevator dings. We edge our way out into the lobby.

"I take it you're back at work." Peter gestures toward my headmistress skirt and heels.

"Yeah." I let out a derisive snort. "Just took the afternoon off for some fun cathartic times at Healing Roots."

He sees straight through me. "You don't look like you're having much fun, kiddo."

My face crumples. God, he looks so fatherly. In a good way.

I will not cry. I will not cry. I will not cry.

Too late. I sink onto the nearest upholstered bench, tears slobbing down my cheeks.

"Hey, hey." Peter sits close by, rubbing my shoulder. "What's going on, hmm?"

I lean into him. He strokes my back. I cry harder.

"Sorry," I gulp.

"Don't be."

"I tried so hard. I tried so *fucking* hard, Peter."

Bless him, he doesn't ask any more questions. Just holds me until

I weep myself dry, then pats my hair and says gently, "Let me give you a ride home."

〜

This could feel creepy, but it doesn't. I lean against the passenger side door of his car, gnawing my thumbnail, my eyes closed against the January post-Snowpocalypse sun.

Peter puts on classical radio. Soothing. I think of Mom, who would rightfully kick ass and take names for me. I'm grateful for that, but it's not what I want right now.

Right now, I just want to be a decent man's daughter.

We pull up to my building. He puts a hand on my arm, and I startle: not only at the touch, but at his gaze intent on my now bare-of-makeup-camouflage face.

"I'm not going to ask for details," Peter says, "because it's none of my business. But I need to know: Are you safe?"

"Yeah." I nod. "I am."

"Good." His vigilant face relaxes. "I'll walk you up."

〜

He doesn't just walk me up. He comes inside and makes me the lunch I didn't have time to eat on my way to my appointment with Laurie.

"You need to preserve your strength." Peter flips a grilled cheese sandwich with one hand while stirring a saucepan of canned tomato soup with the other. "I can tell you're still struggling."

And I can tell it feels good for him, having both the renewed energy to take care of someone and someone to take care of, so I sit at the table and humor him.

"What about you?" I ask. "Are you still struggling?"

"Wouldn't be in therapy three times a week if I wasn't, dear." He sets a plate and bowl in front of me.

"No, I meant with your wife."

Peter raises an eyebrow.

"I'm not trying to be nosy." I stare down into my soup. "Honest. I just—"

"Want to know if there's hope for you and your Atlantic-traversing beau?"

I nod.

"Well," he says, sitting next to me with a sigh, "that probably depends on whether he's responsible for that bruise on your—"

"Just tell me," I snap. "Are you back together, or not?"

Slowly, Peter shakes his head. "We've decided to make the separation permanent."

I'm flooded with sorrow on his behalf, my breath sucked in then pushed out: Oh, no. *No.*

My free hand darts across the table to rest on his arm.

"I'm sorry," I whisper. "I'm so, so sorry."

Now I remember what Mom meant by drowning in empathy. My lungs constrict, unbearably full. My face crumples again, forlorn.

Peter slides his arm out from under my grasp. "Why do you keep apologizing? It's not your fault."

Something cracks inside me. My shoulders slump.

Peter can see it. He takes both my hands in his. Holds them tightly.

"It's not your fault," he repeats.

My eyes burn. I blink and blink and blink. Wait for some subtle, rogue slip—a coy thumb-stroke against the inside of my wrist, a stealthy twine of fingers—but nothing comes. He's safe. He's solid.

We both pull away at the same time. I take a cautious taste of my soup.

"Too warm?" Peter asks.

"No." I give him a small smile. "Perfect."

He waits until I finish the entire bowl before getting up. I walk him to the door shyly.

"Take care of yourself," I tell him.

"You, too."

When we hug again, this time it feels not like a little girl hungrily scrabbling for a daddy figure, but like two grown-ups compassionately rallying each other. As it should be.

"Thanks," I whisper.

⌒〜

When Jascha calls me that night, just after I've gotten Curran to bed, my first thought is: Wait, what? It's Tuesday. So much for the object permanence rulebook.

"Can I take a rain check?" I ask. "It's been a long damn day."

"You're telling me."

"So what are you doing awake at one a.m.?"

"Packing up my stuff."

Oh, shit. "I thought you were going to talk to the property management company."

"I did. They won't budge. Not without proof of steady employment income."

"And the board won't rehire you?"

A long pause. "No. Just got word today."

"Seriously? That's ridiculous. You were gone for what, one extra week? And Tim, bless his reformed asshole heart, was willing to—"

"I quit, Gloria. On short notice. Then came back begging." Jascha sighs. "If I were them, I wouldn't rehire me, either."

"Yeah, but it's not like they've even had time to replace you."

"Please." His voice shakes. "This is hard enough to deal with without you getting stroppy."

He's just called me the British equivalent of bitchy. "I'm not. I'm just affronted on your behalf."

"Well, there's no need to be. I've a plan."

"Which is what?"

"I'll freelance. Move in with my mum."

"Oh, Jasch."

"It's fine. She needs someone there to look after her anyway."

Jascha's putting on his game face in earnest now. Serious downplay. Vera's not in the greatest of health, but I know that if she'd truly needed live-in care he'd never have even contemplated moving abroad.

"And you really think you can pull the freelancing thing together?"

"Sure. I studied graphic design at university along with the fine arts stuff."

Smart guy. Unlike my husband the purist.

My breath relaxes a little. "Well, if that's what you want to do."

"No, it's not what I want to do," Jascha snaps. "But I don't really have any other options, do I?"

It's to his credit that he doesn't say, "*You've* left me no other options," laying on the guilt trip.

He doesn't need to, of course; I'm laying it on myself pretty hard right now. My lips ready to stutter apologies: *I—I'm sorry. I'm so, so sorry.*

Then I think of Peter: his hands gripping mine, his words reminding me that this isn't my fault.

But it's hard not to *feel* at fault; after all, I'm the one who encouraged Jascha to stay on in D.C. To quit his job and leave everything behind. A rash, romantic plan that sounded like such a good idea at the time.

And it was. At least, until the night terrors, the hurried attempts to reorient and soothe, the collision of tender lip and taut knuckles.

"Gloriochka?" Jascha whispers now.

"Yeah?"

"We're doing the right thing. *You* did the right thing. It's just frustrating as hell."

"I know." My voice softens. "You should get some sleep, honey."

"Let me give you my mum's number first."

As he reads off the digits, I scribble them down on the back of one of my medical bills. "When are you headed over there?"

"Tomorrow morning." He yawns. "Technically this morning, I guess."

"Okay. I'll call you from work in the afternoon, see how things are going."

"Won't they mind you running up a long-distance tab?"

"I conference-call the U.K. all the time. Nobody'll check."

"Naughty girl." Jascha's chiding takes on a lascivious tinge.

"Yes, but only on Saturdays." I send a kiss into the phone against the receiver. "Sweet dreams."

CHAPTER THIRTY-TWO

Jascha thought he'd feel incredible shame, being thirty-six years old and living at home again, the car and furniture and accoutrements of adulthood all sold off, but honestly it's not as horrible as he'd expected. He rather likes the lone-wolf quality of self-employment, even with its incessant hustle of ringing old art school mates and former colleagues to drum up business, his marathon scouting sessions punctuated only by coffee breaks and more calls to doctors' offices.

The waiting lists are even longer than in America. Gloria says she'll talk to her assistant Julia, who might have some leads, but he's not holding his breath.

Through it all, his mother remains an unwavering support. He'd come to her doleful-eyed and fearing her reaction. "I'm not like Papa was," he'd insisted. "I'd never deliberately hit a woman. Please, you have to believe me."

He'd expected her to be aghast, or at least give him a stern talking-to, but Vera simply hugged him and waved him inside with a matter-of-fact, "Is no need for melodrama. Of course you can stay."

She pooled her bingo winnings and some extra from her frugality-funded bank account to help Jascha buy a computer for his foray into desktop publishing. She brought him lunch on a tray when he was knee-deep in updating his woefully out-of-date CV. And when he was on the phone with Gloria, she'd look up from across the room where she sat doing her crossword or watching her guilty pleasure, British football, and yell, "Tell that *devushka* of yours to lay off the cigarettes!" Or, "Tell her to eat more so she stops looking like a twig."

Once the cheerful ultimatum was laid down, though, and Gloria had responded in kind ("Tell her I only smoked two, and I gained the equivalent of a freshman fifteen from eating starchy garbage in the hospital."), his mother would always give Jascha the utmost privacy. She'd turn down the telly, or head to the kitchen to tidy some dishes, with a quick, "I leave you to your catching-up." (Thankfully, she went to bed early, so there was no risk of being interrupted on Saturday nights.)

As for Gloria, Jascha misses her tremendously, so much so that there are moments when, during times he knows she'll be out, he'll ring her number just to listen to her voice on her answerphone message. And yet there's something exhilarating about the distance between them. She isn't with him in a mundane, daily sense, but her realness is a marvelous fact that greets him every day. The thought of his girl, his love, across an ocean but very much alive—setting out Scotch eggs for breakfast, dashing to catch the Metro, reading aloud to Curran at night—fills Jascha with a buoyant giddiness.

"Oh, yeah," Gloria says, when he asks her if she feels the same. "It's like a delicious secret in my pocket. I smile in the middle of faculty meetings, thinking about it."

Then she abruptly changes the subject and says, "So, Julia found me a name."

"She did?" The prospect comes as a simultaneous relief and fear-inducer. Jascha's stomach drops.

"Yeah. A specialist in Oxford. Private-pay only."

"There's no way I can—"

"I talked to Mom. She said she'd cover it."

"Well, that's right generous, but I don't want to be some charity case, some object of pity."

"Jesus, would you relax?" Gloria laughs. "If there's anyone she pities, it's me. Says it's the least she can do given the shitty childhood I had."

Yes. He can picture that: Caroline, leaned across a table in intimate urgency, her fawning gaze locked on her daughter. *Oh, sweetheart. Let me be here for you.*

"Okay," Jascha says. "Give me the details."

On the train down to Oxford later that week for his first appointment, Jascha busies himself reading a thick *Learn HTML Today!* bible full of tutorials on web design, apparently the Next Big Thing. Now he knows why Gloria wanted to skive off from her own inaugural therapy session and take him sightseeing; the anticipatory dread and eye-rolly skepticism are surging inside him in equal measure.

He feels better when he enters the therapist's office. Its waiting area looks like any other doctor's surgery: outdated magazines, tatty chairs. Nary a self-help tome or wind chime in sight.

Even better, the woman who greets Jascha looks not like a flowery hippie, but someone's polite but plain-spoken aunt. Sensible shoes, paisley cardigan, hair dyed just a touch too red.

"Nora Blake," she says, thrusting out her hand. "I'm glad you made it."

"So you're a specialist in ... what exactly?" Jascha asks, once they've sat down.

"Complicated grief." She says this as matter-of-factly as Vera did when she told him he could stay.

"Complicated," Jascha repeats, unable to get Tim's sneer of *Of course it is* out of his mind.

Nora nods. "Grief that's so persistent and intense that it takes over your life, even years after the loss."

So there's a name for this torment.

"It's often a combination of post traumatic stress disorder and depression."

"But I'm not a refugee or a Gulf War veteran," Jascha says. "How can I—"

"Trauma reactions aren't limited to those categories. We also see them in people who've experienced natural disasters or assaults." Delicate pause. "Or accidents."

Jascha reflexively flinches.

"Reactions," he says slowly. "You mean like nightmares?"

Another nod. "Or anxiety that comes on when you're faced with reminders of the event."

Rainy roads. Bumper cars. Fiona's baby. Gloria in hospital.

"That happens to me sometimes." Be honest with her. Only way this will work. "Actually, quite a lot."

"And the episodes impact your functioning in your daily life?"

"I accidentally gave my girlfriend a bloody lip in the middle of a flashback." The words explode from him. "Now we're three thousand miles apart. I need to fucking fix this."

To her credit, Nora doesn't blanch or startle.

"Sorry," Jascha says. "Didn't mean to swear at you."

"It's all right." She gives him a dry smile. "I'd swear too if I were in your position."

Whew. "I just ... This ..." He swallows. "It's fixable, right? Please tell me it is."

"With targeted interventions and guidance, absolutely."

Part of said "targeted intervention" is weekly homework. More flashbacks, this time to the hell that was grammar school as a recent Cold War immigrant—all playground taunts of, "You spying on us, Commie?"—but at least the exercises are empirical and concrete, not vague psychobabble.

The first one involves procuring photographs of his late wife and daughter. Not a problem; Jascha's mother counts scrapbooking as one of her hobbies. Color-coordinated albums stand sentry inside the glass doors of her dining room's curio, their archival-quality pages safe from dust.

No cheery stickers and embellishment sparkles for her, though. Vera treats each volume with the reverence of a true archivist, labeling moments in chronological order and precise detail. Here's Elizabeth's first birthday, the sweet snapshots dwarfed by handwritten litanies: the guest list, the gifts given, the recipe for red velvet cake with buttercream frosting she made.

"Don't bend them," she tsks at Jascha when he slides the pictures free from their glued-down protective corners. As if he would ever dream of doing such a thing to his girls.

Here's Marianne, in a yellow bikini with a towel wrapped round her shoulders, wet-haired and laughing. *Mallorca, April 1985.* Their honeymoon.

And here's Elizabeth, aged four, in a staged portrait along with the rest of her class, already with an impish smile, giving the girl in front of her rabbit ears. Cheeky thing. Marianne had been vexed, but he'd thought it fabulous.

The entire hour down to Oxford, Jascha shuffles the photographs. Careful, careful.

"They were beautiful," Nora murmurs when he shows her. "Tell me about them."

"I can't," he insists. "It'll just be fodder for the nightmare."

"Please. This will help. I promise."

Feelings doctor's orders. Might as well have a go.

"Marianne is … was …" Jascha's throat feels like it's closing up.

"Why don't we start with someone else. Ease into it. Can you tell me about your current girlfriend?"

Yes. That Jascha can do.

"She's American, but her accent isn't obnoxious. She reads James Joyce for fun. She has gorgeous dark hair that smells of rosemary-mint." Christ, this is sounding pretentious. "She's a terrible housekeeper, but she gives excellent transatlantic—"

No. You will not confess your long-distance sex life to Auntie Nora. You will *not*.

"She's a, ah, very passionate person." Nice save. "And has an eight-year-old son I adore."

The thought of Curran warms him, unwinds him.

"And Marianne?" Nora says gently.

"Should I use past tense or present?"

"Past, if you don't mind."

"Okay." He takes a deep breath. "She worked as an editor on children's books. Her middle name was Olivia. She grew lavender in the back garden. She always ordered crème brûlée for dessert in restaurants. Is that enough? Can I stop now?"

"Let's try with Elizabeth."

Oh, God. He rubs a hand over his eyes.

"Assuming you're up for it."

Jascha's not, but he's got to try.

"She was born on a Wednesday night, in a snowstorm. She loved doing cartwheels. Her favorite color was cerulean. Very precise. An artist's daughter if ever there was one." Blink blink breathe. "She hated having her hair brushed. She used to put on a bunch of Mare's jewelry and scarves and twirl around to Stevie Nicks. I'm sorry. I've hit my limit. I really need to stop now."

"You did marvelous. A brilliant start."

"Why are we ..." Jascha chokes down a gasp. "Doing this?"

"It's a form of desensitization. To take the venom out of your memories' sting."

"My memories aren't poison," he snaps. "I don't know how you can you even imply—"

"Sorry. A tricky metaphor. Your memories themselves aren't dangerous, but your reactions to being reminded of them are. And working with less potent ones is a good lead-in to conquering the big baddies."

"So you want me to excise everything about them from my mind," Jascha says with a sigh. "Never smell lavender and think of my wife. Never hear that goat-bleating witchy woman and think of my daughter."

"Let me ask you a question." Nora's watery-blue (not cerulean, no) eyes are intent upon him. "If you were to catch a whiff of some Yardley's soap or hear 'Edge of Seventeen' right now, would you feel mildly nostalgic or utterly gutted?"

Jascha ponders her question, acutely aware of the distance between what he'd like his answer to be and what it really is.

"Truthfully, now." She sounds like Gloria.

"The ... the latter."

"Then these exercises will help. I want you to look at your photographs at a specific time each day. Any time will do, as long as it's consistent."

"Shall I set a timer, like my girlfriend does for when she needs to cry but doesn't want her son to see?"

"Yes." Nora gives him a soft smile. "That's fine. No more than fifteen minutes, let's say. And make a list of as many things as you can think of that remind you of them."

"Including things that remind me of the accident?"

"Oh, no, no. Nothing about that. We won't get to it for a while."

Good. "So that's all? Pictures and lists?"

"Right. Notice any emotions that come up for you whilst you're doing the exercise, but don't dwell."

Easier said than done, Auntie. "Okay. I'll … I'll give it a try."

"You need to ring Gloria," his mother says the minute he walks in the door from his appointment. "She phoned three times while you were out."

"Did she say what—"

"Not a word."

Weird. They spoke two nights ago, on Saturday, and she seemed fine, if a little subdued. *Would it break your heart if we skipped tonight's festivities, honey?*

Of course not, he'd said. Then they'd chatted for a bit—about therapy, of all things.

It's kicking my arse, Gloriochka.

Mine, too. I'm gonna need to talk about my dad here soon. Scary shit. I'll hold your hand from afar.

Aww, thanks.

Maybe she had the big session today, and wants to debrief? But it's three o'clock here, which is ten in the morning there. Gloria's probably at her desk at work, issuing school-wide memos and contacting the parents of chronically late pupils.

When Jascha dials her extension, she answers on the first ring. "Hey. Sorry I stalked you. Was Vera annoyed?"

"Nah, it's fine." He heads down the hall to his room, out of his mother's earshot. "Though I can't help wondering what—"

"I'm a week late."

Jascha almost drops the phone. "How? We were so careful."

"Except the one night. When you first had ..."

The nightmare. Shit.

Would it help if we made love? Her hips and hands guiding him. All that slickness and softness and risk.

"Are you sure?" he asks.

"That I'm late? Oh, yeah. Last time I got my period, I was on the plane to London at Christmas with nary a tampon in my carry-on bag."

And now it's the beginning of February.

"But there could be some other reason, right?" Jascha says. "Like all the stress you've been under?"

"Sure." Gloria's voice rises into a forcibly hopeful register. "Probably. I mean, we shouldn't freak."

"Right. No jumping to conclusions."

"I wasn't even sure whether it was worth mentioning for the first few days, but then I hit the one-week mark, and—"

"Thank you. For telling me."

"You're not freaked, are you?"

"No. Just keep me posted."

That night, Jascha sets a timer for fifteen minutes. Shuffles the photos some more.

His gaze lingers on one of a hugely pregnant Marianne clad in a vintage polka dot sundress, her feet propped up on a chaise lounge in the lavender garden, a glass of Pimm's balanced atop her bump.

You're sure it's all right? she kept fretting. *It's so bloody hot out. Just one watered-down one won't hurt, yeah?*

It's only bloody hot out because you're *so bloody hot,* Jascha had said, setting his camera aside and leaning down to kiss her on the mouth.

Marianne had tasted of gin and kiwi. Against his softly cupped palm, Elizabeth had kicked hard.

And now they were both gone. Because of him: his self-absorption, his carelessness.

The timer dings. Jascha wipes his eyes roughly. Goes back to reading about the finer points of designing website tables and utilizing markup tags, all the while praying he'll be able to let go.

CHAPTER THIRTY-THREE

One week's turned into ten days. I'm doing my best not to panic, which is to say that I've gnawed my fingernails to shreds and taken my anxiety medication every five hours like clockwork.

"It's approved for use in pregnancy," I tell Jascha. "I checked with the pharmacist."

"Oh, good."

He's secretly hoping for a positive result. I know he is. Meanwhile, I'm hoping that if I ignore the situation it'll disappear.

Two weeks. I go to therapy, where Laurie informs me that denial is a maladaptive coping mechanism and gently orders me to just pee on a stick already.

I finally do it on a Saturday night after Curran's asleep, around the time Jascha usually calls me. The phone rings right as I'm about to pull down my jeans and rip the test's wrapper open.

I let the machine pick up. "Hey, lovely, it's me. Any signs or portents of you-know-what?"

This is even trickier than when they handed me a plastic cup in the ER, but I pee like my life depends upon it. Which, in a way, it does.

The "Yes, you've done this correctly even though you're a bundle of clumsy nerves" indicator blessedly turns blue. I pull up my zipper, flush, and set the oracle stick on the sink edge.

Then I go into the kitchen, set the timer for three minutes, and call Jascha back.

He's out of breath when he answers. "Close one. Almost woke up my mum."

Yeah, we are *so* not in a position to have a baby.

The timer dings.

"Oh, honey," Jascha murmurs. "Were you in the middle of your ritual cry?"

God, I wish it were only that. "I actually ... umm ... took a test. That's my stick timer."

"So it's finished marinating, or whatever it does?"

I can't stifle a shaky giggle. "Yeah. Fingers crossed." Never mind that we're no doubt crossing them for different outcomes.

Back in the bathroom, I squeeze my eyes shut. "Okay. Moment of truth time."

"Count of three?"

One, two, and ... I look.

A blank circle, white as a cataract-clouded eye. I pick up the stick, not trusting. Scrutinize it for even the slightest hint of blue.

Nope, nope, nope. Thank you, thank you, thank you.

"Gloria?" Jascha's voice trembles.

"We're good. I mean, it's negative."

Jascha lets out his breath slowly.

"You're disappointed, aren't you?" I ask.

"Are you joking? I'm bloody relieved."

"Really? I thought for sure you'd want—"

"To see us sorted out and back in the same flat—hell, even the same country?" His tone softens. "That's what I really want, Gloriochka. And we're nowhere near finished with the work we need to do to get there."

"But we'll get there."

"Damn right we will. Now, tell me: Are your jeans still unzipped?"

My face flushes. I head back to the bedroom, hip-shrug my way out of them, and slide under the duvet. "On the floor, actually."

"Even better. And your knickers?"

"Easily dispensed with."

"Well then lick your fingertips and close your eyes, sweetness."

⟲

It's so much easier like this. Oddly, the geographic distance helps: not just because it inspires a pure, erotic hunger driven by our inability to touch, but also because it eliminates the heartbreak of having to go our separate ways afterwards—one to the couch, one to the bed that should be both of ours—when we're ready for what we wish could be limb-tangled sleep.

Under my duvet with the phone in the crook of my shoulder, there are no nightmares. No bullets to dodge. No risks. Only simple clarity: *Don't comfort me. Don't try to repair my damage. Just talk me through getting off.*

My thighs shudder. My breath catches. I roll over onto my stomach. Rub my free hand across my eyes.

"Better?" Jascha asks.

"Mmm."

"That's a rather inscrutable *mmm*. Was I too—"

"No." I lift my head from the pillow with a satiated gasp. "I'm good."

All I can think is: I'm going to have to be real with Laurie when I see her next time.

⟲

The appointment starts out strong enough. She sweetly asks how I'm doing; I reply with a thoroughly honest sigh of, "Thankful I'm not pregnant. Sick of everything revolving around Jascha's pain. Of it cornering me."

"Into making decisions you normally wouldn't?"

"Into even having to decide." My voice rises in irritation.

"This sounds like a really old feeling for you."

"Old?" I feign puzzlement. "How so?"

"You're stalling," Laurie says. Sharp under all that empathy ooze.

"Yeah," I murmur. "Ancient."

"Childhood ancient?"

I close my eyes. Put up a palm. "Stop fishing. I'm getting to the story, okay? I'll give you your precious narrative. Just let me ..."

My eyes flicker open again. My hand slides down to grip my opposite elbow. Holding myself together.

"This is hard." The words come out in a brittle gulp. "It's gonna be ugly."

"We can go as slowly as you want."

No. Suddenly I want everything spewed out onto the metaphorical table, held up into the light.

"My father," I say. "I think I killed him."

Laurie jumps. Part of me's thrilled I've gotten a reaction; another's terrified that I actually spoke that confession aloud. As if saying it has made it irrefutably true.

"Not literally," I add. "I mean, he put the gun to his own head, not long after I moved to England."

"And yet you feel responsible."

"I could have saved him," I say desperately. "But I didn't."

Laurie's brow furrows. "If you weren't there, how could you possibly intervene to—"

"That's the whole point," I snap. "I *wasn't* there. I deserted him. I was selfish."

"Were you?" She purses her lips. "I'd hardly call pursuing an education and independence at twenty-one years old selfish. If anything, I'd consider it developmentally appropriate."

I return to my skirt-hem picking. "First time in my life anything ever was."

"All the more reason to—"

"You know the mental health techs on Four West?" I blurt out. "Those folks who made sure we ate and took our meds, and looked in on us when we spent too long isolated in our rooms? Who sat and patiently listened to our morose, mumbly rambles?"

Laurie nods. "The ones in the trenches."

Right. "I had their job. Unpaid, unappreciated. Starting when I was Curran's age."

"What about your mother?"

"Eh, she'd pretty much checked out. Angry that she'd had to give up her career to raise me. She was a brilliant cellist. Could have given my namesake a run for her money."

"Your namesake?"

"Well, my middle name. Jacqueline, as in du Pre." I can tell that's not ringing any bells for Laurie. "Tragic British cellist with multiple sclerosis? You know, the Elgar concerto?"

"Sorry." She shakes her head. "I don't …"

"Forget it. Doesn't matter. All you need to know is: bitter and burnt-out." Anticipating Laurie's next question, I keep plowing through. "We're fine now, don't worry. She's sweet as treacle to me. Overcompensates like nobody's business. Paying Jascha's medical bills and mine."

"Thank God for small favors, eh?" There's the wry Laurie I like.

"Abso-freakin'-lutely. But back then …" I drift off.

"You were alone."

"*Left* alone," I correct her. "With my dad."

"What was that like?"

"Horrible. Wonderful. Both." My twitchy hand rises from my lap to my heart, its fingers clutching at the fuzzy wool of my sweater.

"He could have been such a good guy, Laurie. Maybe not a bright, carefree one like my husband. More like Jascha." Or Peter. "If only he'd ... if only there'd been ... I don't even know what."

"Avenues for help? Awareness about mental illness?"

"Sure. Yeah. Something." Jesus, I'm not here for a public policy debate.

"Along with a way for a forced-to-be-wise-beyond-her-years little girl to be heard."

Bile rises in my throat. "I need a break. Can we take a break?"

"Of course."

Laurie's barely spoken the words before I'm pushing myself up from my seat. "Give me five minutes, okay? I'm not ditching. I just need some air."

⁂

I lock myself in her pastel-wallpapered bathroom and retch into the sink. At least it's not morning sickness, right?

Thank God for small favors, redux.

I would sell my soul for a cigarette right about now.

Check the mirror. Is there a stranger staring back?

Nope. Just a wide-eyed, scared-shitless woman.

Not a little girl, unheard. A grown woman with a voice.

If there's any time to be a brash, brave American, this is it. I dig through my purse, pop a Valium, and head back out.

⁂

When I return to her office, Laurie's all vigilant-gazed concern. "Would you like some water? Shall I crack the window?"

"No. No, I'm good." Enough.

I take a seat again. Try to summon *So-where-were-we* nonchalance. Fail.

"He had this girlfriend," I say softly. "At university. First love and all that. Never got over her. Not even years later."

"That's what fed his depression? What it revolved around?"

I nod. "And I had the bad luck to look like her, so ..." A rueful laugh explodes from me. "The older I got, the weirder it got."

"Weirder?" Laurie repeats the word carefully, as if hunting for its elusive subtext.

"By the time I hit my teens, I felt like his mistress. Sitting perched on the edge of his chair's arm in his study, stroking his hair while he rested his head on the desk and cried." My voice shakes with disgust. "And he ate it up. Told me I was the only reason he kept holding on. That I was far too good for the slacker punk guys I dated. I mean, he was right on that count, but ..."

"Did he ever—"

"Nope. Never." I shake my head. "On the one hand, I'm glad, but on the other, it was almost worse. To be constantly looked up and down by eyes that are peeling your layers back like an onion. To get kissed goodnight on the forehead and know what he really wanted was to dip his mouth further down."

My own mouth grimaces at the taste of my words. "It felt so cowardly. Like, come on, you melancholy bastard, just fuck me already and get it over with. Own your own sickness."

I look out the window, which I now wish she'd cracked.

"Don't get me wrong," I whisper. "I have tremendous empathy for the pain he was in. Even more so now that I've been through what I have. But that doesn't ..." My eyes well up. "I mean, Christ. Untreated suffering's not a free pass to treat your kid like she's—"

"No," Laurie says. "It isn't. And the fact that you endured what you did and can still summon empathy is a tremendous testament to your resilience."

Such pretty, validating words. *Thank you,* I should say. But there's more to confess.

"It felt good sometimes. The attention." I turn my head back to her. "He never harped on me for getting a nose ring and drinking at parties like Mom did. He actually listened to what I had to say instead of just brushing me off as a histrionic teenager. Hell, he even got me through AP chemistry." I can't help chuckling. "Is that wrong? That I ate it up, too? That I loved him for that?"

"Not wrong," Laurie says. "Confusing as hell for you, yes, but not wrong. Just utterly human."

"But his motives weren't pure," I say. "I can see that now."

"With the hindsight of a thirty-year-old, yes. But at thirteen, fourteen, fifteen? You were enmeshed in the narrative that says: Dad's the only one who understands me, and I'm the only one who can keep him alive."

God. It sounds so irrational and ridiculous, laid out like that. And yet, I had fervently believed.

"I thought things would let up once I went to college," I tell her. "But he even influenced my decision there. I had acceptances from all over, and yet I picked a place only a weekend's drive from home. You know, in case he ... needed me."

Laurie frowns. "I'm guessing things didn't let up, and he constantly needed you?"

"Yup. Lots of phone calls. Impromptu visits. Pleas for me to come home." I scowl. "I put up with that shit for three more years. And then I got the chance to study abroad in London, and ... "

I swallow. "Sure, I was a total Anglophile, but I also knew that was my ticket out."

Laurie looks impressed. "A brave move."

"Yeah, one he fought all the way. The begging for me not to leave him I could handle—that was business as usual—but when he started poking holes in my confidence, warning me I wouldn't be able to keep up academically ..."

"Ah, so you were only his wise old soul when it suited his ends." To her credit, Laurie says this with an air of curiosity, not contempt.

"Exactly. And I was ready to be done. Seriously done. But ..." My voice cracks. "I still worried about him. About what would happen to him after I left."

I run a hand over my eyes. "I knew it was going to be bad. I had a feeling he was going to sink under. And I was right." My shoulders shudder. "Three months after I moved to London, there I was, with the sweetest British boyfriend in the world—"

"The guy you went on to marry?"

"Uh-huh. So I'm sitting on the floor of my flat studying, all girly flush because we had a date later that night, listening to my roommate singing in the shower. And then I got the call. My boy had to literally pick me up off the rug; I couldn't even stand. He carried me into his bed, and I slept for two days. I was just gutted."

"Not only grieving, but guilty?"

"Yeah. I never talked about that part to anyone—not my mother, not even Bill—but I always felt like I was to blame." I bow my head. "Like my abandoning him did him in."

Laurie pulls her chair forward.

"Gloria," she says. "Look at me."

Warily, I glance up.

"I've worked with chronically suicidal patients for years. The only thing that can stop them is clinical intervention. And even then, I've seen people make attempts on inpatient units. The desire to die can be as potent as the will to live."

I swallow. "So staying may not have made a difference?"

"No. Not unless you count your young, ripe-with-possibility life growing even more controlled and constricted. That difference I can retroactively guarantee."

"But—"

"Magical thinking," Laurie says. "That's the technical term. Creation of cause-and-effect relationships where none logically exist. Staying will keep Dad alive. Or conversely: My leaving is what killed him."

"I just can't help feeling responsible," I whisper.

"Of course you can't. You were tasked with such an enormous responsibility, at such a disturbingly early age."

When she puts it in perspective that way, I'm seized by a sudden surge of empathy: not the drowning kind, but an almost-maternal melt. *Oh, sweetheart,* I hear myself crooning, as I mentally reach out my arms to my solemn, grave-faced girl-self.

And then I sniffle hard, and realize tears are trickling down my cheeks. Not frantic, embarrassed ones like I wept when I sat down on the lobby bench with Peter, but ones of quiet, tender witness.

"Jesus." I lean over to take the tissue Laurie offers me. "I'm a fucking waterworks lately. Almost as bad as right after Bill died."

"You've never cried for yourself before, have you?" Laurie asks gently. "Mourned your lost childhood?"

I can't suppress a snort. "Never occurred to me. Game face, you know? On at all times. Plus in England, that New Age stuff's seen as a total joke."

"Well, how does it feel to honor it now, on unfashionably emotive American soil?"

"Awkward?" I blow my nose. "Necessary?"

She gives me a small smile. I find myself smiling back.

"Self-indulgent, too." My grin deepens. "But you know what? Also kind of good."

⟨୬⟩

"I did it," I say gleefully to Jascha during our next Wednesday night chat. "I talked about my dad, more honestly than I have to anyone, and it didn't shatter me to pieces."

"Brava, lovely. I knew you could."

"How about you and Operation Kick PTSD's Ass?"

"Made my list. Did my fifteen minutes of timed photo-gazing every night this week."

"High-five, baby. Does it feel like the homework's working?"

"Eh, too early to tell. Seems a bit dodgy."

"Don't blow it off, though. I think those psychobabble-pushers are on to something."

"In Auntie Nora we trust?"

"And Hippie-Dippie Laurie."

He chuckles. "Not going to be talking about me next, are you?"

⟨୬⟩

Actually, I am. My existential grapplings with agency and choice and assignation of guilt, Laurie insists, still play themselves out—"reenact," to be precise—in my relationship with Jascha.

Damn it. Can't I just relax into the relief of my twisted magic debunked? Isn't that epiphany—*Hey, I didn't kill my predatory coward of a clinging father after all!*—more than enough self-exploration?

Nope. Not when, as Laurie claims, the aftershocks are rippling across our fragile terrain. More subtly than Jascha's haunted sleep and inadvertent blows, to be sure, but still registering on the Richter scale of—

"Listen," I say to her. "No offense, but your metaphors are starting to strain the bounds of credibility here."

"None taken." She shifts in her chair, the movement like a line break. "Why don't you tell me about the first time you saw Jascha have the nightmare?"

"You mean the time I almost got knocked up trying to calm him down?"

Her normally placid mouth betrays itself with just a hint of frowny frustration. "Yes. That one."

"I was terrified, but not nearly as terrified as he was." Empathy-melt softens my shoulders. "Clutching me. Whimpering my name."

"Bit of an echo there, no?"

"Way more than a bit. But I pushed past it."

"Why?"

"Because I knew this was different. We were—are—lovers. Adults. Equals."

Laurie nods vigorously. "An important distinction. Unresolved trauma likes to drop-kick us into fight-or-flight mode. Convinces us that new situations are reprises of old threats. And it takes strength and self-awareness to talk back to that persuasive siren song." She gestures appreciatively toward me. "Strength that you possessed."

Hmm. Yeah. Guess so. Now I'm nodding, pleased as punch with myself. *Nice one, Gloriochka. Way to smack that shit down.*

And yet …

"That lovely wry smile of yours just faded. What's going on?"

"I went too far," I say slowly. "Tried too hard to fix it for him."

"By initiating unprotected sex."

Laurie pauses. "I mean, you *did* initiate it, right? He didn't pressure you to, or plead in a way that reminded you of your—"

"Oh, no, no, no, no." My protest tumbles out in a defensive cascade. "Jascha's not that kind of guy. At all."

"Which means you weren't cornered, but in fact offered."

Ouch. I see where she's going.

I chew my lip. "Yeeeah."

"How did it feel?"

Christ. Her perennial favorite query, back again.

"Amazing," I say softly, my gaze drifting toward the window once more in reverie.

"In an erotic sense?"

Whoa. "Way to pry there, Laurie."

She blushes. "Sorry. I'm just trying to get an idea of whether—"

I put a hand up. "No. Whatever. It's fine. I can answer."

"You don't have to."

It's a herculean effort not to roll my eyes. "I came, okay? It was hot. Especially after all that awkward fiddling around with condoms and having long serious talks about our dead spouses. To just go for it, not think, run with—"

"So no sense of obligation or duty. No 'Close your eyes and think of England.'" A sly smile. "Pun fully intended."

"Oh, you're funny." I shake my head, chuckling in spite of myself. "Nope. Not even a little bit. It felt like … like giving a gift."

"Freely bestowed."

Warmth floods me. "Yes. Freely bestowed."

"Do you regret giving it?"

"Are you kidding?" I scoff. "I just spent two weeks white-knuckling over the state of my ovaries. Damn right I regret it. I made a stunningly poor choice."

"But an autonomous one."

"I *told* you, I wouldn't have been tempted to make it if it hadn't been for that stupid nightmare!" My voice rises.

"Really," Laurie says coyly. "You're sure."

Jesus. What is this, a therapy session or an interrogation?

"Last week you tell me I'm not responsible; this week you tell me I am." I give my chair's arm a hard thwack. "So which one is it?"

Laurie pauses for a moment. "Both."

Aww, hell.

"Look, there are some situations in which blame can be easily laid. Like with your father."

Now it's legit eyeroll time. "Did you intend *that* pun?"

Laurie claps a hand over her mouth. "God. No. Argh."

"It's okay. I'll find it in my heart to forgive you. Go on."

"Thanks. Sorry. Take two." Poor thing, she's still flustered. "With the knowledge and perspective you have now, what percentage of responsibility would you give him for the way he treated you growing up?"

"One hundred." The answer flies from my mouth, uncontemplated.

"No doubts."

"Nope."

"But back then, I'm guessing, it was way easier to split those percentages along other lines. To shift the blame off this man who simultaneously revered and debased you." She puts on a dismissive tone, waving a careless hand. "'Oh, Dad can't help the way he is. It's his depression, or his grief, or—'"

"Mom being a bitch and not caring enough."

"Bingo."

"Okay," I say, "but you've gotta admit those were contributing factors."

"Sure. But the bottom line is, no person, no entity, forced your father to treat you like his emotional mistress and his teenage eye candy. He threw down that gauntlet all by himself."

My stomach churns. My face contorts into a grimace.

"Disgusting, right? Brutal stuff. Would have devastated you to realize back then, when you were trapped in his orbit."

"So blame serves a protective purpose?"

"You better believe it. Same as magical thinking. We all want to create the most palatable, comfortable narrative possible about our lives. Preserve our dignity and uphold our idols. Make sense out of senselessness."

God, I wish this were just a lit-crit seminar.

"Shall we try another example?"

"Yeah. Sure." Break me some more, Laurie. Go ahead.

"Your late husband's cancer. His untimely death at thirty-one. Whose fault was that?"

"Nobody's. Universe was just being a jerk."

"So you weren't angry at God, or yourself?"

I chew my lip. "Not really. I mean, all I could do was nurse him through chemo and hope for the best."

"Hmm, now this is interesting." Laurie's almost excited, jumping into detective mode. *Let's excavate Gloria's brain!* "Magical thinking got its claws in you over a loss caused by emotional suffering, but not a physical one."

I shrug. "There's no arguing with white blood cells."

"Oh, you'd be surprised how many people think there is. But you didn't buy it."

"I'm a tough sell."

"So I noticed." She leans forward. "How about what you did that night for—with—Jascha?"

How about I pretend to dash off to an emergency work meeting and call our therapeutic adventures done?

No, I shouldn't. If Jascha can keep plugging along on Auntie Nora's nostalgia homework—at my urging, no less—I can sure as hell duke it out with Hippie-Dippie Horrible Pun Laurie.

"That was PTSD's fault," I say.

"One hundred percent? Or less?"

I'm equal parts busted and stumped.

"Look, I'm in total agreement with you that post-traumatic stress is a thief and a liar and a sneaky bitch," Laurie says. "Feel free to hate her guts for stealing your man. But don't give her more power and agency over your life than she deserves."

Whoa. Now there's a metaphor. Is that really what I'm letting happen?

"Okay," I say. "Downgrade her to a contributing factor."

"You look nervous. A bit checked-out and twitchy. Shall we take another break?"

I shake my head no.

"It's starting to sink in, huh?"

"Y-yeah."

"Easy as pie to hold compassionate space for your blameless girlhood self, right, but much harder to make a ruthless examination of your thirty-year-old adult decisions and go, 'Ya know, my motives were understandable and my heart was in the purest of places, but I *chose* this without regard for the potential consequences.'"

And how. "I'd just told him earlier that day, in no uncertain terms, that I didn't want another kid. Not now, not ever. And he'd just barely resurfaced from his delirium. Hardly had it together enough to pull back and think twice, so I ..."

"Made an executive decision."

"For which he thanked me at the time," I add.

"Any idea how he feels about it now?"

"Dunno. We haven't really broached the subject. Too busy breathing sighs of relief that the stick didn't turn blue."

I give her a pointed glance. "Lemme guess. You think I should talk to him?"

"Probably not a bad idea," Laurie says dryly. "You don't have to prostrate yourself in atonement, or come on heavy with apologies, but—"

"At least own it."

She nods. "Not just for him, but for yourself."

Wednesday night check-in's a jolly affair, with all of us playing pass-the-phone. Curran chatters to Jascha about his and Quinn's plans to become professional ninjas; Vera regales me with stories of the trouble Jascha got into as a teen. "But you were perfect angel, right, Gloriochka?"

"With a studded collar for a halo," I laugh.

By the time she puts our favorite troublemaker back on the line, though, I'm filled with apprehension.

"Almost Valentine's Day," Jascha says brightly. "Any requests?"

Just you, unencumbered.

"Not really, but I shudder to think what'll you come up with on your own."

"Schoolgirl outfit?" he suggests. "To go with your headmistress one?"

I snort. "Yeah, no. Is Vera still listening?"

"Don't worry. She just headed off to bed."

"Mum?" Curran taps gently at my arm. "May I watch a bit of telly before I start my homework?"

"Sure, baby," I tell him. "But only until I'm finished with Jascha."

He heads off happily to fetch the remote, and I sprint for the sanctuary of my room.

"Hey, so listen," I say. "While we're on the subject of romance and saucy costumes and—"

"Yeees?" Jascha sounds way too intrigued.

"That night. When you had the ... when we had ..."

"Right." His voice is sheepish now, whether with embarrassment over the nightmare or the pregnancy scare, I'm not sure.

"I just wanted to give you some solace." Be honest. "And to let go a little."

257

"Nothing fundamentally wrong with that impulse, lovely."

"Yeah, but look where it got us. I screwed up, Jasch."

"*You* did? Come on. I'm just as accountable as you are."

"Please. You were too out of your head to even realize we weren't using—"

"And you're talking about yourself as if you're some lounge lizard arsehole who slips tablets in girls' drinks to get them into bed defenseless."

"Okay," I say. "You're right. That sounds insane."

"Beyond insane. Do I need to ring Hippie-Dippie Laurie and give her a lecture about the evils of gaslighting?"

"She wasn't gaslighting me," I say. "We just had a rather ... heated, yet nuanced discussion."

"That made you feel guilty."

"That made me feel justifiably humbled."

"About what?"

"Oh, I dunno," I sigh. "Making a giant deal about never wanting to get pregnant again, then hours later throwing caution to the wind, then keeping us both on pins and needles for weeks waiting to—"

"Gloria." It's Jascha's turn to sigh. "I don't feel played, if that's what you're getting at."

"You don't?"

"No."

Whew. "Good. I was worried you might."

"Don't beat yourself up, sweetheart."

"Oh, trust me, my body's already doing a damn fine job of that."

"What do you mean? You finally got your period?"

"Yup. In the middle of handing Madeline Bingham yet another lecture about smoking."

He snickers. "Do as I say, not as I do, right?"

"Ouch. *Now* who's the lounge lizard asshole?" I curl up on the bed with a mock petulant pout. "Be nice to me. I have cramps."

"Poor lovely. Shall I overnight you an Earl Grey cuppa and some sympathetic head-pets?"

"Yes, please. Along with—"

"Hang on a sec." The phone rustles, and then he calls out. "Mama, what are you doing up?"

Checking on you lovebirds, I expect Vera to shoot back.

But all I hear is the shocked shudder of Jascha's breath. "Fuck. *Fuck.* I have to go."

CHAPTER THIRTY-FOUR

By the time Jascha reaches his mother in the hallway, she's swaying in full-on stumble, one shaky hand pressed to her chest.

Insulin shock? Can't be. We checked her sugars after supper. And besides, insulin shock wouldn't make her wheeze like—

Shit. Why's she wheezing like that?

"Come on," he says. "Let's sit down. I'll ring Dr. Hughson's out-of-hours service."

"*Nichevo*, am fine." Vera flaps her other hand at him as if swatting a fly.

"Don't be ridiculous. You're anything but." Jascha drapes an arm around her. Moves to guide her toward the couch, but she wrenches away with surprising force.

"I said *nyet*, Ivan!" she rasps.

Oh, dear God. She thinks he's his father.

"Mama," Jascha whispers desperately. "It's me. Jascha."

Vera wags a trembling finger at him. "You leave … that boy … alone." Her orders are rattly gasps. "Give me black eye all you want, but don't you … dare …"

The accusation dissolves into a ragged cough, and then a liquidy gag. She collapses against Jascha, her head sinking into his chest. Too heavy to carry, but too overpowered to walk on her own.

"That's it, just lean on me," Jascha soothes as he helps her to the couch at last.

His mother slumps backwards onto an overstuffed cushion. Her eyes woozily blink as she studies his face. "Jascha? Is that you?"

"Yeah, Mamochka." Now his own eyes are blinking. "It's me."

"Did you turn the heating off? So cold in ..." Rattle, gasp. "Here."

Jascha watches her shoulders shiver beneath her dressing gown. Touches her hand to find it clammy.

She's in *some* kind of shock. Damn it.

Jascha turns around to grab the phone from the coffee table. Dials not his mother's GP, but 999.

"Don't go," Vera pleads. "Don't leave me. *Pazhalsta.*" Please.

"Emergency," the voice on the other end of the line answers. "Which service do you require?"

"M-medical. Ambulance. My mother's having a ... a ... some kind of respiratory attack."

"Is she conscious, sir?"

Jascha turns back to to check. Finds Vera slumped on her side, her lips bluish.

He shakes her gently. Her head lolls. Her eyelids flutter as she moans.

"Just barely," he whispers. "Hurry."

The ambulance takes four minutes to arrive. Four minutes that feel like four hours. Four minutes Jascha spends leaned over her, cradling her head in his quavery hands, murmuring wish-fulfillment promises to her in Russian. *They'll be here soon. You'll be fine.*

And then, the siren's wail. The knock at the door.

This can't be happening. It's too surreal. A cruel joke. Face-to-face with medics again, only this time on his feet, as the witness, the distress caller, the reporter of maladies.

"Where—"

"In here." Steady on. Keep your wits. They need you—*she* needs you—to stay calm.

Damn near impossible, watching men in blue gloves turn his mother this way and that, shine their pen-lights in her dazed eyes, press their plastic-covered fingers into the defenseless hollow of her neck.

"Could you step back, please, sir?"

Jascha does as he's told. Listens to the sounds of kit bags being unzipped, diagnostic bits-and-bobs being unwrapped.

His mother remains groggily docile as one medic clips a plastic gauge to her finger, but when the other holds an oxygen mask to her face, she rears up, batting it away as she barks at him. *"Nyet! Nyet!"*

"Lie back, madam."

"Sats are dropping."

No clue what that means—he's never been a fan of television medical dramas, for obvious reasons—but Jascha guesses it can't be good.

"Let them help you, Mama," he calls out to Vera, his voice cracking.

A gurney rolls in. Nimble hands arrange IV drips. Low murmurs brush past him.

Bag her?

Not yet. Let's see if we can stabilize with …

The voices blur. Jascha bows his head. Runs his hands through his hair.

"She on any medications?" one of the blokes asks him.

What *isn't* she on? Jascha leads him to the pharmaceutical tableaux set atop the dining room sideboard.

"Insulin, and this for her blood pressure, and this for ..." His hand gestures spastically toward a bottle whose contents he's blanking on. "I—I can't remember."

"No worries." The medic pats his shoulder. "Just gather them all up for us, and we'll take them in."

Right. Okay. Finally something Jascha can do other than pace and sweat bullets and swallow down the lump in his throat.

He's just swept all the bottles into a Sainsbury's carrier bag when the phone rings on the coffee table.

Gloria? Probably Gloria. Still no time to answer. But—

Someone should know. In case ...

Don't think it. "Hello?"

"Hey, way to scare the shit out of a girl, hanging up like that. What—"

"Vera," he blurts out. "Ambulance. Hospital."

"Jascha?" his mother whimpers from the living room, voice muffled by her oxygen mask, as the medics hoist her onto the gurney.

"Go," Gloria says. "I love you. Call me when you get there."

CHAPTER THIRTY-FIVE

I sleep with the phone on my pillow, but it doesn't ring until five o'clock in the morning.

"Jasch?" I roll over, instantly alert. "How's she doing?"

"Her lung collapsed on the way there." Jascha's voice is one long huffed, trying-not-to-break-down shudder. "She's—she's in the critical care unit."

"Oh, honey. What—"

"Pneumonia and some other thing whose initials I can't remember."

"That's okay. You can figure them out later."

"No, I need to know now. I need to stay on top of this, but my brain won't let me."

"Mine shut down too, with Bill. Just take notes."

"I tried. They're half in Russian, half in English, and none of them make any sense."

"Have you managed to sleep at all? Have you eaten anything?"

"Jesus." A brittle laugh. "You sound just like Vera. Are you channeling her?"

"I'm serious. Have you?"

In the background, I hear the squawk of a page for Dr. Wilson.

"Fifteen minutes dozing in a chair. Bag of crisps and a soda from the vending machine." As Jascha confesses, I can picture him running his hands over his bowed head, eyes glancing up sheepishly. "That counts, right?"

I stifle a yawn. "Nope."

"I can't leave her, Gloriochka. What if she wakes up and I'm not there?"

Argh. I roll back over. "You've got to take care of yourself. It's not optional."

"But—"

"Trust me." I rub a hand over my bleary eyes. "As a former bedside vigil-keeper, I know of what I speak."

That finally chastens him into silence.

"Go home, get a shower, take a quick nap. They'll call you if anything changes."

"You really think that'd be okay?"

"Yes. Crash-and-burn martyrdom won't help either of you."

Jascha sighs. "I guess I could at least nip down to the canteen and grab some lunch."

"What hospital is she in?"

"St. Pancras."

"That's where Bill was. Great people, crap cafeteria. The tuna-fish sandwiches are passable, but don't go anywhere near the curry of the day."

Jascha laughs. "Thanks for the insider tip. I'll put that in my notes."

And then, a long, fraught pause.

"I … I wish you were here."

Me, too. I sit up slowly.

"I'll fly over," I say. "If you want."

"Of course I want, but you can't possibly—"

"Don't worry about me. Don't worry about the logistics. I'll figure them out, okay?"

I've barely hung up when Curran pads in in his pajamas.

"Hey, you." I hold out an arm to him. "Why such an early bird, hmm?"

He leans into my hug. "Phone woke me."

"I'm sorry, lovey."

"Who was it? Miss Julia?"

I swallow. "No. Jascha."

Curran gives me a puzzled look. "But he only rings on Wednesday nights."

"I know, but this was an emergency."

I pat the mattress. He slides under the covers next to me.

The news is gonna devastate this poor kid. He adores "Baba Vera," as he calls Jascha's mother—a compromise nickname for a not-quite-official grandma. When I still lived in London, Jascha would take him over to her place all the time to get spoiled rotten. They'd watch football and eat themselves sick on pastries and play cards for hours while I hung out at home reading in the bathtub. Win-win for everybody.

I prop up on one elbow. "You know how Baba Vera has the problem with too much sugar in her blood, right?"

"Yeah, where she has to jab her fingers with needles all the time." Curran grimaces at the thought.

"Right. Well, now she's got some problems with her lungs."

"That's no big deal. Quinn's got asthma, but he uses his inhaler during PE and that fixes it straightaway."

"We're not talking asthma, sweetie. We're talking lung problems so bad she can't breathe on her own at all."

"Whoa." Curran's eyes widen. "Even Dad never had that."

I nod. "It's serious stuff."

"Is she gonna die?"

How much uncertainty do I want to saddle him with? How much glossing-over do I want to perhaps falsely reassure him with?

"I ..." My voice catches. "I honestly don't know what's going to happen. She's getting really good care, in the same place your dad did, but she's older and frail and ..."

Curran's face crumples, flushed and suddenly tear-blotched. He slams a fist down on my pillow, then buries his head in my shoulder, sobbing in earnest.

"Shh." I stroke his back. "I know it's scary, baby. I know."

"N-not just s-scary," he hiccups. "U-unfair."

"That, too."

"Baba Vera's the nicest lady in the world. Like Dad was the best dad in the world. Why can't horrid people like murderers get all the cancer and stop breathing, so the kind ones don't have to?"

It's way too early in the morning to contemplate the finer points of retribution and random cruelty, so I simply kiss the top of his rumpled head and say, "That's a great question, kiddo. Pint-sized philosopher, you are."

"You know what I think?"

My eyes flicker closed in spite of themselves. "Hmm?"

"I think there should be a limit. Like when we run up a giant fine at the library, and eventually they just say, 'Okay, no more late fees, you're already at twenty dollars or whatever, just give us enough to replace the book.'"

Yes, I'm quite familiar with that scenario. We've got a whole section on the bookcase we call the Shelf of Punctuality Shame. "Uh-huh."

"Well, there should be a limit on bad stuff happening to people, too. I mean, look at Jascha. He lost his wife and his little girl and now he's scared of rain and bumper cars and zillions of other things. You'd think God could be like the library lady, right? Give him a bit of a break. Look down and go, 'You know what, this bloke has been through enough. I'll leave his mum alone.'"

Oh, sweet fucking hell. It's all I can do not to burst into tears myself.

Thankfully, I keep it together, and simply kiss his head again, and say, "One hundred percent agreement from me, angel. Maybe when you and Quinn take over the world, that can be your first ninja policy decree."

He smiles drowsily against the collar of my T-shirt, which is actually Jascha's. "Can I sleep in here with you, till it's time to get ready for school?"

"Of course you can."

I snuggle him until six, when my alarm goes off and I smack it into submission. Gently I then extricate myself from his arms and take the phone into the kitchen.

While coffee brews, I call British Airways to see what's what. No seats available for the ever-popular weekend flights, but amazingly enough there's one economy ticket still left for this evening's Thursday red-eye.

"Would you like to guarantee with a credit card, madam?" the booking agent asks.

"Can we put a hold on the reservation instead? I'll call you right back."

"Unfortunately, at this late juncture, I can't—"

"Please," I whisper. "There's a good chance it's going to be a bereavement fare. All I need is five minutes, to arrange childcare for my son."

"Erm, well." Her voice softens. "In that case, I might be able to make an exception."

No worries about waking Mom; she's a disgustingly chipper morning person.

"Goodness, sweetheart. Shouldn't you still be cursing and hitting the snooze button right about now?"

"I need to go to London. For the weekend. Can you come down and watch Curran?"

"Excuse me?" she splutters.

"Sorry. That came out weird. Jascha—"

"No. Oh, no, no." Mom lets out a brittle laugh. "I've been willing to support you through a lot, Gloria, but I *will* not rearrange my entire life, and watch you rearrange my grandson's, on short notice, just so you can chase your codependent whirlwind romance across the—"

"Mom. Mom. Shut the fuck up and listen, okay? Jascha's mother's on a ventilator with a collapsed lung. He's all alone over there keeping watch."

She gasps, sharply as if her own lung's just collapsed. "Oh. Oh, my God."

"Yeah."

"I'm so sorry. I didn't—"

"Let me get a word in edgewise."

Mom sighs.

"Look," I say. "It's the least I can do to support them. He did the same for me, remember? When *you* asked him to."

Mom sighs again. "Well. Far be it for me turn down an opportunity for quality time with Curran."

"Thank you," I breathe out. "*Thank* you."

⟨∼

I barrel through work that morning with such ruthless, manic efficiency—dispatching students in and out of my office for minor infractions with a brisk, "Just think about the consequences before you act, okay, guys?"; depositing a draft of the monthly parent newsletter on my secretary's desk to photocopy a mere half hour after telling her I'd have it finished before the end of the day—that at lunch time Julia does her nosy edge into my office and asks, "Gloria? Are you feeling all right?"

I startle. Look up, lettuce from my hastily packed sandwich dangling from my teeth.

"I'm fine," I say, mouth full.

Julia gives me a skeptical look.

"No, really." I blot a smudge of mayonnaise from my mouth. "I am."

"Then why were you sniffling in the girls' toilets?"

Wait, she heard that?

I take a sip of my soda. Thunk the can down. "Because my partner's mother might be dying, that's why."

Her face blanches. "I'm so—"

"Yeah, me too. I'm sorry for everything. I'm a compulsive, professional apologizer. But you know what? It doesn't accomplish shit."

Julia takes a step back.

"Sorry," I say. "Am I scaring you?"

"A little." Julia glances down. "Sorry."

We both laugh.

"Oh, Jules, Jules, Jules." I lean back in my chair, pushing my hair off my forehead with both hands. "What a clusterfuck this past six weeks has been."

"Indeed," she says dryly.

"I should nominate you for sainthood. Or at least an MBE. Dame Julia, patroness of exasperating supervisors."

She smiles. "Let me guess. You'll be out for a few days?"

"Just tomorrow and Monday. Unless there's a ..." I swallow. "A funeral."

⟨◞⟩

When school lets out, Mom meets me at my office and we walk over to pick up Curran. He's cheery at first when he spies her—"Ooh, you're staying for the weekend?"—but as we trudge home, his mood deflates.

"Did Mum tell you about Baba Vera? It's so sad, Gran."

"Yes, darling, she did. In fact, that's why—"

I shoot Mom a look that says, *Let's at least wait till we're inside.*

"Why what?" Curran demands, soon as I close the apartment's front door behind us.

Man, it's a mixed blessing having such a tenacious kid.

"Have a seat, honey." I gesture toward the couch.

Curran plops down dejectedly. His lower lip trembles. "She's dead, isn't she?"

"No. I just got an update from Jascha about an hour ago. Baba Vera's still holding on."

"Whew."

"But," Mom says, sitting next to him, "Jascha needs your mum there for a bit. Just like when he came out here to help her, remember?"

"It's only until Monday," I add. "And Gran will stay with you while I'm away."

Curran's brow furrows. "You mean I can't go along?"

I shake my head. "No, baby. It's—"

"I'm not a baby!"

"Well, you certainly are acting like one," Mom tsks.

Great. Thanks. Super-helpful. "Let me handle this, Mom."

I sit down on Curran's opposite side. "This won't be like when we went back at Christmas. No visits with Gran Louise and Granddad

Edward." My former in-laws, whom I secretly call the outlaws. "Or Raj."
His London best friend who used to live downstairs from us. "Or movies
and Monopoly and bounce houses with Jascha."

"I know that." Curran crosses his arms over his chest, giving me
a *What do you think I am, stupid?* glare. "I just want to see Baba Vera."

God, this is hard.

"Curran," I say, "you wouldn't be able to see her even if you did
go with me."

"More fucking hospital rules?"

"Watch your language, young man."

"Mom," I snap. "I *said* let me handle this."

I turn back to Curran. "Yes. She's on a ward for very sick people,
just like your dad was, and they don't allow—"

"Will they let me if she gets worse? If she really is dying?"

"In that case," I say hoarsely, "we'll figure something out."

◦◦

My cab pulls up to Jascha's mother's flat at eight a.m. the next morning.
I bump my wheeled suitcase up the front steps and reach under the mat
for the key Jascha left me, in case he's away at the hospital.

Inside, Vera's pink terrycloth robe still lies draped on the couch
where the paramedics must have left it. The dining room table is
littered with photographs I know are of Jascha's first family, but don't
feel privy to viewing.

I slip quietly down the hall with my carry-on, bound for the
bathroom so I can at least freshen up a bit.

"Gloriochka?"

At the sound of Jascha's drowsy call, I turn to face an open door
and find him sitting up in bed, all tousled-haired and squinty and
boyishly adorable.

I drop my bag on the floor and rush toward him. We kiss and run

272

our hands over each other for a good five minutes, neither one caring how grungy or rumpled the other is. Then we pull back, remembering why I'm here.

"Still no change," he says.

"Better than bad news, at least, yeah?" I settle cross-legged on the mattress, one knee draped comfortingly over his.

Uncomforted, Jascha looks down. "I just don't understand how it happened. *Why* it happened."

"Sometimes there's just not a why to pinpoint, love."

He keeps going as if he hasn't heard me. "She had a doctor appointment on Monday. GP said everything looked good, all things considered. And now ..."

Jascha looks up again. "I did everything I was supposed to, Gloria. Kept a schedule of all her meds. Set timers for her blood sugar tests. Even made her stay home from bridge club when Maeve Kilburn was hosting it with a mild cold."

"Jesus, I can only imagine the challenge that was."

Jascha can't stifle a chuckle. "Worse than getting her to give up Danishes for breakfast. She didn't talk to me for two days." He swallows. "And now she can't talk at all."

"Honey. Please, don't."

"I had a graphic design mockup I was working on for a new client," he says. "Horribly picky, wanted masses of revisions, but a big break for me, you know? So I spent all of Wednesday holed up trying to pull some concepts together. I didn't ignore Vera, but I wasn't exactly checking up on her every hour either. And now I keep wondering whether I missed something, a tiny sign that could have tipped me off that she—"

"Jascha." I grab his face in my palms. "You go down that rabbit hole of second-guessing, and you will *never* come back. So stop it. Right now, do you hear me?"

He nods. "It's just hard not to."

"I know, darlin'." I kiss him on the forehead. "Been there, done that."

From beside his pillow, the phone rings.

We stare at each other for a moment, our eyes full of queries. *Do you think? Could it be?*

"Yes," Jascha says slowly. "Speaking."

I grab his free hand. He squeezes it tight.

"Really?" His eyes widen like Curran's. "When?"

Oh, God.

"Wow. Okay. Thank you." Now he's grinning. "I'll be there soon as I can."

"What—"

"She's off the vent," he says to me. "They're bringing her up out of the sedation."

When we arrive at Vera's room, she's still groggy and wan, sporting chest tube drains and oxygen prongs in her nose and so many IVs the delicate veins on her poor hands are bruised worse than Bill's were. But her eyes are surprisingly lively, and her cracked lips manage a smile.

"Mamochka," Jascha murmurs, his eyes welling up as he leans over to kiss the top of her head. "You're awake."

I feel like an interloper in their intimacy, unsure of what to do or where I fit in. I lean my arms on the bed's guardrails. Give Vera a gentle smile back.

She tilts her face toward me, momentarily puzzled. Finally my presence sinks in, and she rests her cheek against the pillow, and says, in a pained, sandpapery voice that hurts to hear, "Oh, Gloriochka, you came all this way."

My heart somersaults. "Yeah," I say, reaching down to pat her arm. "I sure did."

"How are you feeling?" Jascha presses.

I swear Vera gives a *Do you even have to ask?* eye roll, just before she bursts into a fit of coughing, another excruciating sound. Then, this woman who never forgave me for stamping *F U* on a bingo card in front of her old lady friends, who won't even say *Damn* when Chelsea trumps Arsenal in football, catches her blessed breath and looks straight at me and replies, "Like shit."

For the next three days, Jascha and I tag-team, spelling each other for showers and lunch runs and scheduled work phone calls, alternating nights spent sleeping on a makeshift cot by Vera's side. Jascha helps her sit up so I can guide a straw to her lips, proffering ginger ale to soothe her parched, raw throat; I yell at a nurse to up her morphine drip while Jascha cradles her head against his chest as, six decades of resigned stoicism falling away with pain, she sobs.

We coax her to do her mandated-for-recovery breathing exercises. We sneak her pastries and her own leftover homemade dumplings to combat the dietary tedium of clear broth and Jell-O. We use my international calling card to surprise her with a chat with a beyond-excited Curran. And when she dozes off for a well-deserved afternoon nap, Jascha and I steal a moment and stroll the hospital's outdoor courtyard, holding each other's gloved hands.

Jascha does the talking, mostly; I can tell he's grateful for a chance to finally catch his own constricted breath and (to borrow a word from Hippie-Dippie Laurie) process.

"She was hallucinating that night," he says quietly. "From the decreased blood oxygen levels. Thought I was my dad."

"Oh, shit." He's never spoken much about his father, who

deserted him and Vera when Jascha was in his hell-raising teens, but I get the sense that the guy's departure came as more of a relief than a betrayal.

"Yeah. And then she resurfaces, confused and frightened, calling out for me."

All too familiar. We sit down on a bench.

"It was like watching someone possessed," he says, staring out at the courtyard's turned-off fountain. "I felt so powerless."

Jascha glances over at me. "Is that what my nightmares were like for you?"

I nod.

"I can't believe I ever tried to brush them off. Christ, Gloriochka, I'm so—"

"Don't. Please." I rest my head on his shoulder. "No more looking backwards, okay?"

He leans his cheek against my hair. "Okay."

We sit and listen to the wail of an approaching ambulance siren. I wait for Jascha to slump or stiffen, but he stays steady, keeps calm.

CHAPTER THIRTY-SIX

On Sunday, Gloria's last night in London, Vera orders her and Jascha to take the evening off.

"*Pazhalsta*," she insists when they protest. "Am getting moved to the step-down unit in the morning. No need for 24/7 watch. You need break."

Gloria glances at Jascha. "She makes a good case."

"You're sure, Mama?" he asks, unconvinced.

"Yes." She wags the forefinger that's not saddled with a pulse-ox clip. "Just no funny business in my double bed while I'm gone, you hear?"

❦

Vera needn't worry. They're so exhausted that funny business isn't even on the radar. All he and Gloria do when they leave the hospital is order Indian takeaway and devour it at the dining room table.

"Ohmygod," she says, wincing, when she takes her first bite. "I forgot how spicy it is here."

She carefully slides a photograph of Marianne off to the side. "Sorry. Don't want to spill tikka masala all over your wife."

"I should put those back." Jascha pauses. "I mean, I'm guessing it's uncomfortable for you."

"No, no. I'd love to look at them." Now it's Gloria's turn to pause. "Assuming *you* don't mind."

Jascha shakes his head. Watches as she wipes her hands off with fastidious care to keep from accidentally smearing the photos, and then picks up each one in turn.

"Oh, sweet girl," she half-croons, half-sighs, when she reaches a snapshot of Elizabeth. "Along with a bit sassy, from the looks of it."

"You have no idea," Jascha says.

"Aww, and look at your mom with you at your wedding, with all that auburn hair!" She scrutinizes the photo a bit longer. "Wow, you had a Wedding with a capital W, honey. Tuxedo and everything. Very snazzy."

"Yeah," Jascha says, "we did. Marianne insisted."

"To each her own." Gloria shrugs. "I just threw on a vintage lace dress and some combat boots and called it good."

"Oh, I'll bet it was." Jascha reaches over to stroke the inside of her wrist.

She pulls away. "I'm nothing like Marianne was, am I?"

Now there's a trenchant question.

"Does it really matter?" Jascha asks.

Gloria sighs. "I just can't help wondering."

"Well, there's no need to dwell, because you're like her in the ways that matter."

They both stare down at the image of Mare in her yellow bikini, ocean-drenched and laughing.

"Which are ... what?" Gloria says slowly.

Jascha looks up. "Enormous-hearted. Willing to put up with me. Fierce about your kid."

She gives him what looks mercifully like a satisfied, or at least touched, smile. "Got any pics from your hell-raiser days?"

"Somewhere around here in Vera's archives."

Her smile deepens. "I wanna see."

❧

"Oh, you *were* full of attitude!" she cackles, upon viewing the snap he procures for her of himself at eighteen, sporting spiky hair and a punk chain belt.

"Right after my British naturalization ceremony," Jascha says. "Don't I look thrilled?"

Gloria kicks him playfully under the table. "Ungrateful brat. I cried buckets at mine."

Yes. He can believe it. Can imagine her rushing out of the judge's chambers toward Bill with certificate in hand, all runny mascara and triumphant glee. *It's official, baby! Left that bullshit behind!* Bill lifting her up off the pavement and spinning her around like they're in a trailer for some sappy movie.

"I had a bit of an identity crisis," Jascha says now.

"After your dad left?"

Jesus, Gloria. "Yeah. I guess."

Gloria plucks the photo from the table. Gazes at it for a moment, head slightly tilted, lips slightly pursed, as if about to blow the sullen, overgrown boy Jascha once was a kiss.

"I love him," she says, flipping the image back around to face Jascha. "I love this. Can I take it home with me? For my Valentine's Day present?"

Jascha nods.

❧

Even drowsier now, they lie pressed against each other in Jascha's single bed, shoulder to shoulder, hipbone to hipbone. Folded hands tucked chastely under chins, beneath blankets. Eyes never straying.

"Can you imagine," Gloria says softly, "if we'd met each other back then?"

"I'd have spent all night trying to get up the nerve to talk to you."

"And I'd have gotten in a catfight with your girlfriend in the bathroom of some dive bar."

They both laugh.

"Nah," Gloria says. "We wouldn't have given each other a second glance."

Harsh, but true. At eighteen, an open escape window was what Jascha had craved, not a mirror of his own scruffy posturing and buried frailties.

She sighs deeply. "All I wanted was a cute, gentle English boy who could make it all go away."

"Ditto. I mean, swap out cute for gorgeous and switch the gender, but otherwise …"

"Bill grew up out in rural Kent." Gloria's eyelids are flickering closed now. "In a thatched farmhouse straight out of a tourist brochure. His childhood just … luminous. Joyful. Not a speck of conflict."

"Yeah. Yeah, same with Marianne." Excitement at being understood rises in Jascha, electric and palpable. "Big place in suburban Surrey, with a back garden like a bloody enchanted fairy forest. Lilac bushes and her own Wendy house, all that. No wonder she became a picture-book editor."

"Meanwhile you and I were …"

He nods. "Not saying I resented her for it, mind. I just hoped some of that would—"

"Rub off on you?"

Jascha yawns. "Mmm."

"And now they're gone, and here we are."

Jascha kisses her on the nose. "Indeed. Here we are."

Gloria leans forward to rest her face in his neck. "Holy fuck, you smell good."

"Vindaloo and melancholy. Cologne of the gods."

"Shut up. You do."

"Says the woman with the hair I want to inhale like a line of coke." He nuzzles the top of her head.

She lifts her chin questioningly. "How are things on the …"

"Nightmare front?"

Gloria nods.

Jascha sits up. "Auntie Nora's been making me keep a log. When I have them, my best guess as to what precipitated each one, that sort of thing."

Her gaze follows his to the small spiral notepad on his nightstand. "And?"

"I went two weeks without any. Longest I've ever gone."

"No way." Gloria's face lights up as she gives his arm a congratulatory punch-shake. "That's fantastic, Jasch."

"Eh." He shrugs. "Sounds a bit pathetic, though, when you think about how many years it's been since—"

"Hey. Don't diss your own progress. I used to measure mine by whether I got up in the morning, after Bill died."

"Yeah. *Right* after."

"Okay, look," she says. "Ditch the self-deprecation and just tell me: Can we safely stay in the same bed tonight, or not?"

Jascha's shoulders drop.

"You know, if this stuff with my mum hadn't happened," he says, "I'd be inclined to say yes. But dealing with the medics, riding with her in the ambulance, it … that was a …" He swallows. "I started having them again."

Gloria frowns. "So we're back to square one."

Speaking of dissing progress …

"No," Jascha says. "I really don't think we are. Other stuff that normally triggers me doesn't."

She raises an intrigued eyebrow. "Like what?"

"Adverts in tube stations from Marianne's old publisher. Stevie Nicks on the radio."

Gloria snorts. "Hell, that obnoxious vibrato'd trigger *anybody*."

"Elizabeth was more a fan of her fashion sense," he says. "The lacier and twirlier, the better. She'd improv with a tablecloth if she hadn't a dress-up box handy."

"Look at you," Gloria says. "Not sinking under. Just smiling."

"Nora says I'm 'cultivating resilience.' To quote ye old therapeutic parlance."

"Ooh, that's a good one." She carefully stretches. "Though the only thing we should be cultivating right now is sleep, huh?"

He nods. "Take Vera's bed. Way more comfortable."

"Nah, that's okay." Gloria snuggles up against his pillow. "I want to stay here."

"You sure? That worn-out mattress is older than dirt."

"I don't care." Gloria burrows tighter under the duvet. "It's the next best thing to having you next to me."

"And you call *me* a hopeless romantic."

Jascha switches off the lamp. Leans over to kiss her goodnight.

"Hey," he whispers. "Thank you. For coming over."

"Don't mention it." She yawns. "I totally owed you one."

"No, you didn't. It's not a matter of being even. And you've got way more responsibilities than I had when I—"

"Hush." She grabs his hand. Gives his fingers a tight squeeze. "I did it gladly."

CHAPTER THIRTY-SEVEN

The next day, while Jascha attends a meeting with his finicky design client, I spend my final few hours before my flight home getting Vera settled into her new hospital room.

First up: arranging her collection of get-well cards in a cheery banner above her bed. Maeve Kilburn and the rest of bridge club sent her one of a pastel watercolor scene judiciously embellished with sparkles on its ocean waves, but her favorite is a hand-crayoned sketch of Curran's I brought along in my carry-on, which shows a tally of *Baba Vera: 20, Lung Trouble: 0* on a football stadium scoreboard.

"You're such an angel, Gloriochka," Vera sighs.

"Wouldn't go that far," I say, rolling a tray table closer so she can keep her TV remote and crossword book and tissues handy.

For most of the morning, we watch soap opera reruns. There's a particularly hunky young guy whom Vera alternates between ogling and raspily barking warnings to. "*Nyet*, stay away from the blond girl! She's trouble!"

"Don't yell, honey. You'll get a coughing fit."

Sure enough, her body jackknifes with one, and I return to back-rubbing and straw-proffering duty.

"God, I hate this," she moans.

"I know. It's bullshit. What can I do to help?"

"Lip balm and lotion and hairbrush, *pazhalsta?*" The only thing that soothes her: attending to dignity and vanity.

I work the tangles from her scraggly ends. Gently rub the cream into her rubbed-raw-from-IV-tape hands.

"*Spasiba.* Oh, that's good." Vera closes her eyes for a moment, relishing, then looks up at me again. "What time is flight back to America?"

"Four o'clock." I pull up a chair. "We still have some time."

Her face relaxes with relief. She pats my arm through the guardrail, same as I did for her.

"You are wondering," she says. "Whether I judge you for sending Jascha home. *Da?*"

I bite my lip.

"Be honest, now."

"A … a little."

"Well, I don't. Was hard on him, but it needed to happen."

Thank God. No grudges.

"Did you know how much Jascha was struggling?" I ask.

"He never talked." She gives a rueful smile. "But I knew."

"There's some stuff he won't talk to me about, either." I pause, not sure whether to bring it up. "Like his dad."

Vera scowls. "Less said about that bastard, the better."

So I guessed. "I don't mean to pry. I just—"

"No, no. Is simple fact. Ancient history. Okay to ask." She fiddles with her oxygen tubing in an attempt to adjust the nasal prongs, but the pulse meter on her finger won't let her get a good grip. "This bloody thing. Can you fix?"

"Sure. Of course."

Once I've got her sorted, she launches into her tale. "He was charming bloke. Like Mr. Hunk on telly. Man of principles, eager to escape Stalin."

Vera lets out a bitter laugh. "And yet he was dictator himself."

"What do you mean?"

"Human punching bag. That's what he used me as. Years and years."

"Oh, Vera …" My hand flies to my heart.

"Worst part is, Jascha saw it happen. As little boy. More than once."

Jesus. No wonder he was so scared of hurting me. So utterly mortified when he actually did.

"Thankfully Ivan moved on when Jascha was teenager," Vera continues. "To an English girl half my age. Very … what is word, for someone who convinces easy?"

"Impressionable?"

"*Da,* impressionable. Charmed out of her knickers by the accent."

I shake my head. "Lemme tell ya, it works."

Shit. I did *not* just say that to my boyfriend's mother, did I?

Vera does another finger-wag. "Watch it, young lady."

Yeah, I did. "Sorry. I'll shut up now. Go on."

"We celebrated like we had won lottery. Which you could say we had." She clears her throat to stave off a cough. "But every time I go to church I light a candle for that poor thing. Plus all the others who probably came after."

"You're an amazing woman, Vera," I say. "And you raised an amazing man."

Her eyes flicker with growing fatigue, but they also glimmer with gratitude. "Thank you."

❧

I kiss her goodbye on the forehead. Turn off the television and tuck her blankets around her so she's cozy for her nap.

Then I head downstairs and wait in the lobby for Jascha.

He arrives looking equal parts authoritative and arty, dressed in a blazer and button-down paired with distressed jeans and Doc Martens.

"Tag, you're it." I brush at his shoulders. "Ooh, this is nice."

Jascha blushes. "Guess that and the mockup worked. Got a bonus and a second gig."

Yes! Finally some good news.

His tiniest of delighted smiles fades to concern. "How's Vera?"

"Comfortable. Asleep."

"I'll go sit with her just in case." Of course he will, diligent son that he is.

I take his hand shyly and walk him to the bank of elevators. No long, drawn-out departure gate farewells for us, we decided. Him making a pilgrimage to Heathrow just to see me off is far too impractical given Vera's condition and his recent lack of a car, and besides, this last month apart feels like it's solidified us somehow, stripped us of the need to cling and second-guess and clutch.

Which isn't to say that we're complete stoics. Jascha sighs incredibly deeply while inhaling the scent of my hair one final time; I hold on incredibly hard when I wrap my arms around his waist under his jacket. But when we pull back, there's no sense of breaking apart. Only warmth's tenacious linger.

"Give Curran my love," Jascha says. "And the Cadbury Flakes."

On the flight home, I read a novel in its entirety, sans child interruption. Explain to my curious seatmate, a chatty young college student, how I wound up with two passports. Doze for an hour with my head against the pulled-down window shade, dreaming of a tea party in Marianne's childhood fairy garden, at which I wear ripped black fishnets and a studded belt and one of Jascha's old T-shirts as a dress, and she indulgently, graciously smiles, offering me a cuppa and a plate of cucumber finger sandwiches like we've been best friends for years.

And then, when we're about to land, I pull my Valentine's Day present from my purse, and gaze at Jascha's aloof, world-weary-already-at-eighteen face preserved in all its matte-finish glory, and think: *My love. You've still got a long way to go, but you've come so very far.*

CHAPTER THIRTY-EIGHT

March starts out strong: Vera back at home, lugging an oxygen tank but recuperated enough to return to the bingo hall and bridge club; freelance projects pouring in after Tim's beloved *Observer* arts columnist Veronica finally publishes her "Creatives to Watch" list with Jascha's name at the top.

And then Auntie Nora cuts him down to size with an edict: "It's time."

To pop open the champagne? Jascha wants to cheekily reply, playing dumb even though he knows exactly what she means. Knows, deep down, that she's right.

"Talking about the accident won't break you," Gloria says, during their Wednesday chat the night before his big appointment. "Remember how I thought it would, when I spilled my guts about my dad?"

"Right, but this isn't confessional free-association Auntie Nora's after. She wants me to replay that entire day. In chronological order. In exquisite detail."

Long pause, followed by an apprehensive exhale. "Shiiit."

 ❧

Before they hung up, they'd joked about Gloria overnighting him her bottle of anxiety tablets to fortify himself, but now that Jascha's sat down in Nora's office, he wishes the plan had been a serious one.

"I can see you're nervous," she says, "so I want to be very clear about what our goal in doing this exercise is."

"You mean it's not just masochistic torture for its own sake?"

She shakes her head. "Absolutely not. There's a school of thought that extolls the virtues of emotionally reliving trauma in the name of catharsis, but I didn't study at that one."

Thank God.

"What I'd like you to be able to do is retell what happened, rather than relive it. With the stance of an objective observer."

"Just the facts, ma'am."

"Exactly."

Jascha frowns. "But I can't reduce my wife and child to mere names in a police report."

"I'm not asking you to. I'm just asking you to detach from the layers and layers of emotion surrounding what happened. Temporarily, for the next hour."

"O—okay."

Nora leans down and opens the file cabinet next to her chair. At first Jascha thinks she's merely fishing out a pad and pen to take notes with, but then he realizes that it's a cassette tape machine.

"What—"

"I'm going to record the session. So you can listen to it later."

"Why the hell would I want to do that?"

"Desensitization." Nora puts up a hand. "Again, not to the point of numbness or dismissiveness. Only to the point where those details no longer trigger you or drag you down."

Sounds good. No, sounds amazing.

"Now," she continues, "you may feel some quite strong reactions come up. Anxiety, panic, grief."

"Like in the nightmares?"

"Yes. But I'll do my best to guide you back to an observer stance. To keep you on track."

Nora pops a fresh tape in the machine. Sits back and crosses her legs. "Are you ready?"

Ready as I'll ever be. Jascha nods.

She hits *RECORD*. "Let's begin with some basics. What was the date of the accident?"

"Ninth August, 1991." Memorized. Immortalized, on headstones. A lamb engraved on Elizabeth's, a lavender sprig on Marianne's.

"All right. Why don't you tell me a bit about that day. How you spent it, in the hours leading up to—"

"Working. I was a horrid workaholic in those days." Once Jascha starts talking, he can't stop. "Mare and I always fought about it. I mean, she had a demanding job, moving up the publishing ladder. Far more demanding than mine as a layabout artist. But she put her family first, while I ..." He swallows. "Checked out."

"Check out from the subtext," Nora says gently. "Just try to focus on the literal details."

"We had plans to drive out to Margate that evening, for a seaside holiday weekend. A chance to reconnect and spend some time together, just the three of us."

He looks away. "Marianne had wanted to get an early start, so we'd be settled in before Elizabeth's bedtime. I told her I'd be home by five, but I lost track of time at my studio, so it was more like six-thirty by the time I arrived home. And she was furious."

Jascha glances back at Nora. "How am I doing? Not too much editorializing, is it?"

"You're fine."

Whew. "We'd had a bit of a row already the night before, and some rather clumsy—"

"Concentrate on just that one day. Ninth August."

Jascha looks down. "We argued. Again. 'You've ruined it,' Marianne kept saying. 'The traffic will be rubbish, Elizabeth will get tired and have a tantrum.' On and on.

"So I said to her, 'Do you want to fucking go or not?' And then I turned around to see Elizabeth standing there, her arms full of her cuddly-toy menagerie she planned to take in the car, and you know ..." He smiles ruefully. "You know what she said?"

"Hmm."

"'I still want to fucking go, Daddy.'"

Nora raises an eyebrow. "My, my. Cheeky one, eh?"

"Oh, yeah. We should have scolded her, right, but Marianne and I just looked at each other and laughed and said, in unison, 'Well, then.' And off we went."

"Was the traffic rubbish?"

"Ridiculous. Mare bit her tongue with the *I-told-you-so*'s, to her credit, but I could tell it was taking all she had to hold back."

"And how were the roads otherwise?"

Jascha's shoulders tense. "Fine, until we hit the halfway mark. Then it started raining buckets.

"I pulled off the M2 into a petrol station to fuel up, thinking we could wait it out a bit. Elizabeth was already asleep at that point, poor thing, so Mare and I sat in silence for a while, you know, not wanting to wake her.

"Eventually I nipped into the corner shop and got us some crisps and chocolate, since we'd not had time to eat before we left. We sat in the neon light and crunched away at our prawn and tikka and toffee bars, and I started telling her things I'd never admitted before."

"Like what?"

Jascha rubs a hand over his eyes. "My dad. How he'd bring my mum flowers one day and break her nose the next. Right in front of me, when I wasn't much older than Elizabeth. How relieved we were

291

when he finally left. How afraid I was, of becoming like …"

The words catch in his throat. Jascha looks at Nora, stricken.

"Take a moment," she says. "It's all right."

No, it isn't.

"I was really frank with Marianne," Jascha says. "I think she started to get it, then, why I acted distant as I did. 'If you keep us at arms' length,' she said, 'then there's no chance of arsing things up, am I right?'"

He chuckles. "She could have made a brilliant therapist. Not that that was her—"

"Let's keep moving forward."

Okay. Okay.

"She had me there, you know. And I said yes, that's exactly my daft, scared mind thought. So she goes, 'Your daft, scared mind's out of its mind, Jascha. Because the only way you can possibly arse up is to keep doing what you're doing, thinking it will protect us.'"

He clears his throat. "That floored me. Slapped sense into me. Made me realize: God, I've been beyond daft. Completely irrational. This has to change. So I got out of the …"

Jascha shakes his head. "I got out of the car, and got down on one knee in the dark in the relentless rain, like I was proposing to her. Which I guess I was, in a way, because I said"—here he full-on laughs, still amazed by his own twee earnestness—"'Marianne Olivia Braithwaite Kremsky,' I said, meaning every goddamn word, 'I swear to you, this cowardice ends here.'

"And then I got back in the car, the hem of my trousers dripping, the kind of mess Mare would normally get tetchy about. But right then, she didn't care; I didn't care. We just kissed like we were headed for our honeymoon again, licking chocolate off each other's fingers, brushing tears out of each other's eyes. And then Elizabeth woke up just long enough to murmur, 'Mummy, Daddy, are we there yet?' So

I started up the engine and turned back out onto the motorway."

He closes his eyes. "Never should have. I should have left work earlier, I should have told her fine, fuck it, let's not go. I should have waited all bloody night in the petrol station parking area, I should have—"

"Stop, Jascha. Stop."

Jascha jumps. Blinks until his eyes reopen.

"We'll have plenty of time to unpack those regrets and should-haves later." Nora's voice switches from soothing to precise. "Right now, I want you to focus on the timeline of events."

"What timeline?" he says. "I drove another eight miles. A drunk bastard swerved on the wet road, hit us head-on, and walked away without a single scratch. Meanwhile my girls ..."

Jascha's hand folds into a shaky, furious fist. "They died instantly, Nora."

"And you?" she says quietly.

"Major injuries. Took me six months of rehab to—"

"Stay on ninth August."

"No!" He slams his fist down onto his knee. "I've stayed on ninth August for the last five goddamn years! I want to move past it."

"I know you do," Nora says. "And you will. Just keep going with—"

"I lost consciousness. Woke up on a gurney with medics working on me. Or trying to, at least."

"You fought them?"

"Oh, yeah. Best I could, given how weak I was." His whole body tremble-braces, remembering the struggle. "All I wanted was a glimpse of my family. Alive, dead, getting worked on too. But they ..."

Jascha's throat throbs in its battle to defeat the lump threatening to overtake it. "They held me down so I couldn't sit up. So I couldn't even lift my head. I know now why they did it—I was going into shock, losing heaps of blood—but still." His voice quavers. "How hard would it have been to allow me that one-second glimpse?"

"Step back from the injustice and indignation." Upon seeing the look of resistance on his face, Nora qualifies. "Only for now."

"Fine." He scowls at her. "I passed out again. Woke up on a critical-care unit in Margate. Least I finally made it there, right?"

"Gallows humor," Nora says. "Often a lifesaver."

"Well, I didn't want to be saved. Came up out of the sedation raging."

"Were you told about their deaths straightaway?"

Jascha nods. "The doctors wanted to hold off until I was more stable, but my mum insisted I hear the truth." He lets out a deep breath. "As much as it shattered me, I'm grateful to her for that. For there being no faffing about, no dancing round the subject."

"How did—"

"She told me, through tears. I immediately tried to rip out all my drip lines and tubes. They put me back under. She sat by my bedside all night, planning a funeral I'd be too ill to attend, ringing her friends to ask if they'd light candles for us—Marianne and Elizabeth's souls, and my battered body—at the Orthodox cathedral in London."

Jascha blows out a deep breath, exhausted by the tsunami of words.

"And that," he says, "was the ninth of fucking August, 1991."

Afterwards, there's no triumphant satisfaction akin to Gloria's when she spoke about her dad with Laurie. Only a bled-dry exhaustion, coupled with waves of nausea and prickly faintness.

He wants nothing more than to sleep off this malaise like a hangover, but instead of collapsing into his bed when he gets home,

Jascha sits upright on it with his back against the wall. Puts in his Walkman headphones. Presses *PLAY.*

Ten minutes. That's all his recounted tale clocks in at, even including poignant pauses and Nora's gentle proddings.

Stay focused. Keep going. Keep moving forward.

He keeps going. Every night, the same ritual: Photos. List. Tape.

"Don't overdo it," Nora warns. "One time, and done."

A twisted bedtime story. A Gothic horror-lover's audiobook of choice.

Sounds beyond ridiculous, but strangely, it's working. By mid-March, Jascha's nightmare log records nothing but blank pages since the week his mother went into hospital.

One month. One entire *month* of freedom. Does he dare trust this?

Yes. He has to. Without throwing caution to the wind, of course.

Which is why, on his promised flight back to America for Curran's birthday, Jascha allows himself a few lazy, mindless hours of movie watching and magazine reading, then pulls the Walkman from his messenger bag and listens to his own fervent, tormented voice.

Furious ... raining buckets ... I swear to you ... should have ...

And then, just before they land on the tarmac at Dulles, there comes the lifesaver, the wry comeback, the saving grace: *At least I finally made it there.*

CHAPTER THIRTY-NINE

My kid's so hyper and giddy at the prospect of seeing Jascha again, you'd think he'd just eaten his entire birthday cake himself: jumping up and down in the airport parking garage elevator, skipping down the seating aisles at the arrival gate.

"Somebody's excited," a grandmotherly woman remarks, giving me an *I'm so glad I get to send them home in two weeks* smile.

"Just a little." I smile back.

"Who's he waiting for? His dad?"

I pause for a second. "Yeah. Well, actually, his—"

My words get cut off by Curran's yelp of "Jascha! It's Jascha, Mum!"

Sure enough, there he is, headed toward us down the Jetway.

He waves to Curran. Curran waves back. Looks at me questioningly. "Can I—"

"Go for it."

I watch as Curran barrels over, slamming into Jascha the moment he steps past the check-in desk. They hug for so long all the other passengers have filed out before they pull apart again.

"Argh." Jascha rifles Curran's hair. "Missed you, mate."

Oh, my heart. I stroll over to them. Lean in for a smudgy, delicate kiss.

"How about me, hmm?" I tease. "You miss me?"

"Not in the slightest."

I smack Jascha playfully on the shoulder, then take his hand as we meander toward baggage claim. "Liar."

❧

Scrabble! Monopoly! Video games! The boys want to do it all, but I have to be Mean Mum and force Curran to go to bed at a reasonable hour.

"Big day tomorrow, kiddo," I remind him when he protests. (We're splashing out a bit, with the proceeds from Jascha's latest freelance gig, and renting a nearby indoor playground for an afternoon.)

Jascha does the beloved read-aloud while I pour us two glasses of wine.

"Don't worry," I say when he comes back into the living room. "It isn't that Whole Foods Triple D poison."

He laughs. "I'm not worried."

Only a few sips later, I'm sitting backwards on his lap with my skirt hiked up. Holy hell. Transatlantic phone's got nothing on reunion make-out.

"Wait. Wait. Wait," I huff in between kisses. "You came prepared, right?"

"Best believe I did."

Well, then.

❧

An hour later, we're sprawled on my bed, completely spent.

"Christ, I'm sore." I roll onto my stomach. Reach over to stroke Jascha's hair. "You really—"

Wait, is he asleep?

Sure enough. Can't say I blame him, given that it's three a.m.

right now in London. And given that I'll be wrangling twenty nine-year-old boys—not from a safe administrative distance, but on the front lines—tomorrow, I should sleep too.

Which of course raises the question: Where should I do it?

I hate the thought of taking the couch, not only because it's one of those rock-mattressed, rock-bottom IKEA deals, but also because, yet again, it just feels wrong to split ourselves up. Maybe not as horrible as watching him walk dejectedly out the bedroom door and pad down the hall away from me, but horrible enough.

Okay, so what's the alternative?

I picture Vera with her blackened eyes, her broken nose.

No. Jascha's not his father. Same as I'm not mine just because I spent a weekend at the brain chemo spa on Four West.

Besides, things have mellowed out. Zero nightmares for the last month.

I gaze over at Jascha's blessedly slumber-calm face, and decide to take my chances.

Curran's up at six a.m., leaned over me tugging at my arm.

"Mum, Mum, Mum," he whispers. "When are we gonna do the cupcakes?" Jascha promised him some elaborate decorative scheme that only a fine arts major could come up with, much less skillfully execute.

"Shh," I whisper back. "Poor Jascha had a long day yesterday. Let him get some more rest."

Curran looks disappointed, but then quickly rallies. "I know! I'll make a list of all the things we have to do to get ready, okay?"

"Fantastic." I'm not being facetious; party planning makes my brain hurt worse than therapy with Laurie, so his exuberant organizing will be a real help.

He can't do it all, though. Time to trade cozy boyfriend-in-my-bed mode for Slightly Harried Hostess With the Mostest. I lean over and kiss Jascha on the back of the neck, then begrudgingly crawl out from under the covers and stumble toward the coffeemaker.

By mid-morning, I'm jacked on caffeine and ready to pull my hair out.

"We have to be there for set-up by one." I bark orders as I pace. "Come on, you guys, there are still eight cupcakes left to frost." Sudden shudder of realization. "Shit! I forgot paper plates!"

Jascha glances up from where he's piping green icing into the shape of a dragon. "Don't panic. We have plenty."

"Not the party kind!"

His brow furrows. "There's a party kind?"

"Yeah, they're more heavy-duty, and match the napkins and the streamers and the—"

"Gloria." He gets up, comes over, and places both hands on my shoulders. "Remember when you asked me whether you were at all like Marianne?"

I nod.

"Well, this is one way you're acting like her that's absolutely mad." Jascha plants a kiss on my forehead. "Take a breath. It's a party, lovely, not a White House gala for—"

"Okay, listen." I take a step back from the table, where Curran sits stuffing party favors into cellophane bags, and lower my voice so he won't hear me. "Last year, my kid had nothing for a birthday celebration, because I was too zombified and scattered from grief to pull one together. Not even a storebought cake and supper with Raj from downstairs. So, yes, this *is* the equivalent of a White House gala in his—our—world."

"Hey, Mum," Curran interrupts. "You needn't worry about running out of time. I frosted two whole cupcakes!"

His piped creations look more like dragon turds than actual dragons, but far be it from me to criticize. "Awesome. Six more to go."

"Shall I get you one of your tablets?" Jascha asks me.

"Yes, please."

Two p.m., and the festivities are in full swing. Daredevils spider their way up the rock climbing wall, while their more-sedate-in-comparison classmates bounce in the ball pit and their younger siblings are kept busy and safely out of the way on the preschool play structure.

"This is genius, Glor," Fiona sighs from where she stands at the punch table.

"All his doing." I motion toward Jascha, who's about to start scaling the wall.

"What a love." She leans in conspiratorially. "You know, Jason never got his CV. Is he—"

"Just here for the weekend," I say. "Had to move back to England."

Sotto voce murmur. *"Oh."*

"Yeah." I nod. "Nothing wrong between us. His mom's just not well."

And that's not one hundred percent the truth, but Fiona doesn't need to know one hundred percent of the details.

"Goodness. I'm so sorry." Fee reaches for her paper cup (the *party* kind, mind you) of punch. Moves right on to the next topic. "Listen, I was wondering. Could I possibly take you up on that offer to watch the kids? We've symphony tickets and a dinner invitation next month, and I'm dying to—"

"Sure," I say. And then I pause, realizing there are some full truths she *should* hear. "I just need to …"

"Check your schedule?"

"No. I mean, yes, I will need to, but I also ought to tell you …"

Fiona waves a hand toward the women's restroom. "Do you … shall we talk in there?"

6~

No chance of being walked in on; we're surrounded by boys at the party, and Fiona's the only parent who didn't do a drop-and-run.

"So, okay," I say, soon as the door thumps closed behind us. "I really wish I had a mimosa for this part, but I feel like it's only fair to disclose before I take care of your children."

"You take care of my child on a daily basis," Fiona says, chuckling.

"I don't mean as head of school. I mean in your house, overnight."

"Oh." More sotto voce. "*Oh.* What—"

"That time in January. When Curran stayed with you and my mom picked him up because I was in the hospital."

"Right." She nods.

I grab the sink edge to steady myself. "When I told you I was in for tests to rule out things, and they all came back negative, I wasn't lying. I had them, and they did. But that's not the whole …"

I look down. "This is really hard, Fee."

"Just tell me."

On the count of three. One, two—

I swing my head back up. Stare Fiona straight in her guarded, curious eyes.

"I was in for a mental health issue."

Silence. Is that bad or good?

"A brief one, okay, nothing chronic. I still take anxiety meds every

so often, like today when I was freaking out trying to be Supermom."
I give her a *Surely you know what that's like* smile.

She smiles back. Whew.

"And I go once a week to this therapist in Silver Spring who looks like a total cliché but is actually incredibly helpful."

More silence. Please, please, please …

"That's it?" Fiona finally asks. "You're not impaling babies in your copious spare time, or sleeping with your male sixth-form students?"

"Nope."

"Just having a bit of a rough time and getting yourself sorted."

Bless you, British understatement. "Yep."

She gives a thoughtful nod, as if chewing on this new information. Then she leans over, and gives me a hug, and says, "Wipe that look of terror off your face and consult your schedule. I trust you completely with my kids."

Wow. I'm so gobsmacked and grateful I want to jump headfirst into the ball pit.

Instead I go stand and watch Jascha and Curran attempt to outdo each other rock-climbing. Perfect photo opportunity.

Or would be, if I'd brought the camera. Damn it.

"Gloria!" I turn to see Mom bustling in with two huge gift bags.

This'll be interesting. I made her swear to behave herself around Jascha, but I'm not holding my breath.

She scurries to drop her bounty at the present table, but gets sidetracked chatting with Fiona. For a moment, I'm seized with panic, holding my breath for real. Oh, God. She'll slip up and tell Fee.

Relax, idiot. *You* just told Fee, remember? And it went a million times better than you expected.

Yeah, it sure did. My lips curve into a pleased little grin that deepens the longer my eyes linger on Jascha working his way back down the climbing wall.

"Impressive," I say, after he drops to the floor.

"Not for the faint of heart, either." He grins back at me.

"I actually meant your ass."

Jascha shakes his head. "All that risk-braving athletic prowess, and you're busy looking at—"

"Mmm-hmm."

When we head in opposite directions—him to refill the punch, me to meet the pizza delivery guy outside—our palms swing toward each other and brush. A gesture I know my mother notices as she comes up to me.

"You're certainly giving that lovely Fiona a run for her money," she remarks after kissing me hello.

I sigh. "Not why I'm doing this, Mom. Come give me a hand with the boxes?"

"Of course." She looks chastened. Stays silent not only while I pay for the order, but all the way back to the food table.

"What?" I say, half-scowling, half-laughing, as I pop cardboard tabs to release the aroma of pepperoni.

Her lips purse. "Nothing."

"Oh, don't even."

Mom's gaze flits over to Jascha, who's now playing dodgeball with the kids.

"I'm just concerned about … you know." She drops her voice. "How he's doing. Whether he's still—"

"Going to therapy?" Now my face is a full scowl. "Mom, you get the bills."

"Well, yes, but is he actually making progress?"

"*I* think so."

"And you're not just saying that?"

"Look." I jerk a thumb in Jascha's direction. "If you don't trust my judgment, then go ask him yourself."

CHAPTER FORTY

These boys take no prisoners in dodgeball. Had Jascha known, he'd insisted on padded gear and helmets.

"No head injuries, guys!" He steps out of the fray, both for a break and in self-preservation. "I know your parents signed a waiver, but go easy."

When he hears a muted laugh beside him, Jascha first thinks it's Gloria, but then he turns, startled, to see Caroline.

"You're a saint," she says. "I'd have lost all patience by now."

Did she just pay him a compliment? "Thanks. They're good kids."

"And you've put on quite the party for them. Curran looks thrilled."

Okay, this is definitely a lead-up to something.

"I really do appreciate all that you've done," Caroline says. "For both him and Gloria."

She says this with an edgy sideways glance, as if to say, *I'm sure you don't believe I'm being genuine.*

But Jascha does, and so he glances back at her with what he hopes is reassurance. "Well, I appreciate hearing that."

Christ, could this get any more awkward?

"I'm glad. Because I'd hate for you to think I'm needlessly prying, but …" Caroline leans in closer. "I can't help but wonder how you're … coming along."

And the answer is: Yes.

Her face flushes. "I mean, I get financial statements from the therapist, but those don't exactly give an update."

"Health records are confidential," Jascha says, more sharply than he intends.

"Of course. As they should be." Caroline bites her lip. "But—"

"No," he says, softer now. "It's okay. I get it. If I were in your position, I'd want an update, too." Just like the funding sources for his old gallery, who required an annual report as part of the grant award conditions. *Hey, Arts England, don't have kittens! We're not spending money earmarked for emerging artists on hookers and booze.*

Don't have kittens, Jasch. It's just business.

Except it's not. It's a serious conversation between him and the woman who—maybe, if he's lucky, down the road—could potentially become his mother-in-law.

Thump-thwack. The dodgeball lands at his feet.

"We'd better step out of the line of fire," Jascha says.

After he throws the ball back to the kids, he and Caroline relocate to a corner by the present table.

"Okay, listen," Jascha says, his voice swelling with urgency. "When I … When the …" His hands flail ineptly. "When, you know, *it* happened—"

"The incident in which you left my daughter looking like a domestic violence awareness poster. Yes, I'm well aware."

Ouch. She's veered into pointed hyperbole, but it still hurts.

"I swore to Gloria I would do whatever it took to keep her safe." Jascha feels a surge of sudden eloquence. Like he's getting down on one knee in the rain before Marianne again. "And I'll make the same promise to you. Whatever you need to put your mind at ease—about my treatment, my progress, anything—it's yours."

"Anything," Caroline repeats.

"Absolutely. I'll sign paperwork giving you access to my session notes. You can ring Nora whenever you want, with my blessing."

The more Jascha talks, the more her face relaxes. He watches as her gaze drifts over to Gloria, who's doubled over, laughing with Fiona over God knows what.

"You're really in this for the long haul, aren't you?" Caroline says softly.

Jascha nods. He expects Caroline to say something along the lines of *Good, you'd better be,* but instead she simply chuckles and says, "Well, then, prepare to have your hands full, my dear."

❧

That night, Curran's so knackered from the party that he passes on a read-aloud, preferring to drowsily recount the high points of the day to Gloria and Jascha, who sit on either side of his bed.

"The rock climbing wall," he mumbles, "and the trick candles on the cake, and when Gran won dodgeball …"

Gloria snorts. "Never would have seen that one coming."

"But it was ace. The whole thing was ace. Best birthday party ever."

Curran rolls over onto his back. Stares at them, a query in his eyes, his little face suddenly pensive, even troubled.

"I feel bad saying that, though," he says. "Like it's rude to Dad. Because we had some dead good birthday parties with him too. It's just …"

His gaze fixes on his mother.

"I mean, it's okay, right?" he asks. "To say?"

Gloria swallows so hard Jascha can see the muscles in her throat work.

"Totally okay," she whispers.

"Because Dad would want me to be happy?"

She nods. "But don't get me wrong, kiddo. You can definitely take that line of reasoning too far."

"Like Dad would want me to eat Cadbury Flake bars for breakfast every day?" Curran grins. "Or play Donkey Kong instead of memorize my spelling words?"

"Right," Gloria says with a laugh. "I can guarantee your dad would not agree with those propositions."

Seeming satisfied with her answer, Curran turns to Jascha for his take.

"I agree with your mum," Jascha says.

Nice try, but not good enough, Curran's face replies.

Jascha lets out a sigh. "You know," he says, "your dad and I weren't particularly close. Mostly just shared studio space. But I still got a really good sense of who he was, because he was just the kind of guy where what you saw was what you got."

From across the mattress, he sees Gloria smile, no doubt remembering.

"And what you saw and what you got with your dad," Jascha says, "was not only a kind, thoughtful person, but also a carefree, truly happy one." He shrugs. "I mean, how could he not be, with you and your mum for a family, but still. Sometimes I wanted to ask him, 'What's your secret, mate?' Because even when he was terribly sick, he stayed positive."

"Noble, but infuriating," Gloria murmurs. "I did the freaking out for both of us."

Of that, Jascha has no doubt.

"So," he continues, "while I can't speak to what your dad would or wouldn't want you to do, I know for sure that having the best birthday party ever—even without him here—isn't rude or a betrayal. If anything, it's honoring him."

Now Curran looks completely reassured.

"Okay," he says. "Cool."

After she hugs Curran goodnight, Gloria immediately jumps up and heads down the hall.

Jascha trails behind her. "Honey?"

"I need to set my timer," she says hoarsely.

Already he can see the tears getting a head start forming in her eyes.

"You want company?"

"O-okay."

They enter the kitchen. Gloria grabs the timer from the stove, sets it for exactly five minutes, then plunks it down and drops her face into her palms.

It's brutal to watch. Shades of the old days, in which no parties were thrown and she chain-smoked and chewed her fingernails to shreds and ramble-babbled. Her shoulders quake. Her sobs go gut-deep.

Jascha steps in closer. Wraps his arms around her.

Gloria leans into his chest, hands still pressed to her face. He rubs her back with one palm. Strokes her hair with the other.

The timer dings. They both jump.

She pulls back. Wipes her eyes roughly.

"Thank you," she says.

"My pleasure, lovely."

"No." Gloria reaches out to touch his arm. "I meant thank you for not spewing platitudes or making soothing noises about how everything's going to be all right."

"Kitchen timer time is sacred silence time. I get it."

"And for that, I am forever grateful." Gloria kisses him lightly on the mouth.

"You gonna go read in the bathtub for a bit?"

She nods. "You gonna do Walkman homework?"

He nods back. Waits until he hears the water running to pop in his headphones and settle in on the couch. Auntie Nora will no doubt finger-wag, but he skipped last night. Too tired, too caught up in gleeful catch-up with his loves.

She put her family first, while I ... Best I could, given how weak I was ... Insisted I hear the truth.

"And that," Jascha mouths along, "was the ninth of fucking August, 1991."

He punches the STOP button. Once, and done.

⟳

Gloria returns a half hour later, damp tressed and flushed faced, clad in a short, garnet-colored silk robe that appears new.

Jascha looks her up and down. "Why, hello, gorgeous." He gives the lush fabric's hem a stroke, and then a playful tug. "Have we plans for the evening?"

Her flush deepens. "Sleep, actually. Today kicked my ass."

"In the service of a noble cause, at least."

"Yeah." She lets out a delighted sigh. "Did you see the look on his face, blowing out all those stupid trick candles? Shimmying down that rock wall with you?"

Priceless. They bask in the glow of parental jobs well done, grinning at each other.

And then Jascha clears his throat and addresses the elephant in the room. "So, umm ... I'll take the couch tonight, since you took it last."

Gloria bites her lip. "Actually, I didn't."

"Wait, so we—"

"Slept in the same bed together, like normal people?" She nods.

"Without any problems?"

310

"You were fine. It was fabulous."

"And probably a one-off."

"Jesus, Jasch." Gloria rakes a hand through her tangled hair. "You've worked like a Border collie on a damn agility course, jumping through all of Nora's hoops. You haven't had a nightmare in weeks. Give yourself some credit."

"I *am* giving myself credit," Jascha snaps. "I just don't want to give you another ... I just don't want to be ..."

His spine slumps. He massages his temples. Looks up as Gloria comes over and sits atop the coffee table in front of him. Takes both his hands in hers.

"You're not," she whispers. "You're nothing like him."

Jascha jerks away. "How the hell do you even—"

"Your mom told me. In the hospital."

Jascha swallows. Reaches up to brush his fingers along the corner of her mouth. "That's ... healing up well."

He pauses. "It doesn't still hurt, does it?"

Gloria shakes her head.

"Come to bed with me," she says. "Trust this, for once. Please."

She says this not pleadingly, as she had their final night living here together, but in a grounded tone of encouragement. *Trust this. Trust me. No: Trust yourself.*

Jascha gets up. Takes her hand. Leads her down the hall.

Eight hours later, they wake to each other's drowsy smiles.

"That didn't feel like a one-off," Jascha murmurs, lacing his fingers through hers on the pillow.

Gloria pokes at his calf playfully with her foot. "Told ya."

Sadly, Jascha has to fly back to London that afternoon. Too much work, plus there's his mum.

This flight's a mirror image of the one over: brief period of faffing about, followed by a barely-edible dinner, followed by a pre-doze listen to Ninth of You-Know-What August, 1991.

Looked at each other and laughed … kissing like we were … grateful.

When he moves to put his Walkman back, a folded piece of paper falls from his bag into his lap. Intrigued, Jascha opens it to find it's both a handwritten note and an ersatz protective sleeve for a photograph.

A photograph of a dark-haired teenage girl in ripped fishnets and a plaid chain skirt, perched on the closed boot of a beat-up car, the soles of her Doc Martens firmly planted atop the bumper.

Gloria.

The expression on her face aims for hard, impenetrable, *Don't fuck with me*. But there's something soft about her, almost ethereal— her arched brow scholarly despite the metal ring stuck through it, her mouth curved in the slightest of uplifts, not a smile so much as a momentary quiver of triumph. *Don't worry. I'm not letting the bastards get me down.*

Her note, composed in perfect script, reads:

Thought it was only fair you got a matching relic from me.

xoxo
Gloriochka

P.S. Just because I know you'll ask next Saturday night: No, I don't still have the outfit.

Damn. Jascha shakes his head. Tucks the photo into his bag's front pocket. Reclines as far back as his cattle-car seat will let him, and closes his eyes, still picturing her, adolescent stance of shutdown betrayed by a heart open wide.

CHAPTER FORTY-ONE

April is the cruelest month, to quote a fellow Anglophile expat, and in my case that cruelty can be summed up in three words: Snotty School Fair.

That's not the moniker displayed on its banners and ads, of course; its real name is the D.C. School Choice Expo. (Choice, as in, "Which private option will well-heeled diplomats and federal bigwigs select for their precocious pampered offspring?") But to Julia and me, who are forced to sit behind a table in a windowless, crowded ballroom at the Reston Hyatt for eight hours on a beautiful Saturday afternoon, Snotty School Fair it is.

I shouldn't be cranky. This requirement was, after all, clearly stated in my job description, as was the demographic profile of my student body. But as I field questions from overbearing couples ("Do you track statistics of Ivy League acceptances?" "Georgetown Prep has aftercare and full-day kindergarten—what about you?") and hand info packets to the secretaries of parents too busy to show up in person, I can't help thinking what a load of bullshit this all is.

During a lunchtime lull, I sit nibbling on a HobNob I've appropriated from our set-out dish of British sweets, and watch the few high schoolers who've tagged along with their families. Slouchy shoulders, hands stuffed in jackets, downcast *I'm-so-bored* eyes—and yet, immense yearning underneath.

"God, I miss working full-time with that age group," I sigh to Julia.

"You're joking."

"No." I reach for another chocolate. "I really do."

She shakes her head. "You want to deal with Madeline Bingham? All bloody day?"

"Okay, maybe with a few caveats."

I try to shrug off my own intense yearning as a touch of occupational hazard, but no such luck. I find myself popping into afternoon meetings of the sixth-form literary magazine, the yearbook, the school newspaper, under the guise of extracurricular oversight, but really I just want to sit atop a desk and chat with a bunch of bright, insightful sixteen-year-olds about the evils of censorship and the power of metaphor.

And then I start scanning classified ads. Talking a good game of deflection to myself. *Just checking the employment scene, to gauge Jascha's prospects for when he moves back.*

Yeah, sure, Gloriochka. Checking the employment scene under the *Education* column.

It'd be a big pay cut, teaching. But it'd be a huge boost in other ways. Namely, my ability to take pride in what I do nine-to-five.

In that sense, I envy Jascha. He's got a lot of difficult stuff to deal with—what with his duties tending to Vera and his weekly pilgrimages to hash out the finer points of survivor guilt with Auntie Nora—but his work life is on fire.

No more pretentious claptrap like the South London Subversives show for him. Now, when he's not designing websites for fledgling nonprofits, he's planning an exhibition of photographs and paintings done by ordinary people who've lived through extraordinary situations: civil wars, natural disasters, accidents like his own. *Witness art,* he calls it.

God, I'm so proud. In a way I wish I could be of myself.

"You know," Jascha says slyly one Wednesday night, "I did an artist-in-residence presentation the other week. At a secondary school with a job opening next autumn."

"For a headmistress?"

"Sixth-form English teacher."

Oh, honey. Don't tempt me. "What kind of school?"

"Independent. Quite posh. Out in Harrow. All girls."

"So more elitism." I picture an army of Madeline Binghams.

"Actually, no. They've some massive diversity initiative underway. Scholarships and bursaries for pupils who don't fit the usual Burberry mold."

Girls with nose rings and stony faces. Girls with skin too dark, arms too scarred, family histories too mangled. Girls with nothing but a Tube pass in their wallets.

Girls like I was.

My heart aches, then leaps, then settles again.

No. Don't even think it. Shouldn't even consider it. Can't uproot Curran yet another time. Can't continue zigzagging back and forth across the Atlantic.

"Gloria?" Jascha asks. "Do you want me to—"

"Yeah," I say, in spite of myself. "Send me the info."

❧

When he does, I send mine back. To the school's human resources contact person, in the form of an updated, obsessed-over, immaculately proofread CV.

They call me a week later. "We're quite interested in your qualifications, Ms. Burgess. May we set up an interview time?"

Yes. Yes, you may.

"It can't hurt, right?" I ask Laurie. "I mean, it's just a phone conversation."

"Right," she says. "Treat this as a learning opportunity. A fact-finding mission for your own values."

"So you think I shouldn't take the job if they offer it to me?"

Infuriating smile. "One step at a time."

❦

Okay. Step one: Set your alarm for three-thirty in the morning on a Monday, because the school's headmistress only has a nine a.m. slot free to speak with you.

Step two: Drink half a pot of coffee, even though it will probably make you have to dash to the bathroom in the middle of explaining your take on process-based pedagogy.

Step three: Call Jascha. Get reassured fifteen times, and then told: "Take one of your tablets. Breathe. Ring me back when it's over."

Step four: Take one of your tablets. Dry-heave into your hands.

Step five: Lunge for the receiver. Clear your throat of any interrupted-sleep huskiness that might make you sound more suited for giving transatlantic phone than molding the minds of young scholars.

Step six: Pace your kitchen all through the warm-up pleasantries. Hit your stride and launch into the story of how, last time you taught, you got struggling students not only to read Chaucer, but also to perform a *Canterbury Tales* rap at morning assembly that incorporated Old English and brought the house down.

Step seven: Remind them that you have dual citizenship and will be a hassle-free international hire. Refrain from contemplating the hassle of relocating internationally yet again. Mentally remind yourself that this is a simple learning opportunity. Mere practice.

Step eight: Notice on the microwave clock that you've babbled at your potential new employer for over an hour. Chastise yourself for being so manic and American and loud. Demurely apologize for letting your enthusiasm overtake you. End with a decidedly British, "Lovely to chat with you. Speak again soon, I hope."

Step nine: Hang up. Immediately hit the speed dial. Babble some more at Jascha. Get reminded to breathe again. Apologize for being such a needy pain in the ass. Be told, just as you've told him so often: "Shut up. I love you."

Step ten: Crawl back into bed in the hopes that you'll be able to catch the tiniest sliver of sleep. Toss and turn until six, wondering: What if they don't want me?

And then, more frighteningly: What if they do?

◦∽

A week later, I get asked for a second phone interview. A week after that, they request sample lesson plans.

"This is starting to feel like an *opportunity* opportunity," I tell Laurie.

She gives me another of her smiles. "Easy on the futurecasting, now."

"Please." I can't hold back a snort. "That's not even a damn verb."

◦∽

My instincts turn out correct. The offer they present me on a Thursday afternoon is solid but not stellar: decent salary for London, no relocation package.

I get a long weekend to decide. Hang up flushed and flattered, but resolve to take the entire three days to think it over.

Friday morning starts with another U.K. conference call, this one between me and Yvonne, the Big Boss at Anglo-American Educational Solutions, Ltd. Our monthly check-in.

She's keen to get an update on how Snotty School Fair went, so I rattle off the stats. "We spoke with approximately five hundred families. Fifty of those submitted new student applications."

"*Fifty?*" Yvonne sounds equal parts dubious and guardedly pleased.

"Mmm-hmm."

"That's double the amount we received after the expo last year."

Really? Whoa. "I guess that *Post* profile from Brian Jones stirred up some interest."

"For which I have you to thank. You encapsulated the mission of the school beautifully."

I flush again. Yvonne's not exactly free with the praise—last month she crisply took Julia to task for the page formatting on a report she faxed over—so this is a moment to be savored. *Nailed it, fresh off of Four West. Yeah!*

I'm about to thank Yvonne in return, but she keeps going.

"We've been most impressed with your performance, Gloria. So impressed, in fact, that we're keen to offer you a newly-created position that will commence this summer."

Okaaay. "Doing ... what?"

"Remember our bid on the other six British schools?"

Impossible to forget. It was all management talked about for months. Like we were jostling to host the curricular Olympics.

"Chicago, New York." I tick them off on my fingers. "Boston, L.A., Dallas, and ..." Shit. What's the last one? West Coast, West Coast. "Seattle?"

"Right." Whew. "We just received word. They're all now a part of Anglo-American Ltd."

Ahh, colonialism in action.

"Which of course means we'll need an academic director to supervise the entire lot." Yvonne says this brightly, with an *And I know just the person!* air.

No way. No. Effing. Way.

"I ... umm ... Wow." I scramble for a fortifying sip of coffee. "I'm incredibly honored, Yvonne, but as a single parent, I'm not able to take on a job with constant national travel."

"Well, the consortium will have its own office in Rockville. You'd work there, with the other schools reporting to you via post and email and conference call, just as you and I do currently."

Me, the American Big Boss? I can't even picture it, the prospect's so laughably unimaginable.

Yet Yvonne keeps going, detailing benefits and expectations. "I won't lie. The hours will be rather brutal."

"And the salary's ... commensurate?" I ask delicately.

"Oh, yes."

When she gives me the hard numbers, I almost knock my coffee mug off my desk. They're double what I'm making now, and nearly triple what the girls' school in London just offered.

Umm, wow, redux. My mouth opens to speak, flounders, then closes.

"Give it some thought," Yvonne says, "and we'll speak again Monday."

☙

"What the hell do I do now?" I ask Jascha, whom I of course phone immediately after Yvonne hangs up.

"Whatever you think is the right thing to do."

"Thanks. That's fucking helpful."

"No, I'm serious. You don't need my permission to—"

"I'm not asking you for permission, Jasch. I'm asking you for your opinion."

"Which isn't going to be unbiased in the slightest."

Argh. I tear a sticky note full of scribbled pros and cons off its pad. Affix it to my computer monitor so that the debate I'm facing—$ vs. Ideals—stares me straight in the face.

"Your call, Gloriochka. I'll support you either way."

❧

That knowledge helps, but it doesn't make the decision any easier.

I wind up spending the weekend not in weighty contemplation, but at Fiona's, babysitting Quinn and Bertie and Tess while she and Jason have their symphony date and a swanky hotel overnight. The kids are great, but wrangling the three of them plus Curran has only affirmed my desire to quit while I'm ahead.

By the time I get the older boys to stop pillow-fighting, the three-year-old changed out of his wet pajamas after an accident, and the littlest rocked to sleep, it's past eleven, and I'm beat.

Seeking haggard sanctuary in the massive master bath suite, only place in the house with a proper door that locks, I set the baby monitor on the marble countertop so I can hear Tess if she wakes, toss a Lush bath bomb into Fiona and Jason's jetted soaking tub, and crawl inside.

Oh. My. God. Bliss.

I could fall asleep right here in the pomegranate-scented bubbles, but no. My brain insists on running cost-benefit analyses like I'm some policy wank on *Meet the Press*.

Scenario 1: Big Boss.

Benefits: Money. Tons of money. Enough for a house like this. Enough for us all to have therapy for the rest of our lives should we need it (which, let's be honest, we probably will). Enough to hire an immigration lawyer for Jascha if his job hunt doesn't pan out. Plus: bonus ego stroke.

Cost: Stuck inside the Beltway until the end of time, feeling like a dirty sellout.

Scenario 2: Humble Instructor of Wayward Girls.

Benefits: Jascha! London! Work that makes a difference to something other than Anglo-American Educational Solutions' bottom line!

Cost: Have to leave Mom. Yet more transitions for Curran. Broke-ass broke.

Hmm. What to do? What to do?

(Laurie, at Friday afternoon's session: "This is a wonderfully positive problem to have. Remember that, when you start to feel trapped or cornered.")

I duck my head under the delicious water. Come back up to the sound of Tess fussing on the monitor, and my choice made.

I arrive home the next morning to find a message from Jascha on the answering machine. Afraid it's something racy, given that we missed our own Saturday date, I shoo Curran toward his room to unpack his overnight bag.

"So, umm." Jascha's voice fills the kitchen with wry shyness. "Remember when you asked for my opinion the other day? And I told you it was too biased to share?"

Charmed, I nod along.

"Well, screw bias. Michael Stipe and I are gonna lay it all out for you."

Uh-oh.

Honky-tonk piano kicks in from the stereo in the background, followed by the alt-rock Southern twang of "Don't Go Back to Rockville."

I listen to his entire sing-long performance, laughing so hard I'm doubled over on the counter with tears of hilarity rolling from my eyes. Then I hit *DELETE* to preserve his dignity, and call him back.

"Holy shit, honey. That was priceless."

"Thanks. Probably best I keep my day job, innit?"

"Yeah." I pause. "Especially since I'm ditching mine and taking a monster pay cut."

"What?" Jascha's voice shakes. "You're ... you went with—you decided to—"

"Not waste another year?" My face breaks into a grin. "Yep."

❧

I expect Curran to be if not distressed, then at least a bit mournful at having to move again. But he's remarkably nonplussed. "It's not like we'll never see Quinn again, because his family goes back to England to visit. And Gran will come see us too, right?"

Right. Assuming she's not pissed at me for leaving.

When I finally get up the nerve to tell her over lunch one day, I'm twitchy and tongue-tied. "Please understand, Mom. I—I'm not deserting you. I've loved living so close. Really, I—"

Mom leans across the table and puts a hand on my arm.

"I know," she says softly. "I knew, even when you first came back, that it would be a limited-time-only engagement. An experiment in proving yourself."

"Did I fail?"

Mom shakes her head. "I think you succeeded tremendously. Just in ways you weren't expecting to need to."

"You sound like my therapist."

"No." She takes a sip of her water. "I sound like a mother who knows her stubborn daughter all too well."

I don't need to be in London for staff training until August, but I have to hit the ground running looking for a flat in May.

Jascha scouts out places for me, going to showings and reporting back on the details. "Dreadfully 1970s," he'll say about one place that looked like an adorable steal from the outside. Or: "Underwhelming. You'd be paying for the postcode."

He's searching on his own behalf, too. Now able to take over his therapy bills from my mother, he's started to save up for a deposit on a flat. (He'd balked at first, citing fears about Vera living unsupervised, but Auntie Nora, wise woman that she is, insisted he hire his mother some in-home help and reclaim his independence.)

And holy hell, have housing prices gone up since I left last year. No more trendy Islington for me. (Not that I'm an address snob, but still.)

"If it's so expensive," Curran remarks one night, glancing up from his homework, "why don't you and Jascha just move in together?"

My first thought upon hearing him is: Whoa, those precocious, pragmatic words are not ones I ever expected to come out of my nine-year-old.

My second thought is: Umm, because the last time we tried that, we wound up having to sleep in separate rooms?

And my third: Ya know, the kid has a point.

A point that I decide is worth broaching with Jascha.

"So," I remark casually during a Wednesday night chat, "how's the nightmare log been looking lately?"

His voice swells with pride. "Nothing but blank pages."

"For three months? Wow. That's gotta be a new record."

"Yeah. It's brilliant. Almost makes me wish—"

"You could—"

"*We* could." Jascha's tone reverts to somber. "I mean, if you don't want to, if you don't feel ready, I totally understand."

"Do *you* feel ready?"

Long pause. "I think I will be. By the time you get here."

Another even longer pause, and then we both speak at once.

"You know what? Fuck it. Let's just—"

"Do it."

"Yeah. Let's." Our voices giddy. Not deluded, caution-torn-ragged-in-the-wind giddy, like they were the last time we decided to take such a leap, but swollen with celebratory pride. We've worked our asses off. We've stood some serious darkness down. We've earned this.

In July, just as I'm starting to hyperventilate from the stress of not knowing where exactly I'll live in a month, Jascha finds us a unicorn of a flat: two bedrooms, in a neighborhood near his mother's with decent schools. Not too 1970s, not too sterile and characterless with upgrades. Built-in bookcases and a fireplace and a deep bathtub, all the little things I've missed during the year I've been away.

He describes it to me on the phone in the real estate office, and I scream, "Apply! No, I don't need to see pictures, just apply!" so loudly into his ear that the letting agent asks, "Is there something wrong, sir?" I kiss the envelope full of paperwork when I overnight it to the U.K., praying they'll show some off-kilter mercy and pick a freelance artist and en-route American over their safe stable of City solicitor applicants.

When I find out we got it, I'm in my office packing up. Julia, arms full of new student packets, comes in to find me sobbing with relief into my hands.

"Last time you'll have to see this." I reach for a tissue. "Aren't you glad?"

She smiles. "That I got promoted to your job? Yes. That you'll be gone? No."

"You're just saying that."

"I most certainly am not. This place will be boring as sin without you." Julia hands me another tissue. "Now redo your mascara and get out to the assembly room. We've got one last parent orientation to run together."

~

I sell my IKEA furniture ensemble and car to Julia's daughter, who's just graduated from Georgetown. I drink one last mimosa with Fiona while our kids run in circles around us. I thank Laurie for breaking my brain and opening my heart.

And on my final weekend in D.C., while my mom spends some bonding time with Curran, I take the Metro and then the bus to a neighborhood in Southeast I haven't seen since my high school punk days, and walk into a tattoo parlor, and ask for a phoenix on my shoulder blade.

Guy with ten piercings looks me over, immediately pegging me as a tat virgin. "It's gonna hurt like a bitch in that spot."

"Yeah, I know." No pain, no gain, right?

"Okay." He shrugs. "If you're game."

I am. And he wasn't kidding.

The entire time, I curl my hands into fists and silently mouth *Jesus fucking fuck* like I did while laboring with Curran. I bite my lip and screw my eyes shut and dig my fingernails into my palms, but not once do I scream or even whimper for him to stop.

I am edges made of ink and bone. I am a terrified girl turned firebird.

~

I feel equal parts drained and high by the time I reach the Foggy Bottom Metro station again. At the top of the escalator, I bump straight into the scraggly, paranoid woman Curran was afraid I'd turned into.

She draws back, her eyes narrowed. "You be careful," she mutters to me. "They got cameras everywhere. Careful, you hear?"

I nod. Not just a perfunctory *Yeah, yeah, sure, whatever, crazy lady* indulgence, but one that comes with a held gaze, one which I hope comes across as a deeper affirmation: *I hear you. I see the you behind the wary fear.*

Satisfied, she lets me pass, and I step out into the balmy night air. Across the street, a hip-hop backbeat pours from a car stereo.

I glance back at the station entrance. She's still there, pacing back and forth, head bowed, fingers picking at the frayed threads of her jacket, lips moving in fretful incantations.

My mind conjures its own litany, a silent prayer of gratitude for all the things and people that helped me rise again: Mom. Jascha. Vera. Laurie. Dr. Marshall. Peter. Fiona and Julia. Supportive employers. Health insurance. A roof over my head. A son who kept me going, and a system that never once doubted my ability to raise him.

The phoenix on my shoulder throbs. A welcome breeze lifts the hair off the back of my neck as I turn toward home, exuberantly exhausted, exquisitely aware: There but for the grace of enormous privilege go I.

❧

We fly out in late July, two nights before my birthday, Curran's carry-on bag loaded down with video games, mine with books. I hug my mother goodbye with a cheerful, "See you at Christmas," and head for the boarding line, then turn straight back around and barrel into her arms, burying my face in the curve of her neck.

"Oh, darling girl." She strokes my hair, careful not to jostle the still-fresh tattoo hidden beneath it. "Come on, now. You don't want to miss your plane."

Wet-eyed and stammering, I lift my chin. "T-thank you. For everything."

"My pleasure. Always." Mom kisses me on the forehead. "Now go."

I straighten up. Blink and sniffle my way to composure. Give her a tender, apprehensive smile, then turn back to Curran, who's got a *Great, there goes Mum crying again* look on his face.

"You ready?" he asks. "They've called our flight like fifteen times."

"Yeah," I say, my smile deepening into a grin. "Let's do this."

We give my mother one final wave. March up to the desk with our tickets and passports. Step into the Jetway.

As we head down the makeshift corridor, Curran reaches for my hand. Gives it a hard squeeze.

I squeeze his back. Glance over. "You excited?"

As if I even needed to ask. "Jascha and Baba Vera are going to be there to meet us at Heathrow in the morning, right? You're sure."

"That's what he said." I duck my head to enter the plane. Almost whack a flight attendant with my bag. "Sorry."

Curran's shoulders bunch up with anticipation as we take our seats. "I can't wait."

"Me either, kiddo."

"I don't even know if I'll be able to sleep, I'm so—"

"Please." I lean over to help him adjust his safety belt. "If for nothing else but your poor mother's sanity, just try, okay?"

❧

By the time we land in the morning and reach the hellacious immigration queue, Curran's excitement's dissolved into whining.

"Why's it taaaking so long, Mum?"

"Tourist season," I sigh.

And then realize: I'm in the line for foreign nationals, when I could just as easily stand in the much shorter one for U.K. citizens.

When I jump over, the immigration officer gives me an *Oh, really?* look upon hearing my American accent, but I knock it off his face when I hand him a red passport.

"Thank you, madam." *Click-thunk* goes the date stamp: once for me, and once for Curran.

Back to excited, he grabs my arm and practically drags me toward the exit.

With my free hand, I fluff at my rumpled hair to make it marginally more presentable. "I hope Jascha didn't get stuck in traffic. It's always terrible this time of—"

"He's here!" Curran yelps as we enter the arrivals hall. "See him, Mum?"

Yes. The sweetest thing ever, holding a cup of takeout coffee and a sign that reads: *Welcome Home.*

CHAPTER FORTY-TWO

When Jascha hugs her, Gloria winces.

"Sorry." A wry smile. "Tattoo's still sore."

Ahh, yes. The mystery ink, which she's promised to unveil to him later.

"Where's Baba Vera?" Curran asks as they head for baggage claim. "Is she sick again?"

Nope, just at their flat making some last-minute preparations. "You'll see her when we get there. Don't worry."

"Whew."

He's hired a driver and minivan to ferry their large ensemble of suitcases, so the three of them get to ride in one row together, Jascha squished in the middle.

Gloria rests her hand on Jascha's knee. Curran rests his head on Jascha's shoulder. Traffic on the M4's at a standstill—for which, true to English form, the driver apologizes—but Jascha could sit in it for hours right now, content, with the two of them beside him.

Eventually Gloria's cheek slumps onto Jascha's other shoulder. He reaches an arm around her to steady her while she dozes. Buries his face in her hair for a moment for a quick inhale, then turns to Curran, who's now leaned against the window keeping an eye out for landmarks.

"Cadbury Flakes are in my bag," he whispers. "Hurry and eat one before your mum wakes up."

Curran's eyes widen. "Seriously?"

Jascha nods. Gestures toward the floor where his messenger bag lies.

Curran hauls it onto his lap, unzips it, and scrabbles around until he locates the bounty. For the next fifteen minutes, Jascha's surrounded by stereo snoring and munching.

"Here we are." The driver pulls onto their modest but cozily tree-lined street.

Jascha hurriedly motions for Curran to wipe a chocolate stain from his mouth. Gives Gloria a gentle nudge to wake her.

This time, there's no swearing or swatting away or ultimatums to give her the caffeine so no one gets hurt. She merely yawns, and sits up, and surveys the humble row of terraces.

"Not Georgian Grade Two historically listed like your old place," Jascha says, "but decent enough, innit?"

Gloria chews her lip. "Yeah." Her groggy voice sounds weary. "It's cute."

"Just wait till you see the inside."

⁊

His mother meets them at the door, eager to show Gloria around, but her grand tour gets delayed by the reunion of Curran and his beloved Baba Vera, to whom the boy clings so hard and so long she has to set down her portable oxygen tank.

"*Boshe moi,*" she sighs. "Look how tall you've grown."

"Nine going on nineteen," Gloria says with a laugh. "And dying to see his new room."

"We start at beginning," Vera firmly insists.

She steps back to give them some space. Sweeps a hand toward the main living area. "Your lounge."

Gloria takes it all in: the bookcases filled with paperbacks she'd shipped over a few weeks ago; the cabinet full of board games; the vintage couch Jascha salvaged from a charity shop and had redone in a red paisley print like the one she'd had in her old flat.

"Oh, wow." She strokes the sofa's arm. "Oh, Jasch. This is gorgeous."

"Matching drapes, too." Vera points to the bay window. "Maeve Kilburn made them for me."

Curran glances at Gloria, then shakes his head at Jascha. "Mum's gonna cry again."

"I am not." Halting smile. "Yet."

Jascha takes her hand. Leads her through the dining room with its fresh flowers on the table, and the kitchen with more hand-sewn curtains framing the window above the sink, and Vera's homemade pastries on the counter.

He expects Curran to swipe one, but instead he dashes down the hall to his room before everyone else can catch up.

A moment later, there comes a shout. *"Yes!"*

"I think the glow stars on the ceiling and the Star Wars posters were a hit," Jascha says.

Now Gloria caves and looks teary. "You didn't have to arrange all this."

"I know, but I wanted to."

She squeals at the sight of her longed-for deep English tub. Kisses him on the cheek when she spies the bowl full of Lush bath bombs perched on a glass shelf. Sits down on the end of their new bed, and then sinks back into the pillowtop mattress. "Holy … whoa."

"It's IKEA," Jascha says. "But most decidedly not from the as-is sale corner."

"Heavenly." She stretches out. "If you need me during the next eight hours, I'll be busy testing its softness rating."

"Don't." He flops down next to her. "Naps are the kiss of death for jet lag. Shoot your circadian rhythms to hell."

Gloria scowls as she rolls over to face him. "Thanks for the neuroscience lesson, Auntie Nora."

"Anytime."

They fall into a cozy silence, watching each other.

"All right, you two!" Vera calls from the kitchen. "Save funny business for after I go home."

Jascha chuckles under his breath. Reaches over to tuck a strand of Gloria's hair behind her ear.

"How'd I do?" he whispers. "All right?"

"Better than all right," she whispers back. "Freaking amazing."

The rest of that day is spent making up for lost time: an epic Scrabble smackdown in which Gloria wins with the dubious word *futurecast* ("Shut up, it's a verb in the Self-Help Gospel According to Laurie"); a visit to her former downstairs neighbors in Islington, so that Curran can experience another elated reunion with his friend Raj; a takeaway smorgasbord dinner with the best of REM in the background.

For evening read-aloud, they all pile up on Curran's new bed, Jascha perched on the edge, Gloria curled up with her arm around Curran.

She falls asleep halfway through the first chapter. All the better, since tonight's book pick is full of juvenile scatological humor better enjoyed without an English teacher grumbling about the decline of contemporary children's literature.

"Read the part about toxic fart explosions again," Curran murmurs with a yawn, as he extricates himself from beneath his mother's slumber-heavy grasp. "Please?"

"Sorry, mate. It's half past nine."

Jascha hugs him goodnight. Attempts to nudge Gloria awake like he had earlier in the van, but no luck.

"Mum can stay in here," Curran says. "It's squashy, but I don't mind."

No. She and Jascha will sleep next to each other, even if it means carrying her down the hall.

He's about to drape her arm around his neck and heft her up when she finally startles. "What? Huh?"

"Shh," Jascha says, guiding her to the door with one hand while flipping the light switch with the other.

"Night, Mummy."

"Night, baby," she mumbles, leaned into Jascha.

As they shuffle-stagger toward the bedroom, Gloria recounts in vivid, albeit drowsy, detail the dream she'd been having. "Went back in time … had dinner with James and Virginia."

Joyce and Woolf, respectively. Jascha's hardly a literary scholar, but he knows Gloria well enough to know who her Modernist dream dates would be.

"Did you genuflect before them?" He kisses the top of her head.

"Course. And spilled wine on myself."

Course. Jascha pulls back the duvet. Guides Gloria under it, still in her summer sundress. Nestles in beside her, not only contented by a dream achieved, but also confident—truly so, this time—that the nightmare, banished, will refrain from ransacking it.

CHAPTER FORTY-THREE

"Morning, birthday girl." Jascha gazes over at me with sleepy adoration when I wake, still fully dressed, in our bed. "Any requests for today?"

"Coffee," I say with a yawn.

"That's a given. I meant *special* requests."

"Not particularly." I wriggle closer to him. "Just want to spend the day with you guys."

"Really? I thought for sure you'd want me to take Curran to the cinema so you could read uninterrupted in the bath."

That's what he did last year. Back when things were still fraught with simmery tension and painful awkwardness. (He bought me flowers, too. Tried to pass them off as Curran's idea, but I knew better.)

"Nah." I slip my arms around Jascha's waist. Kiss him lightly on the mouth, then more deeply.

"You know," he murmurs, "you fell asleep on me last night before I could see that tattoo."

"Sorry." I sit up. Turn my back to him, and pull my dress over my head.

"Holy hell." Jascha runs his fingers over my shoulder blade. "That's gorgeous. The lines, the color …" He raises up on one elbow.

Presses his mouth to the ink. "Of course, the artist had a gorgeous canvas to work with."

He's about to dip his head down further when we hear footsteps pad toward us in the hall.

Shit. I hurriedly slide back under the duvet.

"Surprise!" Curran enters carrying a tray. "I made you breakfast."

Complete with a mug of coffee and a card. "Aww, baby. That's too sweet of you."

He sets the tray on the nightstand, impressively managing not to drop or spill it. Hands me the card.

Dear Mummy, it reads, beneath a drawing of me reading a book in the bathtub. *You are the best mum ever, and I hope you have the best birthday ever just like I did. Even without Dad. P.S. You don't look 32.*

"Oh, mercy." I pass it to Jascha. "We should get this framed."

"I can do it for you."

Man of many talents. I roll over to face Curran.

"So hey," I broach. "What do you think about spending the day at that amusement park out in Surrey we never got a chance to visit last summer?"

His eyes light up. He bounces on his heels. "Really?"

"Really."

Then he frowns. "But it's *your* birthday. We should do something you like."

"Well, I'd like for us to all do something fun together." I pause. "As a family."

Curran glances at Jascha. "Can you ride bumper cars now?"

I don't have to look back over my firebird shoulder to tell that Jascha's smiling.

"Yeah," he says softly, his voice lifting in amazement. "I most certainly can."

We head out in the used Volvo Jascha bought in anticipation of Curran's and my return ("Excellent safety record—believe me, I researched," he says dryly.). Windows down, summer sun, radio on. All breezy delight.

He's brought along the high-end camera he once used to take portraits of Marianne and Elizabeth. All day, he snaps photos: Curran's half-delighted, half-terrified scream on a roller coaster; me lasciviously licking an ice cream cone just to mess with him.

Curran puts up with this for a while, but eventually he starts campaigning for our resident documentarian to take a break. "C'mon, let's ride those giant swings. Or the scrambler thingie. Or …"

"Bumper cars?" Jascha gives him a sly smile.

Curran grins back. "Yes!"

As they head for the queue, I grab Jascha's arm. "You know," I whisper, "you don't have to do this if you don't feel—"

"Up for it? Please. I did Walkman homework this morning. I'm good."

And with that, he hands me his camera and disappears with a *Don't worry* wave.

I edge my way past other parents waiting on the sidelines by the ride exit ("Sorry. Sorry." Mustn't forget I'm back in Britain.) so that I can get a front-row view of this Moment with a capital M.

Look at them, my boys, jostling each other playfully as they work their way further toward the entrance to the bump-and-slam arena.

"Wanna go together?" I hear Curran ask.

"Oh, no. I'm taking you on."

Uh-oh. Now *this* is truly camera-worthy. I hook the strap around my neck like a professional, ready to roll.

Once up, Curran and Jascha high-five each other. Jog to their respective cars and yank the safety bars into their laps, then give each other the evil eye.

Crap. I should have grabbed some napkins at the ice cream kiosk, so I'd have ersatz tissues handy now.

The guy in charge of the ride nods to the raring-to-rumble crowd, and flicks the magic switch. I hold my breath and pray.

When the cars jerk into motion, Jascha's face stiffens with shock. My heart sinks, despondently crooning: *Oh, no. Oh, love.*

But then I glance around at the other drivers, and see that they've all got that look on their faces from the jarring jolt of the track set in motion. *Whoa, here we go!* And then it fades. Gives way to exhilarating glee.

Yes, even for Jascha. He steers like a maniac. Plows into Curran. Tips his head back with a triumphant laugh.

Finally. *Finally.*

I could watch this cathartic motorized whirl-bang forever, but I settle for snapping picture after picture after picture till my index finger aches.

One of the photographs I took makes it into Jascha's early August "Witness Art" show at the last minute. My inclusion feels a bit like indulgent nepotism, as if I'm the token tambourine girl in her boyfriend's band, but it's fun to be the creator rather than the muse for a change. Plus, I did witness a kind of art that day. The art of healing.

On opening night, I spend most of my time talking with the other artists, soaking up their stories, humbled. Eventually, though, Tim shows up with his latest conquest, Veronica the *Observer* journalist who put Jascha on her A-list, and I have to be polite and go meet her.

After ten excruciating minutes of syrupy, pretentious fawning ("This is so delightfully innovative, Mr. Kremsky!"), she heads for the ladies' to needlessly refresh her overdone lipstick. I lean over to Tim.

"Never in a million years did I think I'd be saying this to you," I whisper, "but you're too good for her."

Tim laughs. "Umm ... thanks?"

"No, I'm serious. You're a much more genuine soul than I gave you credit for."

Guarded, yet sincere, smile. "Likewise."

☙

On the way home, Jascha and I stop for drinks at a Russian restaurant called Nikita's that holds an amusing place in our hearts as the venue where, pre-fifteen minutes of fame, I plunked a shot glass down and asked him straight up, out of burning curiosity and honest puzzlement: *Why are you so nice to me? Do you want to sleep with me, or what?*

"Repeat performance," Jascha urges me now. "Come on. For nostalgia's sake."

Nostalgia that doesn't involve dead people! Ooh, this is exciting.

"Okay." I sit up. Clear my throat. Ready my lemon vodka.

I get about three words in before we dissolve into laughter. And then silence, piquant as the one that descended after I'd posed that question the first time.

Jascha clears his throat. Lets his fingers lightly play over mine on the table.

"So," he says. "I had an interesting session with Nora this week."

It must have been, if he's referring to her as Nora and not Auntie. "Oh?"

"She thinks I should drive to Margate. For the fifth anniversary of ..." He swallows. "Ninth of fucking August."

Jesus. Bumper cars at the funfair are one thing, but that's ...
"Wow."

"A 'potential corrective experience,' she calls it. Desensitization homework to end all desensitization homework."

"Yeah, well, it sounds like pointless masochism that could needlessly set you back to me."

Jascha frowns. "I agree with her, Gloria. I want to do it."

Shit. "Look, why don't we just take a nice beach weekend in a different town, on a different date? Dover's lovely. We could—"

"No." His jaw sets. "I don't need lovely." His voice sharpens. "I need to arrive in Margate in something other than an ambulance. What part of that don't you understand?"

I almost put a hand up to protest, but again, just as I was while admiring the works of asylum seekers and war veterans earlier tonight, I'm humbled. We share an incredible number of emotional intersection points, Jascha and I, but this is one road—rain-soaked, treacherous—on which, no matter how much I'd like to believe otherwise, our paths irrefutably diverge.

"Okay," I say softly. "How would it work? You'd just drive out there ... alone?"

Jascha shakes his head. "Nora says I should try to approximate the original details as best I can. For, you know, the best—"

"Bang for your trauma trigger buck?" Distaste burns in my mouth.

He shrugs. "In a manner of speaking."

"So we'd leave late on a Friday night. All three of us."

Jascha nods. "Right."

"And we'd tell Curran what, exactly?"

"The truth. That we're headed on holiday to the seaside."

Oh, don't even. "But what if you—what if it's—"

"Too much? I'll hand you the car keys, and we'll keep going." His tone softens. "I won't let things get to the breaking point. Trust me."

I think of my own similar words, urging him to come down the hall to bed. I think of him talking me through my own breakdown. I think of our teenage photograph-selves, aching for their lives to get better.

"Do you remember the name of the place where you were supposed to stay?"

Crooked smile. "Of course I do."

"Then book it."

CHAPTER FORTY-FOUR

For all her initial resistance, Gloria's quite the good sport on the actual evening of their departure: helping Jascha load the car, offering to pick a fight with him in the name of historical accuracy.

"Thanks," Jascha says, "but I'll pass."

He spends the last few minutes before they leave holed up in the bedroom, Walkman headphones clamped on his ears. Auntie Nora's got him down to a once-a-week maintenance schedule, and he already knocked out this week's listen on Tuesday, but Jascha reckons it can't hurt to top up with another. Psychological booster jab.

After so many replays, the main audio narration's faded to a mere hum in his ears, little more than the background noise of cutlery's clink he used to hear when Gloria would empty the dishwasher while on the phone with him.

What jumps out at him now, though, are the discursive asides. Nora's urgings, coupled with his own fury.

Stay on ninth August.

I've stayed on ninth August for the last five goddamn years! I want to move past i—

He startles as, from behind, Gloria slips her arms around him and yanks the headphones from his ears.

"Traffic's gonna be shit, remember?" She kisses him on the side of his neck. "Come on, desensitization rockstar. Let's go."

❧

The drive through London's just teeth-gritting business as usual until they hit the countryside.

Ahh, release from the urban chokehold. Refreshing and uncomplicated as their drive out to the amusement park. The same languid summer trifecta: sun, radio, breeze.

Curran faffs about with his Game Boy in the backseat. Gloria pulls another hefty novel from her bag. Glances over at Jascha questioningly.

He waves a hand at her, as if to say, *Please. Don't worry about me. Get lost in your South African magic realism, or whatever the hell that thing is.*

She gives him a relieved grin. Eagerly cracks the spine and dives in.

See? Everyone's fine.

Keep your eyes on the road.

Jascha turns off the radio so he can concentrate. Or at least try.

Bling bonk sparkle slam, goes the soundtrack to Curran's game. Decidedly not mere background noise.

"Could you turn that down, mate?" Jascha calls back.

"Sure." The volume decreases by a hair at best.

"No. *Actually* down."

Curran sighs. Jascha wills himself not to snap.

The blings blessedly cease. Gloria turns another page. "Thanks, lovey," she murmurs.

God, how he envies her ability to comfortably slouch, flipping through chapters with nary a care, while he grips the steering wheel and sweats bullets.

JENN CROWELL

You're doing this so you can get to that point, remember? Eyes on the prize.

And the road.

The sky's deepened to blue-hour hue now. Sultry, with more than a hint of harbinger. If skies darken, motorways darken. If motorways darken …

No. Don't. Stop it.

Next to him, he hears Gloria chuckle. He glances over at her.

"Curran's out," she says.

Just like Elizabeth. Jascha's throat goes dry.

Speech hurts to scrape out. "Is he still—has he still got his seatbelt on?"

"Yeah." She reaches over. Caresses Jascha's hand that clutches the gearshift. "Relax, okay? He's safe."

For now.

"Check the map for me," Jascha whispers. "Please."

Gloria plucks it from the floorboard. Unfolds the paper rectangle and scans for their current location. "We're almost at the halfway point. You're doing great, babe."

See? Nora was right.

And yet his shoulders still stiffen. And yet his chest still tightens.

"Petrol station's coming up on the left."

He pulls into a parking space. Shuts off the ignition, and rests his head on his arms on the steering wheel.

Gloria reaches over. Rubs his back. "Do you want me to take over?"

"No. No. I just need a breather."

"Well, then, go be chivalrous and bring me some chips and chocolate."

Yes, ma'am. Jascha returns from the shop with his arms loaded. "I got you the sweet chili crisps. And an obligatory Flake for the boy."

"Beautiful."

As he slides back into the driver's seat, Jascha remembers his on-bended-knee proclamation to Marianne. "I can skip the heartfelt proposal, right?"

Gloria smiles. "Absolutely. I'm happy to live in sin for awhile."

"Me, too."

"Are you?" Her smile deepens. "I'd have thought you'd be raring to go on the marriage front."

"It's been one helluva year, Gloriochka." He rubs a hand over his eyes. "Who am I kidding? A helluva five years. That I've spent acting like everything's an emergency, or a tragedy, or too good to last. When in reality ... we've got plenty of time."

"Yeah," Gloria says softly. "Might as well savor it."

As if to prove her point, she sucks a smudge of chocolate from her index finger.

"Hey, now." Jascha reaches for her hand. "Let me take care of that." Devilish pause. "You know, for reenactment purposes."

Gloria snickers. "You're quite selective in what you're choosing to reenact tonight, bucko."

"Damn right I am." He nips playfully at the tip of her thumb.

Once she's done humoring him, Gloria reaches for the map again. Runs her still-damp finger from their starred current location, over to the asterisk eight miles east. Ground zero.

Jascha's gaze traces the distance between. "So close."

"I know. But you can do it."

"I—I'm not sure how."

"Just—"

"No. I mean I'm not sure whether to ..." He trails off. Shifts his head to stare straight into the petrol station's neon sign, blue and ominous as a twirling ambulance light. "Drive past, like it's nothing. Or stop to pay my respects."

"That's your call to make, love."

"I mean, stopping could turn maudlin so easily. Go from respectful to self-flagellating in a matter of seconds."

"Right."

"And driving past doesn't automatically mean I'm treating that spot like it's just another stretch of road, yeah?" He feels like Curran asking permission to enjoy his birthday without his father.

"Not at all."

Okay. Jascha starts the engine.

⟡

Seven miles. Then six. Then five. The countdown a strange throwback to timing Marianne's labor contractions. (*Put that watch away, or I'll strangle you,* she'd growled, in a voice that reminds him retroactively of Gloria.)

Gloria, who sits next to him now, an understatedly reverent copilot, silent keeper of the map.

Four. Three.

At least it's not raining. Thank you, occasionally merciful universe.

Two. A car swerves past them.

Shit shit shit shit.

"We're all right, Jasch. Breathe."

He breathes. Forces his fingers, wrapped round the steering wheel, to unclench.

Gloria rests a steady hand on his knee.

Here the crossroads comes. A pull onto a blameless, bland motorway shoulder and back into the past. Or a simple turn toward the future.

Gloria glances over at him. *Either way,* her eyes promise, *I'll be here.*

Jascha floors the pedal. Keeps on going.

Past the next rest area. Past the Tesco where Marianne had planned to stock up on groceries for their holiday rental's kitchen. Past the hospital to which he'd been rushed.

Past it all, through the dense, flesh-scraping underbrush of memory. Never stopping, not even pausing, till he pulls up at last in front of their seaview cottage.

"Wow," Gloria says. "It's … pink."

Jascha runs his sweaty palms through his hair. Looks over at her. "Out of the PTSD forest and into the candyfloss castle, huh?"

Gloria stifles a laugh with one hand. High-fives him with her other.

He catches her fingers in his. Presses his mouth to her knuckles.

From the backseat, Curran lets out a sleepy groan. Sits up, rubbing his eyes. "We … there … yet?"

"Yeah, mate," Jascha says, swallowing hard. "We're here."

CHAPTER FORTY-FIVE

We kiss our kid goodnight despite his mumbled protests. "The sea air smells so good, Mum." Drowsy roll-over beneath the duvet. "Can't we go down on the beach, for just a little?"

No, we whisper, stroking his hair back from his forehead. *It's late.*

"But—"

Shh. You'll have all weekend.

He's back asleep before we close the door. We embrace in the hallway. Hold on for what feels like all weekend, then head for our room's balcony with a freshly cracked bottle of wine.

We slump cozily on lounge chairs. Our free hands dangle in the space between us, lazily brushing. Night ocean breeze whips the ends of my hair toward Jascha.

He's right about it being a helluva year. Ripe for more dissection, more lapses into mournful contemplation thinly disguised as nostalgia. We could go there, effortlessly and reflexively, if we wanted. But right now what we want is to be who we are: tired parents eager for a respite from the workday grind; triumphant survivors who sent their metaphorical excess baggage packing on a Heathrow carousel.

He does imitations of Veronica the *Observer* columnist that leave me in stitches; I tell him about my plans to visit Julia's brother in his newest group home placement. We kick around ideas for what to do while we're here—more amusement park, or shall we just hit the promenade? I wonder aloud whether my new coworkers will be insufferable and catty; Jascha muses on whether a tattoo artist would work over scar tissue.

And then we set down our empty glasses, and heft ourselves drowsily up to stand at the railing, arms wrapped around each other's waists, edge to edge, cheek to shoulder, watching the muted crash of rendered-harmless waves.

ABOUT THE AUTHOR

Jenn Crowell is the author of the critically acclaimed novels *Necessary Madness, Letting the Body Lead,* and *Etched On Me.* She holds an MFA in creative writing, and lives near Portland, Oregon with her husband and daughter.

Connect with Jenn at her website:

www.jenncrowell.com

www.ingramcontent.com/pod-product-compliance
Lightning Source LLC
Chambersburg PA
CBHW031128120726
47905CB00006B/1606